DECEIVED

By Paul S. Kemp
Star Wars: Crosscurrent
Star Wars: Riptide

THE EREVIS CALE TRILOGY
Twilight Falling
Dawn of Night
Midnight's Mask

THE TWILIGHT WAR
Shadowbred
Shadowstorm
Shadowrealm

DECEIVED

PAUL S. KEMP

LUCAS BOOKS

DEL REY

BALLANTINE BOOKS • NEW YORK

Star Wars: The Old Republic: Deceived is a work of fiction. Names, places, and incidents either are products of the author's imagination or are used fictitiously.

2012 Del Rey Mass Market Edition

Copyright © 2011 by Lucasfilm Ltd. & ® or ™ where indicated.

All Rights Reserved. Used Under Authorization.

Excerpt from *Star Wars: Fate of the Jedi: Outcast* by Aaron Allston copyright © 2009 by Lucasfilm Ltd. & ® or ™ where indicated. All Rights Reserved. Used Under Authorization.

Published in the United States by Del Rey, an imprint of The Random House Publishing Group, a division of Random House, Inc., New York.

DEL REY is a registered trademark and the Del Rey colophon is a trademark of Random House, Inc.

Originally published in hardcover in the United States by Del Rey, an imprint of The Random House Publishing Group, a division of Random House, Inc., in 2011.

ISBN 978-0-345-51139-3
eBook ISBN 978-0-345-52988-6

Printed in the United States of America

www.starwars.com
www.lucasarts.com
www.delreybooks.com

9 8 7 6 5 4 3 2 1

Del Rey Mass Market Edition: June 2012

For Jen, and Riordan, and Roarke

ACKNOWLEDGMENTS

My thanks to Shelly, Sue, Leland, and David,
for all their help and encouragement.

THE **STAR WARS** NOVELS TIMELINE

OLD REPUBLIC
5000–33 YEARS BEFORE
STAR WARS: A New Hope

Lost Tribe of the Sith
Precipice
Skyborn
Paragon
Savior
Purgatory
Sentinel

3954 *YEARS BEFORE STAR WARS: A New Hope*

The Old Republic: Revan

3650 *YEARS BEFORE STAR WARS: A New Hope*

The Old Republic: Deceived

Lost Tribe of the Sith*
Pantheon
Secrets

Red Harvest

The Old Republic: Fatal Alliance

1032 *YEARS BEFORE STAR WARS: A New Hope*

Knight Errant

Darth Bane: Path of Destruction
Darth Bane: Rule of Two
Darth Bane: Dynasty of Evil

RISE OF THE EMPIRE
1000–0 YEARS BEFORE
STAR WARS: A New Hope

67 *YEARS BEFORE STAR WARS: A New Hope*

Darth Plagueis

33 *YEARS BEFORE STAR WARS: A New Hope*

Darth Maul: Saboteur*
Cloak of Deception
Darth Maul: Shadow Hunter

32 *YEARS BEFORE STAR WARS: A New Hope*

STAR WARS: EPISODE I
THE PHANTOM MENACE

Rogue Planet
Outbound Flight
The Approaching Storm

22 *YEARS BEFORE STAR WARS: A New Hope*

STAR WARS: EPISODE II
ATTACK OF THE CLONES

22-19 *YEARS BEFORE STAR WARS: A New Hope*

The Clone Wars
The Clone Wars: Wild Space
The Clone Wars: No Prisoners

Clone Wars Gambit
Stealth
Siege

Republic Commando
Hard Contact
Triple Zero
True Colors
Order 66

Shatterpoint
The Cestus Deception
The Hive*
MedStar I: Battle Surgeons
MedStar II: Jedi Healer
Jedi Trial
Yoda: Dark Rendezvous
Labyrinth of Evil

19 *YEARS BEFORE STAR WARS: A New Hope*

STAR WARS: EPISODE III
REVENGE OF THE SITH

Dark Lord: The Rise of Darth Vader

Imperial Commando
501st

Coruscant Nights
Jedi Twilight
Street of Shadows
Patterns of Force

The Han Solo Trilogy
The Paradise Snare
The Hutt Gambit
Rebel Dawn

The Adventures of Lando Calrissian
The Force Unleashed
The Han Solo Adventures
Death Troopers
The Force Unleashed II

*An eBook novella
**Forthcoming

REBELLION
0–5 YEARS AFTER
STAR WARS: A New Hope

Death Star
Shadow Games

0

> **STAR WARS: EPISODE IV**
> **A NEW HOPE**

Tales from the Mos Eisley Cantina
Tales from the Empire
Tales from the New Republic
Allegiance
Choices of One
Galaxies: The Ruins of Dantooine
Splinter of the Mind's Eye

3 YEARS AFTER STAR WARS: A New Hope

> **STAR WARS: EPISODE V**
> **THE EMPIRE STRIKES BACK**

Tales of the Bounty Hunters
Shadows of the Empire

4 YEARS AFTER STAR WARS: A New Hope

> **STAR WARS: EPISODE VI**
> **THE RETURN OF THE JEDI**

Tales from Jabba's Palace

The Bounty Hunter Wars
  The Mandalorian Armor
  Slave Ship
  Hard Merchandise

The Truce at Bakura
Luke Skywalker and the Shadows of
  Mindor

NEW REPUBLIC
5–25 YEARS AFTER
STAR WARS: A New Hope

X-Wing
  Rogue Squadron
  Wedge's Gamble
  The Krytos Trap
  The Bacta War
  Wraith Squadron
  Iron Fist
  Solo Command

The Courtship of Princess Leia
A Forest Apart*
Tatooine Ghost

The Thrawn Trilogy
  Heir to the Empire
  Dark Force Rising
  The Last Command

X-Wing: Isard's Revenge

The Jedi Academy Trilogy
  Jedi Search
  Dark Apprentice
  Champions of the Force

I, Jedi
Children of the Jedi
Darksaber
Planet of Twilight
X-Wing: Starfighters of Adumar
The Crystal Star

The Black Fleet Crisis Trilogy
  Before the Storm
  Shield of Lies
  Tyrant's Test

The New Rebellion

The Corellian Trilogy
  Ambush at Corellia
  Assault at Selonia
  Showdown at Centerpoint

The Hand of Thrawn Duology
  Specter of the Past
  Vision of the Future

Fool's Bargain*
Survivor's Quest

*An eBook novella
**Forthcoming

THE STAR WARS NOVELS TIMELINE

 NEW JEDI ORDER
25–40 YEARS AFTER
STAR WARS: A New Hope

Boba Fett: A Practical Man*

The New Jedi Order
  Vector Prime
  Dark Tide I: Onslaught
  Dark Tide II: Ruin
  Agents of Chaos I: Hero's Trial
  Agents of Chaos II: Jedi Eclipse
  Balance Point
  Recovery*
  Edge of Victory I: Conquest
  Edge of Victory II: Rebirth
  Star by Star
  Dark Journey
  Enemy Lines I: Rebel Dream
  Enemy Lines II: Rebel Stand
  Traitor
  Destiny's Way
  Ylesia*
  Force Heretic I: Remnant
  Force Heretic II: Refugee
  Force Heretic III: Reunion
  The Final Prophecy
  The Unifying Force

35 *YEARS AFTER STAR WARS: A New Hope*

The Dark Nest Trilogy
  The Joiner King
  The Unseen Queen
  The Swarm War

 LEGACY
40+ YEARS AFTER
STAR WARS: A New Hope

Legacy of the Force
  Betrayal
  Bloodlines
  Tempest
  Exile
  Sacrifice
  Inferno
  Fury
  Revelation
  Invincible

Crosscurrent
Riptide

Millennium Falcon

43 *YEARS AFTER STAR WARS: A New Hope*

Fate of the Jedi
  Outcast
  Omen
  Abyss
  Backlash
  Allies
  Vortex
  Conviction
  Ascension
  Apocalypse

*An eBook novella
**Forthcoming

DRAMATIS PERSONAE

Adraas; Sith Lord (human male)
Angral; Sith Lord (human male)
Arra Yooms; child (human female)
Aryn Leneer; Jedi Knight (human female)
Eleena; servant (Twi'lek female)
Malgus; Sith Lord (human male)
Ven Zallow; Jedi Master (male, species unknown)
Vrath Xizor; mercenary (human male)
Zeerid Korr; smuggler (human male)

A long time ago in a galaxy
far, far away. . . .

DECEIVED

CHAPTER 1

FATMAN SHIVERED, her metal groaning, as Zeerid pushed her through Ord Mantell's atmosphere. Friction turned the air to fire, and Zeerid watched the orange glow of the flames through the transparisteel of the freighter's cockpit.

He was gripping the stick too tightly, he realized, and relaxed.

He hated atmosphere entries, always had, the long forty-count when heat, speed, and ionized particles caused a temporary sensor blackout. He never knew what kind of sky he'd encounter when he came out of the dark. Back when he'd carted Havoc Squadron commandos in a Republic gully jumper, he and his fellow pilots had likened the blackout to diving blind off a seaside cliff.

You always hope to hit deep water, they'd say. *But sooner or later the tide goes out and you go hard into rock.*

Or hard into a blistering crossfire. Didn't matter, really. The effect would be the same.

"Coming out of the dark," he said as the flame diminished and the sky opened below.

No one acknowledged the words. He flew *Fatman*

alone, worked alone. The only things he carted anymore were weapons for The Exchange. He had his reasons, but he tried hard not to think too hard about what he was doing.

He leveled the ship off, straightened, and ran a quick sweep of the surrounding sky. The sensors picked up nothing.

"Deep water and it feels fine," he said, smiling.

On most planets, the moment he cleared the atmosphere he'd have been busy dodging interdiction by the planetary government. But not on Ord Mantell. The planet was a hive of crime syndicates, mercenaries, bounty hunters, smugglers, weapons dealers, and spice-runners.

And those were just the people who ran the place.

Factional wars and assassinations occupied their attention, not governance, and certainly not law enforcement. The upper and lower latitudes of the planet in particular were sparsely settled and almost never patrolled, a literal no-being's-land. Zeerid would have been surprised if the government had survsats running orbits over the area.

And all that suited him fine.

Fatman broke through a thick pink blanket of clouds, and the brown, blue, and white of Ord Mantell's northern hemisphere filled out Zeerid's field of vision. Snow and ice peppered the canopy, frozen shrapnel, beating a steady rhythm on *Fatman*'s hull. The setting sun suffused a large swath of the world with orange and red. The northern sea roiled below him, choppy and dark, the irregular white circles of breaking surf denoting the thousands of uncharted islands that poked through the water's surface. To the west, far in the distance, he could make out the hazy edge of a continent and the thin spine of snowcapped, cloud-topped mountains that ran along its north–south axis.

Motion drew his eye. A flock of leatherwings, too small to cause a sensor blip, flew two hundred meters to starboard and well below him, the tents of their huge, membranous wings flapping slowly in the freezing wind, the arc of the flock like a parenthesis. They were heading south for warmer air and paid him no heed as he flew over and past them, their dull, black eyes blinking against the snow and ice.

He pulled back on the ion engines and slowed still further. A yawn forced itself past his teeth. He sat up straight and tried to blink away the fatigue, but it was as stubborn as an angry bantha. He'd given the ship to the autopilot and dozed during the hyperspace run from Vulta, but that was all the rack he'd had in the last two standard days. It was catching up to him.

He scratched at the stubble of his beard, rubbed the back of his neck, and plugged the drop coordinates into the navicomp. The comp linked with one of Ord Mantell's unsecured geosyncsats and fed back the location and course to *Fatman*. Zeerid's HUD displayed it on the cockpit canopy. He eyed the location and put his finger on the destination.

"Some island no one has ever heard of, up here where no one ever goes. Sounds about right."

Zeerid turned the ship over to the autopilot, and it banked him toward the island.

His mind wandered as *Fatman* cut through the sky. The steady patter of ice and snow on the canopy sang him a lullaby. His thoughts drifted back through the clouds to the past, to the days before the accident, before he'd left the marines. Back then, he'd worn the uniform proudly and had still been able to look himself in the mirror—

He caught himself, caught the burgeoning self-pity, and stopped the thoughts cold. He knew where it would lead.

"Stow that, soldier," he said to himself.

He was what he was, and things were what they were.

"Focus on the work, Z-man."

He checked his location against the coordinates in the navicomp. Almost there.

"Gear up and get frosty," he said, echoing the words he used to say to his commandos. "Ninety seconds to the LZ."

He continued his ritual, checking the charge on his blasters, tightening the straps on his composite armor vest, getting his mind right.

Ahead, he saw the island where he would make the drop: ten square klicks of volcanic rock fringed with a bad haircut of waist-high scrub whipping in the wind. The place would probably be underwater and gone next year.

He angled lower, flew a wide circle, unable to see much detail due to the snow. He ran a scanner sweep, as always, and the chirp of his instrumentation surprised him. A ship was already on the island. He checked his wrist chrono and saw that he was a full twenty standard minutes early. He'd made this run three times and Arigo—he was sure the man's real name was not Arigo—had never before arrived early.

He descended to a few hundred meters to get a better look.

Arigo's freighter, the *Doghouse,* shaped not unlike the body of a legless beetle, sat in a clearing on the east side of the island. Its landing ramp was down and stuck out of its belly like a tongue. Halogens glared into the fading twilight and reflected off the falling snow, turning the flakes into glittering jewels. He saw three men lingering around the ramp, though he was too far away to notice any details other than their white winter parkas.

They spotted *Fatman*, and one waved a gloved hand.

Zeerid licked his lips and frowned.

Something felt off.

Flares went up from the freighter and burst in the air—green, red, red, green.

That was the correct sequence.

He circled one more time, staring down through the swirl of snow, but saw nothing to cause alarm, no other ships on the island or in the surrounding sea. He pushed aside his concern and chalked his feelings up to the usual tension caused by dealing with miscreants and criminals.

In any event, he could not afford to mess up a drop of several hundred million credits of hardware because he felt skittish. The ultimate buyer—whoever that was—would be unhappy, and The Exchange would take the lost profits from Zeerid in blood and broken bones, then tack it on to the debt he already owed them. He'd lost track of exactly how much that was, but knew it was at least two million credits on the note for *Fatman* plus almost half that again on advances for Arra's medical treatment, though he'd kept Arra's existence a secret and his handler thought the latter were for gambling losses.

"LZ is secure." He hoped saying it would make it so. "Going in."

The hum of the reverse thrusters and a swirl of blown snow presaged the thump of *Fatman*'s touching down on the rock. He landed less than fifty meters from Arigo's ship.

For a moment he sat in the cockpit, perfectly still, staring at the falling snow, knowing there'd be another drop after this one, then another, then another, and he'd still owe The Exchange more than he'd ever be able to pay. He was on a treadmill with no idea how to get off.

Didn't matter, though. The point was to earn for Arra, maybe get her a hoverchair instead of that wheeled antique. Better yet, prostheses.

He blew out a breath, stood, and tried to find his calm as he threw on a winter parka and fingerless gloves. In the cargo hold, he had to pick his way though the maze of shipping containers. He avoided looking directly at the thick black lettering on their sides, though he knew it by heart, had seen such crates many times in his military career.

DANGER—MUNITIONS.
FOR MILITARY USE ONLY.
KEEP AWAY FROM INTENSE HEAT
OR OTHER ENERGY SOURCES.

In the crates were upward of three hundred million credits' worth of crew-served laser cannons, MPAPPs, grenades, and enough ammunition to keep even the craziest fire team grinning and sinning for months.

Near the bay's landing ramp, he saw that three of the four securing straps had come loose from one of the crates of grenades. He was lucky the crate hadn't bounced around in transit. Maybe the straps had snapped when he set down on the island. He chose to believe that rather than admit to his own sloppiness.

He did not bother reattaching the straps. Arigo's men would have to undo them to unload anyway.

He loosened his blasters in their holsters and pushed the button to open the bay and lower the ramp. The door descended and snow and cold blew in, the tang of ocean salt. He stepped out into the wind. The light of the setting sun made him squint. He'd been in only artificial light for upward of twelve hours. His boots crunched on the snow-dusted black rock. His exhalations steamed away in the wind.

Two of the men from Arrigo's freighter detached themselves from their ship and met him halfway. Both were human and bearded. One had a patched eye and a scar like a lightning stroke down one cheek. Both wore blasters on their hips. Like Zeerid, both had the butt straps undone.

Recognizing neither of them rekindled Zeerid's earlier concerns. He had a mind for faces, and both of the men were strangers.

The drop was starting to taste sour.

"Where's Arigo?" Zeerid asked.

"Doin' what Arigo does," Scar said, and gestured vaguely. "Sent us instead. No worries, though, right?"

No Scar shifted on his feet, antsy, twitchy.

Zeerid nodded, kept his face expressionless as his heart rate amped up and adrenaline started making him warm. Everything smelled wrong, and he'd learned over the years to trust his sense of smell.

"You Zeerid?" Scar asked.

"Z-man."

No one called him Zeerid except his sister-in-law.

And Aryn, once. But Aryn had been long ago.

"Z-man," echoed No Scar, shifting on his feet and half giggling.

"Sound funny to you?" Zeerid asked him.

Before No Scar could answer, Scar asked, "Where's the cargo?"

Zeerid looked past the two men before him to the third, who lingered near the landing ramp of Arigo's ship. The man's body language—too focused on the verbal exchange, too coiled—reinforced Zeerid's worry. He reminded Zeerid of the way rooks looked when facing Imperials for the first time, all attitude and hair trigger.

Suspicion stacked up into certainty. The drop didn't just smell bad, it *was* bad.

Arigo was dead, and the crew before him worked for some other faction on Ord Mantell, or worked for some organization sideways to The Exchange. Whatever. Didn't matter to Zeerid. He never bothered to follow who was fighting who, so he just trusted no one.

But what did matter to him was that the three men standing before him probably had tortured information from Arigo and would kill Zeerid as soon as they confirmed the presence of the cargo.

And there could be still more men hidden aboard the freighter.

It seemed he'd descended out of atmospheric blackout and into a crossfire after all.

What else was new?

"Why you call that ship *Fatman*?" No Scar asked. Arigo must have told them the name of Zeerid's ship because *Fatman* bore no identifying markings. Zeerid used fake ship registries on almost every planet on which he docked.

" 'Cause it takes a lot to fill her belly."

"Ship's a she, though. Right? Why not *Fatwoman*?"

"Seemed disrespectful."

No Scar frowned. "Huh? To who?"

Zeerid did not bother to answer. All he'd wanted to do was drop off the munitions, retire some of his debt to The Exchange, and get back to his daughter before he had to get back out in the black and get dirty again.

"Something wrong?" Scar asked, his tone wary. "You look upset."

"No," Zeerid said, and forced a half smile. "Everything's the same as always."

The men plastered on uncertain grins, unclear on Zeerid's meaning.

"Right," Scar said. "Same as always."

Knowing how things would go, Zeerid felt the calm he usually did when danger impended. He flashed for a moment on Arra's face, on what she'd do if he died on Ord Mantell, on some no-name island. He pushed the thoughts away. No distractions.

"Cargo is in the main bay. Send your man around. The ship's open."

The expressions on the faces of both men hardened, the change nearly imperceptible but clear to Zeerid, a transformation that betrayed their intention to murder. Scar ordered No Scar to go check the cargo.

"He'll need a lifter," Zeerid said, readying himself, focusing on speed and precision. "That stuff ain't a few kilos."

No Scar stopped within reach of Zeerid, looking back at Scar for guidance, his expression uncertain.

"Nah," said Scar, his hand hovering near his holster, the motion too casual to be casual. "I just want him to make sure it's all there. Then I'll let my people know to release payment."

He held up his arm as if to show Zeerid a wrist comlink, but the parka covered it.

"It's all there," Zeerid said.

"Go on," said Scar to No Scar. "Check it."

"Oh," Zeerid said, and snapped his fingers. "There is one other thing . . ."

No Scar sighed, stopped, faced him, eyebrows raised in a question, breath steaming out of his nostrils. "What's that?"

Zeerid made a knife of his left hand and drove his fingertips into No Scar's throat. While No Scar crumpled to the snow, gagging, Zeerid jerked one of his blasters free of its hip holster and put a hole through Scar's chest before the man could do anything more than take a surprised step backward and put his hand on the grip of his own weapon. Scar staggered back two more steps, his mouth working but making no sound, his right arm held up, palm out, as if he could stop the shot that had already killed him.

As Scar toppled to the ground, Zeerid took a wild shot at the third man near the *Doghouse*'s landing ramp but missed high. The third man made himself small beside the *Doghouse*, drew his blaster pistol, and shouted into a wrist comlink. Zeerid saw movement within the cargo bay of Arigo's ship—more men with ill intent.

No way to know how many.

He cursed, fired a covering shot, then turned and ran for *Fatman*. A blaster shot put a smoking black furrow through the sleeve of his parka but missed flesh. Another rang off the hull of *Fatman*. A third shot hit him square in the back. It felt like getting run over by a speeder. The impact drove the air from his lungs and plowed him face-first into the snow.

He smelled smoke. His armored vest had ablated the shot.

Adrenaline got him to his feet just as fast as he had gone down. Gasping, trying to refill his lungs, he ducked behind a landing skid for cover and wiped the snow from his face. He poked his head out for a moment to look back, saw that No Scar had stopped gagging and started being dead, that Scar stayed politely still, and that six more men were dashing toward him, two armed with blaster rifles and the rest with pistols.

His armor would not stop a rifle bolt.

A shot slammed into the landing skid, another into the snow at his feet, another, another.

"Stang!" he cursed.

The safety of *Fatman*'s landing ramp and cargo bay, only a few steps from him, somehow looked ten kilometers away.

He took a blaster in each hand, stretched his arms around to either side of the landing skid, and fired as fast he could he pull the trigger in the direction of the onrushing men. He could not see and did not care if he hit anyone, he just wanted to get them on the ground. After he'd squeezed off more than a dozen shots with no return fire, he darted out from the behind the skid and toward the ramp.

He reached it before the shooters recovered enough to let loose another barrage. A few bolts chased him up the ramp, ringing off the metal. Sparks flew and the smell of melted plastoid mixed with the ocean air. He ran past the button to raise the ramp, struck at it, and hurried on toward the cockpit. Only after he'd nearly cleared the cargo bay did it register with him that he wasn't hearing the whir of turning gears.

He whirled around, cursed.

In his haste, he'd missed the button to raise the landing ramp.

He heard shouts from outside and dared not go back. He could close the bay from the control panel in the cockpit. But he had to hurry.

He pelted through *Fatman*'s corridors, shouldered open the door to the cockpit, and started punching in the launch sequence. *Fatman*'s thrusters went live and the ship lurched upward. Blasterfire thumped off the hull but did no harm. He tried to look down out of the canopy, but the ship was angled upward and he could not see the ground. He punched the control to move it forward and heard the distant squeal of metal on metal. It had come from the cargo bay.

Something was slipping around in there.

The loose container of grenades.

And he'd still forgotten to seal the bay.

Cursing himself for a fool, he flicked the switch that brought up the ramp then sealed the cargo bay and evacuated it of oxygen. If anyone had gotten aboard, they would suffocate in there.

He took the controls in hand and fired *Fatman*'s engines. The ship shot upward. He turned her as he rose, took a look back at the island.

For a moment, he was confused by what he saw. But realization dawned.

When *Fatman* had lurched up and forward, the remaining straps securing the container of grenades had snapped and the whole shipping container had slid right out the open landing ramp.

He was lucky it hadn't exploded.

The men who had ambushed him were gathered around the crate, probably wondering what was inside. A quick head count put their number at six, so he figured none had gotten on board *Fatman*. And none of them seemed to be making for Arigo's ship, so Zeerid assumed they had no intention of pursuing him in the air. Maybe they were happy enough with the one container.

Amateurs, then. Pirates, maybe.

Zeerid knew he would have to answer to Oren, his handler, not only for the deal going sour but also for the lost grenades.

Kriffing treadmill just kept going faster and faster.

He considered throwing *Fatman*'s ion engines on full, clearing Ord Mantell's gravity well, and heading into hyperspace, but changed his mind. He was annoyed and thought he had a better idea.

He wheeled the freighter around and accelerated.

"Weapons going live," he said, and activated the

over-and-under plasma cannons mounted on *Fatman*'s sides.

The men on the ground, having assumed he would flee, did not notice him coming until he had closed to five hundred meters. Faces stared up at him, hands pointed, and the men started to scramble. A few blaster shots from one of the men traced red lines through the sky, but a blaster could not harm the ship.

Zeerid took aim. The targeting computer centered on the crate.

"LZ is hot," he said, and lit them up. For an instant pulsing orange lines connected the ship to the island, the ship to the crate of grenades. Then, as the grenades exploded, the lines blossomed into an orange cloud of heat, light, and smoke that engulfed the area. Shrapnel pattered against the canopy, metal this time, not ice, and the shock wave rocked *Fatman* slightly as Zeerid peeled the ship off and headed skyward.

He glanced back, saw six, motionless, smoking forms scattered around the blast radius.

"That was for you, Arigo."

He would still have some explaining to do, but at least he'd taken care of the ambushers. That had to be worth something to The Exchange.

Or so he hoped.

DARTH MALGUS strode the autowalk, the steady rap of his boots on the pavement the tick of a chrono counting down the limited time remaining to the Republic.

Speeders, swoops, and aircars roared above him in unending streams, the motorized circulatory system of the Republic's heart. Skyrises, bridges, lifts, and plazas covered the entire surface of Coruscant to a height of kilometers, all of it the trappings of a wealthy, decadent civilization, a sheath that sought to hide the rot in a co-coon of duracrete and transparisteel.

But Malgus smelled the decay under the veneer, and he would show them the price of weakness, of complacency.

Soon it would all burn.

He would lay waste to Coruscant. He knew this. He had known it for decades.

Memories floated up from the depths of his mind. He recalled his first pilgrimage to Korriban, remembered the profound sense of holiness he had felt as he walked in isolation through its rocky deserts, through the dusty canyons lined with the tombs of his ancient Sith fore-bears. He had felt the Force everywhere, had exulted in it, and in his isolation it had showed him a vision. He had seen systems in flames, the fall of a galaxy-spanning government.

He had believed then, had *known* then and ever since, that the destruction of the Jedi and their Republic would fall to him.

"What are you thinking of, Veradun?" Eleena asked him.

Only Eleena called him by his given name, and only when they were alone. He enjoyed the smooth way the syllables rolled off her tongue and lips, but he tolerated it from no others.

"I am thinking of fire," he said, the hated respirator partially muffling his voice.

She walked beside him, as beautiful and dangerous as an elegantly crafted lanvarok. She clucked her tongue at his words, eyed him sidelong, but said nothing. Her lavender skin looked luminescent in the setting sun.

Crowds thronged the plaza in which they walked, laughing, scowling, chatting. A human child, a young girl, caught Malgus's eye when she squealed with delight and ran to the waiting arms of a dark-haired woman, presumably her mother. The girl must have felt his gaze. She looked at him from over her mother's shoulder, her small face pinched in a question. He stared at her as he walked and she looked away, burying her face in her mother's neck.

Other than the girl, no one else marked his passage. The citizens of the Republic felt safe so deep in the Core, and the sheer number of beings on Coruscant granted him anonymity. He walked among his prey, cowled, armored under his cloak, unnoticed and unknown, but heavy with purpose.

"This is a beautiful world," Eleena said.

"Not for very much longer."

His words seemed to startle her, though he could not imagine why. "Veradun . . ."

He saw her swallow, look away. Whatever words she intended after his name seemed stuck on the scar that marred her throat.

"You may speak your mind, Eleena."

Still she looked away, taking in the scenery around them, as if memorizing Coruscant before Malgus and the Empire lit it aflame.

"When will the fighting end?"

The premise of the question confounded him. "What do you mean?"

"Your life is war, Veradun. *Our* life. When will it end? It cannot always be so."

He nodded then, understanding the flavor of the conversation to come. She would try to disguise self-perceived wisdom behind questions. As usual, he was of two minds about it. On the one hand, she was but a servant, a woman who provided him companionship when he wished it. On the other hand, she was Eleena. *His* Eleena.

"You choose to fight beside me, Eleena. You have killed many in the name of the Empire."

The lavender skin of her cheeks darkened to purple. "I have not killed for the Empire. I fight, and kill, for you. You know this. But you . . . you fight for the Empire? Only for the Empire?"

"No. I fight because that is what I was made to do and the Empire is the instrument through which I realize my purpose. The Empire is war made manifest. That is why it is perfect."

She shook her head. "Perfect? Millions die in its wars. Billions."

"Beings die in war. That is the price that must be paid."

She stared at a group of children following an adult, perhaps a teacher. "The price for what? Why constant war? Why constant expansion? What is it the Empire wants? What is it *you* want?"

Behind his respirator, he smiled as he might when entertaining the questions of a precocious child.

"Want is not the point. I serve the Force. The Force is conflict. The Empire is conflict. The two are congruent."

"You speak as if it were mathematics."

"It is."

"The Jedi do not think so."

He fought down a flash of anger. "The Jedi understand the Force only partially. Some of them are even powerful in its use. But they fail to comprehend the fundamental nature of the Force, that it is conflict. That a light side and a dark side exist is proof of this."

He thought the conversation over, but she did not relent.

"Why?"

"Why what?"

"Why conflict? Why would the Force exist to foment conflict and death?"

He sighed, becoming agitated. "Because the survivors of the conflict come to understand the Force more deeply. Their understanding evolves. That is purpose enough."

Her expression showed that she still did not understand. His tone sharpened as his exasperation grew.

"Conflict drives a more perfect understanding of the Force. The Empire expands and creates conflict. In that regard, the Empire is an instrument of the Force. You see? The Jedi do not understand this. They use the Force to repress themselves and others, to enforce their version of tolerance, harmony. They are fools. And they will see that after today."

For a time, Eleena said nothing, and the hum and buzz of Coruscant filled the silent gulf between them. When she finally spoke, she sounded like the shy girl he had first rescued from the slave pens of Geonosis.

"Constant war will be your life? Our life? Nothing more?"

He understood her motives at last. She wanted their relationship to change, wanted it, too, to evolve. But his dedication to the perfection of the Empire, which allowed him to perfect his understanding of the Force, precluded any preeminent attachments.

"I am a Sith warrior," he said.

"And things with us will always be as they are?"

"Master and servant. This displeases you?"

"You do not treat me as your servant. Not always."

He let a hardness he did not feel creep into his voice. "Yet a servant you are. Do not forget it."

The lavender skin of her cheeks darkened to purple, but not with shame, with anger. She stopped, turned, and stared directly into his face. He felt as if the cowl and respirator he wore hid nothing from her.

"I know your nature better than you know yourself. I nursed you after the Battle of Alderaan, when you lay near death from that Jedi witch. You speak the words in earnest—*conflict, evolution, perfection*—but belief does not reach your heart."

He stared at her, the twin stalks of her lekku framing the lovely symmetry of her face. She held his eyes, unflinching, the scar that stretched across her throat visible under her collar.

Struck by her beauty, he grabbed her by the wrist and pulled her to him. She did not resist and pressed her curves against him. He slipped his respirator to the side and kissed her with his ruined lips, kissed her hard.

"Perhaps you do not know me as well as you imagine," he said, his voice unmuffled by the mechanical filter of his respirator.

As a boy, he had killed a Twi'lek servant woman in his adoptive father's house, his first kill. She had committed some minor offense he could no longer recall and that had never mattered. He had not killed her because of her misdeed. He'd killed her to assure himself that he *could* kill. He still recalled the pride with which his adoptive father had regarded the Twi'lek's corpse. Soon afterward, Malgus had been sent to the Sith Academy on Dromund Kaas.

"I think I do know you," she said, defiant.

He smiled, she smiled, and he released her. He replaced his respirator and checked the chrono on his wrist.

If all went as planned, the defense grid should come down in moments.

A surge of emotion went through him, born in his certainty that his entire life had for its purpose the next hour, that the Force had brought him to the moment when he would engineer the fall of the Republic and the ascendance of the Empire.

His comlink received a message. He tapped a key to decrypt it.

It is done, the words read.

The Mandalorian had done her job. He did not know the woman's real name, so in his mind she had become a title, the Mandalorian. He knew only that she worked for money, hated the Jedi for some personal reason known only to herself, and was extraordinarily skilled.

The message told him that the planet's defense grid had gone dark, yet none of the thousands of sentients who shared the plaza with him looked concerned. No alarm had sounded. Military and security ships were not racing through the sky. The civilian and military authorities were oblivious to the fact that Coruscant's security net had been compromised.

But they would notice it before long. And they would disbelieve what their instruments told them. They would run a test to determine if the readings were accurate.

By then, Coruscant would be aflame.

We are moving, he keyed into the device. *Meet us within.*

He took one last look around, at the children and their parents playing, laughing, eating, everyone going about their lives, unaware that everything was about to change.

"Come," he said to Eleena, and picked up his pace. His cloak swirled around him. So, too, his anger.

Moments later he received another coded transmission, this one from the hijacked drop ship.

Jump complete. On approach. Arrival in ninety seconds.

Ahead, he saw the four towers surrounding the stacked tiers of the Jedi Temple, its ancient stone as orange as fire in the light of the setting sun. The civilians seemed to give it a wide berth, as if it were a holy place rather than one of sacrilege.

He would reduce it to rubble.

He walked toward it and fate walked beside him.

Statues of long-dead Jedi Masters lined the approach to the Temple's enormous doorway. The setting sun stretched the statue's tenebrous forms across the duracrete. He walked through the shadows and past them, noting some names: Odan-Urr, Ooroo, Arca Jeth.

"You have been deceived," he whispered to them. "Your time is past."

Most of the Jedi Order's current Masters were away, either participating in the sham negotiations on Alderaan or protecting Republic interests offplanet, but the Temple was not entirely unguarded. Three uniformed Republic soldiers, blaster rifles in hand, stood watchful near the doors. He sensed two more on a high ledge to his left.

Eleena tensed beside him, but she did not falter.

He checked his chrono again. Fifty-three seconds.

The three soldiers, wary, watched him and Eleena approach. One of them spoke into a wrist comlink, perhaps querying a command center within.

They would not know what to make of Malgus. Despite the war, they felt safe in their enclave in the center of the Republic. He would teach them otherwise.

"Stop right there," one of them said.

"I cannot stop," Malgus said, too softly to hear behind the respirator. "Not ever."

STILL HEART, still mind, these things eluded Aryn, floated before her like snowflakes in sun, visible for a moment, then melted and gone. She fiddled with the smooth coral beads of the Nautolan tranquillity bracelet Master Zallow had given her when she'd been promoted to Jedi Knight. Silently counting the smooth, slick beads, sliding them over their chain one after another, she sought the calm of the Force.

No use.

What was wrong with her?

Outside, speeders hummed past the large window that looked out on a bucolic, beautiful Alderaanian landscape suitable for a painting. Inside, she felt turmoil. Ordinarily, she was better able to shield herself from surrounding emotions. She usually considered her empathic sense a boon of the Force, but now . . .

She realized she was bouncing her leg, stopped. She crossed and uncrossed her legs. Did it again.

Syo sat beside her, callused hands crossed over his lap, as still as the towering statuary of Alderaanian statesmen that lined the domed, marble-tiled hall in which they sat. Light from the setting sun poured through the window, pushing long shadows across the floor. Syo did not look at her when he spoke.

"You are restless."

"Yes."

In truth, she felt as if she were a boiling pot, the steam of her emotional state seeking escape around the lid of her control. The air felt charged, agitated. She would have attributed the feelings to the stress of the peace negotiations, but it seemed to her something more. She felt a doom creeping up on her, a darkness. Was the Force trying to tell her something?

"Restlessness ill suits you," Syo said.

"I know. I feel . . . odd."

His expression did not change behind his short beard, but he would know to take her feelings seriously. "Odd? How?"

She found his voice calming, which she supposed was part of the reason he had spoken. "As if . . . as if something is about to happen. I can explain it no better than that."

"This originates from the Force, from your empathy?"

"I don't know. I just . . . feel like something is about to happen."

He seemed to consider this, then said, "Something *is* about to happen." He indicated with a glance the large double doors to their left, behind which Master Dar'nala and Jedi Knight Satele Shan had begun negotiations with the Sith delegation. "An end to the war, if we are fortunate."

She shook her head. "Something other than that." She licked her lips, shifted in her seat.

They sat in silence for a time. Aryn continued to fidget.

Syo cleared his throat, and his brown eyes fixed on a point across the hall. He spoke in a soft tone. "*They* see your agitation. They interpret it as something it is not."

She knew. She could feel their contempt, an irritation in her mind akin to a pebble in her boot.

A pair of dark-cloaked Sith, members of the Empire's delegation to Alderaan, sat on a stone bench along the wall opposite Aryn and Syo. Fifteen meters of polished marble floor, the two rows of Alderaanian statuary, and the gulf of competing philosophies separated Jedi and Sith.

Unlike Aryn, the Sith did not appear agitated. They appeared coiled. Both of them leaned forward, forearms on their knees, eyes on Aryn and Syo, as if they might spring to their feet at any moment. Aryn sensed their derision over her lack of control, could see it in the curl of the male's lip.

She turned her eyes from the Sith and tried to occupy her mind by reading the names engraved on the pedestals of the statues—Keers Dorana, Velben Orr, others she'd never heard of—but the presence of the Sith pressed against her Force sensitivity. She felt as if she were submerged deep underwater, the pressure pushing against her. She kept waiting for her ears to pop, to grant her release in a flash of pain. But it did not come, and her eyes kept returning to the Sith pair.

The woman, her slight frame lost in the shapelessness of her deep blue robes, glared through narrow, pale eyes. Her long dark hair, pulled into a topknot, hung like a hangman's noose from her scalp. The slim human man who sat beside her had the same sallow skin as the woman, the same pale eyes, the same glare. Aryn assumed them to be siblings. His dark hair and long beard—braided and forked into two tines—could not hide a face so lined with scars and pitted with pockmarks that it reminded Aryn of the ground after an artillery barrage. Her eyes fell to the thin hilt of the man's lightsaber, the bulky, squared-off hilt of the woman's.

She imagined their parents had noticed brother and sister's Force potential when they had been young and shipped them off to Dromund Kaas for indoctrination. She knew that's what they did with Force-sensitives in the Empire. If true, the Sith sitting across from her hadn't really *fallen* to the dark side; they'd never had a chance to rise and become anything else.

She wondered how she might have turned out had she been born in the Empire. Would she have trained at Dromund Kaas, her empathy put in service to pain and torture?

"Do not pity them," Syo said in Bocce, as if reading her thoughts. Bocce sounded awkward on his lips. "Or doubt yourself."

His insight surprised her only slightly. He knew her well. "Who is the empath now?" she answered in the same tongue.

"They chose their path. As we all do."

"I know," she said.

She shook her head over the wasted potential, and the eyes of both Sith tracked her movement with the alert, focused gaze of predators tracking prey. The Academy at Dromund Kaas had turned them into hunters, and they saw the universe through a hunter's eyes. Perhaps that explained the war in microcosm.

But it did nothing to explain the proposed peace.

And perhaps that was why Aryn felt so ill at ease.

The offer to negotiate an end to the war had come like a lightning strike from the Sith Emperor, unbidden, unexpected, sending a jolt through the government of the Republic. The Empire and the Republic had agreed to a meeting on Alderaan, the scene of an earlier Republic victory in the war, the number and makeup of the two delegations limited and strictly proscribed. To her surprise, Aryn was among the Jedi selected, though she was stationed perpetually *outside* the negotiation room.

"You have been honored by this selection," Master Zallow had told her before she took the ship for Alderaan, and she knew it to be true, yet she had felt uneasy since leaving Coruscant. She felt even less at ease on Alderaan. It wasn't that she had fought on Alderaan before. It was . . . something else.

"I am fine," she said to Syo, hoping that saying it would work a spell and make it so. "Lack of sleep perhaps."

"Be at ease," he said. "Everything will work out."

She nodded, trying to believe it. She closed her eyes on the Sith and fell back on Master Zallow's teachings. She felt the Force within and around her, a matrix of glowing lines created by the intersection of all living things. As always, the line of Master Zallow glowed as brightly as a guiding star in her inner space.

She missed him, his calm presence, his wisdom.

Focusing inward, she picked a point in her mind, made it a hole, and let her unease drain into it.

Calm settled on her.

When she opened her eyes, she fixed them on the male Sith. Something in his expression, a knowing look in his eye, half hidden by his sneer, troubled Aryn, but she kept her face neutral and held his gaze, as still as a sculpture.

"I see you," the Sith said from across the room.

"And I you," she answered, her voice steady.

CHAPTER 2

MALGUS LET his anger build with each step he took toward the Temple's entrance. The Force responded to his emotional state, caught him up in its power until he was awash in it. He sensed the seed of fear growing in the soldiers' guts.

"I said *stop*," the lead soldier said again.

"Do nothing," Malgus said to Eleena over his shoulder. "These are mine."

She let her hands fall slack to her sides and fell in behind him.

The three guards spread out into an arc as they approached him, their movements cautious, blaster rifles ready. The entrance to the Temple, a fifteen-meter-tall opening in the edifice's façade, loomed behind them.

"Who are you?" the guard asked.

The last word hung in the air, frozen in time, as Malgus drew on the Force and augmented his speed. The hilt of his lightsaber filled his hand and its red line split the air. He crosscut the guard before him, putting a black canyon in his chest, continued the swing through the guard on his left, and with his left hand used a blast of power to drive the third guard into the Temple wall hard enough to crush bones and kill him.

Malgus felt the sudden surge of terror in the two soldiers up on the ledge to his left, felt them take aim in sweaty hands, start to squeeze triggers. He flung his lightsaber at them, guided it with the Force in a flickering red arc that cut both of them down, then recalled the blade to his hand. He deactivated it and hung it from his belt.

The roar of a rocket pack drew his attention. On a ledge above the Temple's entrance, the Mandalorian rode the fire on her back to a high window on one of the Temple's upper tiers and disappeared within. He trusted that she would join him for the combat inside.

He checked his chrono, watched the numbers evaporate. Twenty-nine seconds.

Eleena took the station to his right, and they entered the Temple.

The setting sun at their back reached through the huge doorway and extended their shadows before them, giant, dark heralds marking the path ahead. Within the Temple was a stillness, a peace soon to be shattered.

Malgus's boots rapped against the polished stone floor. The hall extended before them for several hundred meters. Two rows of elegant columns reached from floor to ceiling on either side, framing a processional down the hall's center. Ledges and balconies, too, lined both sides.

Malgus felt the presence of more guards and Jedi to his right, his left, and before him.

He checked his chrono. Twelve seconds.

Motion above and to his right, then to the left, drew his eyes. Curious Padawans looked down from the ledges above.

Ahead, half a dozen robed and hooded Jedi dropped

from the balconies and took station in the hall. Another Jedi descended the grand staircase at the end of the hall. His Force signature radiated power, confidence—a Master.

As one, the seven Jedi moved toward Malgus and Eleena, and Malgus and Eleena moved toward them.

More and more Padawans gathered on the balconies and walkways above, sparks of light-side blasphemy flickering in Malgus's perception.

The more powerful Force signatures of the approaching Jedi pressed against Malgus, and his against theirs, the power of each distorting the other by its presence.

In his mind, the countdown continued.

The space between him and the Jedi diminished.

The power within him grew.

They stopped at two meters. The Jedi Master threw back his hood to reveal blond hair graying at the temples, a handsome, ruddy face. Malgus knew his name from his intelligence briefings—Master Ven Zallow.

In appearance, Zallow was everything Malgus—with his pale skin, scars, and hairless pate—was not. With respect to the Force, Malgus was everything Zallow was not.

The six Jedi Knights accompanying Zallow spaced themselves around Malgus and Eleena, to minimize maneuvering room. The Jedi eyed him cautiously, the way they might a trapped predator.

Eleena put her back to Malgus's. Malgus felt her breathing, deep and regular.

Silence ruled the hall.

Somewhere, a Padawan cleared his throat. Another coughed.

Zallow and Malgus stared into each other's eyes but exchanged no words. None were necessary. Both knew what would unfold next, what must unfold.

The chrono on Malgus's wrist began to beep. The slight sound rang out like an explosion in the silent vastness of the hall.

The sound seemed to free the Jedi to act. Half a dozen green and blue lines pierced the dimness as all of the Jedi Knights ignited their lightsabers, backed off a step, and assumed a fighting stance.

All except Zallow, who held his ground before Malgus. Malgus credited him for it and inclined his head in a show of respect.

Perhaps the Jedi Knights thought the beeping chrono indicated a bomb of some kind. In a way, Malgus supposed, it did.

From behind, another sound broke the silence. The whine of the hijacked drop ship's approaching engines.

Malgus did not turn. Instead, he watched the events behind him by watching the events before him.

The Jedi Knights stepped back another step, looking past Malgus, uncertainty in their expressions. Eleena pressed her back against Malgus. No doubt she could see the drop ship by now as it roared downward, toward the Temple.

Zallow did not step back and his eyes stayed on Malgus.

The sound of the drop ship's engines grew louder, more acute, a prolonged, mechanical scream.

Malgus watched the eyes of the Jedi Knights widen, heard the shouts of alarm from throughout the hall, then the screams, all of them soon overwhelmed by the roar of the reinforced drop ship slamming at speed into the front of the Temple.

Stone shattered and the Temple's floor vibrated under the impact. Metal bent, twisted, and shrieked. People, too, bent, twisted, and shrieked. The explosion colored the hall in orange—Malgus could see it reflected in Zallow's eyes—and the sudden flame drew the oxygen toward it in a powerful wind, as if the conflagration were a great pair of lungs drawing breath.

Malgus did not turn. He had seen the attack thousands of times on computer models and knew exactly what was happening from the sounds he heard.

The drop ship's enormous speed and mass allowed it to retain momentum and it skidded along the Temple floor, gouging stone, trailing fire, toppling columns, collapsing balconies, crushing bodies.

Still Malgus did not move, nor Zallow.

The drop ship skidded closer, closer, the sound of metal grinding over stone ever louder in Malgus's ears. More columns collapsed. Eleena pressed against him as the flaming, shredded vessel slid toward them. But it was already losing speed and soon came to a halt.

Dust, heat, and smoke filled the hall. Flames crackled. Shouts of pain and surprise penetrated the sudden silence.

"What have they done?" someone called.

"Medic!" screamed someone else.

Malgus heard the explosive bolts on the specially reinforced passenger compartment of the drop ship blow outward and hit the floor like metal rain, heard the hatch clang to the floor.

For the first time, Zallow looked past Malgus, his head cocked in a question. Uncertainty entered his expression. Malgus savored it.

A prolonged, irregular hum sounded as the fifty Sith warriors within the drop ship's compartment activated their lightsabers. The sound heralded the fall of the Temple, the fall of Coruscant, the fall of the Republic.

Malgus flashed on the vision he'd seen on Korriban, of a galaxy in flames. He threw back his hood, smiled, and activated his lightsaber.

* * *

ZEERID LET *Fatman* fly free and blazed away from Ord Mantell's surface. He kept his scanners sweeping the area, concerned that the pirates might have allies in another ship somewhere, but he saw no signs of pursuit. In time, he let himself relax.

The pink of Ord Mantell's clouds and upper stratosphere soon gave way to the black of space. Planetary control did not ping him for identification, and he would not have responded anyway. He did not answer to them. He answered to The Exchange, though he'd never met any serious player in the syndicate face-to-face.

Receiving his instructions through a handler he knew only as Oren, he flew blind most of the time. He got his assignments remotely, picked up cargo where he was told, then dropped it off where he was told. He preferred it that way. It made it feel less personal, which made him feel less dirty.

He took care to return the emphasis on privacy, ensuring that The Exchange knew little about him other than his past as a soldier and pilot. As far as they knew, he had no friends and no family. He knew that if they learned of Arra, they would use her as leverage against him. He could not allow that. And were any harm to ever come to her . . .

Once again, he realized that he was holding the stick too tightly. He relaxed, breathed deeply, and composed his thoughts. When he felt ready, he plugged in the code for the secure subspace channel he used to communicate with Oren. He waited until he heard the hollow sound of an open connection.

Oren did not waste time with a greeting. "The drop went well, I presume?"

From his voice, Zeerid made Oren as a human male,

probably in his forties or early fifties, though he could have been using voice-disguising technology.

"No," Zeerid said, and exhaled a cloud of smoke. "The drop was an ambush."

A moment of silence, then, "The purchaser's agents ambushed you?"

Zeerid shook his head. "I don't think so. These were men I hadn't seen before. Pirates, I think. Maybe mercs. I think they killed the purchaser's men and commandeered the ship."

"Are you certain?"

Anger bled into Zeerid's tone. "No, I'm not certain. What's certain in this work? Ever?"

Oren did not respond. Zeerid lassoed his emotions and continued.

"I'm only certain that the pilot I expected, a fellow named Arigo, was not there. But his ship was. I'm only certain that eight men with blasters and hostile attitudes tried to burn holes through me."

"Eight men." Oren's voice was tight. Not a good sign. "What happened to them?"

Zeerid had the impression that Oren was noting everything he said, filing it away in memory so he could sift it for any inconsistencies later.

"They're dead. I sniffed out the attack before they sprang it."

"That seems . . . convenient, Z-man."

Zeerid stared out the canopy at Ord Mantell's star and controlled the flash of temper. He knew that if Oren suspected him of double dealing, or just didn't believe his story, a word from the man would turn Arra into an orphan.

"Convenient? Let me tell you what's convenient, Oren. Word is that lots of deals have been going sour because The Exchange won't play nice with the other syndicates, including the Hutts. And nothing explains lots of deals going sour except a leak. That tells me The Exchange is venting Oh-two."

Oren did not miss a beat. Zeerid almost admired him. "If one of my fliers thought there might be a leak, he might also think it an ideal time to make a play for some goods himself. Especially if he had heavy debts. Make it look like an ambush of, say, eight men. After all, there's a ready excuse at hand—this strife with the other syndicates you mentioned."

"He might," Zeerid said. "But only if he was stupid. And stupid I am not. Listen, you gave me the drop coordinates on Ord Mantell. Send someone there, a surveillance droid. You'll see what I left there. But do it quick. Someone is going to clean up that mess before long, I'd wager."

"So . . . how did you manage to kill eight men?"

The discussion was about to take a turn for the worse. "They were too close to one of the shipping containers full of grenades when it blew up."

Oren paused. "One of *our* shipping containers blew up?"

Zeerid swallowed hard. "I lost it in the escape. The rest of the cargo is intact."

A long silence followed, an abyss of quiet. Zeerid imagined Oren flipping through the file cabinet of his mind, cross-referencing Zeerid's story with whatever other pertinent facts Oren already knew or thought he knew.

"This wasn't my fault," Zeerid said. "You find your leak, you'll find who's at fault."

"You lost cargo."

"I *saved* cargo. If I hadn't sussed this out, the whole shipment would have been lost to pirates."

"It would have been recovered. It is difficult to recover exploded grenades. Do you agree?"

"I would have been dead."

"You are replaceable. I ask again: Do you agree?"

Zeerid could not bring himself to respond.

"I choose to interpret your silence as agreement, Z-man."

Zeerid glared at the speaker while Oren continued: "At best, you will get paid only half for the job. The amount of the lost cargo will be set against that and added to your marker. It was already in excess of two million credits, if I remember correctly. The note on the ship and some loans against your gambling."

Oren always remembered correctly. The job would net negative for Zeerid. He wanted to punch something, someone, but there was no one in the cockpit but him.

"This makes me look bad, Z-man," Oren said. "And I very much dislike looking bad. You will make this up to me."

Zeerid did not like the sound of that. "How?"

A pause, then, "By doing a spicerun."

Zeerid shook his head. "I don't run spice. That was our understanding—"

Oren's voice never lost its calm, but the edge on it could have gouged armor. "The understanding has changed, contingent, as it was, on your successful completion of assignments. You owe us a large sum of credits and you owe me a large sum of face. You will make up both with a few spiceruns. That's where the credits are. So that's where you will be."

Zeerid said nothing, could say nothing.

"Are we clear, Z-man?"

Zeerid scowled but said, "Clear."

"Return to Vulta. I will be in touch soon. I have something in mind already."

I'll bet you do, Zeerid thought but didn't say.

The channel closed and Zeerid let fly with a sleet

storm of expletives. When he had finally vented, he cleared Ord Mantell's gravity well and its moons, set a course for Vulta, and engaged the hyperdrive.

"I'm a spicerunner, now," he said, as the black of space turned to the blue of hyperspace.

The treadmill under his feet had just picked up speed.

ARYN FELT dizzy. A rush of emotion flooded her. She could not name it, categorize it. It was just a wash of inchoate, raw feeling. She was swimming in it, sinking.

"Something is happening, Syo," she said, her voice tight. "I don't know what it is, but it is not good."

MASTER ZALLOW and the six Jedi Knights near Malgus leapt back and up, flipping at the top of the arc of their leaps, and landed in a crouch twenty meters away.

"May the Force be with you all," Zallow shouted to his fellow Jedi, and lit his blade.

Dozens more Jedi poured out of the hallway behind him and flowed down the staircase, the blades of their lightsabers visible through the smoke and dust, a forest of green and blue oriflammes. The Jedi did not shout as they charged, but the rumble of their boots and sandals on the floor sounded like rolling thunder.

"Stay near me," Malgus said over his shoulder to Eleena.

"Yes," she said, her blasters already in hand.

Malgus's Sith charged out of the carcass of the drop ship, their collective roar the sound of a hungry, rage-filled beast. The red lines of their blades cut the dust-covered air. Lord Adraas, a political favorite of Darth Angral and constant irritant to Malgus, led them. Like all of the Sith warriors save Malgus, a dark mask obscured his face entirely.

Malgus used his distaste for Adraas to further feed his

anger. He had requested that Darth Angral allow him to lead the attack alone, but Angral had insisted that Adraas lead the drop ship team.

Discarding his cloak, discarding the remaining restraints on his rage, Malgus joined the Sith charge, taking position before Adraas. Emotion fed his power, and its swell fairly lifted him from his feet. He felt the power of the dark side around him, within him.

Blaster bolts crisscrossed the battlefield from left and right as two platoons of Republic soldiers emerged from somewhere above and to the side and fired into the Sith ranks.

Malgus, nested deeply in the Force, perceived the dozens of bolts and their trajectory with perfect clarity. Without breaking stride he whipped his blade left, right, angled it ten degrees, and turned three bolts back on the soldiers who'd fired them, killing all three. A soldier had exploded a grenade in his face in the Battle of Alderaan, so he enjoyed killing soldiers when he could. Behind him, Eleena's twin blasters answered to the left and right with bolts of their own, picking off two more soldiers.

The Sith and Jedi forces closed, Sith battle lust facing the calm of the Jedi, the floor of the Temple the arena where centuries of indeterminate strife would at last reach a conclusion. Those strong in the Force would survive and their understanding of the Force would evolve. Those weak in the Force would die.

Malgus sought Master Zallow but could not make him out from the crowd of faces, dust, flames, and glowing blades. So he chose a Jedi at random from the crowd, a human male with a blue blade and a short beard, and targeted him.

Waves of power distorted the air and dopplered sound as the Jedi and Sith forces crashed into one another and intermixed in a chaotic, roaring tangle of bodies, light-sabers, and shouts.

Malgus augmented his strength with the Force, took a two-handed grip on his blade, and unleashed an over-hand slash designed to split the Jedi in half. The Jedi sidestepped the blow and crosscut with his blue blade at Malgus's throat. Malgus got his blade up in time, par-ried, and slammed a kick into the Jedi's mid-section. The blow folded the Jedi in half, sent him reeling backward five paces. Malgus leapt into the air, flipped, landed be-hind him, and drove his blade through the Jedi. Roaring with battle lust, Malgus sought another opponent.

A flash of lavender skin drew his gaze—Eleena. She ducked under a saber slash and dived to her side, firing half a dozen blaster shots as she did so. The Padawan who'd tried to kill her, a female Zabrak, the horns of her head gilt with colored pigments, deflected the shots as she closed in for another blow. Eleena flipped to her feet, still firing, but the Padawan deflected every shot and drew nearer.

Malgus drew on the Force and with a blast of power drove the Padawan across the hall and into one of the towering columns of stone, where she collapsed, blood leaking from her nose. Eleena continued firing, her eyes darting here and there over the battlefield as she sought targets.

The battle turned ever more chaotic. Jedi and Sith leapt, bounded, rolled, and flipped as red lines inter-sected with those of blue and green. Blasts of power sent bodies flying through the air, against walls, pulled loose rocks from the ceiling and sent them crashing into flesh. The hall was a cacophony of sound: shouts, screams, the hum of lightsabers, the intermittent sound of weapons-fire. Malgus walked in its midst, reveled in it.

He watched Lord Adraas leap into the middle of a

squad of Republic soldiers and punctuate his landing with an explosion of Force energy that cast the soldiers away like dry leaves.

Malgus, not to be outdone, picked a Jedi Knight at random, a human female ten meters away, held forth his left hand, and discharged veins of blue lightning from his fingertips. The jagged lines of energy cut a swath through the battle, harvesting two Padawans as they went, until they caught up to the Jedi Knight and lifted her off her feet.

She screamed as the lightning ripped into her, her flesh made temporarily translucent from the dark power coursing through her. Malgus savored her pain as she died.

He caught Adraas eyeing him and gave him a mocking salute with his lightsaber.

The high-pitched sound of Eleena's blasters drew his attention. She bounded past him and over the slain female Jedi Knight's corpse, a lavender blur firing rapidly. Putting her back to a column, she crouched and sought targets for her blasters. She met his eyes, winked, and signaled behind him. He whirled to see a score or more Republic soldiers rushing into the hall from a side room, blaster rifles tracing hot lines through the battlefield. Eleena answered with shots of her own.

Before Malgus could dispatch the soldiers, the Mandalorian rose from somewhere behind them, her jetpack spitting fire, her head-to-toe silver-and-orange armor gleaming in the fire of the hall. Hovering in the air like an avenging spirit, she discharged two small missiles from wrist mounts. They struck the floor near the Republic soldiers and blossomed into flame. Bodies, shouts, and loose rock flew in all directions. Still hovering, she spun a circle in the air while flamethrowers mounted on her forearm engulfed another group of soldiers.

Malgus knew the battle had turned, that it soon would be over. He glanced around, still seeking Zallow, the only opponent in the field worthy of his attention.

Before he could locate the Jedi Master, three more Jedi swarmed him. He parried the chop of a human male, leapt over the low slash of an orange-skinned Togruta female, severed the hand of the third, a female human, disarming her, then grabbed her by the throat with his free hand and slammed her into the floor with his Force-enhanced strength.

"Alara!" said the human male.

Leaping high over the male's cross-slash, Malgus landed behind the Togruta, who parried his lightsaber strike but could not defend herself against a Force blast that sent her skidding across the hall and into a pile of rubble.

Malgus roared, the lust for battle so pronounced that he would have killed his own warriors were there no Jedi left to slay. He wanted, needed, to kill another and to do so with his hands.

He ducked under a slash from the male, lunged forward, and took the Jedi by the throat. He lifted him from his feet and held him suspended in the air, gagging. The Jedi's brown eyes showed no fear, but did show pain. Malgus roared, squeezed hard, then dropped the body and stood over it, blade at his side, breath coming hard. The battle still swirled around him and he stood in its center, the eye of the Sith storm.

Malgus finally spotted Master Zallow ten paces away, whirling, spinning, his green blade a blur of precision and speed. One Sith warrior fell to him, another. Lord Adraas landed before him, trying to take Malgus's kill for himself. Adraas ducked low and slashed at Zallow's knees. Zallow leapt over the blow and unleashed a blast of energy that sent Adraas skidding on his backside across the hall.

"He is mine!" Malgus shouted, charging through the battlefield. He repeated himself as he passed Adraas. "Zallow is mine!"

Zallow must have heard Malgus, for he turned, met his eyes. Eleena, too, must have heard Malgus's shouting. She emerged from behind the column, deduced Malgus's intent, and fired several shots at Zallow.

Zallow, his eyes on Malgus throughout, deflected the bolts with his blade and sent them back at Eleena. Two struck her, and as she collapsed Zallow used a Force blast to drive her body against a column.

Malgus halted in mid-stride, his rage temporarily abated. He turned and stared at Eleena's fallen form for a long moment, her lavender body crumpled on the floor, her eyes closed, two black circles marring the smooth purple field of her flesh. She looked like a wilted flower.

Anger refilled him, overcame him. A shout of hate, raw and jagged, burst from his throat. Power went with it, shattering a nearby column and sending a rain of stone shards through the room.

He returned his gaze to Zallow and stalked toward him, his rage and power surging before him in a palpable wave. Another Jedi stepped in front of him, blue blade held high. Malgus barely saw him. He simply extended a hand, pushed through the Jedi's insufficient defenses, seized his throat with the Force, and choked him to death. Tossing the body aside, he moved toward Zallow.

Zallow, for his part, moved toward Malgus. A Sith warrior bounded at Zallow from his left, but Zallow leapt over the Sith's blade, spun, slashed, and cut down the Sith.

Zallow and Malgus closed. They halted at one meter, studied each other for a moment.

A human male Jedi Knight separated from the swirl of battle and stabbed at Malgus. Malgus sidestepped the blue line of the blade, punched the man in the stomach, doubling him over, and raised his own blade for a killing blow.

Zallow bounded forward and intercepted the downstroke. Zallow and Malgus stared into each other's faces and the rest of the battle fell away.

There was only Malgus and his rage, and Zallow and his calm.

Their blades sizzling in opposition, each used the Force to press against the strength of the other, but neither had an obvious advantage. Malgus shouted rage into Zallow's face. Only a furrowed brow and the tight line of his mouth betrayed the tension behind Zallow's otherwise tranquil expression.

Feeding off the anger from Eleena, Malgus shoved Zallow away and unleashed an onslaught of overhand slashes and crosscuts. Zallow backed off, parrying, unable to respond with blows of his own. Malgus tried to split Zallow's head but Zallow blocked again and again.

Malgus spun into a high, Force-augmented kick that hit Zallow in the chest and sent him flying backward ten meters. Zallow flipped and landed upright in a crouch near two of Malgus's Sith warriors.

They lunged for him and Zallow parried one blow, leapt over the second, and spun a rapid circle, cutting down both Sith.

Malgus, burning with hate, flung his lightsaber at Zallow. He guided its trajectory with the Force, and it spun a sizzling path through the air at Zallow's neck. But Zallow, riding the momentum of his attack on the second Sith, leapt into the air and over the blade.

While Zallow was still in the air, Malgus unleashed a blast of energy that caught the Jedi unprepared and sent him crashing downward into a pile of rubble. He lay there, prone.

Malgus did not hesitate. He mounted the column of his anger, shouting with hate, and leapt twenty meters into the air toward Zallow. Mid-jump, he used the Force to recall his blade to his hand, took a reverse two-handed grip, and prepared to pin Zallow to the Temple floor.

But Zallow rolled out of the way at the last moment and Malgus's blade sank to the hilt in the stone of the Temple's floor. Zallow leapt up and over Malgus, landed in a crouch, reactivated his lightsaber, and pelted across the floor back at Malgus.

Eschewing speed and grace for power, Zallow loosed a flurry of rapid strikes, slashes, and lunges. Malgus parried one blow after another but could not find an opening to mount his own counterattack. Lunging forward, Zallow slashed crosswise, Malgus parried, and Zallow slammed the hilt of his saber into the side of Malgus's jaw.

A tooth dislodged and his respirator was knocked askew. Malgus tasted blood, but he was too deep in the Force for the blow to do real damage. He staggered backward a step, as if the blow had stunned him.

Seeing an opening, Zallow stepped forward and crosscut for Malgus's throat.

As Malgus knew he would do.

Malgus turned his blade vertical to parry the blow and spun out of the blade lock. Reversing his lightsaber during the spin, he rode it into a stab that pierced Zallow's abdomen and came out the other side.

Zallow's expression fell. He hung there, impaled by the red line. He held Malgus's eyes, and Malgus saw the flames of the burning Temple reflected in Zallow's green irises.

"It is all going to burn," Malgus said.

Zallow's brow furrowed, perhaps with pain, perhaps with despair. Either way, Malgus enjoyed it. He waited for the light to disappear from Zallow's eyes before jerking his blade free and allowing the body to fall to the floor.

THE SHOCK hit Aryn with little warning, the sensation as sudden and powerful as a blaster shot. Her body spasmed. The tranquillity bracelet in her hand, the bracelet given her by Master Zallow, snapped in her clenched fist and the tear-shaped bits of coral rained to the floor.

She doubled over, moaned. Her stomach sank. Her vision blurred. The room spun. Her legs dissolved under her and she felt herself slipping, falling, sinking. A fist formed in her throat, throttling the cry that wanted release and allowing it loose only as an aborted, grief-ridden wail.

Through their connection in the Force, she felt the sharp stab of agony that Master Zallow experienced, felt her own breath hitch in sympathy as he took his final breath and died. The line of his life, usually so bright in her mind's eye when she felt the Force, usually so close to her own line, vanished from her perception.

Beside her, Syo's sharp, surprised intake of breath told her that he had felt something, too.

Despite her pain, the rising despair, the reality settled on her immediately. She had seen it in the eyes of the Sith male.

"What was that?" Syo asked, his voice seemingly far away, but his question fat with ugly possibilities.

She lifted her head, her long hair dangling before her

face, and stared across the room. Both Sith were standing, their bodies tensed, knowledge in their eyes.

"We are betrayed," she answered, her voice a hiss.

She left it unsaid that her Master, the man who had been a father to her, was dead.

She was surprised to find her legs sturdy under her as she stood up straight. A group of people stood near her. No, not people. They were statues, Alderaanian statues. She was on Alderaan for peace negotiations with the Sith.

And the Sith had betrayed them. She had fought the Sith on Alderaan before, during the battle for the planet. She would do so again. Now.

"How do you know this, Aryn?"

But Syo's voice, his doubt, did not erode her certainty.

"I *know*," she spat.

The Sith knew, too. They had known all along. She could see it in their faces.

Her view distilled down until it consisted entirely of the two Sith and nothing else. A roar filled her ears, the crashing surf of grief and burgeoning rage. She heard a voice calling her name from some distant place, repeating it as if it were an invocation, but she paid it no heed.

Both Sith eyed her, their stances ready for combat. The man wore the same contemptuous sneer, the curve of his thin lips uglier than the scars that lined his face.

"Aryn!" It was Syo calling her name. "Aryn! Aryn!"

They knew. The Sith knew.

"They knew all along," she said, speaking as much to herself as Syo.

"What? Knew what? What has happened?"

She did not bother to answer. She fell into the Force, drawing on its power.

Time seemed to slow. She felt as if she existed outside herself, watching. Her body moved across the antechamber, her boots scattering the coral of her bracelet. Violence filled her mind as she moved among the statues of men and women of peace.

"Aryn!" Syo called. "Do not."

She did not reach for her lightsaber. Her need would not allow for such antiseptic justice. She would avenge Master Zallow's death with her bare hands.

"No clean death for you," she said through the wall of her gritted teeth.

Some distant part of her recognized her emotional slippage, recognized in passing that Master Zallow would not have approved. She did not care. The pain was too deep, too fierce. It wanted expression in violence and the two Sith in the room became the focus of its need.

The male Sith reached for his lightsaber. Before he could activate it, Aryn unleashed a blast of power that lifted both Sith from their feet and blew them into the wall. Two Alderaanian statues, caught in the effect of her power, slammed into the wall to either side of the Sith and shattered into chunks.

The Sith must have used the Force to cushion their impact, for neither appeared hurt. Both leapt to their feet and spaced themselves apart for combat. Hilts came to hands and their lightsabers made red lines in the air. The male held his blade high over his head in an unusual style, awaiting her charge, light on the balls of his feet. The female held hers low, in a variant on the medium style.

Behind her, Aryn heard the hum of Syo activating his blade. She did not slow her advance. Using the Force, she jerked the male's hilt from his hand and brought it flying into her own grasp. Then she tossed it aside, and his sneer melted in the heat of his surprise.

She advanced on him, heedless of the woman, imagining the feel of her hands on his throat. He answered her approach with a blast of power, but she made a V with her hands, formed a wedge with her will, and deflected the blast to either side of her. More statues toppled, shattered. The female Sith, caught in the deflected blast, was thrown backward ten paces.

She closed to five paces, four. The male Sith took a fighting stance. They would fight not with lightsabers but with their hands—close, bloody work.

Aryn used the Force to augment her strength, her speed. She felt it flowing within and around her, turning her body into a weapon—

"Aryn Leneer!" a commanding voice said, Master Dar'nala's voice. "Jedi Knight Aryn Leneer!"

Syo, too, called to her. "Aryn! Stop!"

The combination of Dar'nala's and Syo's voices penetrated the haze of her emotional state. She faltered, slowed, stopped. Reason elbowed its way past her emotional turmoil, and she gave voice to her thoughts. Without taking her eyes from the male Sith, she said, "The Sith have betrayed us, Master Dar'nala. The negotiations were a ploy."

Dar'nala did not speak for a moment. Then, "You . . . felt this?"

Tears fought to fall from Aryn's eyes but she forced them back. She nodded, unable to speak.

Master Dar'nala's next words hit Aryn like a punch in the stomach.

"Listen to me, Aryn. I know. *I know.* But hear me now—Coruscant is in Imperial hands."

Aryn's breath went out of her. The statement did not make sense. Coruscant, the heart of the Republic, had fallen to the Empire?

"What?" Syo asked. "How? I thought—"

"That cannot be," Aryn said. She must have misheard.

She turned from the male Sith, who had recaptured his sneer, to face the leader of the Jedi delegation

Master Dar'nala stood in the archway, her skin a deeper red than usual. Senator Am-ris and a senior Jedi Knight, Satele Shan, flanked her. The Senator, a Cerean whose ruff of white hair topped the cliff of his furrowed brow, towered over the other two. His worried eyes looked out from a wrinkled face but focused on nothing. He looked lost.

Satele, on the other hand, looked as tightly wound as an ion coil, her gaze fixed straight ahead, her auburn hair mussed, the veneer of her neutral expression unable to mask the emotion boiling beneath it.

Neither Am-ris nor Satele seemed to notice the destruction in the hall. Both looked dazed—blank-eyed refugees wandering through the ruins of events. Only Dar'nala seemed composed, her hands clasped before her, her eyes noting the details in the room—the broken sculptures, the position of Aryn relative to the two Sith.

Aryn wondered what had transpired in the negotiation room. For a fleeting moment, hope rose in her, hope that her fellow Jedi had perceived the Sith betrayal and arrested or killed the Sith negotiators, but that hope faded as the lead Sith negotiator, Lord Baras, emerged from the chamber and stood near Dar'nala.

His wrinkled face could not hold the smugness he felt. It leaked out around the raised corners of his mouth. His dark hair, combed back off a widow's peak, matched his dark robes and eyes. In a haughty baritone, he said, "It can be, Jedi Knight. And it is. Coruscant has fallen."

Satele visibly tensed; her left hand clenched into a fist. Am-ris sagged. Dar'nala closed her eyes for a moment, as if struggling to maintain her calm.

"As of now," Lord Baras continued, "Coruscant belongs to the Empire."

"How—?" Aryn began, but Dar'nala raised a hand.

"Say nothing more. *Say nothing more.*"

Aryn swallowed the question she wished to ask.

"Deactivate your lightsaber," Dar'nala said to Syo, and he did. The female Sith did the same.

"What happened here?" Lord Baras asked, his eyes on the Sith brother and sister, the ruin in the room.

The male Sith bowed, used the Force to pull his lightsaber hilt to his hand, and hooked it to his belt. "A slight disagreement, Lord Baras. Nothing more. Please forgive the tumult."

Baras stared at the male Sith for a time, then at the female. "It is well that the disagreement did not lead to bloodshed. We are, after all, here to discuss peace."

He seemed almost about to burst out laughing. Am-ris whirled on him. Satele grabbed the Senator's cloak, as she might a leash, to keep him from getting too close to Baras.

"Peace! This entire proceeding was a farce—"

"Senator," Dar'nala said, and took Am-ris by the arm. But Am-ris would have none of it. His voice gained volume as he gave vent to his anger.

"You did not come here to discuss peace! You came here to mask a sneak attack against Coruscant. You are dishonorable liars, worthy of—"

"Senator!" Dar'nala said, and her tone must have reached Am-ris, for he fell silent, his breath coming fast and hard.

Lord Baras appeared untroubled by Am-ris's outburst. "You are mistaken, Senator. The Empire *is* here to discuss peace. We simply wished to ensure that the Republic would be more amenable to our terms. Should I understand your outburst to mean that the Republic is no longer interested in negotiating?"

While Am-ris reddened and sputtered, Dar'nala broke in.

"Negotiations will continue, Lord Baras."

"You are ever the voice of wisdom, Dar'nala," Baras said. "The Empire will expect a return to the negotiation table at this time tomorrow. If not, matters will go . . . poorly for the people of Coruscant."

Dar'nala's skin darkened further but her voice remained placid. "Our delegation will discuss matters and contact you tomorrow."

"I shall look forward to that. Rest well."

Am-ris cursed Baras in Cerean and Baras pretended not to hear.

As the Republic entourage picked its way among the rubble in the hall, among the rubble in their hearts, Aryn felt the mocking eyes of the Sith male upon her and could barely contain a shout of rage. Before leaving the room, she knelt and picked up one of the coral beads from her shattered bracelet.

CHAPTER 3

MALGUS SURVEYED the ruin. The shell of the drop ship still smoked and burned in places. Bits of blackened metal dotted the hall. Walls and columns had been reduced to piles of jagged rubble. Cracks veined the walls and ceiling. Light from the day's dying sun traced dust-filled lines from roof to floor. Bodies, many of them Sith, but more of them Jedi and Republic military, lay strewn about the floor, amid the rubble. A few groans sounded here and there. The Mandalorian stood in the Temple's shattered entrance. She held her helmet under her arm and the sun glinted on her long hair. Her eyes moved across the destruction, the hard line of her mouth showing no emotion. She must have felt Malgus's eyes on her. She met his gaze and nodded. He returned the gesture, one warrior acknowledging another. She pulled her helmet back on, turned, ignited her jetpack, and lifted off into Coruscant's sky. The Empire would see to her payment.

Of the fifty Sith warriors who had assaulted the Temple, perhaps a score remained on their feet. Malgus was displeased but not surprised to see Lord Adraas among the living. They, too, shared a look across the ruin, but no mutual gesture acknowledged their kinship as warriors. Neither credited the other with anything.

With the battle over, the remaining Sith warriors assembled near the drop ship and raised their fists in a salute to Malgus, shouting a victory cry amid their fallen foes. For a moment, Adraas stood among them and did nothing, merely stared at Malgus, then he, too, reluctantly joined the salute. Malgus let his tardiness pass.

For now.

Malgus acknowledged the salute with a nod.

"You are servants of the Empire," he said. "And of the Force."

They shouted once more in response.

Malgus kicked the hilt of Zallow's weapon out of his way, deactivated his own lightsaber, stepped over Zallow's body, and strode among the rubble, among the fires, among the dead, until he reached Eleena. He felt the eyes of his warriors on him, the eyes of Adraas, felt the change in sentiment come over them. He did not care.

He knelt and cradled Eleena in his arms. She remained warm, breathing. The puckered blaster wounds Zallow had given her looked like black mouths in the skin of her shoulder and chest. She appeared to have no broken bones.

"Eleena. Open your eyes. Eleena."

Her eyes fluttered open. "Veradun," she whispered.

Hearing her pronounce his name before other Sith surprised him, and his hand closed into a fist so tight it made his knuckles ache. She must never—never—behave familiarly with him in front of other Sith.

She must have sensed his anger for she blanched, cowered, staring at his closed fist, her eyes wide.

That she understood her transgression diffused his anger. He unrolled his fist and extended his hand.

"Can you stand?"

"Yes. Thank you, Master."

He lifted her roughly to her feet, heedless of her wounds. She winced with pain and leaned on him. He allowed it. Her breath came in pained gasps.

"Summon a medical team from *Steadfast*," he ordered Adraas.

Adraas's eyes narrowed. No doubt he thought the task beneath him.

"You heard Darth Malgus," Adraas said to a nearby Sith warrior. "Summon a medical team."

"No," Malgus said. "You do it, Adraas."

Adraas stared at him for a moment, anger in his eyes, before he pulled a curtain over his irritation and turned his face expressionless. "As you wish, Darth Malgus."

From outside, explosions like thunder sounded, the steady drumbeat of intense bombardment. Angral's fleet had begun its attack on Coruscant.

"I signaled to Darth Angral that the Temple was secure," Adraas said, the faintest hint of defiance in his tone. "You seemed . . . preoccupied with other things at the time."

Adraas's gaze fell on Eleena, then returned to Malgus.

Malgus glared at Adraas, one fist clenched, and fought down the flash of anger. He would not allow Adraas's borderline insubordination to diminish the rush he felt at his victory.

"I will forgive your arrogation of power this once, but do not overstep again," Malgus said. "Now remove yourself from my sight."

Adraas colored with rage, his mouth a thin line of anger, but he dared not say another word. He gave a half bow and stalked off.

Malgus made his grip on Eleena gentler as they turned to look outside. The ruined entrance of the Temple, widened by the drop ship crashing through it, opened onto clear sky. Together, he and Eleena watched Imperial bombers streak out of the orange-and-red clouds and light Coruscant aflame.

"Go see it, Master," Eleena whispered to him. "It is your victory. I am fine. Go."

She was not fine and he knew it. But he also knew that he had to see.

He left her and walked the hall until he reached the shattered entranceway. The statues of the Jedi that had lined the processional lay toppled, broken at his feet. He looked out on the culmination of his life.

Imperial ships swarmed the air. Bombs fell like rain and exploded into showers of red and orange and black. Gouts of smoke poured into the sky. The few native speeders that remained in the air were pursued by Imperial fighters and shot down. Hundreds of fires filled Malgus's field of vision. A skyrise burned, a pillar of flame reaching for the heavens. Secondary explosions sent deep vibrations moaning through the ground. Malgus occasionally caught the sounds of distant, panicked screaming. A handful of Republic fighters got airborne but they were quickly swarmed by Imperial fighters and blown from the sky.

He opened a communications channel to *Darkness,* Angral's command cruiser.

"Darth Angral, you have heard that the Jedi Temple is secure?"

The sound of a busy bridge served as background noise to Angral's response. "I have. You have done well, Darth Malgus. How many warriors died in the assault?"

"Adraas did not tell you?"

Angral did not answer, merely waited for Malgus to answer the original question.

"Perhaps thirty," Malgus said at last.

"Excellent. I will send a transport to pick up you and your men."

"I would rather you wait."

"Oh?"

"Yes. I wish to see Coruscant burn."

"I understand, old friend. I will ensure the bombers spare the Temple. For now."

The channel closed and Malgus sat down cross-legged in the doorway of the Temple. Soon, several of the Sith warriors took station around him. Together, they bore witness to fire.

IN LESS than half a standard hour, an Imperial medical transport cut through the smoke and flame and other Imperial ships that filled the sky to set down in a cloud of dust on the large processional outside the Jedi Temple. The two pilots, visible through the transparisteel of the cockpit, saluted Malgus.

A belly door slid open and two men in the gray-and-blue of the Imperial Medical Corps hustled down the ramp. Both carried cases of supplies and instruments and both had the soft physiques of men who—despite their warrior training—had not seen hard work in some time. Bipedal medical droids, their polished silver bodies reflecting the fires burning in the cityscape, walked behind them, each pulling a treatment cart with a tri-level gurney behind it.

Malgus rose and approached them. The doctors' eyes widened at his appearance—his scarred mien alarmed most—and they gave crisp salutes.

"There are several wounded within," Malgus said. "The Twi'lek female is my servant. Care for her as you would me."

"An alien, my lord?" asked the older of the two men, his jowls dotted with a day's growth of gray beard. "As

I'm sure you know, Imperial medical facilities in-theater are restricted—"

Malgus took a step toward him and the doctor's mouth snapped shut.

"Care for her as you would me. Do you understand?"

"Yes, my lord," the doctor said, and the medical team hurried past.

More explosions rocked the urban landscape. A bomb struck a power station, and an enormous flare of plasma jetted half a kilometer into the sky. A flight of ISF interceptors, notable for their bent wings, streaked over the Temple. The Sith around him cheered.

Eleena emerged from the Temple, her mouth tight with pain. The doctor trailed after her, worry creasing his brow.

"Please, mistress," the doctor said, eyeing Malgus with terror. "Please."

Eleena's eyes widened as she took in the scale of the bombardment, the destruction. Malgus stepped before her.

"Go with the doctors," he said. "There's an Imperial medical ship, *Steadfast,* in orbit with the rest of the cruiser fleet. Await me there. I will come when I am finished here."

"I do not require care, Master."

"Do as I command," he said, though his voice was not harsh.

She swallowed, smiled, and nodded.

"Thank you, my lord," the doctor said to Malgus. "Come, mistress." He took Eleena gently by the arm and escorted her aboard the transport while bombs fell and the Republic died.

After the medical team had triaged and loaded the wounded, the Sith loaded their own dead aboard. The bodies would be taken to Dromund Kaas or Korriban for proper rites. Malgus wished Adraas had been among them.

After the transport lifted off, Adraas, masked once more, came to Malgus's side.

"What of the Jedi bodies?" Adraas asked.

Malgus considered. The Jedi had fought well, especially Zallow. They misunderstood the Force, but he nevertheless wished to treat them honorably. "Make the Temple their tomb. Bring the whole thing down."

"I will request a bomber to—"

Malgus shook his head and turned on Adraas. They stood about the same height, and Adraas did not quail before Malgus's appearance.

"No," Malgus said. "There are more than enough explosives still on the drop ship. Use them."

"This is an order . . . my lord?"

Malgus held his calm with difficulty. "Sith should destroy the Jedi Temple, not Imperial pilots. Do you disagree, Adraas?"

Adraas seemed not to have considered this. Malgus was not surprised. Adraas, too, misunderstood the Force, and he had little sense of honor. Still, he did as he was told.

"It will be done, my lord."

Presently, the charges were set and Malgus held a remote detonator in his hand. He eyed the Temple one last time, its towers, the stacked tiers of the central structure, the toppled statues, the great entryway made into a rough and jagged sneer by the passage of the drop ship. The rest of his Sith forces stood gathered around him.

"Should we remove to a safe distance?" Adraas asked.

Malgus regarded him with contempt. "This is a safe distance."

"We are twenty meters away from the entrance," Adraas said.

Staring into Adraas's face, Malgus activated the detonator. A series of low booms sounded, starting deep within the Temple and drawing closer as the charges exploded in sequence and undermined the Temple's foundation.

A strong gust of dust and loose debris blew out of the entrance. The explosions on the upper levels began, grew louder, fiercer. Stone cracked. Large chunks fell from the Temple's façade and crashed to the ground. Flames were visible through the entrance. A whole series of explosions followed in rapid succession, the sound of the snapping spine of the Jedi Order.

The huge edifice, a symbol of the Jedi for centuries, began to fall in on itself. The towers collapsed in its wake, the huge spires crumbling as if in slowed motion. A jet of fire and bits of rock moving faster than the speed of sound exploded out of the now-collapsing entrance.

Instead of taking cover, Malgus fell into the Force, raised both of his hands, palms outward, and formed a transparent wall of power before himself and his warriors. His fellow Sith joined him, mirroring his gesture, mirroring his power. Rocks and debris pelted into the shared barrier, the speeding shrapnel of ruin. The jet of flame struck it and parted around it, water to a stone.

The Temple continued its slow demise, falling inward, shrinking into a shapeless mound of rubble and ruin. And then it was over.

A thick cloud of dust hung like a funeral shroud over the mountain of shattered stone and steel that had been the Jedi Temple. There could have been Jedi survivors in the Temple's lower levels. Malgus did not care. They were either crushed or trapped forever.

"And so falls the Republic," Malgus said.

The Sith around him cheered.

* * *

NO ONE among the Republic delegation to Alderaan spoke until they had cleared the hall. No one seemed to know what to say. Aryn struggled to keep their collective emotional turmoil at bay. Like her, they were bouncing randomly among grief, rage, and disappointment. Even Dar'nala was struggling to stay centered, though she appeared outwardly calm.

Dar'nala finally broke the silence, her tone, at least, all business.

"We need to reach Master Zym as soon as possible. I need his counsel."

"How can we be sure he is alive?" Satele asked. "If Coruscant is fallen . . ."

As one the delegation faltered. Syo and Aryn shared a look of shock. It had not occurred to Aryn that Master Zym, too, might have been lost.

"I would have felt it if he were . . . dead," Dar'nala said, nodding as if to assure herself. "Arrange a secure communications link, Satele."

"Yes, Master Dar'nala."

"No one is to leave here," Dar'nala said to all of them. Aryn saw that the Master's eyes were bloodshot. "When word of the attack reaches the public, the press will want comment. We are to give none until we have settled on our course. I will speak for this delegation for now. Agreed?"

All nodded, even Senator Am-ris.

"This will ultimately be a decision for the Republic to make, Senator," Dar'nala said. "The Jedi will advise, of course."

Am-ris slouched when he spoke, weighed down by events. "I will discuss matters with the acting head of the Senate," he said.

"The Senate may not exist as of today," Dar'nala said.

"You may have to act in its stead. Your advisers here can assist you. We will support you and whatever decision is ultimately made."

Worry lines creased Am-ris's forehead. He swallowed, nodded.

They walked through the empty corridors, despondent. The High Council building had been vacated for the negotiations. Even the Alderaanian guards typically stationed within the structure had been relegated to posts outside. Though the windows looked out on courtyards of manicured grass and shrubs, gently flowing fountains, and elegant sculptures, Aryn nevertheless felt as if they were walking through a tomb. Something had died within the building.

Her thoughts churned. All of them seemed to be on the edge of saying something, yet no one said anything. Aryn finally gave voice to what she imagined all of them must be thinking.

"We cannot let this aggression stand, Master."

Satele and Syo gave small nods of agreement. Dar'nala stared straight out a window at the Alderaanian countryside.

"I fear we will have no choice. The Chancellor is dead—"

"Dead?" Aryn asked.

"We saw it happen," Satele said, nodding, her voice tight. "He said an Imperial fleet attacked Coruscant. It seems the attack focused on the Senate and the Jedi Temple."

"I doubt they stopped there," Am-ris said.

"There were Padawans in the Temple," Syo said.

Satele continued. "We have no idea of the numbers of the Imperial forces or what other damage they may have wrought."

"We cannot surrender Coruscant," Aryn said.

The statement appalled everyone into silence.

"I agree," Dar'nala said at last. "It should not come to that."

"*Should* not?" Syo asked.

Aryn could scarcely believe what she was hearing. The Jedi had been duped, had failed in their charge to protect the Republic. Master Zym should have foreseen the Sith plan. She stared out the windows as they walked, barely seeing the Alderaanian landscape, the nearby river.

She had fought Imperial forces on Alderaan, had beaten them into retreat. She wanted nothing more than to fight them again now.

Dar'nala's voice brought her back to the present. "How did you know the Sith had attacked Coruscant before we exited the negotiation room, Aryn?"

"I didn't," Aryn admitted. "Not with certainty. I only knew that . . ." She tried and failed to keep the emotion from her voice. "Master Zallow had been killed. And when I saw the look in the eyes of the Sith . . ."

Syo moved a step closer to her, as if he would protect her from her grief.

"Master Zallow is dead, then," Dar'nala said, stiffening. Her words sounded tight, the grief leaking through her control. "You are certain?"

Aryn nodded but said nothing more, simply built a wall of her will to hold back tears. Syo seemed to want to offer her comfort, but instead he did nothing.

"We all mourn him, Aryn," Dar'nala said. "And the others lost today."

Aryn could not keep the anger from her voice. "Yet you would have us return to negotiate with those who did this."

Dar'nala stopped in her tracks, turned to face Aryn. Aryn knew she had overstepped. Dar'nala's voice remained level, but the heat in her eyes could have set Aryn afire.

"There are billions of people on Coruscant. Children. Their lives depend upon us acting judiciously, not rashly. Your emotions are controlling your tongue. Do not let them control your thinking."

"She is right, Aryn," Senator Am-ris said and put a hand on Aryn's shoulder. "We must think of the good of the Republic."

Aryn knew both of them were right, but it did not matter. She would get justice for Master Zallow, one way or another.

"Forgive me, Master," she said. "Senator."

"I understand," Dar'nala said, and the group started walking again. "I understand all too well."

ZEERID TRIED and failed to sleep in his chair for a few hours while *Fatman* pelted through the blue tunnel of hyperspace. Instead, he worried over his next job. More, he worried about the job after that, and the one after that. He worried about his daughter, about how she'd get the care she needed when he—he saw it as inevitable now—died on one of his jobs. The hole he lived in seemed to be getting deeper all the time, and he got no closer to digging his way out.

The instrumentation beeped a signal to indicate the end of the jump. He de-tinted the cockpit canopy as the ship came out of hyperspace and blue gave way to black.

The ball of Vulta's star burned in the distance. Vulta was visible through the canopy, its day side shining like a green-and-blue jewel against the dark of space.

Arriving in Vulta's system made him feel immediately lighter. The part of him that kept work at bay reasserted itself. The thought of seeing Arra always did that for him.

He engaged the engines and *Fatman* sped through the empty space between him and his daughter. When he neared the planet, he turned the ship over to the autopilot and waited for planetary control to ping him.

While waiting, he called up a news channel on the HoloNet. His small in-cockpit vidscreen showed images of the peace negotiations on Alderaan. He'd forgotten about them. Since mustering out, the war between the Empire and the Republic had become little more than background noise to him. He knew Havoc Squadron had accounted well for itself on Alderaan, but not much more.

Footage of the Sith delegation entering the council building filled the screen, commentary, then footage of the Jedi delegation doing the same. He thought he saw a familiar face among the Jedi.

"Freeze picture and magnify right."

The vidscreen did as he'd ordered, and there she was—Aryn Leneer. She still wore her long, sandy hair loose, still had the same green eyes, the same hunched posture, as if she were bracing herself against a storm.

Which she was, Zeerid supposed, given the keenness with which she felt the emotions of those around her.

He hadn't seen her in years. They had become friends during the months they'd served together on Balmorra. He'd come to know that she could fly pretty well and fight *very* well. He respected that. And because he fought pretty well and flew still better, he thought she had respected him. She never drank with Zeerid and the commandos, but she always hit the cantina with them. Just watching them.

Zeerid had assumed she came along because she liked the emotional temperature of the commandos when they drank—relief and joy at having survived another mission. She always had an openness to her face, an expression in her eyes that said she *understood*. Her openness had drawn drunk soldiers like sweet flies to nectar honey. They'd wanted to look in her eyes and confess something. Zeerid imagined it must have been exhausting for her. And yet she'd always been there for them. Every time.

The vid cut to a shot of Coruscant and a commentator said, "Until today, when an attack . . ."

The ship's comm unit chimed receipt of a signal and Zeerid killed the vid. Expecting planetary control, he reached for it but stopped halfway when he realized it was the encrypted subspace channel he used with The Exchange.

He considered ignoring the hail. Speaking to Oren so near to Vulta would soil his reunion with Arra. He did not want business on his mind when he saw his daughter.

The steady, red blink of the hail continued.

He relented, cursed, and hit the button to open the channel, hit it so hard that he cracked the plastoid. He tensed for what he would hear.

"What?" he barked.

For a moment Oren said nothing, then, "If voice analysis didn't show it to be you speaking, I might have assumed I'd hailed someone else."

"I have something else on my mind right now."

"Oh?" Oren paused, as if awaiting a more thorough explanation. Zeerid offered none, so Oren continued: "As I alluded to before, I have something urgent. Delivery requires someone with extraordinary piloting skills. Someone like you, Z-man."

"I just finished a job, Oren. I need time—"

"This job will wipe your slate clean."

Zeerid sat up in his chair, not sure he'd heard correctly. "Say again?"

"You heard me."

Zeerid had heard him; he just couldn't believe it. Mere hours ago, he imagined he could never get clear of The Exchange. Now Oren was offering him just that. He tried to keep his voice steady.

"This just a drop?"

"It is a drop."

"What's the cargo?" He tried not to choke on the next word. "Spice?"

"Yes."

"Where is it going?"

He figured it had to be heading to some seriously hot hole of a planet for Oren to have offered to clear his debt.

"Coruscant." Oren pronounced the name reluctantly, as if he expected Zeerid to balk.

"That's it?"

"Did you hear what I said?"

"I did. You said 'Coruscant.' So what's the catch?"

"The catch?"

"Coruscant ain't exactly a hot LZ. It's a vacation compared with what I'm used to. So what's the catch?"

"You haven't caught the holo?"

"I've been in hyperspace."

"Of course." Oren chuckled. "The Empire attacked Coruscant."

Zeerid leaned in close, once more not sure he had heard correctly. Oren's simple statement and the flat tone in which he delivered it did not seem to have the wherewithal to carry the import of the words Zeerid thought he'd heard.

"Repeat? There were peace negotiations taking place on Alderaan. I just saw them on the holo. What do you mean by 'attacked'?"

"I mean *attacked*. An Imperial fleet is in orbit around

the planet. Imperial forces occupy Coruscant. No one knows much else because the Empire is jamming communications out of Coruscant."

Zeerid's thoughts still could not quite wrap around the idea. How could the Empire have attacked any of the Core Worlds, much less the capital?

"How could they have gotten past the defense grid? It doesn't make sense."

"I neither know nor care about the particulars, Z-man. Though I gather it was a surprise attack that occurred right in the midst of the peace negotiations. If nothing else, one can appreciate the Empire's boldness. You fought against the Empire, didn't you, Z-man?"

Zeerid nodded. He had traded shots with Imperial forces many times, originally as a commando in the Republic army, then as . . . whatever he was now. For a moment, he flashed on the ridiculous notion that he should re-up with the army. He chided himself for stupidity.

"You can get the rest from the holo," Oren said. "Meanwhile, start planning for this drop."

The drop. Right.

"You want me to fly a ship full of spice into a freshly conquered world occupied by the Empire? You said they locked down comm traffic. They'll have orbital traffic to a minimum, too. I can't sneak through that, even flying dark. They'll blow me out of space."

"You'll find a way."

"I'm open to suggestions."

"I have faith you'll figure something out."

"At the least we should wait until matters settle. The Empire will probably allow regular commercial ship traffic to resume in a week or so. At that point—"

"That will not work."

"It's got to work."

"No. The cargo needs to move immediately."

Zeerid was starting to like things less and less. His sense of smell picked up something turning to rot. "Why?"

"You don't need to know."

"I do if I'm hauling it. Which I haven't even decided yet."

Oren fell silent for a moment. Then, "This is engspice."

Zeerid blew out a sigh. No wonder the job would wipe his slate clean. Chem-engineered spice was not only especially addictive, it also altered users' brain chemistry such that only more of the same "brand" of engspice could satisfy their need. Mere spice would not do. Dealers called engspice "the leash," because it gave them a monopoly over their users. They could charge a premium, and did.

"We have a buyer on Coruscant whose supply is running low. He needs this order to get to Coruscant quickly, Empire or no Empire. You know why."

Zeerid did know why. "Because if the users can't get their brand of engspice, they'll go through withdrawal. And if they get through that . . ."

"They break their addiction to the brand and our buyer loses his market. His concern over this is great, understandably."

"Which means The Exchange got to name its price."

"Which works well for you, Z-man. Don't sound so contemptuous."

Zeerid chewed the corner of his lip. He felt a bit nauseated. On the one hand, he could be free with just this run. On the other hand, he'd seen an engspice den on Balmorra once, while serving in the army. Not pretty.

"No," Zeerid said. For strength, he stared through the cockpit canopy at Vulta, where his daughter lived, and shook his head. "I can't do it. Spice is bad enough. Engspice is too much. I'll earn my way out of this some other way."

Oren's voice turned hard. "No, you won't. You can die trying to make this drop, or you can die not making this drop. You understand my meaning?"

Zeerid ground his teeth. "Yes. I understand it."

"I'm glad. Look at it this way. If you make the drop, you're even with The Exchange. Maybe you even walk away, huh? If you don't make the drop, you're dead and who cares?"

Oren chuckled at his own cleverness, and Zeerid wished for nothing more than to choke the bastard.

"Then I need more," Zeerid said. If he was going to get dirty, he wanted enough credits in hand to buy a shower for his conscience. "Not just a clean slate. I want two hundred thousand credits on top of wiping out the debt, and I want a hundred of it paid before I land on Vulta, which means you've got a quarter of an hour."

"Z-man . . ."

"This is non-negotiable."

"You need some play money, huh?"

"Something like that."

"Very well. Done. The first one hundred will hit your account before you touch down."

Zeerid bit his lip in anger. He should have asked for more. "When do I go?"

"The cargo is en route to Vulta now. And when I say it's time to go, you move your tail."

"Fine." Zeerid drew a deep breath. "You done talking, Oren?"

"I'm done."

"Then I've got one more thing."

"What is it?"

"The more I come to know you, the more I want to shoot you in the face. Just so you heard it from me at least once. Two hundred thousand or no two hundred thousand."

"This is why I like you, Z-man," Oren said. "Put your ship down as *Red Dwarf* and follow the docking instructions. I will contact you when the cargo is ready."

"You loading *Fatman,* or am I flying something else?"

"I don't know yet. Probably we'll load *Fatman* in the usual way—a modified maintenance droid. You'll know when I know."

"If it ain't *Fatman,* make kriffing sure it's something else fast."

"I will be in touch."

"Fine," Zeerid said, though it wasn't fine. He closed the channel, sat back in his chair, and stared out into space.

DAR'NALA DISMISSED Aryn and Syo, presumably so she, Satele, and Senator Am-ris could take private counsel with Master Zym. With nothing to do and nothing more to say, Aryn returned to her chambers to . . .

To what?

She did not know what to do. She felt as if she should be doing something, but she had no idea what. So she ate without tasting, paced the floor, and meditated, trying to keep the pain at bay by staying busy.

When that did not work, she checked the HoloNet for news. Unsurprisingly, the reports were filled with breathless speculation about the Imperial attack on Coruscant and what it meant for the peace negotiations. She could not bear the sound of the newscasters, so she muted the vidscreen.

There was no footage of Coruscant post-attack so Aryn assumed the Empire must have jammed communications. Instead, the footage showed old images of the Republic's capital. Millions of speeders, swoops, and aircars moved in organized lines above the landscape of duracrete and transparisteel. Thousands of pedestrians strode the autowalks and plazas.

The image changed to a view of the Jedi Temple taken from an airborne recorder. Aryn could not take her eyes from the image, the towers, the tiered layers of the structure. Towering statues of old Masters, lightsabers pointed skyward, lined the broad avenue that led to the enormous doors to the Temple.

She remembered the sense of wonder she'd felt walking under those statues for the first time, side by side with Master Zallow. She'd been a child and the Temple and the statues had seemed impossibly big.

"This will be your home now, Aryn," Master Zallow had said, and smiled at her in his way.

She wondered how the Temple looked now, after the attack, wondered if it even still stood.

She imagined Master Zallow, commanding the Jedi Knights and Padawans, fighting Sith warriors in the shadows of those statues, just as she had fought the Sith warrior in the midst of the Alderaanian statues. She imagined him falling, dying.

Tears welled anew. She tried to fight them but failed. She could not level out her emotional state, wasn't even sure she wanted to. The pain of Master Zallow's death was all she had left of him.

A thought struck her, and the thought transformed into an urgent need. An idea rooted in her mind, in her gut, and she could not unseat it.

She wanted to know the name and face of Master Zallow's murderer. She wanted to *see* him. She *had* to see him. And if she could see the Sith, learn his name, then she could avenge Master Zallow.

The more she pondered the notion, the more needful it became.

But she could learn nothing on Alderaan, as part of a *peace* negotiation. She knew what Zym, Dar'nala, and Am-ris would decide, what they must decide. They would put up a show of negotiating, then they would accept whatever terms the Sith offered. They would betray the memory of Master Zallow, of all the Jedi who had fought and fallen at the Temple.

It was obscene, and Aryn would not be party to it.

Unable to contain her emotion, she shouted a stream of expletives, one after another, a wide and long river of profanity of the kind she had not uttered since her adolescence.

Moments later, an urgent knock sounded on her door.

"Who is it?" she called, her voice still rough and irritable.

"It is Syo. Are you . . . well? I heard—"

"It was the vid," she lied, and powered off the vidscreen. "I want to be alone now, Syo."

A long silence, then, "You don't have to carry this alone, Aryn."

But she did have to carry it alone. The memory of Master Zallow was her weight to bear.

"You know where to find me," Syo said.

"Thank you," she said, too softly for him to hear.

She passed the hours in solitude. Day gave way to night and no word came from Master Dar'nala or Satele. She tried to sleep but failed. She dreaded what the morning would bring.

She lay in her bed, in darkness, staring up at the ceiling. Alderaan's moon, gibbous and hazy, rose and painted the room in lurid light. Everything looked washed out, ghostly, surreal. For a moment she let herself feel as if she'd stepped into a dream. How else could matters have transpired so? How else could the Jedi have failed so?

Master Dar'nala's voice replayed in her mind, over and over: *I fear we will have no choice.*

The pain of the words came from the fact that they were correct. The Jedi could not sacrifice Coruscant. The Republic and the Jedi Council would accept a treaty. They had to. All that remained was to negotiate terms, terms that must be favorable to the Empire. In the end, the Empire's betrayal, the Sith betrayal, would be rewarded with a Jedi capitulation.

While Aryn recognized the reasonableness of the course, she nevertheless could not shed the feeling that it was *wrong*. Master Dar'nala was wrong. Senator Am-ris was wrong.

Such a thought had never entered her mind before. It, too, brought pain. Everything had changed for her.

Her fists balled with anger and grief, and she felt more shouts creeping up her throat. Breathing deeply, regularly, she sought to quell her loss of control. She knew Master Zallow would not have approved it.

But Master Zallow was dead, murdered by the Sith.

And soon he would be failed by the Order, his memory murdered by political necessity.

Her mind walked through memories of Master Zallow, not of his teachings, but of his smiles, his stern but caring reprimands of her waywardness, the pride she knew he'd felt when she was promoted to Jedi Knight.

Those were the things that had bonded them, not pedagogy.

The hole that had opened in her when she'd felt his death yawned still. She feared she might drain away into it. She knew the name of the hole.

Love.

She'd loved Master Zallow. He'd been a father to her. She had never told him and now she never could. Losing something she loved had ripped her open in a way she had not expected. The pain *hurt,* but the pain was right.

The Order had wrought a galaxy in which good capitulated to evil, where human feelings—Aryn's feelings—were crushed under the weight of Jedi nonattachment.

What good was any of it if it brought matters to this?

Her racing thoughts lifted her from bed. She was too restless for sleep. She put her feet on the carpeted floor, hung her head, tried to gather the thoughts bouncing chaotically in her brain.

She realized that she still wore her robes, not her nightclothes. She crossed the room and stepped through the sliding doors to her balcony. The brisk wind mussed her hair. The scent of wildflowers and loam saturated the air. Insects chirped. A night bird cooed.

It would have been peaceful under other circumstances.

A hundred meters down, the Alderaanian landscape unrolled before her, a meadow of tall grasses, shrubs, and slim apo trees that whispered and swayed in the breeze. She could not see the walls of the compound through the vegetation.

It was beautiful, Aryn allowed. Yet she still had the sense that she was standing at the scene of a crime. The cool night air and calm setting did nothing to assuage the feeling that the Jedi had failed catastrophically. She gripped the top of the balcony so tightly that it made her fingers ache.

Beyond the compound, in the distance, the surface of a wide, winding river shimmered in the moonlight. The running lights from a few boats dotted its surface. She watched their slow, hypnotic traverse over the water. The sky, too, was dotted with traffic.

She found it infuriating that life went on as it had for

everyone else, while for her, everything had changed. She felt as if she had been hollowed out.

"Thinking of jumping?" a voice said, a gentle smile in the tone.

She started before placing the voice as Syo's. For a moment, he had sounded exactly like Master Zallow.

Syo stood on the balcony of his own chambers, five meters to her right. He had to have been there the whole time. Perhaps he could not sleep, either.

"No," she said. "Just thinking."

His usual calm expression was marred by a furrowed brow and worried eyes. "About Master Zallow?" he asked.

Hearing someone else speak her master's name at that moment pierced her. Emotion welled in her, put a fist in her throat. She nodded, unable to speak.

"I am sorry for you, Aryn. Master Zallow will be missed."

She found her voice. "He was more to me than just a master."

He nodded as if he understood, but she suspected he did not, not really.

"To speak of nonattachment, to understand it, that is one thing. But to practice it . . ." He stared at her. "That is another."

"Are you lecturing me, Syo?"

"I am reminding you, Aryn. All Jedi must sacrifice. Sometimes we sacrifice the emotional bonds that usually link people one to another. Sometimes we sacrifice . . . more, as did Master Zallow. That is the nature of our service. Don't lose sight of it in your grief."

She realized that there was more separating her from Syo than five meters of space. Her grief was allowing her to see for the first time.

"You do not understand," she said.

For a time he said nothing, then, "Maybe I don't. But I'm here if you need to talk. I am your friend, Aryn. I always will be."

"I know that."

He was silent for a moment, then stepped back from the ledge of his balcony. "Good night, Aryn. I'll see you in the morning."

"Good night, Syo."

He left her alone with her thoughts, with the night.

Sacrifice, Syo had said. Aryn had already sacrificed much in her life, and Master Zallow had sacrificed all. She did not turn from sacrifice, but sacrifice had to have meaning. And she saw now that it had all been for nothing. Always she had quieted her needs, her desires, under the weight of sacrifice, nonattachment, service. But now her need was too great. She owed Master Zallow too much to let his death go unavenged.

Dar'nala and Zym and Am-ris and the rest of them could accede to onerous Sith terms to save Coruscant. That was a political matter. Aryn's matter was personal, and she would not shirk it.

She returned to her room and flicked on the vidscreen. More commentary on the attack, a Cerean pundit offering his analysis of how it changed the balance of power in the peace negotiations. Aryn watched the vids to distract her, barely saw them.

Vids.

"Vids," she said, sitting up.

The Temple's surveillance system would have recorded the Sith attack. If she could get to it, she could see Master Zallow's murderer.

Assuming the Temple still stood.

Assuming the recording had not been discovered and destroyed.

Assuming the Jedi did not surrender Coruscant to the Empire.

It should not come to that, Master Dar'nala had said. *Should not.*

Aryn would not leave her need to chance, not this time.

She *was* thinking of jumping after all.

Having made the decision, she knew she had to act on it immediately or let doubt assail her certainty. She rose, feeling light on her feet for the first time in hours. She gathered her pack, tightened her robes, and stepped back out onto the balcony. The wind had picked up. The leaves hissed in the breeze. The next step, once taken, was irrevocable. She knew that.

She spared a glance at Syo's room, saw it was dark.

Heart racing, she turned and leapt into the open air, following her thoughts groundward, untethered from the Order, from nonattachment, from everything save her need to right a wrong.

Using the Force to slow her descent, she hit the ground in a crouch and sped off. No one had seen her leave and no one would mark her absence before dawn. She would be at her ship and gone well before that.

She'd need to figure a way to get to Coruscant, and she had an idea of who could help her. She wanted those surveillance vids. And then she wanted to find the Sith who'd murdered Master Zallow.

The Order might be forced to betray what it stood for, but Aryn would not betray the memory of her master.

CHAPTER 4

THE REST of the Sith force had returned to the fleet, but Malgus lingered. He stood alone among the ruins of the Jedi Temple. He powered off his comlink, putting him out of touch with Imperial forces, and communed in solitude with the Force. Walking the perimeter of the ruins, he loitered over the destruction, pleased at his victory but flat with the realization that he had defeated his enemy and no obvious replacement was apparent.

He longed for conflict. He knew this of himself. He *needed* conflict.

There would be more battles with the Jedi and the Republic, of course, but with the capture and razing of Coruscant, the fall of the Republic was a certainty, only a matter of time. Soon his Force vision would be realized, then . . . what?

He would have to trust that the Force would present him with another foe, another war worth fighting.

Scaling a mound of rubble, he found a perch that offered an excellent view of the surrounding urbanscape. The cracked face of the statue of Odan-Urr lay atop the mound beside him, eyeing him mournfully.

There, astride the ruins of his enemy, Malgus waited

for the Imperial fleet to begin the incineration of the planet.

An hour passed by, then another, and as twilight gave way to night the number of Imperial ships prowling the sky over Coruscant began to thin rather than thicken. Bombers returned to their cruisers, and fighters took up not attack but patrol formations.

What was happening? The Imperial fleet did not have the resources to manage a long-term occupation of Coruscant. Imperial forces had to raze the planet and move on before Republic forces could gather for a counterattack.

And yet . . . nothing was happening. Malgus did not understand.

He activated his comlink and raised his cruiser, *Valor*.

"Darth Malgus," said his second in command, Commander Jard. "We have been unable to raise you for hours. I was concerned for your well-being. I just dispatched a transport to search for you at the Temple."

"What is happening, Jard? Where are the bombers? When will the planetary bombardment begin?"

Jard stumbled over his reply. "My lord . . . I . . . Darth Angral . . ."

Malgus's hand squeezed the comlink as he surmised the meaning behind Jard's stuttering response. "Speak clearly, Commander."

"It seems the peace negotiations are continuing on Alderaan, my lord. Darth Angral has instructed all forces to stand down until matters there crystallize."

Malgus watched a patrol of Mark VI interceptors fly over. "Peace negotiations?"

"That is my understanding, Darth Malgus."

Malgus seethed, stared at a smoke plume thrown up by a burning skyrise. "Thank you, Jard."

"Will you be returning to *Valor*, my lord?"

"No," Malgus said. "But get that transport to me *now*. I require an audience with Darth Angral."

THE TERMS of the negotiations prohibited either the Imperial or Republic delegations from posting external security around the High Council building and compound. Instead, both had their extended delegations posted in nearby cities.

Moving with Force-augmented speed, Aryn easily avoided the Alderaanian guards posted on the grounds of the compound. A canine with one of the guard teams must have caught her smell. It growled as she passed, but before the guards could turn on their infrared scanners, Aryn was already a hundred meters away. She did not exit through any of the checkpoints. Instead, she picked her way among the gardens until she reached the compound's walls, veined in green creepers blooming with yellow and white flowers.

Without slowing, she drew on the Force, leapt into the air, and arced over the five-meter wall. She hit the ground on the other side, free.

To her surprise, she did not feel a pull to turn back. She took this as a sign that she had made the right decision.

The High Council building perched atop a wooded hill. Winding roads, streams, and scenic footpaths led down the hill to a small resort town nestled at its foot. Lights from the town's buildings blinked through the trees and other foliage. The susurrus of traffic and city life carried up the hill.

It was late, but not so late that she couldn't hail an aircar taxi and get to the spaceport before her absence was noted.

Without looking back, she sped off into the night.

When she reached town, she located a line of automated aircar taxis parked outside an open-air eatery filled with young people. A Rodian chef manned the central grill, his arms a whirl of cleavers and knives. The smell of roasted meat, smoke, and a spice she could not place filled the air. Music blared from speakers, the bass causing the ground to vibrate. She kept her hood drawn over her face and hopped into the first taxi in line. The anthropomorphic droid driver put an elbow on the seat and turned to face her. It wore a ridiculous cloth hat designed to make it look more human. Given her own fragile emotions, Aryn was pleased to have a droid driver. Droids were voids to her empathic sense.

"Destination, please."

"The Eeseen spaceport," she answered.

"Very good, mistress," it said.

The door of the taxi closed, the engine started, and the car climbed into the air. The town fell away underneath them.

The droid's social programming kicked in, and it tried to make small talk designed to put a passenger at ease. "Are you from Alderaan, mistress?"

"No," Aryn said.

"Ah, then may I recommend that you try—"

"I have no need for conversation," she said. "Please drive in silence."

"Yes, mistress."

Once the taxi took position at commercial altitude and fell into a lane, the droid accelerated the taxi to a few hundred kilometers per hour. They'd make the spaceport in half an hour. She considered powering on the in-car vidscreen but decided against it. Instead, she looked out the window at other traffic, at the dark Alderaanian terrain.

"Spaceport ahead, mistress," said the droid.

Below and ahead, the Eeseen spaceport—one of many on Alderaan—came into view. Aryn could not have missed it. Its lights glowed like a galaxy.

One of the larger structures on the planet, the spaceport was really a series of interconnected structures that straddled fifty square kilometers. The main hub of the port was a series of tiered, concentric arms that twisted around a core of mostly transparisteel, which locals called "the bubble." It was very much a self-contained city, with its own hotels, restaurants, medical facilities, and security forces.

From above, Aryn knew, the spaceport looked similar to a spiral-armed galaxy. It could dock several hundred ships at a time, from large superfreighters on the lower-level cargo platforms to single-being craft on the upper platforms. A tower for planetary control stuck out of the top of the bubble like a fat antenna.

Due to the late hour, most of the upper docking platforms were dark, but the lower levels were bright and busy with activity. As Aryn watched, a large cargo freighter descended toward one of the lower platforms, while two others began their slow ascent out of dock and into the atmosphere. Shipping firms often did much of their work at night, when in-atmosphere traffic was reduced.

Watching it all, Aryn was once more struck with the oddity of the fact that life for everyone else in the galaxy went on as it had, while the Republic itself was in grave danger. She wanted desperately to scream at all of them: *What do you think is going to happen next!*

But instead she kept it inside, an emotional pressure that she thought must soon pop an artery.

Dozens of speeders, swoops, and loader droids flew,

buzzed, crawled, and rolled along the port's many docks and in the air around the landing platforms. Automated cranes lifted the huge shipping containers carried in the bays of freighters.

Even from half a kilometer out, Aryn could see the lines of people and droids riding the autowalks and lifts within the spaceport's central bubble. The whole structure looked like an insect hive. A portion of the bubble near the top housed a luxury hotel. Each room featured a balcony that looked out on Alderaan's natural beauty. Seeing them, Aryn thought of her exchange with Syo.

"A Jedi must sacrifice," she said.

She was about to do exactly that.

"I'm sorry, mistress," said the droid. "Did you say something?"

"No."

"What entrance, mistress?"

"I need to get to level one, sublevel D."

"Very good, mistress."

The aircar descended from the traffic lane to stop at one of the entrances on level one of the spaceport. The droid offered his hand, which featured an integrated card scanner, and Aryn ran her credcard. The Order would be able to track her from its use, but she had no other way to pay. She stepped out of the aircar and hurried through the automated doors of the port.

Once inside, she moved rapidly, barely seeing the other sentients on the walkways and lifts. Conversation occurred around her, but, lost in her thoughts, she heard it only as a distant buzz. Music blared from a darkened cantina. A young couple—a human man and a Cerean woman—walked arm-and-arm out of a restaurant, heads close together, laughing at some shared secret. Droids whirred past Aryn, carting cargo and luggage.

"Pardon me," they said as they whizzed past.

Vidscreens hung in strategic places throughout the facility. She eyed one, saw a view of Coruscant, which then cut to the High Council compound on Alderaan. She avoided looking at any other vids as she went.

She kept her eyes focused on nothing, hoping that the late hour would spare her any contact with other members of the Jedi delegation who might be stationed at the spaceport. She feared the sound of their voices would pop the bubble of her emotional control.

Hurrying along the corridors, lifts, and walks, she reached the level where she'd landed her Raven and let herself relax. She raised her wrist comlink to her mouth, thinking to hail T6, but a voice from behind called to her and shattered her calm.

"Aryn? Aryn Leneer?"

Her heart lurched as she turned to see Vollen Sor, a fellow Jedi Knight, emerging from a nearby lift and hurrying to catch up with her. Vollen's Padawan, a Rodian named Keevo, trailed behind him, a satellite in orbit around the planet of his Master. Both wore their traditional robes. They wore their lightsabers openly, outside their robes, as they would in a combat environment.

She tensed. Perhaps Master Dar'nala had noticed her absence and deduced her intent. Perhaps Vollen and Keevo had come to stop her.

She let her hand hover near the hilt of her lightsaber.

BY THE time the transport set down near the Temple, Malgus had followed enough communication chatter to understand what had occurred. And what he had learned only incensed him further.

He bounded onto the transport and stood in the small, rear cargo bay.

"Leave the bay open as you fly," he ordered the pilot over the transport's intercom.

"My lord?"

"Go to a hundred meters up and circle. I want to see the surface."

"Yes, Darth Malgus."

As the transport lifted him away from the ruins of the Jedi Temple, wind whipped around the bay and pawed at his cloak. He stood at the edge of the ramp and used the Force to anchor himself in place. From there, he surveyed Coruscant, the planet that should have been destroyed.

Most of the urbanscape was lit, so night did not hide the destruction. A haze of smoke hung like a funeral shroud over the still smoldering ruins. The air carried the faint, sickly sweet tang of burned bodies and melted plastoid. He tried to guess the number of the dead: in the tens of thousands, certainly. A hundred thousand? He could not know. He did know that it should have been billions.

Shafts of steel stuck like bones out of piles of shattered duracrete. Here and there droid-assisted excavation teams sifted through the rubble, seeking survivors or bodies. Frightened faces turned up to watch the transport pass.

"You should be dead," Malgus said to them. "Not merely frightened."

Quadrant after quadrant of Coruscant had been reduced to rubble.

But not enough of it.

Most buildings still stood and most of the planet's people still lived. The Republic had been wounded, but not killed.

And there was nothing more dangerous than a wounded animal.

Malgus had difficulty containing the anger he felt. His fist reflexively clenched and unclenched.

He had been misled. Worse, he had been betrayed. A score of his warriors had died for no reason other than to strengthen the Empire's negotiating posture.

Sirens screamed in the distance, barely audible over the wind. Far off, unarmed Republic medical ships whirred through the sky. Speeders and swoops dotted the air here and there, the traffic light and haphazard.

Malgus had learned that Darth Angral had dissolved the Senate and declared martial law. But with the planet pacified, Angral had allowed rescuers to save whom they could. Malgus imagined that Angral would soon allow free civilian movement. Life would start again on Coruscant. Malgus did not understand Angral's thinking.

No. He did not understand *the Emperor's* thinking, for it must have been the Emperor who had decided to spare Coruscant.

Nothing was as it should be. Malgus had intended, *had expected,* to turn Coruscant into a cinder. He knew the Force intended him to topple the Republic and the corrupt Jedi who led it. His vision had shown him as much.

Instead, the Emperor had given the Republic a slight burn and begun to negotiate.

To negotiate.

A squad of ten Imperial fighters sped past, their wings reflecting the red glow of a nearby medical ship's sirens. Smoke plumes from several ongoing fires snaked into the sky.

Malgus might have hoped that the Emperor planned to force the Republic to surrender Coruscant to the Empire, but he knew better. The fleet had temporarily secured the planet, but they did not have the forces to hold it for long. The planet was too big, the population too numerous, for the Imperial fleet to occupy it indefinitely. Even a formal surrender would not end the resistance of Coruscant's population, and an insurgency among a population so large would devour Imperial resources.

No, they had to destroy it or return it. And it looked as if the Emperor had decided on the latter, using the threat of the former as leverage in negotiations.

The pilot's voice sounded over the intercom. "Shall I continue the flyover, my lord?"

"No. Take me to the Senate Building. Notify Darth Angral of our imminent arrival."

He had seen all he needed to see. Now he needed to hear an explanation.

"Peace," he said, the word a curse.

ZEERID FINALLY noticed the ping from Vulta's planetary control. He watched it blink, half dazed, having no idea how long they had been signaling him. He shook his head to clear up his thinking, called up the fake freighter registry Oren had told him to use, ran it through *Fatman*'s comp, and used it to auto-respond to the ping. In moments he received approval to land and docking instructions.

"Welcome to Vulta, *Red Dwarf*," said the controller. "Set down on Yinta Lake landing pad one-eleven B."

Zeerid tried to let the heat of atmospheric entry burn away thoughts of Oren, of The Exchange, of engspice. He tried instead to focus only on the one hundred thousand credits that should be awaiting him, and what he could do with them.

By the time the ship cleared the stratosphere and entered Vulta's sky traffic, he had once more begun to

distance himself from work and the persona that it necessitated.

But stripping away the vice-runner was getting harder
to do all the time. The hole was getting too deep, the
costume too sticky. He would be ashamed if his daughter ever learned how he earned a living.

He gave *Fatman* to the autopilot and went to the small
room below the cockpit that he'd converted to his quarters.

His time in the army had taught him the value of organization, and his room reflected it. His rack was neatly
made, though no one ever saw it but him. His clothes
hung neatly from a wall locker beside the viewport. He
kept extra blasters of various makes stowed about the
room, and a lockbox held enough extra charger packs
to keep him firing for a standard year. The top of his
small metal work desk was clear, with nothing atop it
but a portcomp and a stack of fraudulent invoices. Integrated into the floor beside it was a hidden safe. He exposed it, input the combination, and opened it. Inside
was a bearer payment card with the mere handful of
spare credits he'd been able to stash, and, more important, a small holo of his daughter.

Seeing the holo summoned a smile.

He picked it up. He always noticed the same three
things about the image: Arra's long curly hair, her smile,
as bright as a nova despite her handicap, and the wheelchair in which she sat.

He could have chosen a holo that didn't include the
chair, but he hadn't. It pained him to see her in it and it
would continue to pain him until he got her out of it.

And that was the point.

The holo reminded him of his purpose. He looked at
the holo before he went to sleep in his quarters and he
looked at it when he awakened.

He hated the wheelchair. It was the sin he needed to expiate.

Val and Arra had been coming to see him on planetside leave. He'd still been in the army then. Val had been suffering dizzy spells but she had insisted on coming anyway and he, desperate to see his wife and daughter, had done nothing to discourage her. She'd had an episode while driving and careered into another aircar.

The accident had killed Val and left Arra near death. Her legs had been crushed from the impact, and the doctors had been forced to remove them.

He'd mustered out of the army to grieve for Val and take care of Arra, not thinking much beyond just getting through one day and then the next. He'd had no pension, no property, and soon learned that even with his piloting skills he could not find legit work that paid anywhere near what he needed and was going to need. Not only had Arra's immediate post-crash care resulted in enormous medical bills, but ongoing rehab cost just as much.

Desperate, despondent, he'd taken a leap, jumping into the atmosphere and hoping he hit deep water. He called on some old acquaintances he'd known before his tour in the army, and they'd put him in contact with The Exchange. When he'd heard their offer, he'd hopped on the treadmill, thinking he could make it work.

His debts had only grown since. He'd gone into debt to an Exchange-owned holding company for *Fatman,* and he pretended to have a gambling problem against which he sometimes took additional loans. In truth, the credits from the loans went to Arra's ongoing care.

But he was treading water there, too. He could barely make interest payments and while he tried to keep his head above water, Arra remained in a prehistoric, unpowered wheelchair. Zeerid did not make enough to purchase her even a basic hoverchair, much less the prosthetic legs she deserved.

He'd once heard tell of technology in the Empire that could actually regrow limbs, but he refused to think much about it. If it existed somewhere, the cost would put it well beyond his means.

He just wanted to get her a hoverchair, or legs if he could hit a big job. She deserved at least that and he planned to see to it.

The engspice run to Coruscant was the start, the turning point. The front-end money alone could get her a hoverchair, and with his slate wiped clean afterward, he could actually start making real credits without all of it going to paying down debt.

Credits for prosthetics. Credits for regrown legs, maybe.

He'd see her run again, play grav-ball.

He returned the holo to the safe and stripped out of his "work" clothes, sloughing away Z-man the spice-runner to reveal Zeerid the father, and dropped them into a hamper. After he landed, he'd activate the small maintenance droid he kept aboard; it would clean and sweep the ship and launder his clothing.

He threw on a pair of trousers, an undershirt, and his ablative armor vest, then took a collared shirt from its hanger and sniffed it. Smelled reasonably clean.

He swapped out his hip holsters with their GH-44s for a single sling holster he'd wear under his jacket and fill with an E-11, then secured two E-9 blasters, one in an ankle holster, one in the small of his back.

Arra had never seen him holding a blaster since he had mustered out, and, fates willing, she never would. But Zeerid never went anywhere unarmed.

Before leaving his quarters, he sat at the portcomp, logged in, and checked the balance in the dummy account he used with The Exchange.

And there it was—one hundred thousand credits, newly deposited.

"Thank you, Oren."

He transferred the credits to an untraceable bearer card. It was more than he'd ever held in his hand before.

VRATH SAT on one of the many metal benches found in Yinta Lake's spaceport on Vulta. Droids sped past. Sentients went by in groups of two and three and four. Someone's voice blared over a loudspeaker.

Like every spaceport on every planet in the galaxy, the place was abuzz with activity: droids, holovids, vehicles, conversations. Vrath tuned it all out.

A large vidscreen hanging from the ceiling showed the latest news on the right side, and the latest ship arrivals and departures on the left. He watched only the arrivals. The board tracked every ship to which planetary control gave docking instructions, the scroll moving as rapidly as the activity in the port. Vrath was waiting for one name in particular.

An exercise of will, the firing of certain neurons, caused his artificial eyes to go to three-times magnification. The words on the screen grew clearer.

The Hutts' mole in The Exchange had given Vrath a ship's name, which meant he had a pilot, which meant he could find the engspice and keep it from ever getting to Coruscant.

The Hutts wanted the addicts on Coruscant freed of their reliance on their competitor's engspice so they could be hooked on Hutt engspice, a new market for the Hutts, as Vrath understood matters.

In truth he found it surprising that The Exchange had been able to find a pilot crazy enough to make a run to Coruscant, a world on Imperial lockdown. The Exchange must have had a flier with uncommon skill.

Or uncommon stupidity.

The overhead vidscreen showed the same news footage that every vidscreen and holovid in the galaxy must have been showing: another story on the peace negotiations on Alderaan. A Togruta female—Vrath knew she was a Jedi Master but could not recall her name—was giving an interview. She looked stern, unbowed as she spoke. Vrath could not make out her words. The sound of engines and people made it impossible to hear. He could have activated the auditory implant in his right ear to pick up the vid's sound, even through the noise, but he really did not care what the Jedi had to say. He did not care how the war between the Republic and Empire went, so long as he could thread the needle between them and make his credits.

He hoped to retire soon, maybe to Alderaan. If he could take out the engspice, the Hutts would compensate him well. Who knew? Maybe this would be his last job, after which he'd get drunk, fat, and old, in that order.

He alternated his attention between the news and the arrivals board until he saw the name he was waiting for—*Red Dwarf*.

He slung the satchel that held his equipment over his shoulder, stood, and walked to the *Red Dwarf*'s landing pad. Lingering among the bustle, he watched unobtrusively as the beat-up freighter set down on the landing pad. He noted the modified engine housings. He suspected *Fatman* was fast.

He reached into his pack and took the nanodroid

dispenser in hand. He ordinarily preferred to use an aerosolized version of the tracking nanos, but the port was too crowded for it.

Ready, he waited.

THE SENATE building came into view, a dome of transparisteel with a tower atop its center aimed like a knife blade at the sky. Most of the windows were dark. The transport headed for the landing pad atop the building. Halogens washed the roof in light. Malgus saw a squad of Imperial guards, gray as shadows in their full armor, and a single, uniformed naval officer near the landing pad. The officer held his hand over his hat to keep the wind from blowing it off.

Malgus did not wait for the ship to touch down. When the transport was still two meters up, he leapt out of the open cargo bay and landed before the officer, whose eyes went wide at the sight of Malgus's method of debarkation.

The young officer, his gray uniform neatly pressed, his hair neatly combed under his hat, had probably not so much as fired a blaster in years. Malgus did not bother to disguise his contempt. He tolerated the officer and his ilk only because they provided necessary support to those who did the actual fighting for the Empire.

"Darth Malgus, welcome," the attaché said. "My name is Roon Neele. Darth Angral—"

"Speak only if you must, Roon Neele. Pleasantries annoy me at the best of times. And this is not the best of times."

Neele's mouth hung open for a moment, then closed.

"Excellent," Malgus said, as the transport put down and its weight vibrated the landing pad. "Now take me to Darth Angral."

"Of course."

They walked across the roof to the turbo lift. Armored Imperial troops flanked the door to either side of it. Both saluted Malgus. Neele and Malgus rode the lift down several floors in silence. The doors opened to reveal a long, wide hallway lined with office doors to the right and left, and ending in a large pair of double doors on which were engraved the words:

THE OFFICE OF THE CHANCELLOR OF THE REPUBLIC

Two more armed and armored Imperial soldiers stood guard at the doors.

The arc-shaped reception desk immediately before the lift—presumably the domain of the Chancellor's secretary—sat empty, the secretary long gone.

Roon indicated the Chancellor's office but did not move to exit.

"Darth Angral has commandeered the Chancellor's office. He is expecting you."

Malgus exited the lift and strode down the hall. The offices to either side of him stood empty, all of them showing signs of a hurried evacuation—spilled cups of caf, papers lying loose on the carpeted floor, an overturned chair. Malgus imagined the shock the occupants must have felt as they watched Imperial forces pour out of the sky. He wondered what Angral had done with the Senators and their staffs. Some, he knew, had been killed in the initial attack. Others had probably been executed afterward.

When he reached the end of the hall, the Imperial soldiers saluted, parted, and opened the doors for him. He stepped inside and the doors closed behind him.

Angral sat at the desk of the Republic's Chancellor, on the far end of an expansive office. His dark hair, shot through with gray, was neatly combed, reminiscent of Roon Neele's. Elaborate embroidery decorated the color of his cloak. His angular, smooth-shaven face reminded Malgus of a hatchet.

Art from various worlds hung on the walls or sat on display pillars—bone carvings from Mon Calamari, an oil landscape painting from Alderaan, a wood sculpture of a creature Malgus could not identify but that reminded him of one of the mythical zillo beasts of Malastare. An opened bottle of blossom wine sat on Angral's desk in a crystal decanter. Two chalices sat beside it, both half full with the rare, pale yellow spirit. Angral knew that Malgus did not drink alcohol.

Two large, high-backed leather chairs sat before the desk, their backs to the doorway. Anyone could have been seated in them. Behind the desk, a floor-to-ceiling transparisteel window looked out on the urbanscape. Plumes of black smoke curled into a night sky mostly empty of ships and underlit by the many fires burning across the planet. To Malgus, the black lines of smoke looked like the scribbles of giants. A maze of duracrete buildings extended out to the horizon.

"Darth Malgus," Angral said, and gestured at one of the chairs. "Please sit."

Words burst from Malgus before he could stop them. "We hold Coruscant in our fist and need only squeeze. Yet I understand that peace negotiations are continuing."

Angral did not look surprised at the outburst. He sipped his blossom wine, put the chalice back down. "Your understanding is correct."

"Why?" Malgus put an accusation in the question. "The Republic is on its knees before us. If we stab it, it dies."

"Using it as a lever in peace negotiations—"

"Peace is for bureaucrats!" Malgus blurted, too hard, too loud. "It is not for warriors."

Still Angral's face held its calm. "You question the wisdom of the Emperor?"

The words cooled Malgus's heat. He took hold of his temper. "No. I do not question the Emperor."

"I'm pleased to hear it. Now *sit*, Malgus." Angral's tone left no doubt that the words were not a suggestion.

Malgus picked his way through the artwork. Before he had gotten halfway across the office, Angral said, "Adraas has beaten you here."

Malgus stopped. "What?"

Adraas rose from one of the chairs before the desk, revealing himself, and turned to face Malgus. He no longer wore his mask, and his face—unmarred and handsome, like Master Zallow's, and with a neatly trimmed goatee—wore smugness with comfort.

Malgus recalled the look on Zallow's face when the Jedi had died, and imagined replacing Adraas's current expression with one that echoed Zallow's death grimace.

"Darth Malgus," Adraas said, his false smile more sneer than anything. "I am sorry I did not announce myself before your . . . outburst."

Malgus ignored Adraas and addressed Angral directly. "Why is he here?"

Angral smiled, all innocence. "Lord Adraas was giving me his complete report of the attack on the Temple."

"*His* report?"

"Yes. He spoke highly of you, Darth Malgus."

Adraas took the other chalice on Angral's desk, sipped. "He? Spoke highly of me?"

Malgus did not play Sith politics well, but he suddenly felt as if he had walked into an ambush. He knew Adraas was a favorite of Angral's. Were they setting Malgus up?

They certainly could use his condemnation of the peace talks against him.

With effort, he got himself under control and sank into the seat beside Adraas. Adraas, too, sat. Malgus endeavored to choose his words with care.

"The attack on the Temple could not have gone better. The plan *I* developed worked perfectly. The Jedi were caught completely unawares." He turned to face Adraas. "But your report should have been approved by me before it came to Darth Angral." He turned back to Angral. "Apologies, my lord."

Angral waved a hand dismissively. "No apologies are necessary. I solicited his report directly."

Malgus did not know what to make of that and did not like that he did not know. "Directly? Why?"

"Do you believe that I owe you an explanation, Darth Malgus?"

Malgus had misstepped again. "No, my lord."

"Nevertheless I will give you one," Angral said. "The reason is simple. I was unable to locate you."

"I had powered down my comlink while—"

Adraas interrupted him and Malgus had to restrain the impulse to backhand him across the face.

"We assumed you to be checking on the well-being of your woman," Adraas said.

"*We* assumed?" Malgus said. "Do you presume to speak for Darth Angral, Adraas?"

"Of course not," Adraas said, his tone infuriatingly unworried. "But when we could not locate you, Darth Angral asked me to speak for you."

And there it was, unadulterated and out in the open. Not even Malgus could miss it. Adraas had essentially admitted that he wished Malgus's spot in the hierarchy, and Angral's participation suggested that he sanctioned the power grab.

Malgus's voice went low and dangerous. "It will take more than words to speak for me, Adraas."

"No doubt," Adraas said, and answered Malgus's stare with one of his own. His dark eyes did not quail before Malgus's anger.

Angral watched the exchange, then leaned back in his chair.

"Where were you, Darth Malgus?" Angral asked.

Malgus did not take his eyes from Adraas. "Assessing the post-battle situation around the Temple, my lord. Trying to understand . . ."

He stopped himself. He'd almost said, *Trying to understand why the Empire has not razed Coruscant.*

"Trying to understand the planetside situation more clearly."

"I see," Angral said. "What of this woman Adraas mentioned? I understand from Adraas's report that she was a liability to you during the attack on the Temple?"

Malgus glared at Adraas. Adraas smiled behind the rim of the chalice as he drank his wine.

"Adraas is mistaken."

"Is he? Then this woman isn't a liability to you? She is an alien, isn't she? A Twi'lek?"

Adraas sniffed with contempt, turned away from Malgus, and sipped his wine, the gestures perfectly capturing the Empire's view of aliens as—at best—second-class sentients. Angral shared that view and had just let Malgus know it.

"She is," Malgus answered.

"I see," Angral said.

Adraas placed his wine chalice on Angral's desk. "An excellent vintage, Darth Angral. But right at the end of its cellar life."

"I think so, too," Angral said.

"Let things linger around overlong and they can turn rancid."

"Agreed," Angral said.

Malgus missed nothing, but could say nothing.

Adraas snapped his fingers as if he had just remembered something. "Oh! Darth Malgus, I do regret that I had to refuse your woman treatment aboard *Steadfast*."

A tic caused Malgus's left eye to spasm. His fingers sank into the arms of the chair and pierced the leather. "You did what?"

"Priority is to be given to Imperial forces," Adraas continued. "Human forces. I'm sure you understand."

Malgus had had enough. To Angral, he said, "What is this? What is happening here?"

"What do you mean?" Angral asked.

"The Twi'lek woman is planetside," Adraas said, as if no one else had spoken. "I'm sure the care she receives will be . . . adequate."

"I mean what is happening here, now, in this room," Malgus said. "What is your purpose in this, Angral?"

Angral's expression hardened, and he set down his glass with an audible clink. "My purpose?"

"Who is this woman to you, Darth Malgus?" Adraas pressed. "Her presence at the battle for the Jedi Temple caused you to make mistakes."

"Passions can lead to mistakes," Angral said.

"Passions are power," Malgus said to Angral. "The Sith know this. Warriors know this." He fixed his gaze on Adraas, and the words came out a snarl. "What mistakes do you mean, Adraas? Name them."

Adraas ignored the question. "Do you care for her, Malgus? Love her?"

"She is a servant and you are a fool," Malgus said, his anger rising. "She satisfies my needs when I require it. Nothing more."

Adraas smiled as if he'd scored a point. "She is your slave, then? A mongrel harlot who satisfies you because she must?"

The smoldering heat of Malgus's brewing anger ignited into open flame. Snarling, he leapt from his chair, activated his lightsaber, and unleashed an overhand strike to split Adraas's head in two.

But Adraas, anticipating Malgus's attack, bounded to his feet, activated his own lightsaber, and parried the blow. The two men pressed their blades against the other before Angral's desk, energy sizzling, sparks flying.

Malgus tested Adraas's strength.

"You have been hiding your power," he said.

"No," Adraas answered. "You are just too blind to see the things before your eyes."

Malgus summoned a reserve of strength and pushed Adraas back a stride. They regarded each other with hate in their eyes.

"That will be all," Angral said, standing.

Neither Malgus nor Adraas took his eyes from the other and neither deactivated his blade.

"*That will be all*," Angral said.

As one, both men backed off another step. Adraas deactivated his lightsaber, then Malgus.

"You should have sent her to my ship for care," Malgus said, aiming the comment at Adraas, but intending it for both of them.

Angral looked disappointed. "After all of this you still say such things? Very well, Malgus. The woman is in a Republic medical facility near here. I will have the information sent to your pilot."

Malgus inclined his head in grudging thanks.

"As for you, Lord Adraas," Angral said, "I accept your report of the battle."

"Thank you, Darth Angral."

Angral drew himself up to his full height. "You will, both of you, follow my commands without question or hesitation. I will deal harshly with any deviation from that order. Do you understand?"

Angral had directed the rebuke at both of them, but Malgus understood it to be intended for him.

"Yes, Darth Angral," they said in unison.

"You are servants of the Empire."

Malgus, stewing, said nothing.

"Both of you leave me, now," Angral said.

Still seething, Malgus walked for the door. Adraas fell in a stride behind him.

"Darth Malgus," Angral called.

Malgus stopped, turned. Adraas stopped as well, keeping some space between them.

"I know you believe that conflict perfects one's understanding of the Force." He made Malgus wait a beat before adding, "I will be curious to see if events validate your view."

"What events?" Malgus asked, and then understood. Angral would let Adraas make his play for Malgus's role in the hierarchy. He intended to see who would prevail in a conflict between Malgus and Adraas, a conflict conducted in the shadows, by proxy, according to all the ridiculous political rules of the Sith.

Subtle, backhanded conflict was not Malgus's strength. He glared at Adraas, who glared back.

"That will be all, then," Angral said, and Malgus walked toward the doors.

"Adraas, remain a moment," Angral said, and Adraas lingered.

Malgus looked over his shoulder to see Adraas watching him.

Malgus walked out of the office alone, the same way

he had walked in. He had been made a fool and was being played for Angral's amusement.

Worse, the victory he had so dearly won would be for nothing, a mere lever for the Emperor to wield in peace negotiations. After negotiations were concluded, the Empire would leave Coruscant.

In the hall outside, he slammed a fist down on the secretary's desk, putting a crack on the marble top.

CHAPTER 5

AS VOLLEN and Keevo approached, Aryn realized what she was doing and let her hand fall to her side. She would not fight another Jedi, not ever. Besides, she sensed no hostility in them.

She tried to clear the emotion from her face as Vollen and Keevo avoided a train of cargo droids and approached her. Vollen's brown hair hung loose over bloodshot eyes. He had not shaved, and the circles darkening the skin under his brown eyes pronounced his need for sleep. Aryn imagined she must look much the same. Her own emotional state made it hard to maintain her empathic shields. Both Vollen and his Padawan sweated apprehension. It came off them in waves.

"Hello, Vollen, Keevo."

Both of them returned her greeting.

"What are you doing here at this hour, Aryn?" Vollen asked.

For a moment, she had no words. She thought it strange that she had known the question would be coming, yet she had not rehearsed an answer. Perhaps she had not wanted to lie. So she didn't.

"I'm doing something . . . something Master Zallow wants me to do."

Tension visibly flowed out of Vollen's expression. Relief from both of them flooded Aryn.

"Then Master Zallow survived the Sith attack," Vollen said, making a fist and grinning. "That is wonderful news. I know you have remained close with him." He turned to his Padawan. "You see, Keevo. There is hope yet."

The Rodian nodded. Nictitating membranes washed his large, dark eyes. The oil moisturizing his pebbly green skin glistened in the overhead lights.

"There is always hope," Aryn said, and ignored how false the words sounded to her. She could not bring herself to break their hearts with the truth. Let them feel some relief, even if only for a time.

A pair of cargo droids wheeled past, beeping in droid-speak.

Vollen stepped closer to her and lowered his voice, as if discussing a conspiracy. "So what is happening in the hall of the High Council? We heard the negotiations would continue. How can Dar'nala justify that? We should be planning a counterattack. The entire Sith delegation should be taken into custody."

Keevo put his hand on the hilt of his lightsaber and mouthed something in Rodian that Aryn took to be agreement. The Rodian looked around as if concerned someone might have overheard.

Aryn felt the creeping pressure of their suppressed anger, their disappointment. They felt betrayed, deceived. She heard in their words the echo of her own thoughts and started to utter agreement. But before the words had cleared her lips, she saw how the words, the thoughts, if given free rein, would fragment the Jedi Order.

For the first time, the consequences of her decision

struck her, but even as they did, she knew she could make no other choice. Hers was the sacrifice. Other Jedi, however, could not make the same choice or the Order would disintegrate.

"Trust that Master Dar'nala knows what she is doing," she said.

Vollen made a dismissive gesture and went on as if Aryn had not spoken. "There are many of us ready to act, Aryn. If we can coordinate with the surviving members of the Order on Coruscant, we can—"

"Vollen," Aryn said, her voice soft but her intent sharp.

He stopped talking, met her eyes.

"Do as Master Dar'nala says. You must, or the Order falls. Do you understand?"

"But negotiating with the Sith after this is madness! We are at our weakest. We must retake the initiative—"

"Do as she says, Vollen. I should not even have to say that." She spoke in a firm, clear voice, to break the conspiratorial spell that Vollen and Keevo had cast with their whispers. "You took an oath. Both of you did. Do you intend to break it?"

Vollen colored. Keevo shifted on his feet and dropped his eyes.

"No," Vollen said.

Aryn was swimming in Vollen's frustration, and her own. She felt like a hypocrite.

"Good," she said, and touched his shoulder. "Things will work out. The Council knows what it is doing. We are an instrument of the Republic, Vollen. We will do what is best for the Republic."

"I hope you're right," Vollen said, sounding unconvinced. Keevo nodded agreement.

Aryn could take no more of her own falsity.

"I must go. Be well, Vollen. And you, Keevo. May the Force be with you both."

Her recitation of the familiar parting seemed to reassure them.

"And you," Vollen said.

"Be well, Aryn Leneer," Keevo said in high-pitched Basic.

"You still haven't said where you're going," Vollen said.

"No, I haven't," Aryn said. "It's . . . personal."

She turned and headed for her ship. As she walked, she activated her comlink and hailed her astromech.

"Tee-six, get the ship ready for launch."

The droid acknowledged receipt and queried about a flight plan.

"None," Aryn said, and the droid let out a long-suffering beep.

When she reached the landing bay, T6, the dome of his orange head sticking out of the PT-7's droid socket, beeped a greeting. The Raven starfighter was already in pre-launch and the hum of the warming engine coils made the pad vibrate under her feet.

She stood there for a time, staring at the ladder that led into her cockpit, listening to the hum of the engines, thinking that if she got in and took off, she could never come back.

She thought back to the pain she'd felt when Master Zallow had died. She had felt it physically, a searing shock in her abdomen that burned away doubt. Closing her eyes, she inhaled deeply, a new, clean breath, and shed her outer Jedi robes, the robes she'd earned under Master Zallow's tutelage.

She could not avenge him as a Jedi. She could and should avenge him as his friend.

"What are you doing, Aryn?" Vollen called from behind her.

She turned to see that Vollen and Keevo had followed her to her ship. Vollen wore a concerned frown.

"Are you following me?" Aryn asked.

"Yes."

"Don't," she said.

"What are you doing, Aryn?"

She put one hand on the ladder to her cockpit. "I already told you, Vollen. Something for Master Zallow."

"But your robes? I don't understand."

She could offer no explanation that would satisfy him. She turned, climbed the ladder to the cockpit, and pulled on her helmet. Thankfully, T6 held any questions it might have had.

Vollen and Keevo walked toward the ship. Aryn felt Vollen's alarm, his uncertainty. He stopped when he reached Aryn's robes. He looked as if he were standing over a grave. Perhaps he knew what it meant that Aryn had left them there.

"Tell Master Dar'nala I am sorry," she called to him. "Tell her, Vollen."

Vollen and Keevo did not come any closer. It was as though the discarded robes demarcated some boundary they could not cross.

"Sorry for what?" Vollen called. "Aryn, please tell me what you're doing. Why are you leaving your robes?"

"She will understand, Vollen. Be well."

She lowered the transparisteel canopy on the cockpit and could not hear whatever Vollen said in response. The engines grew louder and Vollen stood on the landing pad, staring up at Aryn. Keevo stood beside him, his dark eyes on Aryn's robes.

"Get us out of here, Tee-six," she said. "Set a course for Vulta, in the Mid Rim."

She knew someone there, once. She hoped he was still there. If anyone could get her to Coruscant, it was the Z-man.

The droid beeped agreement, and the Raven's engines lifted it from the pad.

She looked down one last time to see Vollen gathering her robes with the same delicacy he might use to bear a fallen comrade.

MALGUS REPLAYED the exchange with Adraas and Angral again and again in his mind. His anger remained unabated when he stepped off the lift onto the roof of the Senate Building and strode toward his transport, ignoring the guards who saluted him as he stalked past. The transport pilot waited on the lowered landing ramp.

"You received a location from Darth Angral?" Malgus asked the pilot. "A hospital?"

"Yes, my lord."

"Take me there."

He boarded the transport, the doors whispered closed, and the ship soon lifted off into the hazy destruction of Coruscant's night sky. They did not have far to fly. In under a quarter hour the pilot's voice carried over the intercom.

"Coming up on the facility now, my lord. Where shall I set down?"

Below, Malgus saw the multistoried rectangle of the medical facility. Swoops, aircars, speeders, and medical transports crowded the artificially lit landing pad on its roof. Dozens of people moved among the vehicles—doctors, nurses, medics, the wounded. Bodies lay on gurneys here and there.

On the ground level the scene was much the same. Vehicles and people clotted the artery of the road and a

mass of people thronged the main entrance to the facility.

"Set down at ground level," Malgus ordered.

Some of the people on the roof noticed the transport's
Imperial markings. Faces stared skyward, uncertain,
frightened, and a few people ran for the lifts. One
tripped over a gurney and fell. Another ran into a medic
and knocked him flat.

"Darth Angral temporarily commandeered this hospital to triage Imperial wounded," the pilot said over the
intercom. "They've all been moved to *Steadfast* by
now."

"Not all of them," Malgus said, but not loudly enough
to be heard over the intercom.

"There are a lot of people down there, my lord. I don't
see a clear spot to land."

Malgus stared down at them, his rage bubbling.
"Land. They will move."

The transport wheeled around, hovered, and began to
descend. The crowd below parted as the ship neared the
duracrete. Malgus could hear the shouting of the crowd
through the bulkheads.

"My lord, should I send for some troops? To guard
you?"

"I do not require a guard. Keep the ship secure. I will
not be long." Malgus pressed the switch that opened the
side door of the transport, and a cacophony of sirens
and angry shouts poured through the opening.

Malgus, his own anger more than a match for that of
the crowd, discarded his cloak, revealing his scarred
face and respirator, and stepped out onto the landing
ramp.

Upon seeing him, the crowd fell mute. Only the sirens
continued to howl. A sea of faces stared up at him, pale
in the streetlights, frightened, smeared with dust and

blood, but above all, angry. Their collective rage and fear washed over him. He stood before it, eyeing one of them after another. None could hold his gaze.

He walked down the ramp and into their midst. They gave way before him. The moment he put his foot on the road the shouting renewed.

"Monster!"

"Murderer!"

"We need medical supplies!"

"He is alone. Kill him."

"Coward!"

His presence among them focused their rage. As the tumult grew, he could not distinguish individual words. He heard only a single, prolonged, hate-filled roar, a wave of fists and bared teeth. It echoed his own emotion, fed it, amplified it.

From somewhere ahead, a fist-sized piece of duracrete arced over the crowd toward him. Without moving, he stopped it in mid-flight with the Force. He let it hang suspended in the air for a moment, so the crowd could see it, before he used the Force to crush it to pieces.

The crowd went silent again as the pebbles and dust rained down on the road, on their heads.

"Who threw that?" Malgus asked, the heat of his anger stoked.

Sirens wailed. A cough from somewhere. Fearful eyes everywhere.

Malgus raised his voice. "I said who threw that?"

No response. The crowd's anger turned to anxiety.

"Disperse," Malgus said, his own anger building as theirs receded. "Now."

Perhaps sensing his anger, those near him started to back away. Some at the fringe of the crowd turned and fled. Most held their ground, though they looked uncertainly at one another.

"We have family inside."

"I need care," someone else shouted.

Malgus fell into the Force as his brewing anger bubbled to the surface. "I said disperse!"

When the crowd did not respond to his demand, he slammed a fist into his palm and let anger-fueled power explode outward from his body. Screams sounded as the blast shoved everything away from him in all directions.

Bodies flew backward, slammed into one another, into the walls, against and through windows. The transport he'd rode on lurched from the blast. The doors of the medical facility flew from their mounts and crashed to the ground.

The sirens continued to wail.

Partially vented, he came back to himself.

Moans and pained whimpers sounded from all around him. A child was crying. Bodies lay scattered about like so many rag dolls. Shattered glass covered the ground. Speeders and swoops lay on their sides. Loose papers stirred in the wind.

Unmoved, Malgus walked the now-clear path into the medical facility.

Inside, patients and visitors cowered behind chairs, desks, one another. Malgus's breathing was the loudest sound in the room. No one dared look at him.

"Where are the Jedi?" someone said.

"The Jedi are dead in their Temple," Malgus said. "Where I left them. There is no one to save you."

Someone wept. Another moaned.

Malgus found an overweight human man in the pale blue uniform of a hospital worker and pulled him to his feet by his shirt.

"I am looking for a Twi'lek woman with a scar on her throat," Malgus said. "She suffered two blaster wounds and was brought here earlier today. Her name is Eleena."

The man's eyes darted around as if they were seeking escape from his head. "I don't know of any Twi'lek. I can check the logs."

"If harm has come to her here . . ."

A heavyset nurse, her red hair pulled back into a tight bun, rose from behind a desk. Her uniform looked like a blue tent on her stout body. Freckles dotted her face. "I know the woman you mean. I can take you to her."

Malgus cast the man to the floor and followed the nurse through the corridors. The air smelled of antiseptic. Walls and floors were clean white or silver.

Staff and medical droids hurried through the halls, barely noticing Malgus, despite his disfigurement. A female voice over the intercom almost continually called doctors to this or that treatment room, or announced codes in various places in the facility.

Malgus and the nurse took a lift up to a treatment ward, walking past rooms overcrowded with patients. A woman's crying carried through the hall. Moans of pain sounded from other rooms. A team of surgeons hurried past, their faces hidden behind masks spattered with blood.

The nurse did not look at Malgus when she spoke.

"The Twi'lek woman was dropped at the doors by an unmarked transport. We did not realize she was . . . Imperial."

Malgus grunted. "You would not have treated her had you known?"

The nurse stopped, turned on her heel, and stared Malgus in his scarred face.

"Of course we would have treated her. We are not savages."

Malgus did not miss the woman's subtle emphasis on *we*.

He decided to allow the nurse her moment of defiance. Her spirit impressed him. "Just take me to her."

Eleena lay in a bed in a small treatment room with three other patients. One of them, an elderly man, was curled up in a fetal position on the bed, moaning, his sheets bloody. Another, a middle-aged woman with a lacerated face, watched Malgus and the nurse enter, her expression vacant. The third appeared to be asleep.

A fluid line was hooked to Eleena's unwounded arm and several cables—cables!—connected her to monitoring equipment. The facility must have been stretched to use such dated technology. Her blaster wounds, at least, had been treated and bandaged. The arm with the wounded shoulder had been stabilized in a sling.

Eleena saw him, sat up, and smiled.

He realized that she was the only person in the galaxy who smiled when she saw him.

"Veradun," she said.

Seeing her face and hearing her voice affected him more than he liked. The anger drained out of him as if he had a hole in his heel. Relief took its place and he did not fight it, though he realized that he had let his feelings for her grow dangerously strong.

When he looked at Eleena, he was looking at his own weakness.

Angral's words bounced around his consciousness.

Passions can lead to mistakes.

He had to have her, and he had to stay true to the Empire.

He had to square a circle.

He resolved to find a way.

He went to her bedside, touched her face with his callused hand, and started disconnecting her from the fluid line and cables.

"You will be treated aboard my ship. In proper facilities."

A man's voice from behind him said, "You there! Stop! You can't do that!"

Malgus looked over his shoulder to see a male nurse standing in the doorway. The man quailed when he saw Malgus's visage but he held his ground.

"She is not cleared for discharge." The man started into the room as if to stop Malgus, but the female nurse who had led Malgus to Eleena interposed her wide body.

"Leave them be, Tal. They are leaving."

"But—"

"Leave it alone."

Malgus could not see the fat nurse's face but he imagined her trying with her expression to communicate to the male nurse that Malgus was a Sith. He asked Eleena, "Can you walk?"

Before she could answer, he scooped her up in his arms.

"I can walk," she said halfheartedly.

He ignored her, brushed past the nurses and into the corridor. For a time, Eleena looked into the rooms they passed, at the wounded, the dying. But soon it became too much and she buried her head in Malgus's chest. Malgus enjoyed the feel of her in his arms, the warmth she radiated, the musky smell of her.

"You are thoughtful," she whispered. The feel of her breath on his ear sent pangs of desire through him.

"I am thinking of geometry," he said. "Of squares and circles."

"That's an odd train of thought."

"Perhaps not as odd as you think."

When they exited the facility, she saw the dozens of bodies strewn about the ground. Medical teams hovered over several, treating their wounds. Faces turned to

Malgus, eyes wide, but no one said a word as he walked toward the transport.

"What happened here? To these people? It was not like this when I arrived."

Malgus said nothing.

"They are afraid of you."

"They should be."

When they got aboard the transport, Malgus instructed the pilot to fly them to *Valor,* the orbiting cruiser he commanded. Then he laid Eleena down on a reclinable couch and covered her with a blanket. She touched his hand as he tucked her in.

"There is gentleness in you, Veradun."

He pulled his hand away from her and stood. "If you ever call me Veradun in public again I will kill you. Do you understand?"

Her smile melted in the heat of his anger. She looked as if he had punched her in the stomach. She sat up on her elbow. "Why are you saying this?"

His voice came out loud and harsh. "Do you understand?"

"Yes! Yes!" She threw off the blanket, rose, and stood before him, her body quaking. "But why are you so angry? Why?"

He stared into her lovely face, swallowed, and shook his head. His anger was only partly her fault. He was angry at Adraas, Angral, the Emperor himself. She was just a convenient focus for it.

"You must do as I ask, Eleena," he said, more softly. "Please."

"I will, Malgus." She stepped forward, raised a hand, and traced the ruined lines written in the skin of his face. Her touch put a charge in him.

"I love you, Malgus." She peeled away his respirator to reveal the ruins of his mouth. "Do you love me?"

He licked his scarred lips, his thoughts whirling, again no words coming.

"You don't have to answer," she said, smiling, her voice soft. "I know that you do."

ZEERID CHECKED his appearance in the small mirror in the ship's refresher and chided himself for neglecting to shave. He activated the ship's maintenance droid and stepped out into the bustle of the docks.

Cargo carts and droids whipped past at breakneck speeds, signal horns clearing the path before them. Treaded droids motored along the walkways. Crew members and dockworkers plied their trade, loading and unloading crates of cargo with the help of crane droids. One of the dockmasters, a fat human with a bald head but a long beard and mustache, walked among the chaos, occasionally shouting an order to someone on the dock, occasionally mouthing something into his comlink. He carried a huge torque wrench in one hand and looked as if he wanted to whack something, or someone, with it. The air smelled faintly of vented gas and engine exhaust, but mostly it smelled like the lake.

The city of Yinta Lake ringed the largest freshwater lake on the planet, Lake Yinta. Geothermal vents kept the water warm even in winter and the differential between the water temperature and the autumn air caused the lake to sweat steam, so the air always felt thick, greasy. It reminded Zeerid of decay, and every time he returned he felt as though the city had decomposed a little more in his absence.

Yinta Lake had begun as an unnamed winter getaway for the planet's wealthy—those who'd made their fortunes in arms manufacturing—the mansions forming a thin ring around the lakeshore. Back then, the ring had been called the wealth belt.

Over time, the presence of the wealthy had attracted a middling-sized spaceport to bring offworld goods to the onworld money. That had brought workers, then merchants, then the not-so-wealthy, then the very poor.

And by then the unnamed vacation spot had become Yinta, a town, and it had not stopped growing since. Now it was a metropolis—Yinta Lake—an accretion disk of people and buildings that collected around the gravitational pull of the lake.

In time, shipping had polluted the lake's water, the wealthy had mostly fled, and the city had begun a slow spiral into decrepitude. The once grand mansions on the shore of the lake had been sold off to developers and converted to cheap housing. The wealth belt had become slums and loading docks.

Zeerid had grown up in the slums, smelling the acrid, rotting odor of the lake every day of his childhood. He had provided better for his daughter, but not by much.

The deep, bass boom of a horn carried across the city, the call of one of the enormous flatbed cargo ships that moved goods and people across the lake and up and down the river that fed it. Zeerid smiled when he heard it. He'd awakened to that sound almost every day of his childhood.

He stepped into the tumult, feeling oddly at home and very much looking forward to seeing his daughter.

FROM THE haircut, muscular build, and upright posture, Vrath made the pilot as former military. Vrath, too, was ex-military, having served in the Imperial infantry.

The man smiled as he walked and Vrath found that he liked the man immediately.

Too bad he'd probably have to kill him.

Holding the nanodroid solution dispenser in a slack arm, Vrath knifed through the crowd toward the pilot.

He cut in front of him, slowing him, just another body in the press, and squeezed a dollop of the suspension on the ground at their feet.

Vrath pasted on a fake grin and held up his other hand in a frantic wave to no one.

"Rober! Rober, over here!"

He hurried off as if to meet someone but watched the pilot sidelong throughout.

The pilot never even looked down, did not seem to notice Vrath at all. Suspecting nothing, the man stepped in the oily suspension Vrath had left on the floor before him. Others stepped in it afterward, but that would not matter. In moments all traces of it were gone.

Vrath fell in behind the pilot and took the targeted nano-activator from his pack.

ZEERID SHOULD not have been smiling, and certainly should not have been at ease. He knew, as he always did, that he was one mistake, one unlucky break away from someone discovering Arra and using her against him. Or worse, harming her. The thought made him sick to his stomach.

He could not let himself get sloppy.

He hopped on the back of a droid-driven cargo cart and rode it until he neared one of the port's exits. The spaceport and all the vehicles in it rusted in the moisture-rich air of Yinta Lake; the brown smears on walls and in corners looked like bloodstains.

The exit doors slid open, and he hopped off the cargo cart. The collective voice of the streets hit him immediately. The shouts of air taxi drivers vying for fares— Yinta Lake had to have more taxis than any other city in the Mid Rim—street vendors hawking all manner of foods, vehicle horns, the rush of engines.

"Heading to the inner ring, sir?" said one of the taxi drivers, a tiny slip of a man. "Hop right in."

"Lowest rates in Yinta, sir," said another, a gray-haired old-timer, cutting in front of the first.

"Vinefish fresh off the grill," shouted a vendor. "Right here. Right here, sir."

To his right, a Zeltron woman, perhaps lovely once, but now just haggard, leaned against a wall. When she smiled, she showed the stained teeth of a spice addict.

He winced. Shame warmed his cheeks.

Only the hundred thousand in his pocket and what it could do for Arra kept him on course.

Aircars and speeders lined the street, even a few wheeled vehicles. He pushed through the throng of pedestrians and picked his way through the buzz of traffic to a public comm station across the street.

ONCE THE pilot had cleared the spaceport, Vrath surreptitiously pointed the activator at him and powered it on. The nanodroids adhering to the pilot's boot came to life.

The press of another button synced the activator to the particular signature of the droids on the pilot and only those droids. He did not want to pick up any of the others that had adhered to other pedestrians.

The bodies of the tracking nanodroids, about the size of a single cell and engineered in a hook shape, would contract to embed themselves in the pilot's boot sole. From there, they would respond to Vrath's ping from a distance of up to ten kilometers. Their power cells would keep them responsive for three standard days.

More than enough, Vrath knew. The Exchange had to get the engspice to Coruscant quickly or the market would be lost. He'd be surprised if they didn't try to move the spice tonight.

He watched the pilot cross the street and head to a public comm station. Turning his ear in the direction of the station, Vrath activated his audio implant.

ZEERID CLOSED the doors of the station for privacy, cutting off the outside noise, and tapped in Nat's number. He never called her from his ship's comm unit or his personal comlink for fear that someone in The Exchange was monitoring him. An excess of paranoia had saved his life more than once, most recently on Ord Mantell.

Nat did not answer so he left her a message.

"Nat, it's Zeerid. I'm onplanet. If you get this soon, bring Arra and meet me at Karson's Park in an hour. I can't wait to see you both."

He disconnected and hailed a taxi.

A thin Bothan driver, his face reminiscent of an equine, stared at him in the rearview mirror.

"Where to?"

"Just drive. Stay low."

"Your credits, pal."

EVEN FROM afar, Vrath was able to listen through the synthplas walls of the commstation. By the time the call was finished, he had a name for the pilot—Zeerid—and names of people the pilot appeared to care about—Nat and Arra.

He climbed into an air taxi and monitored the tracking droid activator. The droid driver looked back at him.

"Where to, sir?"

"Karson's Park, eventually," Vrath said. "But for now, follow my instructions precisely."

"Yes, sir."

Zeerid had shown discretion in calling Nat from a public comm station, so Vrath expected him to take a winding route, maybe change vehicles a few times. He settled in for a long ride.

Even if he lost him, he knew how to find him again.

THE AIRCAR lifted off the ground and merged with traffic. Zeerid had the driver take a series of abrupt turns for about ten minutes. Throughout, he kept his eyes behind him, trying to see if anyone was following. For a time, he thought another taxi might have been tailing him, but it fell away and did not return.

The glowing sign for a casino he knew, the Silver Falcon, shone ahead.

"Right here, driver."

He paid the Bothan, hopped out, headed into the casino's front door and out its back. There, he hailed another taxi and went through the same exercise.

Still no one that he could see. He breathed easier.

He hailed another taxi, one that could house a hoverchair, this one droid-driven.

"Where to, sir?"

Even the droid showed some rust from the air. Its head squeaked when it turned.

"I need to purchase a hoverchair."

The droid paused for a moment while its processors searched the city directory.

"Of course, sir."

The taxi lifted off and took him to a medical supply reseller. Medical devices filled the cavernous warehouse, tended to by a single elderly man who reminded Zeerid of a scarecrow.

There, eighty-seven thousand credits got Zeerid a used hoverchair sized for a seven-year-old and a crash course on how to operate it. Zeerid could not stop smiling while the wholesaler's utility droid loaded the chair in the back of the taxi.

"Don't see bearer cards all that often," the old man said, eyeing Zeerid's method of payment.

"Credits are credits," Zeerid said. He knew what the man must have been thinking.

"True. I used to be a nurse, you know. That chair is a good device."

"She'll love it," Zeerid said.

The old man rubbed his hands together. "If that's all then, sir. I'll just need you to fill out a few forms. The bearer card is untraceable, as you know."

"Can we do it another time?" Zeerid said, and started walking for the door. "I really have to go."

The old man tried his best to keep up the pace. "But sir, this is a regulated medical device. Even for resale I need your name and an onplanet address. Sir! Please, sir!"

Zeerid hopped into the taxi.

"I'll come back tomorrow," he said, and closed the cab door. "Karson's Park," he said to the droid.

"Very good, sir."

CHAPTER 6

THROUGH THE window of the taxi, Zeerid saw Karson's Park below. Benches surrounded a large pond in which greenbeaks swam. Walking paths zagged through a small wood. Picnic tables dotted the grass here and there. Public athletic courts, most of them cracked but still usable, formed the geometric meeting grounds where the neighborhood's youth met and played.

Zeerid checked his chrono as the aircar set down. Right on time.

He paid the driver, threw on a billed hat, unloaded the hoverchair, and pushed it before him as he entered the park. The chair felt light in his hands, though he thought he might just have been excited. He headed straight for the walkway and benches around the pond.

Ahead, he saw Nat pushing Arra in her wheelchair. Arra was tossing to the greenbeaks the processed feed sold by the utility droids that cleaned the park. She laughed as the greenbeaks quacked and squabbled over the feed nuggets. To Zeerid, the sound of her joy was like music.

He spared a quick glance around, seeing many pedestrians and a few droids but nothing that gave him concern.

"Nat!" he called, and waved to them. "Arra!"

He thought his voice sounded different planetside than it did on *Fatman,* and he approved of the change. It wasn't the voice of a spicerunner, not even the voice of a soldier. Instead, it was the gentle voice of a father who loved his daughter. Arra made him better. He knew that. And he needed to make sure he saw her more often.

Nat turned Arra's chair and both of their eyes widened at the sight.

"Daddy!" Arra said.

Of all the words in the galaxy, that was the one he liked to hear most. She wheeled toward him, leaving Nat and the still-squabbling greenbeaks behind.

"What is that?" she asked as she came closer. Her eyes were wide, her smile bright.

He knelt down and scooped her out of her chair in a hug. She felt tiny.

"It is my surprise for you," he said.

Arra's face pinched in a question. "And what is that?" she asked, tapping the armor vest he wore under his clothes.

He felt his cheeks warm. "Something for work. That's all."

She seemed to accept that. "Look, Aunt Nat. A hover-chair!"

"So I see," said Nat, walking up behind her.

"Is it for me?" Arra asked.

"Of course it is!" Zeerid answered.

Arra squealed and gave Zeerid another hug, dislodging his hat. "You are the best, Daddy. Can I try it out right now?"

"Sure," Zeerid said, and set her down in it. "The controls are right here. They're intuitive, so—"

She manipulated the controls and was off and flying before he could say another word. He just watched her go, smiling.

"Hello, Nat," he said.

His sister-in-law looked worn, too young for the lines on her face, the circles under her eyes. She wore her brown hair in a style even Zeerid knew was five years out of date. Zeerid wondered how he must look to her. Probably just as worn.

"Zeerid. That was very nice. The chair, I mean."

"Yeah," Zeerid said. "She seems to be enjoying it."

Arra flew the hoverchair after some greenbeaks and they fled into the water.

"Careful, Arra!" he called.

"I'm fine, Daddy," she said.

He and Nat stood there, next to each other but with an abyss between them.

"Been a while," Nat said. "She needs to see you more often."

"I know. I'm trying."

She seemed to want to say something but held off.

"How's work?"

"I am a waitress in a casino, Zeerid," she scoffed. "An old waitress. Work is hard. My feet hurt. My back hurts. I'm tired. And our apartment is the size of an aircar."

He could not help but take all of it personally. "I will try to send more."

"No, no." She waved to punctuate the words. "If it wasn't for the credits you do send, we'd go hungry. It's not that. I just . . . feel like I'm on a treadmill, you know? Can't stop running but I'm going nowhere."

He nodded. "I hear you."

Arra called to him. "Look, Daddy!"

She flew the hoverchair in a tight circle, laughing the whole way.

"Careful, Arra," he said, but smiled.

"Wait until you've got the hang of that, Peashooter," Nat said.

They stood together in silence for a time. Then Nat's voice turned serious. "How did you afford the chair, Zeerid?"

He did not look at her, fearful that she'd see the ambivalence in his face.

"Work. What else?"

"What kind of work?"

He did not like the tone of the question. "Same as always."

She turned on him, and the stern expression on her face channeled Val so well he almost crumbled.

"You've been sending us one hundred, two hundred credits a month for almost a year now. Today you show up with a hoverchair that I *know* costs more than the aircar I drive."

"Nat—"

"What are you into, Zeerid? You have this ridiculous hat on, armor."

"The same—"

"Do you think I'm blind? Stupid?"

"No, of course not."

"I can guess at what you do, Zeerid. Arra has already lost her mother. She can't lose her father, too. It will crush her."

"I'm not going anywhere," he said.

"You're not hearing me. You think she'd rather have legs than have her father? That hoverchair more than you? She *glows* when she knows you are coming to see us. Listen to me, Zeerid. Whatever you're doing, give it up. Sell that ship of yours, take a job planetside, and just be a father to your daughter."

He wished he could. "I can't, Nat. Not yet." He turned to face her. "One more run and everything changes. One more."

She stared back at him, her skin pale from too little sun and inadequate nutrition. "I told her not to marry a soldier, much less a pilot."

"Val?"

"Yes, Val."

"Nat—"

"You don't know when to stop, Zeerid. You never have. All of you, you put on that armor, get in that cockpit, and you think you're invulnerable, that a blaster can't kill you, that your ship can't get shot out of the sky. It can, Zeerid. And if yours does, it'll hurt Arra more than the accident that took her legs."

He could think of nothing to say because he knew she was right. "I'm going to buy her a sweet ice. You want one?"

She shook her head and he walked toward the concession stand. He felt Nat's eyes on his back the whole way.

VRATH WATCHED Zeerid walk away from the woman, his sister-in-law, and head to the vendor stands to get a sweet ice for his daughter.

His daughter.

Small wonder that Zeerid operated with such concern for being followed. Vrath knew what an organization like The Exchange, or one like the Hutts, could do to a man with a family. A young child was a lever waiting to be pulled, the marionette strings to make a man dance.

A man living the life Zeerid and Vrath lived had to have either enough power—or a patron with enough power—to protect his family, or his family was at risk. Zeerid had neither power nor patron. Vrath respected the fact that Zeerid had managed to keep his daughter out of the game for so long. No mean feat.

But now she was in it, a piece on the board.

Vrath would not use her, of course. As a matter of professional pride, Vrath never resorted to threats or harm to a man's family, much less a child. It lacked precision, something a bomber pilot would do, not a sniper.

And Vrath was still a sniper in his soul. One shot, one kill, no collaterals.

He turned away from Nat and Arra to locate Zeerid and found him standing directly behind him, a red sweet ice in one hand, a green in the other, and eyes like spears.

"Do I know you, friend?" Zeerid said. His eyes took in Vrath's clothes, his bearing.

Vrath slouched some, adopted as harmless a look as he could. "I don't think so. You from around here?"

Zeerid took a step closer, angling his body for a strike.

Vrath had to fight down the instinct to shift his own stance to eliminate the off-angle of Zeerid's approach. Zeerid would recognize it. And Vrath could not afford to kill Zeerid now, not until he used Zeerid to locate the engspice.

"What were you looking at, friend?" Zeerid asked.

"Daddy!" Arra called, but Zeerid's eyes never left Vrath's face.

"I was just watching the greenbeaks. I like to feed 'em." He reached into his pocket and grabbed a handful of the feed pellets he'd purchased from one of the park's droids.

"Daddy, I want the green 'ice!" Arra said.

Seeing the feeding pellets, Zeerid visibly relaxed, though not entirely. "Of course," he said. "Sorry, pal."

"Is that your daughter?" Vrath asked, nodding at Arra.

"Yes," Zeerid answered, and the hint of a smile curled his lips.

"She seems very happy," Vrath said. "Have a great day, sir."

Vrath walked past Zeerid and fell in with the runners, bikers, and other sentients using the park. As he did, he chided himself for taking his eyes off Zeerid. The man clearly had a nose for trouble.

ZEERID TURNED to watch the man walk away. Something about him felt off, but Zeerid could not quite put his finger on it. He'd seemed overly interested in Arra and Nat, and he'd had a coldness to his eyes, despite the stupid grin.

"Daddy! It's melting!"

Arra steered the chair over to him and he handed over the sweet ice, wiping his hands clean on his jacket.

"Thank you," she said and took a bite. "Mmm. Deeeeeeelicious!"

He smiled at her, and when he looked back, he could not spot the man anywhere.

"Who was that?" Nat asked when she walked over.

Zeerid absently offered Nat the other sweet ice, still looking in the direction the man had walked. "I don't know. Nobody."

Nat must have picked up on Zeerid's concerns. "Are you sure?"

"Yes," he said, and forced a smile. "I'm sure."

Only he wasn't.

"I think I'll walk you both home, okay?"

"Hooray!" Arra said.

"What is it?" Nat asked. She still had not taken the sweet ice.

"Nothing," he said, not wanting to alarm her. "Can't I walk my girls to their door?"

"I'm not walking," Arra said, grinning. "I'm flying."

* * *

ARYN'S RAVEN came out of hyperspace. She'd left her robes and her regrets back on Alderaan.

"Straight on to Vulta, Tee-six."

The astromech took over the flying and the Raven knifed through space. Vulta appeared through the canopy, a lone planet circling its star. The sun's light glinted off the many artificial satellites in orbit and the space traffic moving to and from the planet.

"Ping planetary control with our official Republic credentials," she said to T6. "Request a pad at the Yinta Lake spaceport."

The droid whistled an affirmative.

Aryn would soon know if her absence had been noted. If so, her credentials would probably be no good.

T6 gave a satisfied series of beeps as landing instructions scrolled across Aryn's HUD.

"Take us down, Tee-six. And also link into the planetary directory and find me an address for Zeerid Korr."

She had not seen Zeerid in years. He could be dead. Or he might be unwilling to help her. They'd been good friends: Aryn had been the only person Zeerid had told about his wife's death before he'd mustered out. Aryn had helped him come through the initial shock. And she could still feel the intense grief, the despair he'd endured upon hearing the news. It was similar to what she'd felt when Master Zallow had died. Zeerid had been grateful for her sympathetic ear, she knew. But she was going to be asking him for a lot.

T6 beeped a negative. No Zeerid Korr in the directory.

Aryn clenched a fist as the planet grew larger.

"His wife had a sister. Natala . . . something. Natala . . . Yooms. Try her, Tee-six."

In moments T6 had an address. She lived near the

lakeshore in Yinta Lake and had legal guardianship over a nine-year-old girl named Arra Yooms.

"Arra?"

Aryn knew Arra was the name of Zeerid's daughter. If Natala had custody of the girl, then Zeerid could very well be dead. Her plan began to crumble. She had no one else to whom she could turn. If Zeerid was dead, then so, too, was her opportunity to avenge Master Zallow.

She had no choice but to try. She did not know how she could get through the Imperial blockade at Coruscant without help.

The Raven descended through the atmosphere in a shroud of heat and flame. When she emerged into the blue sky of Vulta's stratosphere, she could see below them the large blue oval of Lake Yinta and the ring of urbanism that surrounded it.

T6 put them into the flow of the sky traffic, and they headed for their landing pad in Yinta Lake. From there, she'd find Natala.

ZEERID FELT like a father as he walked Nat and Arra back to their apartment near the lake. He felt like a failure when he saw what a hole it was. They lived in one of the mansions converted to subsidized housing by the planetary authority. Rust, broken glass, chipped stone, addicts, and drunks seemed omnipresent.

"It looks worse than it is," Nat said to him, softly enough that Arra could not hear.

Zeerid nodded.

"Did you hear what happened on Coruscant?" Nat said, apparently wanting to change the subject. "It's all over the 'Net."

"I heard."

"How do you think it will turn out?"

He shrugged.

As they walked, he kept his eyes open for anyone suspicious but saw no one. Still, he could not shed the feeling that something had gone awry. The man in the park just smelled wrong.

They took a rickety lift up several floors. Zeerid did not enter the apartment and Nat did not invite him in. Arra turned her hoverchair, maneuvering in the small space like a pro.

"You are a pilot's daughter," he said.

She beamed. "I love you, Daddy."

"And I love you."

He lifted her out of the chair and squeezed her so hard she squealed. He felt the absence of her legs like a hole in his heart. He didn't want to let her go but knew he must.

He could see a bit of the tiny two-room flat over Nat's shoulder. One window, a galley kitchen.

"Will you come back soon, Daddy?" Arra asked as he lowered her back into the chair.

"Yes," he said, as unequivocal as a blaster shot. "Soon." He stole her nose and she giggled. "I'll give this back to you when I return."

Nat, standing beside her, stroked her hair. "Time for homework, Arra. Then bedtime."

"All right, Aunt Nat. Bye, Daddy," she said, her eyes watering. She was trying to be strong.

Zeerid knelt. "I will be back soon. Within days. All right?"

She nodded and he mussed her hair. She turned the hoverchair and headed for her room.

He filed the image of her face in the file cabinet of his memory.

"She loves that chair," Nat said. "You did good, Zeerid."

"I'm going to get you both out of here," he said, determined to make it so. "After this next job——"

Nat held up a hand and shook her head. "I don't want to hear about the job. I just want you to promise that you won't take unnecessary chances."

"I promise," he said.

"We'll see you when you come back. We're fine here, Zeerid. It doesn't look like much, but we're fine."

He reached into his jacket and took out the bearer card. "There are over thirteen thousand credits on this. Take it. Buy something nice for you and Arra."

She eyed the card as if it might bite her. "Thirteen thousand . . ." She looked him in the face. "How'd you come by this amount of money?"

He ignored the question and held up the card until she took it.

"Thank you, Nat. For everything." He hugged her, the gesture as awkward as always. She felt too thin, as threadbare as an old sweater. He vowed to himself then and there that he was getting both of them out of the slum. He'd do whatever he had to do.

"Take care of yourself, Z-man," Nat said.

"I will. And I'll be back soon."

To that, she said nothing.

The moment the door closed and the locks clicked into place, he flipped the switch in his brain. Zeerid the father fled before Z-man the soldier and smuggler.

The man at the park had been all wrong, from his hair, to his clothes, to the coldness in his eyes. He could have been nobody. Or he could have been somebody.

Zeerid decided that he would linger in the apartment building for a while, out of sight, just to be sure Nat and Arra were safe.

He took station on their floor and settled in. He hadn't

done sentry duty since he was a new recruit. Felt good,
though.

VRATH SAT in the aircar taxi on the street outside the
decrepit apartment building. The smell of rotten fish
and dirty lake filled the air. He watched for a long time,
monitoring Zeerid's movements with the tracker. Zeerid
had stopped moving. Perhaps he shared an apartment
there with Nat and Arra.

He gave it a while longer, then decided to take a look.
He paid the droid driver, hopped out of the aircar,
dodged the few ramshackle speeders and the public
speeder bus that flew low through the street, and headed
across to the apartment building.

ZEERID'S EYES adjusted to the dim lights that flickered
intermittently in the hallway. The door to Nat and
Arra's flat was about halfway down the corridor. There
was no other way in or out of the apartment. All he
needed to do was take a boresighting down the hall.

The far end of the hallway ended in a cracked glass
window. The near side ended in the lift and a door to the
stairs. Other than scaling the building from the outside,
the lift and the stairs were the only way onto the fourth
floor. He could cover both.

He thought about just lingering in the hallway and
putting the muzzle of his blaster into the belly of anyone
who looked at him sideways. But that wouldn't do. He
did not want to draw too much attention to himself and
he did not want to cause a scene unnecessarily. He finally decided to take station on the emergency stairwell
to the side of the lift. He propped the door open so he
could see the lift, the hall, and the stairs.

A good field of fire, he decided.

He took the E-9 blaster pistol—small, compact, but with decent power—held it in his front jacket pocket, and waited.

Minutes passed, turned to half an hour, to an hour, and he began to think his paranoia had ill served him. The building did not see a lot of foot traffic. A near-obsolete utility droid came up the creaky lift and vacuumed the floor, ignoring Zeerid altogether. When it completed its sweep, it retired to a utility closet next to the lift.

Zeerid sat alone with only uncomfortable thoughts for company in a stairwell that smelled of urine and vomit. He had let his daughter down. To try and give her a better life, he had turned himself into the kind of man he once would have regarded with contempt. And what did she have to show for it? A decrepit apartment and an absentee father who could die on his next run.

And a hoverchair, he reminded himself. But still . . .

He had to get out of the life. But there was no walking away until he'd cleared his debt with The Exchange. So he'd make a last run to Coruscant—

The door to the stairwell on the ground floor opened with an angry squeal. At almost the same moment, he heard the rumble of the lift coming up the shaft.

Alert and tense, he went to the railing at the edge of the stairwell and peered down. Light from the fluorescent fixture attached to the ceiling two floors above him did little to illuminate the stairwell. Shadows coated the lower floors but Zeerid thought he saw a form there, humanoid, and watched it start up the stairs.

Meanwhile, the chime of the lift announced its arrival on the fourth floor.

Cupping his blaster in his hand, Zeerid flattened himself against the wall near the doorway of the stairwell.

The footsteps coming from below continued their slow ascent. They stopped from time to time, as if the person was unsure of his or her destination, or was stopping to listen.

The lift doors opened and Zeerid heard the soft susurrus of quiet movement. The lift doors closed.

The footsteps on the steps started again, stopped.

Zeerid waited a three-count and poked his head around the doorway to give him a view of the hallway.

A cloaked figure stole down the corridor, about the size of the man he'd met in the park. He was checking the doors for apartment numbers. Zeerid could not see the figure's hands. He shot a look back at the stairwell, heard nothing, and stole out into the hallway.

The figure stopped before Nat's apartment and consulted a palm-sized portcomp, as if confirming an address.

Zeerid had seen all he needed to see. He brandished the E-9.

"You! Move away from that door."

The figure turned toward him, reached for something at waist level. Zeerid did not hesitate. He pulled the trigger, and the muffled whump of the E-9 sounded like a polite cough.

In near-perfect time with Zeerid pulling the trigger, the motion so fast that it was blurry, the figure whipped free a silver cylinder that grew a glowing green line and deflected the E-9's bolt into the floor.

Before Zeerid squeezed off another shot, the figure cocked its head and deactivated the lightsaber.

"Zeerid?"

A woman.

Zeerid did not lower his weapon or his temperature. He could not make sense of the lightsaber. A Jedi?

"Who are you?" he asked.

The figure threw back her hood to reveal long sandy hair and the warm green eyes that Zeerid had never forgotten. The heat and tension went out of him in a rush.

"Aryn? Aryn Leneer? What are you doing here?"

"Looking for you," she said. She motioned at the door to Nat's apartment. "I thought I would try your sister-in-law's—"

"Are you alone? Did someone follow you?"

She looked taken aback by the rapid-fire questions. "I . . . yes. No."

"How did you find me?"

"Luck. I remembered your sister-in-law's name. I hoped she could help me find you."

"Stay there," he said, and hurried back down the hall to the stairwell. He looked down and saw nothing and no one. Whoever had been on the stairs was gone.

He told himself that it was probably just a resident coming home.

He turned to find himself staring into Aryn's concerned face. She looked much as she had when she'd held him while he cried over Val's death.

"What is wrong?" she asked.

No doubt she could feel his apprehension.

"Probably nothing. I'm overreacting, I think."

She smiled her smile but he saw something new in her eyes—a hardness. He did not need to be a Force-user to know that something was different.

"What happened to you?" he asked. "I just saw you on the 'Net. I thought you were on Alderaan."

A veil fell over her eyes and closed her off. He'd never seen it before, not from her, though he imagined his own expression looked much the same when he was working.

"I was. That's part of what I want to talk about. I need your help. Can we go somewhere and talk?"

"This really is not a good time, Aryn."

"It's important."

He had a flash of fear, thinking the Jedi had caught wind of the engspice delivery, had learned that he was to deliver it, and were intent on stopping him. But she said nothing about engspice.

"It's a personal issue, Z-man. Not something for the Order."

He breathed easier, even smiled at how silly his name sounded when she said it. Maybe it sounded that silly all the time. He shot a glance back down the hall at Nat's apartment.

Closed and secure, like all the other doors in the hall. A blaster shot and an activated lightsaber had not even merited an open door.

He had to get them both out of there. It was no place for a child.

Aryn touched his arm. "Are you all right?"

He let out a long breath and tried to shed some stress. He *was* overreacting. Since arriving on planet, he had taken all of the precautions he usually took. No one he didn't want to know knew of his relationship to Arra or Nat, much less where they lived. Aryn had stumbled on him only because they were friends from way back and she knew Nat's name. The man in the park had probably been nobody, just a random passerby.

"No, I'm all right. I do know a place we can talk. For old times' sake. But I may have to cut it short. I'm expecting a call."

Zeerid could get the ping from Oren at any time.

They walked out to the street and waited with a small crowd for a public speeder bus to arrive. They boarded and it pulled away. Zeerid watched Nat and Arra's building vanish below them. He tried to fill the pit in his stomach by telling himself that they would be fine.

* * *

VRATH LINGERED outside the stairwell entrance to Zeerid's apartment. His tracker had shown him Zeerid's location before he'd gotten halfway up the stairs.

An ambush or just extreme cautiousness?

Leaning against the crumbling brick wall, he eyed the tracker. It showed Zeerid moving away on the speeder bus. Vrath had seen the woman who had accompanied him. It wasn't Nat.

He activated his comlink and raised the rest of his team, all of whom were stationed at or near the Yinta Lake spaceport.

"He's mobile, on a speeder bus, heading in your direction. I'm en route."

ZEERID AND Aryn rode the airbus in silence to a stop near the hulking, rusty geometry of the spaceport. From there, they walked the busy street to a casino Zeerid knew, the Spiral Galaxy, where Nat worked. An overpowering sea of smoke, shouts, flashing lights, and music greeted them. No one would overhear them there.

Zeerid led Aryn to the bar area, found a corner table that allowed him a view of the rest of the room, and sat. He waved off the server before the young man ever reached their table. Aryn glanced around the casino, tiny furrows lining her brow. She looked to have aged ten years since he'd last seen her. He imagined he looked much the same to her, if not worse. He was surprised she had recognized him. But then, maybe she hadn't recognized him by sight so much as by feel.

He leaned back in the chair and spoke loud enough to be heard over the ambient sound. "You said you needed my help?"

She nodded, leaned forward to put her elbows on the

table. She looked past him as she spoke, and he had the impression she was reciting something she had rehearsed. "I need to get to Coruscant as soon as possible."

He chuckled. "That makes two of us."

His response threw her off. "How do you mean?"

"Never mind. Coruscant isn't exactly Jedi-friendly at the moment."

"No. And this . . . isn't sanctioned by the Order."

Her response threw *him* off. He'd never known Aryn to buck orders.

"Really?"

"Really."

"You'll want to wait until the negotiations on Alderaan are completed, right? See how things shake out? In a week—"

"I can't wait."

"No? Why?"

She sat back in her chair as if to open some distance between them, room for a lie maybe. "I need to get something from the Temple."

"What?"

"Something personal."

He leaned forward, closing the gap between them, reducing the room for falsehoods. "Aryn, we haven't seen each other in years. You show up out of a nebula and tell me you want my help to get to a world just conquered by the Empire and that getting you there isn't sanctioned by the Jedi Order."

He let her stew in that for a moment before continuing. "Maybe I want to help you. Maybe I *can*."

She looked up at that, hope in her eyes.

"You were there for me when I went through a tough time. But I need to understand what's really happening here."

She smiled and shook her head. "I missed you and didn't know it."

He felt his cheeks warm and tried to hide his discomfiture. Of course, he could hide nothing from her. She would feel the warmth her words put in him.

She slid her chair forward and crossed her hands on the table. He was very conscious of how close her hands were to his. It seemed he had missed her, too.

"The attack killed someone I cared about."

The sinking feeling he felt surprised him.

"A husband?" Could Jedi even marry? He didn't know.

She shook her head. "My master. Ven Zallow."

"I'm sorry." He touched her hand in sympathy and it put such a charge through him that he pulled away. Surprisingly, he did not see pain in her expression, but anger.

"The Temple will have vids of the attack. I need to see how he died."

"It could've been bombs, Aryn. Anything."

She shook her head before he finished his sentence. "No. It was a Sith."

"You know this?"

"I know it. And I want to see that Sith, know his name."

Insight dawned. "You want to kill him."

She did not gainsay it.

He blew out a whistle. "Blast, Aryn, I thought you'd come here to arrest *me*."

"Arrest you? Why?"

"Never mind," he said. "No wonder the Order didn't sanction your going to Coruscant. What would this do to the peace negotiations? You're talking about assassinating someone."

The coldness in her eyes was new to him. "I'm talking

about avenging my master. They murdered him, Zeerid. I will not let it stand. Do you think I don't know exactly what I am doing? What it will cost?"

"No, I don't think you know."

"You're wrong. I want help from you, Zeerid, not a lecture. Now, I need to get to Coruscant. Will you help?"

He'd been working alone since he'd mustered out. Preferred it that way. But working with Aryn had always felt . . . right. If he was going to fly with anyone, it would be her.

His comm buzzed. He checked it, saw an encrypted message from Oren, decrypted it.

Goods are aboard Fatman. *Leave immediately. Cargo is hot.*

He looked across the table at Aryn. "Your timing is good."

Her eyes formed a question.

"I'm flying to Coruscant, too. Right now."

"What?" She looked dumbfounded.

He pushed back his chair and stood. "Coming?"

She stayed in her chair. "You're flying to Coruscant? Now?"

"Right now."

She stood. "Then yes, I'm coming."

"Whatever you flew here, you need to leave it. We're taking only my ship."

Aryn tapped on her comlink and spoke over the sound of the casino.

"Tee-six, put the Raven in lockdown. I am going off-planet. Monitor our usual subspace channel, and I will contact you when I can."

The droid's answering beeps were lost to the cacophony.

They started picking their way through the crowd.

Aryn took him by the bicep and pulled his ear to her mouth. "It can't be coincidence, you know. Consider the timing. The Force brought us here at this moment so that we can help each other. You see that, don't you?"

At a table near them, bells rang and a Zabrak raised his arms high, shouting with joy.

"Jackpot!" the Zabrak said. "Jackpot!"

Zeerid decided that he had to tell her. He shouted over the noise. "If the Force brought us together, then the Force has an odd sense of humor."

Her eyes narrowed in a question. "What are you talking about?"

He dived in. "Listen, what I'm doing makes what you're doing look like charity work."

Her expression fell and her body leaned backward slightly. "What do you mean?"

"I'm going to give you another chance to ask that question before I answer it. Before you do, realize that I would make this run whether you came or not, Aryn. I am not proud of it, but I have to do it. Now, do you want to know?"

"Yes," she said, and blinked. "But later. Right now— and do not look around—there are people watching us."

An effort of will kept his eyes on her. Oren had told him the cargo was hot, but he didn't realize it was *that* hot. He feigned a smile. "Where? How many?"

"Two that I can see. A human male at the bar, brown jacket, long black hair. To my right, a human male in a long black coat and gloves."

"You sure?" He nodded as if he was agreeing with something she said.

"Mostly."

"How do we play it?" he asked her.

Funny how they so easily fell back into old roles. She giving the orders and he obeying them.

"We play dumb and make for the spaceport. We'll evaluate as we go. Then . . ."

"Then?"

Her hand went under her cloak, to the hilt of her lightsaber. "Then we improvise."

He took mental stock of all the weapons he bore and their location on his person.

"Good enough," he said, and they headed for the exit.

CHAPTER 7

THE SHUTTLE took Eleena and Malgus skyward to Malgus's cruiser, *Valor*. Malgus stared out one of the viewports as they broke through the atmosphere. He felt Eleena's eyes on him but did not turn to her. His thoughts were on the Force, on the Empire, and how the two seemed to be diverging before his eyes. The question for him was singular—what would he do about it?

The pilot's voice carried over the speaker. "Darth Malgus, Darth Angral wishes to speak to you."

Malgus cocked his head in a question. He looked to Eleena but she looked away, out a viewport at the receding surface of Coruscant.

"Put him through."

The small vidscreen in the shuttle's passenger compartment lit up and projected a holographic image of Darth Angral. He sat at the same desk in the Chancellor's office from which he had previously lectured Malgus. Malgus wondered if Adraas remained there still.

"My lord," Malgus said, though the words felt false.

"Darth Malgus, I see you have recovered your . . . companion. I am pleased for you."

"I am returning her to *Valor*, then I will return to the surface to assist—"

Angral held up a hand and shook his head. "There is no need for that, old friend. Your presence on Coruscant is no longer necessary. Instead, I need you to command the blockade and ensure the safety of the hyperspace lanes."

"My lord, any naval officer could—"

"But I am ordering you to do this, Darth Malgus."

Malgus stared at the image of Darth Angral for a long while before he trusted himself to answer. "Very well, Darth Angral."

He cut off the connection, and the image sank back into the screen.

A headache rooted in the base of his skull. He could feel the veins in his head pulsing, each beat amplifying his disillusionment, his growing rage.

He did not need to be skilled in political maneuvering to understand that Angral ordering him into an unimportant role was a way of sending the clear message that he was out of favor. Angral had used him just long enough to ensure the success of the sacking of Coruscant, and now he was being edged aside in favor of Lord Adraas. In the span of a day he had gone from the conqueror of Coruscant to a second-tier Darth.

He glanced over at Eleena once more, wondering how much of it she understood.

She did not look at him, just continued to look out the viewport.

PEDESTRIANS THRONGED the misty street outside the casino. The smell of the lake was strong: dead fish, other organic decay. Zeerid swept the crowd with his eyes, seeking anyone else that struck him as suspicious. He saw twenty men in the crowded street who might have been eyeing him.

"I can't make anyone in this crowd," he said.

Two drunk Houks staggered by, shouting a song in their native tongue. A young Bothan revved his swoop engine and blasted into the air. Ubiquitous aircar taxis lined the street. Private aircars and a public speeder bus flew above them.

"Keep moving," Aryn said. "No urgency, though."

The spaceport occupied several blocks beginning across the street from them. Digital billboards affixed to its side played advertisements for everything from vacation homes to energy bars to debt relief counseling. Zeerid sympathized with that last.

Moving with forced casualness, they cut across the street, eliciting the honk of a signal horn and a raised fist, and headed for the nearest entrance to the spaceport.

"Don't look back," Aryn said. "They're there."

"How do you know?"

"I know."

The doors to the spaceport opened. Baggage trams pulled by droids rolled through the doors, followed by a dozen or so recent arrivals of several different sentient species. The doors closing behind them cut short the pitches of the taxi drivers.

VRATH SAT on a bench inside the spaceport, pressed between a female Rodian on his left and a male Ithorian on his right. The Ithorian smelled like leather and hummed a tune through his two mouths.

Vrath endured, and watched Zeerid and the woman enter the spaceport. Zeerid glanced around, suspicion in his eyes. But Vrath had spent years perfecting his own

inconspicuousness, a skill invaluable to a sniper, and
Zeerid's eyes moved over and past him.

He whispered commands, the sound inaudible above
the commotion of the spaceport. The implant in his jaw
amplified the words and sent them to the earpieces of his
team.

"He is wary. Keep your distance."

Vrath did not want Zeerid to sense danger and bolt
before Vrath located the cargo. His team had stolen
aboard Zeerid's ship hours earlier and searched it.
They'd found nothing and, other than a routine visit
from one of the port's maintenance inspection droids,
no one had been aboard since. Two of his team were
stationed near the ship, keeping an eye on it.

Vrath watched Zeerid and the woman with his pe-
ripheral vision and, using his audial implant, listened to
them as best he could over the sounds of the port.

ZEERID STUDIED the faces of those around them, looking for anyone else who might be watching them. Faces
blurred into one another. He felt as if their pursuers
were breathing right down his neck. Unable to stop himself, he turned and shot a glance backward.

Through the sea of faces, he glimpsed the two men
Aryn had described in the casino. Both saw him looking
at them.

He looked away, cursing himself.

"They know we know," he said.

Aryn was staring at a wall-mounted vidscreen that
showed a news piece about the negotiations on Alderaan.

A BREAKTHROUGH IN NEGOTIATIONS? read the cap-
tion.

A human man, his dark hair combed back over a

wrinkled face, was speaking. Zeerid did not recognize him. The tag below his image named him LORD BARAS.

"Did you hear what I said, Aryn?"

She pulled her eyes away from the screen with difficulty. "I heard you. What do you think they want?"

Zeerid had made a lot of enemies since signing on with The Exchange, but he figured those pursuing them wanted the engspice.

"They want the cargo we're taking to Coruscant," he said.

They hopped on an autowalk that sped them across the port. Through the transparisteel windows along one wall, they could see freighters and other small starships sitting on the port's landing pads. Crane droids loaded and unloaded cargo.

He used the reflection in the transparisteel to determine if the men were still behind them. They were. But he still could not tell if there were more or just the two.

"They just got on the autowalk behind us," Zeerid said, as the men followed them onto the belt.

"Tell me what it is, Zeerid. The cargo."

He did not hesitate, though he did not look at her when he answered. Instead, he stared at his own reflection in the transparisteel. "Engspice."

She said nothing for a time, and he disliked the import of the silence.

"How did you get into running engspice?" she asked finally.

He disliked even more the accusation he heard in her tone and turned to face her. "How did you fall out with the Order and go off looking to murder? It's a long story, yes? Well, so is this."

She stared into his face, those open green eyes. He saw more pain in them than he'd ever seen before. "You're right. I'm sorry, Zeerid. I didn't mean—"

"I'm not proud of it, Aryn."

"I know."

She would know. She would sense his guilt, his ambivalence.

"We do what we do," she said.

"We do what we must."

"Right," she said. "What we must."

They switched walks, took an autostair up a floor. He continued to watch the two men behind them. They made no move to close the distance between them.

"What are they waiting for?" Aryn asked.

Zeerid had wondered the same thing but realization soon dawned. "They don't know whether I know where the spice is."

Ahead, he saw the landing pad where *Fatman* as *Red Dwarf* was docked. A long cargo tram rolled past. A platoon of maintenance droids trudged near it. A man and woman before it waved to each other, smiled, embraced, and moved on.

Another two men near it drew his attention. One sat on a chair near the door that led out to the landing pad. A portcomp sat open on his lap, but he paid it no heed. The second faced the transparisteel window, ostensibly looking out on the landing pad. Zeerid imagined him watching them approach in its reflection.

"Do you know where it is?" Aryn asked.

"It's on my ship," he said. "The Exchange uses jacked maintenance droids to sneak illicit cargo onto their mules."

VRATH WALKED beside a Twi'lek women carrying a small travel bag. He stayed close to her and let his body language suggest that they were together. When he heard Zeerid's words via his audial implant, he cursed himself for missing the obvious—the maintenance droid had been hijacked with stealth programming to load the engspice.

Vrath did not have the firepower on hand to destroy Zeerid's ship, so he'd have to do things the hard way.

"The cargo is on the target's ship and the target is not to get aboard," he said, his words loud enough that the Twi'lek looked at him askance and moved away.

"Keene," he said to the driver of the speeder he had stationed outside. "Be ready with an evac off the target's landing pad."

Vrath drew his blaster and pushed through the crowd. "Everybody down!"

THE MAN facing the transparisteel window turned while the man on the bench set aside his portacomp and stood.

"Here they come," Zeerid said.

Aryn let her hand fall to the hilt of her lightsaber. "I see them."

Zeerid glanced back and saw the two men who had trailed them out of the casino moving at a jog, then a run, through the crowd. Both reached behind their backs for weapons.

A third man Zeerid had not noticed before, but who looked vaguely familiar to him, shouted for everyone to get down and fired a blaster shot into the high ceiling.

Panic gripped the crowd. Screams erupted from all around and people dived to the ground or ducked behind benches and chairs. The dozens of droids in the vicinity stopped in their work and glanced about in confusion, their programming leaving them slow to respond to the unexpected.

The two men between Aryn and Zeerid and the ship had blasters in hand, firing as they approached. Aryn's lightsaber hummed to life, spun a rapid arc before them, and deflected the shots into the ceiling and floor.

More screams. The acrid stink of discharged blasters.

Zeerid pulled his blaster from under his armpit and put two shots into one of the two men. The impact blew the man from his feet and left a charred shirt and two black holes in his chest.

Zeerid grabbed Aryn and pulled her down behind the box-shaped body of a stationary maintenance droid while the surviving man in front of them returned fire and the three men closing from behind opened up. A shot grazed the sole of Zeerid's boot and left it smoking and black. The droid they sheltered behind vibrated under the impact of multiple shots.

"Do not move, droid," Zeerid said.

But it could not have moved had it wished to. Smoke rose from the holes in its body, and sparks shot out.

"We have to get to my ship," Zeerid said.

"The authorities will be coming . . ."

Zeerid shook his head. "Too many questions, Aryn. I've got engspice aboard. They'll seize the ship and arrest us both. We have to go. *Now.*"

The men from behind were closing, using benches, chairs, and the bodies of passersby and droids for cover as they closed the distance. The screams and shouts of the civvies made it hard to think.

"I just want the cargo," one of the men, the leader apparently, shouted above the tumult.

For answer, Zeerid popped up from behind the droid and fired three quick shots. He hit no one but he drove all three of the men behind them to the ground. He whirled on the man before them just in time to see the red muzzle flare of the blaster shot that slammed into his chest and sent him sliding three meters along the floor. The impact blew the breath from his lungs and left him gasping. Black smoke spiraled up from the hole ablated in his armored vest.

He'd been hit before and kept his wits, despite the pain and difficulty breathing.

"I'm hit," he said.

He rolled over onto this stomach and fired as rapidly as he could pull the trigger at the three men behind them. They responded in kind. Blaster bolts put holes in the floor around him. Chunks of floor tile flew into the air. He could barely hear anything over the sound of blasterfire and the screams of the civvies.

A shot from the attack's leader, the man who looked so familiar, caught Zeerid's shoulder. Once more his armor spared him serious injury but the impact sent a jolt of pain down the length of his arm, left his hand numb, and sent his blaster skittering over the floor.

It stopped directly before a Zeltron female who lay flat on the floor. He met her wide-eyed gaze and saw the mindless fear. She made no move toward the blaster.

He rolled for cover away from the woman as more and more shots from the three men caged him in. Near him, a civilian moaned, presumably hit in the crossfire. A woman shrieked.

He had to get clear.

But before he could stand Aryn was over him, her blade a blur of motion that formed a cocoon of green light around them, deflecting blaster shots in all directions. She grabbed him under his armpit and helped him to his feet while still deflecting shots.

"Up," she said. "Up."

He still had not caught his breath enough to reply, but with her assistance he got to his feet. His right arm hung from his shoulder like a slab of meat. Reaching behind to the small of his back, he pulled the E-9 he kept there and took it in his left hand.

"The ship," he said, still struggling for air.

Aryn gestured at a cargo tram near the three men

shooting at them from behind. The six cars of the tram rushed toward the men, propelled by Aryn's power. They scrambled aside, and Aryn and Zeerid dashed for *Fatman*.

The single man standing between them and the ship fired once, twice, and Aryn deflected both shots. Zeerid leveled the E-9 and fired. The shot hit the man in the brow and he fell backward, eyes wide open, blood pooling, dead.

As they pelted to the ship, more blaster shots rang out and Aryn's blade hummed. The energy of the weapon caused Zeerid's hair to stand on end.

They bounded over the dead man and through the transparisteel doors to the landing pad. The doors slid shut behind them, shutting off the screams of the civvies. Zeerid was grateful for it. Blaster shots thudded into the doors. The sound of speeders, swoops, and other nearby ships put a thrum in the air.

Shots rang out from above and to the right. A bolt clipped Aryn in the calf and knocked her legs out from under her.

An unmarked open-topped speeder flew in from the right, the pilot, a human male, firing over the side.

Zeerid crouched, one hand on Aryn, as he fired three shots with the E-9, trying to target one of the grav-thrusters on the speeder but hitting only the surrounding fuselage. The shots did no damage so he targeted the cockpit. Trying to avoid Zeerid's fire, the pilot overcompensated and the speeder turned hard right. While the pilot scrambled to regain control, Zeerid grabbed Aryn with his good arm and pulled her to her feet.

"I'm all right," she said. "Go, go."

Sirens screamed in the distance, presaging the arrival of the port authorities.

Supporting each other arm in arm, they limped to the

entry door and Zeerid punched in the code. Behind them, the doors to the landing pad slid open. Shots rang off the hull of *Fatman*. Zeerid fired a few blind bolts behind him. Aryn deflected another two shots into the bulkhead.

The ship's door slid open too karking slow. Zeerid grabbed Aryn and climbed in before the door was all the way open. He hit the button to close it and the door stopped and reversed itself.

"I've got to get us out of here. You're all right?"

"I'm fine," she said.

The wound on her calf was ugly but looked like a graze. The pink, raw meat of her flesh was bordered by black lines of charred skin.

He pelted through *Fatman*'s corridors until he reached the cockpit, slammed himself into the pilot's seat, and fired up the engines. His numb arm made it difficult, but he managed. He looked out of the cockpit for the speeder, saw it above him.

He'd ram it if it didn't get out of the way.

The thrusters engaged and *Fatman* rose off the pad. The speeder wheeled to the side. The pilot fired wildly at the cockpit, but *Fatman*'s transparisteel canopy turned the shots without so much as a mark.

Zeerid considered blowing the speeder from the air with *Fatman*'s plasma cannons, but the falling debris might hurt an innocent.

"Consider yourself fortunate, fella."

When he had ten meters of altitude, he engaged the ion engines and *Fatman* blazed skyward. He monitored the scanners to ensure no one was following them.

When he saw nothing, he let himself uncoil. He tested his arm, found it unbroken, just badly bruised. The feeling was already beginning to return to his hand.

Once the ship broached the atmosphere, he gave her

to the autopilot and hurried back to the hold to check on Aryn.

VRATH HOLSTERED his still-warm weapon while he watched Zeerid's ship lift into Vulta's night sky. The ship's ion engines flared blue and the freighter sped into the darkness and mingled with the rest of the night traffic.

He cursed as he surveyed the ruins of their ambush: two of his men dead, one wounded, the authorities en route, and he'd neither seized nor destroyed the engspice.

The Hutts would be unhappy.

Hundreds of faces stared out at them through the transparisteel windows of the spaceport. Behind the faces, he saw security droids and blue-uniformed security officers speeding along the autowalks. Some of the gawkers turned to the officers, pointed fingers outside at Vrath and his men. He could hear sirens in the distance.

"Time to get clear, boss," said Deron.

Vrath nodded. He regretted leaving his dead behind, but their identities would tell the authorities nothing. They'd all been surgically altered several times over. Their current identities would not be traceable to the Hutts.

Keene set the speeder down on the landing pad. Vrath, Deron, and Lom hopped in.

"Move," Vrath said.

Keene brought the speeder up and punched the acceleration. The wind whipped over them. Keene kept the speeder low and mixed with the traffic in the heart of Yinta Lake. Vrath kept an eye behind them for pursuit but saw none.

"We are clear," he said.

Keene slowed the speeder and changed course, heading for their safehouse.

Lom started a stream of expletives that lasted three minutes. When he finished, Deron said, "The Hutts said nothing about Jedi involvement."

"No, they didn't," Vrath agreed, though he doubted his contact with the Hutts had known.

"What are the Jedi doing with a spicerunner?" Deron asked.

Vrath shook his head, pondering. Jedi involvement made no sense, unless . . .

"Maybe the Jedi want to put their agent on Coruscant and they're using a spicerunner to get her there."

Deron harrumphed, seemingly unimpressed with the explanation.

"So how do they get through the Imperial blockade and get to Coruscant? He can't just fly up to an Imperial cruiser."

"No," Vrath said, still thinking. "He can't. But he's got to have something in mind. The spice needs to get there and get there fast."

"Right."

Vrath made up his mind. "Keene, get me to *Razor*."

"Why? What are you going to do?" Deron asked.

"I'm going to fly right up to an Imperial cruiser."

"Huh?"

Vrath did not waste time with further explanation. The authorities would be searching for them once they analyzed video of the battle in the spaceport. Probably The Exchange already had the video, too. They'd be hunting Vrath and his team also.

"Get to your ships and get offplanet," Vrath said. His team had landed in the bush outside Yinta Lake, and had not registered with planetary control.

"We rendezvous in three standard days at the usual place on Ord Mantell."

He would get one more chance at stopping the eng-spice.

ZEERID FOUND Aryn limping through the corridors toward the cockpit.

"We're away," he said. "Safely, it seems. I got nothing but normal traffic on the scanners."

"Good. Now what?"

"Now we go to Coruscant."

She said, "How will we get through the Imperial blockade?"

"Ah. Well, that's complicated. Why don't you go take care of that leg?"

"Why don't you take care of that arm?"

"I need to eyeball the cargo. You don't need to come."

"I think I won't."

He nodded. "Medbay is forward and starboard."

She smiled. "Kolto for your cuts."

"Kolto for your cuts," he echoed, a soldier's phrase for medical care in the field.

"There's food in the galley," he said. "Protein bars and glucose supplements, mostly. Help yourself."

"You're still eating like a soldier."

"I still do lots of things like a soldier."

Just not the most important things.

She headed off and he headed toward the cargo bay, sneaking up on the crates as if they were an easily startled animal. They were small, maybe a meter on a side, tiny in the otherwise empty hold. He didn't know what he had expected. Something bigger, he supposed. They seemed like a great deal of trouble for such small containers. He ran his hands over them and decided he did not want to see the spice after all.

He headed back to the cockpit to pilot his ship. The hail from Oren was already blinking. He punched it.

"Go," he said.

"Our hackers have the film from the spaceport. I have seen your little incident."

"Incident? I was shot. Twice."

"Facial recognition on the apparent leader of the hit team gives an ID of Vrath Xizor." Oren chuckled. "Apparently he's an elementary school teacher from the Core."

"I think we can safely assume that is fake. Who is he, Oren?"

"Free agent, we think. Probably works for the Hutts. They wouldn't want the engspice to get to Coruscant. They're . . . at odds with our buyer."

The Hutts. It seemed they were into everything.

"Is that all you have?" Zeerid asked him.

"That's all I have. How are you planning to get the spice to Coruscant, Z-man?"

"I'm not telling you a kriffin' thing, Oren. You have a leak in your organization. I'll get it there. That's all you need to know."

Oren chuckled. "Good-bye, Z-man."

Behind him, Aryn cleared her throat. Zeerid could not bring himself to make eye contact with her. He started punching coordinates into the navicomp and Aryn eased into the copilot's seat. It had been a long while since anyone had shared the cockpit with him. She had bandaged up her calf.

"Bandage looks good," he said.

"Thanks." She eyed the math in the navicomp. "That's not going to get us to Coruscant."

"No," he said. "It's going to take us to the Kravos system."

"That's a dead system," she said. "On the edge of Imperial space."

He nodded. "Supply convoys stop there to skim the gas giants for hydrogen."

"I don't understand. What's the plan to get to Coruscant?"

"I thought you had the plan," he said.

"What?"

He smiled. "I'm joking."

"Not funny. The plan, Zeerid."

He nodded. "It's dangerous."

Aryn seemed unbothered. She stared out the cockpit as they flew into the velvet of space, waiting for him to explain. He tried.

"I'm going to piggyback *Fatman* on an Imperial ship."

"What does that mean?"

"It means what it sounds like. I heard about it in flight school, back in the service."

"You *heard* about it?"

Zeerid continued as if she had said nothing. "Centuries ago, smugglers used to jump into and out of hyperspace milliseconds after a Republic ship, say a big supply ship, heading for Coruscant. Smuggler comes out of hyperspace and goes cold except for thrusters."

Aryn considered it. "Hard to pick up on sensors."

"Right, but only if you come out in the supply ship's shadow. And only if you come out and get cold right away."

"You'd have to know right where they'd come out."

"And they did then. And we do now."

Zeerid knew all the details of every hyperspace lane in the Core. If he knew where the Imperial ships entered hyperspace and their ultimate destination, he knew where they would come out.

"Then what?"

"Then you latch on."

Aryn's eyes looked as wide as a Rodian's. "You latch on?"

"An electromagnetic seal. That part's easy to do."

"They'll feel it."

Zeerid nodded. "Gotta be a big enough ship and you've got to latch onto a cargo bay or something similar. Something likely to be empty. Then, once you get through the atmosphere, you disengage the seal and float away into clear sky."

It sounded ridiculous when he spoke it aloud. He could not believe he was contemplating it.

Aryn blew out a sigh, stared out the cockpit. "This is your plan?"

"Such as it is. You have something better?"

"Who's ever done it?"

"No one I know. When the Republic learned of it, they adjusted their sensor scans to look for it. No one's done it in centuries."

"But the Empire won't know about it."

"So I hope."

He tried hard not to see the doubt in her expression. It echoed his own.

"This is all I've got, Aryn. It's this or nothing."

She stared out the cockpit, the turn of her thoughts visible behind the green veil of her eyes.

Fatman was almost clear of gravity wells.

"I can still drop you somewhere," he said, hoping she would not take him up on it. "You don't have to hitch a ride with me."

She smiled. "This is all I've got, too, Z-man."

"Aren't we a pair, then."

She chuckled, but it faded quickly.

"Aryn? You all right?"

"I feel like I left Alderaan a lifetime ago," she said. "It's been hours."

"A lot can happen in a handful of hours," he said.

She nodded, drifted off.

"Aryn?"

She came back to him from wherever she'd been. "I'm with you," she said. "And I think I can help make this work."

CHAPTER 8

VRATH TURNED *Razor's* navicomp loose, and it generated a course to Coruscant. Even if Zeerid jumped into hyperspace right away—which Vrath doubted—Vrath's modified Imperial drop ship would still beat *Fatman* to Coruscant. His work required much travel. *Razor* had the best hyperdrive credits could buy.

When the navicomp had finished its calculations, he engaged the hyperdrive and the ship blazed through hyperspace. He dimmed the cockpit and watched a bulkhead-mounted chrono tick away the seconds, the minutes. After a short time, he disengaged the hyperdrive and the black of normal space replaced the cerulean churn of hyperspace. In the distance, day-side Coruscant gleamed against the black of space.

The planet, entirely coated in duracrete and metal, always reminded Vrath of a giant cog, the mainspring of the Republic. He wondered what would befall the Republic now that the spring had been fouled.

For a moment, he turned nostalgic for his time in the Imperial Army, when he had turned Republic soldiers into rag dolls at over three hundred meters. He'd had fifty-three confirmed kills before getting thrown out of the service and regretted not one. He'd hated everything about the service except for the killing and how he felt after winning a battle. He imagined how it must feel for Imperial forces to walk as conquerors on Coruscant's surface, for the navy to own the space around the jewel of the Republic.

Even from a distance, Vrath could see the silver arrows of two Imperial cruisers patrolling the black around Coruscant. A third orbited a moon. Ordinarily a flotilla of satellites whirled around the planet, too, but Vrath saw none. Perhaps the Empire had destroyed them as part of its forced communications blackout of the planet.

Two of the dozen or so fighters escorting the nearest cruiser, the new Mark VII advanced interceptors, peeled off and sped toward Vrath's ship. He made sure his weapons systems were powered down and put his communications gear on open hail. Almost before he lifted his hand from the control panel, the navy pinged him.

"Unidentified vessel," said a stern voice that sounded like every Imperial communications officer he'd heard during all his time in the corps. "You are in restricted space. Power down your engines and deflectors completely and prepare to be towed. Any deviation from that instruction will result in your immediate destruction."

Vrath did not doubt it. "Message received. Will comply." He powered down his engines and deactivated his deflectors. "I need to speak to the OIC. I have information of interest to the Empire."

The fighters buzzed his drop ship. One of them swooped around and under *Razor.* As it pulled out in front of him, it activated an electromagnetic tow. A glowing blue line formed between the two ships, and the Mark VII started pulling him through space. The other fighter maintained position behind *Razor* so he could blow Vrath from space should it prove necessary. Ahead, the tunnel of the cruiser's landing bay loomed.

THE FIGHTER pulled Vrath through the throat of the cruiser's landing bay until they reached an isolated landing pad where two dozen troopers in full gray battle armor awaited him, along with a tall, red-headed naval officer. He nodded at them through the canopy, unstrapped from the chair, disarmed himself of both his blaster and his knives, and headed out.

By the time *Razor*'s landing ramp clanged off the metal deck of the cruiser, he was staring at the dead eyes of fourteen TH-17 blaster rifles.

"Secure him," the naval officer said.

Two of the armored troopers shouldered their weapons and rushed him. He did not resist as one put flex binders on his wrists and the other patted him down.

"He is unarmed," the one said, his voice the modulated mechanical sound of the helmet's speaker.

"Search the ship," the naval officer said. "I want to see his flight records."

"Yes, sir," responded the troopers, and seven of them boarded the ship to search.

"There is nothing of interest aboard," Vrath said. "I came from Vulta. That's as far back as the records go."

The naval officer smiled, a tight, false gesture, and walked up to Vrath. His unwrinkled uniform smelled freshly cleaned. The freckles on his pale face looked like a pox.

Vrath could have killed him with a high kick to the trachea, but he thought it unwise.

"I am Commander Jard, first officer of the Imperial cruiser *Valor*. You are under arrest for flying in restricted space. Whether your punishment is execution or mere imprisonment is entirely at my discretion and depends upon how satisfied I am with the answers you provide to my questions."

"I understand."

"What is your name? Where did you come from?"

He barely remembered the name his mother had given him. He offered the one his profession had most recently given him. "Vrath Xizor. As I said, I flew here directly from Vulta."

"What brought you here, Vrath Xizor?"

"I have information of interest to the OIC."

The naval officer cocked his head. "Are you military, Vrath Xizor?"

"Former. Special detachment from the Four Hundred and Third. Company E."

"An Imperial sniper?"

Vrath was impressed that Jard knew his unit designation. He nodded.

"Well, Vrath Xizor of the Four Hundred Third, you may tell me your information."

"I would prefer to speak directly to the captain."

"Darth Malgus will not—"

"Darth? The commander is a Sith?"

Jard looked hard at Vrath.

"He will want to hear what I have to say," Vrath said. "It concerns the Jedi."

Jard studied his face. "Put him in the brig," he said to another soldier standing behind Vrath. "If Darth Malgus wishes to speak to you, he will do so. If he does not, then he does not."

"You're making a mistake—"

"Shut up," one of the troopers said, and cuffed him in the back of the head.

Three troopers escorted Vrath out of the landing bay and into a nearby lift. Vrath did not resist. It had been years since he'd been aboard an Imperial ship, and they remained exactly as he remembered—antiseptic, purely functional killing machines.

Just like him.

"This one was a sniper detached from the Four Hundred Third," said one of the troopers to another.

"Or so he says."

"That true?" said another. "I heard things about that unit."

Vrath said nothing, merely stared into the tinted slit of the trooper's helmet visor.

"Some kind of supermen is what I heard."

The trooper holding his shoulder gave him a shake. "This one don't look like much."

Vrath only smiled. He didn't look like much—deliberately so.

The soldiers trekked him deeper into the bowels of the ship. The corridors narrowed, and blue-uniformed security personal started to appear at doors that answered only to certain keycodes. Vrath had been in Imperial brigs many times, usually for insubordination.

Before they reached the bridge one of the troopers—the one with a sergeant's symbol on his shoulder plate—held up a hand for the others to stop. He cocked his head to the side as he listened to something over his helmet's speaker. He glanced at Vrath as he listened.

"Confirmed," he said to whomever he was speaking. Then, to his men, "Darth Malgus wants him on the bridge."

The three men shared a look and reversed course.

"Lucky you, Four Hundred Third," said the trooper holding him.

Exploding into motion, Vrath drove a kick into the chest plate of the trooper in front of him, sending him flying into the sergeant and knocking both of them hard against the wall. Then he spun behind the third while slipping his bound arms over the trooper's head. He maneuvered the binders under the neck ring of the helmet and squeezed, not enough to kill, just enough to make a point.

The man's gags sounded loud in his helmet speaker. His fingers clawed at Vrath's arms. He was probably starting to see spots.

Vrath released him and shoved him away. The entire exchange had taken perhaps four seconds. The two men he'd knocked against the wall had their rifles aimed at his head.

Vrath held out his arms for them to take. "Don't look like much," he said.

FATMAN CAME out of hyperspace in the Kravos system. Zeerid immediately engaged the ion engines and flew the freighter into the system's soup.

Debris from a partially dispersed accretion disk around the system's star filled the black with ionized gas and debris. Some fluke of solar system evolution had resulted in an orange gas giant forming a few hundred thousand kilos outside the far border of the disk.

Zeerid wheeled *Fatman* through the swirl, deftly dodging asteroids and smaller particles. He maneuvered the ship to the end of the disk and maintained his position, though it taxed his piloting skill.

"Now what?" Aryn asked.

"We wait. And when an Imperial convoy heading to Coruscant comes through, we roll the dice."

"How will we know it's heading for Coruscant?"

"We won't know, strictly speaking. But Imperial Navy regs call for a convoy heading to an occupied world to have an escort of at least three frigates. If we see that, it's probably heading to Coruscant."

"And if we don't see that?"

Zeerid preferred not to think about it. "We will."

"What if you're wrong? What if the convoy isn't heading to Coruscant?"

"Then it'll jump where it's jumping and we'll jump to Coruscant, bare naked and within range of an Imperial fleet. You're not the modest sort, are you?"

He tried to convey with his grin a confidence he did not feel.

She only shook her head and stared out at the gas giant.

They waited. A medical transport came through and Zeerid ignored it. A single cruiser came through later and still they waited. After several hours, Zeerid's instruments showed another hyperspace distortion.

A convoy appeared, three supply superfreighters and four frigates bristling with weapons.

"That's our ride," he said. "You ready?"

"I'm ready," she said.

THE LIFT doors opened to reveal a short corridor that led to the double doors of the cruiser's bridge. A pair of armored soldiers stood near the lift, awaiting Vrath's arrival. Two more stood down the corridor before the bridge doors.

The three troopers who had escorted Vrath to the lift handed him off to those in the hall.

"He's dangerous," the sergeant said. "Watch him."

"Yes, sir," said the two troopers in the corridor, their expressions unreadable behind their helmets. They flanked Vrath but did not touch him as they led him to the bridge. The double doors opened to reveal the dimly lit, multi-leveled oval chamber of the cruiser's bridge.

A score of naval officers—all human—sat at their posts, hovered over their compscreens. A huge viewscreen to the left provided a magnified view of Coruscant and the surrounding space. The hum of low, curt conversation and the thrum of electronics filled the air.

A swivel-mounted command chair sat on the center of the bridge on a raised platform. Commander Jard stood beside it, one hand on its armrest, conferring with the man who sat in it. Jard glanced at Vrath and spoke to the man, whom Vrath assumed to be Darth Malgus. He activated his audial implant to hear the exchange.

"My lord," Jard said. "The prisoner I spoke of is here."

Malgus turned his eyes to Vrath and whatever smugness Vrath had felt over showing up some troopers sank under the weight of that gaze. Malgus rose and strode across the bridge toward Vrath. He stood well over two meters, and the black cape he wore looked like a pavilion tent.

He never took his eyes from Vrath's face as he approached. Scars lined his face, and a network of blue veins made a patchwork of his bald pate. He was so pale he could have been a corpse, the walking dead. The small respirator he wore hid his mouth and lips. But it was his eyes that cowed Vrath. Malgus was all eyes. The sum of him, of his power, radiated outward from his bloodshot gaze.

He dismissed the guards who flanked Vrath and, with a gesture, used the Force to pry open the binders on Vrath's wrists. They fell to the floor of the bridge with a dull clang.

"You mentioned a Jedi to Commander Jard." His voice, deep and rough, sounded like stones grinding together.

"I did . . . my lord." Malgus's mere presence pulled the last words out of him.

"Explain."

Vrath found it more difficult than he would have

imagined to compose his thoughts. "A freighter is en route to Coruscant. A Jedi is aboard."

"Just one?"

"As far as I know just one, yes," Vrath said, nodding. "A woman. Human, mid-thirties, I'd say. Long, light brown hair. She is flying with a man named Zeerid Korr. As far as I know, they are the only crew."

"How do you know this woman is a Jedi?"

Vrath was starting to feel cold. He had to work to keep his voice steady. "I saw her using a green light-saber. I saw her do things with the Force." He held up his hands to show Malgus his wrists, still red from the binders Malgus had unlocked. "Things like this."

Malgus eased half a step closer to Vrath and Vrath felt decidedly overwhelmed. "Tell me then, Vrath Xizor, what else is aboard this ship and why and when it is coming to Coruscant?"

Vrath bumped up against the doors behind him. He considered lying but did not think he could pull it off.

"Engspice, my lord. The ship is carrying engspice."

He saw connections being made, conclusions being drawn, and more questions forming in the deep wells of Malgus's eyes.

"This Zeerid Korr is a spicerunner?"

"He is."

"Why would a Jedi associate with a spicerunner, Vrath Xizor?"

"I . . . don't know, my lord."

"And you?" Malgus loomed over him, all dark eyes, all dark armor, all dark power. "Are you a spicerunner? A business rival, maybe?"

The lie exited his mouth before wisdom could stop it. "No, no, I am a former Imperial. A sniper. I'm . . . I'm just doing my part for the Empire, my lord."

Malgus inhaled deeply, exhaled, the mechanical sound

heavy with disappointment. "You are a poor liar. You are a rival spicerunner, or a killer in service to one of the syndicates that runs spice."

Vrath dared not deny it. He stood there, frozen, pinioned by Malgus's eyes.

"When is this freighter due to arrive?" Malgus asked. "And how do they plan to get through the blockade?"

Vrath found his mouth was dry. He cleared his throat. "They are coming soon. Today. They must."

"Because of the engspice?"

Vrath could not meet Malgus's eyes. "Yes. I don't know how they intend to get through, but I know they will try."

Malgus stared at him for a long second that felt like an eternity to Vrath.

"You will remain on the bridge, Vrath Xizor. If this freighter and the Jedi it carries show up, I will overlook your illegal flight into restricted space. Perhaps I will even compensate you for your service. But if the ship doesn't show then I will devise a . . . suitable punishment for a spicerunner found in restricted space. Does that seem to you unreasonable?"

Vrath choked on his response. "No, my lord."

"Excellent."

Malgus turned from Vrath and Vrath felt as though the air had become easier to breathe. Malgus took a seat in his command chair and spoke to Commander Jard.

"Commander, intensify all scanning until further notice. Any unusual readings are to be reported to me. And dispatch a squad of fighters to put eyes on all incoming ships."

"Most of the fighter fleet is otherwise assigned, my lord."

"Use shuttles then."

"Yes, my lord," answered Jard.

Vrath stared at the cruiser's viewscreen, hoping that Zeerid had not scratched the run for some reason. Or just as bad, that Zeerid had somehow beaten him to Coruscant and already snuck through the blockade.

He had never before felt so vulnerable.

"WE HAVE to jump right on their heels, Aryn."

Aryn did not bother to respond. She dwelled in the Force, floated in and on the warm network of lines that connected all things, one to another. Her consciousness expanded to see and feel everything near her. She focused on her perception of the passage of time, first on how it felt as she moved through it, then on spreading it, stretching it, until she could linger in a millisecond as if it were a moment, then a minute. To Zeerid it would appear that she were a blur of motion, existing simultaneously in multiple places. To her, it felt as if the universe around her had stilled. She smiled, seeing the moments that hung before her, each millisecond a long moment in which she could think, in which she could act. The effort taxed her, and she knew she could not maintain it for long.

"Watch the scanner," Zeerid said, his words a lifetime in the utterance.

She did not watch the scanner. Her body could respond faster than any machine. Instead she watched the viewscreen. The Imperial ships had finished their hydrogen skim and now maneuvered into a formation suitable for a hyperspace jump, the supply ships within the ring of the frigate escort.

She tensed.

"They're forming up," Zeerid said. The waves of his tension crashed against her but she dammed them off, did not allow them to disrupt her focus.

She watched, waited, waited . . .

As one, the Imperial ships began to stretch in her perception. For a nanosecond, all of them seemed to stretch to infinity, their rear engines a hundred thousand kilometers off *Fatman*'s bow, their forms reaching across and through an incomprehensible distance. She knew it was illusion, that is was a trick of her perception caused by the moment they entered hyperspace seeming to freeze before her eyes.

She engaged *Fatman*'s hyperdrive and the black night of space turned blue.

"Now, Aryn! Now!" Zeerid said, but he was far too late.

They were already gone.

She remained immersed in the Force as *Fatman* surged through hyperspace. The ordinary maddening churn slowed to a crawl of spirals and whorls, the script of the universe writ large in characters of blue, turquoise, midnight, and lavender. She fancied there might be meaning in the lines, an important revelation that hung before her, just beyond the reach of her consciousness.

She lost track of the slow passage of time. Zeerid spoke to her from time to time but his words bounced off her perception, ricocheted without her comprehension. In time, something he said penetrated her understanding.

"Coming out, Aryn. Be ready."

She watched Zeerid, moving in slow motion, pull back on the lever that engaged the hyperdrive.

She readied herself, and the moment the blue of hyperspace started to fade into black, she pushed a series of buttons and switches that turned *Fatman* cold except for life support, thrusters, and the small amount of power they'd need to create an electromagnetic bond.

The blue disappeared in favor of the midnight of space, and she returned to normal perception.

"Engaging thrusters," Zeerid said. "Well done, Aryn."

Sweat soaked her robes, pasted them to her body. She felt as if she had not slept in days.

"Now it gets fun," Zeerid said.

The trailing freighter in the convoy, five times the size of *Fatman,* flew right before them. They had jumped out within the ring of frigates and gone cold so fast the frigates would not have perceived their arrival. They were directly under one of the freighters, a kilometer beneath its underside, maybe less.

In the distance, the metal-and-duracrete sphere of Coruscant floated in space. The rest of the convoy spread out before them. The trailing freighter's ion engines fired, and it started to head out.

"Not so fast," Zeerid said.

He punched the thrusters and *Fatman* lurched toward the freighter until its underside filled their field of vision. It started to pull away.

Zeerid hit the thrusters again.

"There it is," he said, closing on the freighter's cargo bay. His hands flew over the instrument panel, using one thruster then another to angle the ship, finally flipping *Fatman* over so that her flat ventral side faced a flat spot on the Imperial freighter. As they closed, Zeerid flipped a switch, using *Fatman*'s deflector array to form an electromagnetic field. He killed the thrusters and they coasted in.

"Brace," he said.

Fatman closed a few hundred meters more and then the electromagnetic field did the rest, pulling them tight against the Imperial ship. Aryn felt barely a lurch.

"As soft as a kiss," Zeerid said, and eased back in his seat. He looked over at Aryn, all grins, seemingly unsurprised by his success. "Let's take a ride."

* * *

MALGUS FELT a flash of discomfort, the irritating needle stab of a light-side user, the feeling oddly similar to that which he had felt when he'd fought Master Zallow in the Temple. The feeling lasted barely an instant and disappeared, leaving only a sensory ghost in its wake.

"Are you all right, my lord?" Jard said.

Malgus waved a hand dismissively. He sat in the command chair and the viewscreen of *Valor* showed the distant silver-and-white triangles of an Imperial convoy just out of hyperspace.

"Magnify the convoy," he said, and the image grew large enough to see the ships—blocky freighters escorted by the much smaller, sleeker navy frigates. He saw nothing out of the ordinary.

Jard monitored incoming transmissions and ships' registries from the command lectern at which he stood.

"All appears in order, Darth Malgus."

Malgus examined the convoy's details on his own command readout. They bore medical supplies, spare parts, and a contingent of Imperial soldiers. All perfectly ordinary.

"They are requesting landing instructions, my lord."

"Provide it to them. But have the shuttles put eyes on them."

"We could delay them, my lord. If you think something is amiss."

"No. Let's get those supplies on the ground so they can be distributed."

"Yes, my lord."

ARYN AND Zeerid both hunched in their seats and said nothing, as if their silence within the cockpit would somehow assist *Fatman* in passing through the blockade. Zeerid radiated both apprehension and excitement.

The angle at which *Fatman* had connected to the freighter restricted their field of vision to seventy or eighty degrees. The system moved into and out of their view, one small slice at a time. The convoy was on an approach vector and moving at less than one-half. Aryn could see the tail end of the starboard side of another freighter fifteen kilometers away.

"Can anyone see us?" she asked, her voice almost a whisper.

"Not at that distance," Zeerid said. "We just look like part of the line of the ship. We'll cut loose during atmospheric entry. Their sensors will be blacked out and we'll be gone before they're wise to us. I think we're going to make it, Aryn."

She nodded. She thought so, too.

Seconds slogged by, stretched into minutes.

"We have to be getting close," Zeerid said.

Motion near the tail end of the nearby freighter drew Aryn's eye. A small ship moved slowly around the freighter. Its tri-winged configuration told her it was an Imperial shuttle. She watched it for a time, unconcerned, until another came into view, this one cruising underneath the freighter.

"What are those shuttles doing?" she asked.

He frowned. "I have no idea."

They watched the shuttles move methodically along the length and breadth of the tail section of the freighter.

"They're checking its exterior," Aryn said, and she felt Zeerid's level of apprehension rise as he realized the same thing.

"Maybe it suffered damage in hyperspace," Zeerid said. "Could be they're just checking the one."

"Could be," Aryn said, and knew that neither of them believed it.

Zeerid cleared his throat, rubbed the back of his neck.

"If we get seen, we either make a dash for the atmosphere and try to get lost under it, or we jump into hyperspace."

"I need to get to the planet."

Zeerid nodded. "Me, too. It's unanimous then. We'll make a dash."

MALGUS SAT in his chair and watched his shuttles slide around the freighters, sand flies to banthas. None had reported seeing anything unusual.

One of the junior officers on a scanner called Commander Jard to him. The two conferred briefly, and Jard returned to his command lectern near Malgus.

"What is it?" Malgus asked.

"An anomalous reading from the *Dromo*," Jard said. "An unusual magnetic signature."

Malgus saw Vrath tense and lean toward them.

"Halt them and send the shuttles over."

"My lord, it could just be an engine malfunction, scanner noise."

Malgus thought not. "Do it, Commander."

Jard raised the *Dromo* on the ship-to-ship. "Freighter *Dromo*, come to a full stop immediately."

He cut off the connection before the *Dromo*'s captain could protest, then dispatched the shuttles.

"If there's anything to it," Jard said. "We'll soon know."

ARYN AND Zeerid watched first one then another shuttle peel away from the other vessel and start toward them. Zeerid cursed as their freighter began to slow.

"Are we stopping?" Aryn asked.

Zeerid nodded, licked his lips. "I think we go hot right now. I don't want a cold ship when they spot us."

"If you fire up the engines, their scanners will pick us up."

"They're going to see us anyway. Those shuttles are coming. Let's fire her up and make our run. You ready?"

Aryn watched the shuttles close the gap between them. She nodded. "Ready."

Zeerid pushed buttons and flipped switches. *Fatman* came back to life.

THE COMMUNICATIONS officer spun in his chair. "Sir, secured communication from Darth Angral. Shall I put it through?"

"What have the shuttles found?" Malgus asked Jard.

"Not there yet, my lord."

Vrath turned his head sideways, as if he heard better out of one ear than another.

"Anomalous reading just flared and vanished," the scan officer said.

"Vanished?" Jard asked.

"I'm getting something else," said the scan officer.

"Darth Malgus," said the communication officer. "Darth Angral insists I put him through."

"Put him through," Malgus said irritably, and slapped the comm button. He put a wireless earpiece in his ear so Angral's words would be heard only by him.

"What is it, my lord?"

Darth Angral's smooth voice carried over the connection. "Malgus, how goes the patrol?"

"I am in the middle of something, Darth Angral. I beg you to be brief."

Before Angral could reply, the scan officer said, "Engines. Sir, I think there's a ship hiding in the *Dromo*'s shadow."

"That's it!" Vrath said. "That is them!"

"Alert the shuttles," Jard said. "Now."

* * *

"ENGINES READY to burn," Zeerid said.

The shuttles, perhaps a kilometer or two away, either spotted them or got word of *Fatman*'s presence. One peeled left, the other right. *Fatman*'s thrusters pushed it off the freighter. Zeerid engaged the ion drives and *Fatman* screamed through the space between the two shuttles. He throttled the freighter's engines to full and headed straight for the next nearest freighter.

Aryn had flown with Zeerid many times but had forgotten what an instinctive flier he was. He seemed to consult his instruments only rarely, instead relying on intuition, experience, and his own reflexes.

A bit like Force-piloting without the Force, she supposed.

Fatman twirled a spiral as it closed on the nearest freighter and pelted along its exterior.

"Give me a hug," Zeerid muttered.

Aryn gripped the armrests of her chair, expecting the red lines of the frigates' plasma cannons to light the sky at any moment, but no fire came. She checked the scanner. No fighters yet, either.

"What are they waiting on?" she said.

Zeerid ran *Fatman* along the bulkhead of the freighter, close enough that Aryn felt as if she could have reached out and touched it. She imagined the crew of the Imperial freighter ducking low as *Fatman* buzzed them.

"Too much traffic and we're staying too close," he said, whipping *Fatman* over and past the bridge of the freighter. "They don't want to hit their own ships."

JARD'S VOICE was tense with urgency. "That's a Corellian XS freighter, my lord."

Vrath nodded and pointed at the viewscreen. "That's

the one I told you about, Darth Malgus. Shoot him down!"

Malgus used a blast of power to throw Vrath against the far wall.

"Shut your mouth," Malgus said to him.

"Are you speaking to me?" Angral asked in his earpiece.

Malgus had forgotten about Angral. "Of course not, my lord. Give me a moment, please."

He muted the earpiece and eyed the viewscreen. He could not shoot the freighter down in the midst of the convoy. *Valor*'s armaments could inadvertently hit an Imperial ship. The frigates would be in the same situation. Their formation was designed to thwart attacks from outside the convoy, not attacks from within.

"Keep the ship on screen. Pursue at full and order the rest of the convoy to get clear."

"Yes, my lord," Jard said, and made it happen.

Valor's engines fired on full and the cruiser lurched after the freighter.

Vrath climbed to his feet, favoring his side.

Possibilities played out in Malgus's mind. With a Jedi aboard, shooting the freighter down could undermine the peace negotiations. Of course, the mere fact that a Jedi was inbound to Coruscant arguably undermined the peace process already.

Malgus stared at the viewscreen, watched the cruiser gain on the freighter. In moments he would get a clear field of fire.

The Empire needed war to thrive. He knew that.

He needed war to thrive. He knew that, too.

He had it within his power, possibly, to reignite the war.

He saw Coruscant in the viewscreen beyond the freighter and imagined it in flames.

The flashing light on his console reminded him that Darth Angral was waiting.

"Hail the freighter," he said.

Jard looked puzzled. "I doubt they will answer."

"Try, Commander."

ARYN DID not need to consult her scanner display to know that the ships of the convoy were peeling away to give the cruiser and frigates a clear field of fire. Zeerid said nothing, merely handled the stick, worked the instrument panel, and occasionally consulted the scanner readout. *Fatman* banked hard right, jumped away from the near freighter, and covered the short gulf of empty space between it and the next. Zeerid was frog-hopping along the convoy, all while trying to get *Fatman* closer to the planet.

But the convoy was starting to break up. The freighters and frigates accelerated away from one another. And above them all loomed the enormous bulk of the Imperial cruiser, waiting for its chance.

"I'm running out of ships, Aryn. We have to make a run for the atmosphere."

Before them, the glowing orb of Coruscant's night side hung in the deep night of space. The sun crested behind the planet, and Coruscant's horizon line lit up like it was on fire.

"Do it," she said. "No, wait. They're hailing us. Holo."

"You're kidding?"

Aryn shook her head and Zeerid activated the small transmitter mounted in his instrument panel.

A hologram of an Imperial bridge took shape. Crew sat at their stations, their images clear in the holo's resolution. Two human men stood in the foreground, one a thin redhead in the uniform of a naval officer, one a towering, bulky figure of a man who wore a heavy black cape and whose eyes seemed to glow in the light of the bridge's instrumentation. The eyes studied Zeerid with such intensity that it made him uncomfortable even through the holo. A respirator clung to the man's face, covering his mouth. His pale skin looked as gray as a corpse's.

"Power down entirely," said the tall man, his voice as raw as an open wound. "You have five seconds."

Aryn leaned in close to see the hologram better. The man's eyes moved from Zeerid to her and even across the distance he felt their power. She recognized him. He had fought in the Battle of Alderaan.

"He is Sith," Aryn said. "Darth Malgus."

Motion behind Malgus caught Aryn's eye, a third man, short, arms crossed across his chest. She and Zeerid almost bumped heads as they eyed the holo. Aryn recognized him. So did Zeerid, it seemed.

"That's the man that ambushed us in the spaceport," Zeerid said. "Vrath Xizor."

"He alerted them we were coming."

Zeerid stared at the holo then leaned back, eyes wide. "Stang, Aryn. That's the same man I saw in Karson's Park on Vulta."

"Where?"

"He knows I have a daughter."

"You have two seconds," Malgus said.

Zeerid hit the TRANSMIT button. "To hell with you, Sith."

He cut off the transmission, unleashed a rain of expletives, and put *Fatman* into a rapid spin that turned Aryn light-headed and would make it as difficult as possible for targeting computers to lock on.

CHAPTER 9

MALGUS STARED at the holotransmitter, now dark, on which he had communicated with the freighter, the freighter that had a Jedi aboard.

Torn, he thought of Eleena, of Lord Adraas, of Angral, of the flawed Empire that was taking shape before his eyes and how it fell short of the Empire as it should be, an Empire congruent with the needs of the Force.

"They will be clear of the convoy shortly, Commander Jard," said Lieutenant Makk, the bridge weapons officer.

Malgus watched the freighter dance among the now-separating ships of the convoy, trying to hug what vessels it could as it skipped toward Coruscant.

He thought he should shoot it down and hope that the death of a Jedi over Coruscant would destroy the peace talks and restart the war.

He should do it.

He knew he should.

"I think he's going to try to make the planet," Jard said. "Why doesn't he just jump out?"

Members of the bridge crew shook their heads at the

pilot's foolishness. Were he wise, he would have jumped into hyperspace and fled.

"His need to get to the planet outweighs the risk of his getting shot down," Malgus said, intrigued.

"All this for spice?" Jard said.

"Perhaps it is the Jedi's need that drives them."

"Curious," Jard observed.

"Agreed," Malgus said. With difficultly, he let curiosity murder temptation. "Get close enough to use the tractor beam. There is more to this than mere spicerunning."

"Yes, my lord."

Malgus tapped the earpiece and reopened the channel with Darth Angral.

"What is happening there?" Angral asked, his tone perturbed.

Malgus offered a half-truth. "A spicerunner is trying to get through the blockade."

"Ah, I see." Angral paused, then said, "I have received a communiqué from our delegation on Alderaan."

The mere mention of the delegation caused Malgus a flash of rage, a flash that almost caused him to reconsider his decision to capture, rather than destroy, the freighter.

Angral continued: "A member of the Jedi delegation has left Alderaan without filing a flight plan and without reporting her intent to her superiors. The Jedi have reason to believe that she may be heading to Coruscant. Her activities are unauthorized by the Jedi Council and she is to be treated no differently from the spicerunner you are pursuing now."

"She?" Malgus asked, eyeing the freighter on the viewscreen, recalling the woman he had seen in the vidscreen. "This rogue Jedi is a woman?"

"A human woman, yes. Aryn Leneer. Her actions,

whatever they may be, are not to be attributed to the Jedi Council or the Republic. The Emperor wants nothing to affect the ongoing negotiations. Do you understand, Darth Malgus?"

Malgus understood all too well. "The Jedi delegation told Lord Baras of this rogue Jedi? They sacrificed one of their own to ensure that the negotiations continued smoothly?"

"Master Dar'nala herself, as I understand it."

Malgus shook his head in disgust. He felt a hint of sympathy for Aryn Leneer. Like him, she had been betrayed by those she believed in and served. Of course, what she believed in and served was heretical.

"If this Jedi does attempt to reach Coruscant and she falls into your hands, you are to destroy her. Am I clear, Darth Malgus?"

"Yes, my lord."

The freighter broke free of the convoy into open space and flew an evasive path toward Coruscant. Perhaps the pilot thought to escape in the planet's atmosphere.

"Engage the tractor beam," Commander Jard said, and Malgus did not gainsay the order.

He cut the connection with Angral.

He had disobeyed an order, taken the first step down a path he had never before trod. He still wasn't sure why.

THERE WAS nothing between *Fatman* and Coruscant but open space, and that meant fire would be incoming. Aryn watched the distance to the planet's atmosphere shrink on her scanner. She sat hunched, braced against the plasma fire she knew must soon come. She thought they might make it until *Fatman* lurched and lost half of its velocity, throwing Aryn and Zeerid forward in their seats.

"What's that?" Aryn said, checking the instrument panel.

"Tractor beam," Zeerid said, and pushed down hard on the stick. *Fatman* dived, her nose facing the planet, and Aryn could see the night side of Coruscant, the lines of light from the urbanscape like glowing script on the otherwise dark surface.

The ship was not accelerating. Alarms wailed and *Fatman*'s engines screamed, battling with the tractor beam but losing decisively.

The cruiser started to reel them in.

Cursing, Zeerid cut off the engines and *Fatman*'s reverse motion increased noticeably. Through the canopy, Aryn watched the distant stars move past them in reverse. She imagined the cruiser's landing bay opening as they approached, a mouth that would chew them up.

She cleared her mind, thought of Master Zallow, and readied herself to face the Sith Lord and whatever else she might find on the cruiser. She reached into her pocket, traced her fingers over the single stone she'd brought from Alderaan, the stone from the Nautolan calming bracelet Master Zallow had given her. The cool, smooth touch of it helped clear her mind.

"I'm sorry, Zeerid," she said.

"I was coming anyway, Aryn. And you didn't get me caught. I got you caught. And anyway don't apologize yet." His hands flew over the instrument panel. "No Imperial tractor beam is holding my ship. I have to get back to Vulta and my daughter."

He ratcheted up the power to the engines, though he didn't yet engage them. The ship vibrated as Zeerid backed up the power and held it just before the exchange manifolds, a river of energy gathering behind a dam.

"What are you going to do?" Aryn asked, though she suspected she knew.

"Shooting this cork out of the bottle," he said, and diverted more power to the engines. He made as though he were shaking a bottle of soda water. "Get yourself strapped in, Aryn. Not just the lap. All five points."

Aryn did so. "You could tear the ship in half," she said. "Or the engines might blow."

He nodded. "Or we might break loose. But for that to work, I need to get oblique to the pull at the correct moment." He checked the scanner. "You're not so big," he said to the cruiser.

His even tone and steady hands did not surprise Aryn. He seemed to thrive under stress. He'd have made a decent Jedi, she imagined.

She checked the distance between the cruiser and *Fatman*, the speed the beam was pulling them.

"You have five seconds," she said.

"I know."

"Four."

"Do you believe that's helpful?"

"Two."

He tapped another series of keys and the engines whined so loudly they overwhelmed the alarm.

"One second," she said.

In her mind's eye, she imagined *Fatman* snapping in two, imagined she and Zeerid perishing in the vacuum, their dying sight pieces of *Fatman* flaming like pyrotechnics as they cut a path through Coruscant's atmosphere.

"And . . . we go!" Zeerid said.

He twisted the stick leftward at the same moment that he released all of the pent-up power into the engines.

The sudden rush arrested the backward motion of the ship and *Fatman* bucked like an angry rancor. Metal creaked, screamed under the stress. Somewhere deep within the ship, something burst with a hiss.

For a fraction of a second the ship hung in space, perfectly still, engines wailing, their power warring with the tractor beam's pull. And then *Fatman* tore loose and streaked free. The sudden acceleration pressed Aryn and Zeerid into the back of their seats.

Fire alarms sounded. Aryn checked the board.

"Fires in the engine compartment, Zeerid."

He was talking to himself under his breath, handling the stick, watching the scanner, and might not have heard her.

"He's right behind us," Zeerid said.

"Get into the atmosphere," she said. "That cruiser has no maneuverability outside a vacuum. We can ditch somewhere, get lost in the sky traffic before they can dispatch a fighter."

"Right," he said, and slammed down on the stick.

Fatman dipped her nose and Coruscant once more came into view, tantalizingly close.

Smoke wafted into the cockpit from the rear, the smell of seared electronics.

"Aryn!"

"I'm on it," she said, and started to unstrap herself.

"Chemical extinguishers are in wall mounts in every corridor."

ON THE main screen, Malgus watched the freighter's engines flare blue. The ship shook loose of the tractor beam's noose and dived toward the planet like a blaster shot. A murmur went through the bridge crew.

"Pursue, helm," Commander Jard said.

The helmsman engaged the engines and accelerated after the freighter.

"The tractor has failed, my lord," Commander Jard said to Malgus, checking the command readout. "We will have it up again in moments."

Malgus watched the freighter open some distance between it and the cruiser, and made up his mind. He had crossed a line and started down a road when he had first engaged the tractor beam. But the time was not yet right to walk farther down that road. He could not afford to let the Jedi, Aryn Leneer, get to Coruscant, lest Angral start to perceive motives in Malgus that Malgus would not yet acknowledge in himself.

"No," he said. "They'll be in the atmosphere in a moment. Shoot them down."

"Very good, my lord." Jard looked to the weapons officer. "Weapons free, Lieutenant Makk." Jard looked to Malgus. "Shall I alert the planetary fighter wing, my lord?"

"That shouldn't be necessary, provided Lieutenant Makk does his job."

"Very good, my lord."

Red lines from *Valor*'s plasma cannons filled the space between the ship, the fire so thick that the lines seemed to bleed together into a red plane.

ARYN GOT halfway out of her seat when an explosion rocked the ship. *Fatman* lurched and Aryn fell to the floor.

"Back in your seat," Zeerid said. "Weapons are hot on that cruiser."

Aryn climbed into her seat and got the lap strap on. The moment the buckle clicked into place, Zeerid went evasive. Coruscant spun in the viewscreen as *Fatman* spun, wheeled, and dived. The red lines of plasma fire lit up the black of space. Zeerid went hard right, down, then left.

The ship knifed into the atmosphere.

"Divert everything but the engines and life support to the rear deflectors."

Aryn worked the instrument panel, doing as Zeerid ordered.

Another explosion rocked the ship.

"The deflectors aren't going to take another one," she said.

Zeerid nodded. The orange flames of atmospheric entry were visible through the canopy. Plasma bolts knifed over them, under, to the left. Zeerid cut *Fatman* to the right as they descended, risking a bad entry that could burn them up.

The smoke in the cockpit thickened.

"Masks?" Aryn asked, coughing.

"There," Zeerid responded, nodding at a ship's locker between their seats. Aryn threw it open, grabbed two masks, tossed one to Zeerid, and pulled the other one on herself.

"You've got the stick," Zeerid said while he pulled on his mask.

Aryn grabbed the copilot's stick and continued *Fatman*'s spiraling descent toward Coruscant.

Fire from the cruiser hit the ship on the starboard side and caused the freighter to spin wildly. Aryn felt dizzy, sick.

"I have the stick," Zeerid said, his voice muffled by the mask. He got the spin under control and drove *Fatman* almost vertically into the atmosphere. The cockpit grew hot. Flames engulfed the ship. They must have looked like a comet cutting through the sky.

"Too steep," Aryn said.

"I know," Zeerid said. "But we've got to get in."

The unrelenting fire from the cruiser struck the freighter again, the impact shoving them through the stratosphere. The flames diminished, vanished, and Coruscant was once more visible below them.

"We're through," Aryn said.

Without warning the engines died and *Fatman* went limp in the air, spinning, falling, but with no power.

Zeerid cursed, slammed his hand against the instrument panel, trying frantically to refire them, but to no avail.

"They can still hit us here," he said, and unbuckled his belts. "I got nothing but thrusters. Get to the escape pod."

"The cargo, Zeerid."

He hesitated, finally shook his head and unbuckled her straps. "Forget the cargo. Move."

She stood and another bolt hit *Fatman*. An explosion rocked the rear of the ship. Another. They were going down. Alarms wailed. The ship was burning, falling through the sky. Zeerid hit the control panel to engage the thrusters and keep the ship in the air.

For the moment, at least.

"THEY ARE dead in the air," Lieutenant Makk announced. "Drifting on thrusters."

Commander Jard looked to Malgus for the kill order. Vrath, too, looked on with interest.

The freighter hung low over Coruscant's atmosphere. It limped along on thrusters, trailing flames from its dead ion engines. They could rope them back in with the tractor.

"Shoot them down," Malgus ordered.

Out of the corner of his eye, he saw Vrath smile and cross his arms over his chest.

EXPLOSIONS IN the rear of *Fatman* started to spread, the secondary explosions working their way forward in a series of dull booms. They would never make it to the escape pod.

Aryn activated her lightsaber. "Grab hold of something."

"What are you doing?"

"Getting us out."

"What?"

She did not bother to explain. Bracing herself and holding on to her seat strap, she stabbed her blade through the transparisteel of the cockpit canopy and opened a gash. The oxygen rushed out of the cockpit while the pressure equalized. Their masks allowed them to breathe, despite the thin atmosphere. The cold startled Aryn.

She used her blade to cut a door out of the canopy. The thin air whipped by, whistling.

"We're fifty kilometers up, Aryn!" Zeerid said, his voice rising for the first time. "The velocity alone—"

She grabbed him by the arm and gave him a shake to shut him up. "Do not let go of me no matter what. Do you understand? No matter what."

His eyes were wide behind the lenses of his mask. He nodded.

She did not hesitate. She sank into the Force, cocooned them both in a protective sheath, and leapt out of the ship and into the open air.

The wind and velocity tore them backward. They slammed into the ship's fuselage and whipped through the flames pouring out its sides. At almost the same moment, plasma fire from the cruiser above them hit *Fatman* dorsally and the ship exploded into an expanding ball of flame. The blast wave sent them careering crazily through the sky and set them to spinning like a pinwheel. For an alarming moment, Aryn's vision blurred and she feared she would lose consciousness, but she held on to awareness with both hands and fought through it.

Zeerid was shouting but Aryn could not make it out.

Her stomach crawled up her throat as they plummeted, spinning wildly, toward the planet below. Her perspective alternated crazily from flaming pieces of *Fatman,* to Coruscant below, to the sky above and the distant silhouette of the Imperial cruiser, to *Fatman* again. The motion was pulling the blood from her head. Sparks blinked before her eyes. She had to stop the spinning or she would pass out.

She made her grip a vise around Zeerid and used the Force first to slow, then to stop the spin. They ended up hand in hand, passing through clouds, falling at terminal velocity toward Coruscant's surface.

MALGUS WATCHED the freighter disintegrate into flaming debris over Coruscant. He expected the faint touch of the Jedi's Force signature to disintegrate with it, but he felt it still.

"Magnify," he said, leaning forward in the command chair. The image on the viewscreen grew larger.

Chunks of jagged steel and a large portion of the forward section of the ship burned their way toward the surface.

"Did an escape pod launch before the ship exploded?"

"No, my lord," Jard said. "There were no survivors."

But there had been. The Jedi, at least, had survived. He could still feel her presence, though it was fading with distance, a splinter in the skin of his perception.

He considered dispatching fighters, a search party, but decided against it. He was not yet sure what he would do about the Jedi, but whatever it was, he would do it himself.

"Very good, Commander Jard. Well done, Lieutenant Makk." He turned to Vrath. "You are done here, Vrath Xizor."

Vrath shifted on his feet, swallowed, cleared his throat. "You mentioned the possibility of payment, my lord?"

Malgus credited him with bravery, if nothing else. Malgus rose and walked over. He stood twenty centimeters taller than Vrath but the smaller man held his ground and kept most of the fear from the slits of his eyes.

"It is not enough that you've killed a rival and destroyed the engspice your employer wished to prevent reaching the surface?"

"I did not—"

Malgus held up a gloved hand. "The petty squabbles of criminals hold little interest for me."

Vrath licked his lips, drew himself up straight. "I brought you a Jedi, my lord. That was her on the holo."

"So you did."

"Will I . . . be paid, then?"

Malgus regarded him coolly, and the small man seemed to withdraw into himself. The fear in his eyes expanded, the knowledge that he was a lone prey animal surrounded by predators.

"I am a man of my word," Malgus said. "You will be paid."

Vrath let out a long breath. "Thank you, my lord."

"You may take your ship to the planet. The coordinates will be provided to you and I will arrange for payment there."

"And then I can leave?"

Malgus smiled under his respirator. "That is a different question."

Vrath took half a step back. He looked as if he had been slapped. "What does that mean? I . . . will not be allowed to leave?"

"No unauthorized ships may leave Coruscant at this time. You will remain on the planet until things change."

"But, my lord—"

"*Or* I can blow your ship from space the moment it leaves my landing bay," Malgus said.

Vrath swallowed hard. "Thank you, my lord."

Malgus waved him away. Security escorted him from the bridge.

AFTER THE chaos of the cockpit, the quiet of the fall seemed oddly incongruous. Aryn heard only the rush of the wind, the steady thump of her heartbeat in her ears. Zeerid's fear was a tangible thing to her, and it fell with them.

She felt free, exhilarated, and the feeling surprised her. To the east Coruscant's surface curved away from them and the morning sun crept over the horizon line, bathing the planet in gold. The sight took her breath away. She shook Zeerid's arm and nodded at the rising sun. He did not respond. His eyes stared straight down, iron to the magnet of the planet's surface. Aryn allowed herself to enjoy the view for a few seconds before trying to save their lives.

The drag increased as the thin air of the upper atmosphere gave way to the thicker, breathable air of the lower. Below them, Coruscant transformed from a brown-and-black ball crisscrossed with seemingly random whorls of light, to a distinguishable geometry of well-lit cities, roads, skyways, quadrants, and blocks. She could make out tiny black forms moving against the urbanscape, the ants of aircars, speeders, and swoops, but far fewer than ordinary. Plumes of smoke traced twisting black lines into the air. Large areas of Galactic City lay in ruins, dark lesions on the skin of the planet.

The Empire must have killed tens of thousands. More, perhaps.

The wind changed pitch, whistled past her ears. She

fancied she heard whispers in it, the soul of the planet sharing its pain. Her clothing flapped audibly behind her.

Below, she could distinguish more and more details of Coruscant's upper levels: the lines of skyscrapers, the geometry of plazas and parks, the orderly, straight lines of roads.

She let herself feel the descent and used the feeling to fall into the Force. Nestled in its power, she marshaled her strength. She pulled Zeerid toward her. Unresisting, he felt as limp as a rag doll in her hands. She drew him to her, under her, wrapped her arms and legs around him.

"Ready yourself," she shouted in his ear. "Nod if you understand."

His head bobbed once, tense and rapid.

The buildings below grew larger, more defined. They descended toward a large plaza, a flat trapezoid of duracrete with stratoscrapers anchoring each of its corners.

"I will slow us," she shouted. "But we will still hit with some force. I will release you before we hit. Try to roll with the impact."

He nodded again.

She lowered her head, angled her body, and tried to use the wind resistance to create some slight motion forward, rather than entirely downward. The ground rushed up to meet them.

They passed through the ring of skyrises, plummeting past the roofs, windows, balconies. Given the hour, she doubted anyone saw their descent.

She reached out with the Force, channeled power into a wide column beneath them. She conceptualized the power as somewhat similar to what she would use when augmenting a leap, except that instead of a sudden rush of power to drive her upward, she instead used the power in a gentler, passive fashion. She imagined it as a balloon, soft and yielding at first, but providing ever-increasing resistance as they fell farther into it.

They slowed and Zeerid shifted in her grasp. Perhaps he did not believe it.

Pressure built behind Aryn's eyes, an ache formed in her head.

The balloon of her power slowed them further. She could see benches in the plaza, a fountain. She could distinguish individual windows in the skyrises around them. They were five hundred meters up and still falling fast.

The pressure in her brain intensified. Her vision blurred. The ache in her head became a knife stab of pain. She screamed but held on, held on.

Four hundred meters. Three hundred.

They slowed still more and Aryn feared she could not bear any more.

Two hundred.

A second stretched into an eternity of pain and pressure. She thought she must burst.

"Hang on, Aryn!" Zeerid said, his voice muffled by the mask. He was rigid in her arms.

Fifty meters.

They were still going too fast.

Twenty, ten.

She dug deep, pulled out what power she could, and expended it in a final shout, an expulsion of power that entirely arrested their descent for a moment. They hung in the air for a fraction of a second, suspended only by the invisible power of the Force and Aryn's ability to use it.

And then they were falling free.

She released Zeerid and they both hit the duracrete feetfirst, the shock of impact sending jolts of pain up Aryn's ankles and calves. She rode the momentum of the fall into a roll that knocked the wind from her and tore a divot of skin from her scalp.

But she was alive.

She lifted herself to all fours, every muscle screaming, legs quivering, blood dripping from her scalp. She tore off her mask.

"Zeerid!"

"I'm all right," he answered, his voice as raw as old leather. "I can't believe it, but I am all right."

She sagged back to the duracrete, rolled over onto her back, and stared up at dawn's light spreading across the sky. The long thin clouds, painted with the light of daybreak, looked like veins of gold. She simply lay there, exhausted.

Zeerid crawled over to her, cursing with pain throughout. He peeled off his mask and lay on his back next to her. They stared up at the sky together.

"Is anything broken?" she asked him.

He turned to look at her, shook his head, looked back at the sky. "If we get out of this, I'm becoming a farmer on Dantooine. I swear it."

She smiled.

"I'm not joking."

She held her smile; he began to chuckle, louder, and the chuckle turned into a laugh.

She could not help it. A wide smile split her face, followed by a chuckle, and then she joined him in full, both of them giggling hysterically at the dawn sky of a new day.

VRATH'S HANDS sweated on *Razor*'s stick. Despite Malgus purporting to be a man of his word, Vrath felt certain the Imperial cruiser would shoot him from space after he exited the landing bay. For a moment, he considered veering off deeper insystem, accelerating to full to get out of Coruscant's gravity well, then jumping into hyperspace, but he did not think he would make it.

More important, he feared that even if he did make it, Malgus would hunt him down on principle. Vrath knew that Malgus would do it because Vrath would have done the same. He'd looked into the Sith Lord's eyes and seen the same relentlessness he tried to cultivate in his own. He would not cross Malgus.

He let the ship's autopilot ride the coordinates provided to him by *Valor* into Coruscant's atmosphere. It would put him down in one of Galactic City's smaller spaceports, probably one commandeered by Imperial soldiers.

Presently, the spaceport hailed him and sent him landing instructions. He affirmed them and sat back in his chair.

He resolved that he would not leave *Razor* once he put down on Coruscant. He wanted no further interaction with conquering Imperials. He wanted only to wait until peace negotiations on Alderaan were concluded, however long that might take, and then get off Coruscant.

MALGUS KNEW Aryn Leneer had somehow survived the destruction of her ship and he suspected she had survived the descent to Coruscant's surface. He did not want Angral to learn of her escape. Such knowledge would be . . . premature.

He would need to track her down. To do that, he needed to determine why she had returned to Coruscant in the first place.

"I will be in my quarters," he said to Commander Jard.

"If anything requires your attention, I will alert you immediately."

When he reached his quarters, he found Eleena sleeping. Her blasters, tucked into their holsters, lay on the bed beside her. She slept with one hand on them. He watched the steady rise and fall of her chest, the half smile she wore even while sleeping. She had shed the sling on her arm.

Staring at her, he acknowledged to himself that he cared for her. Deeply.

And that, he knew, was his weakness.

He stared at her and thought of the Twi'lek servant woman he had murdered in his youth . . .

He realized that his fists were clenched.

Shaking his head, he closed the door to the room in which Eleena slept and started up the portcomp at his work desk. He wanted to learn more of Aryn Leneer, so he linked to several Imperial databases and input her name.

Her picture came up first. He studied her image, her eyes. She reminded him of Eleena. But she looked different from the woman he had seen on the vidscreen on *Valor*'s bridge. The change was in her eyes. They'd grown harder. Something had happened to her in the interim.

He scrolled through the file.

She was a Force empath, he saw. An orphan from Balmorra, taken into the Jedi academy as a child. He scrolled deeper into her file and there found her motivation.

A picture of Master Ven Zallow stared out of the screen at Malgus, a day-old ghost.

Aryn Leneer had been Master Zallow's Padawan. Zallow had raised her from childhood.

He scrolled back up to Aryn's image. Back then, her green eyes had held no guile, no edge. He could tell by looking at her that she left herself too open to pain. Her Force empathy would have only increased her sensitivity.

He leaned back in the chair.

She had felt her Master die, had felt Malgus drive his blade through him.

That was what had changed her, changed her so much that she had abandoned her Order and rushed across space to Coruscant.

Why?

He saw the faint reflection of his own face in the comp-screen, superimposed over hers. His eyes, dark and deeply set in the black pits of his sockets. Her eyes, green, soft, and gentle.

But not anymore.

They were the same, he realized. They had both loved and their love had brought them pain. In a flash of understanding, he knew why she had come to Coruscant.

"She is looking for me," he said.

She would not know she was looking for him because she had no way to know who had killed her Master. But she had come to Coruscant to find out, to avenge Zallow.

Where would she go first?

He thought he knew.

He inhaled deeply, tapped his finger on the edge of the desk.

She was hunting him. He admired her for that. It seemed very . . . unlike a Jedi.

Of course, Malgus would not sit idle while she sought him out.

He would hunt *her*.

CHAPTER 10

A SQUAD of six Imperial fighters, bent wing interceptors, zoomed overhead, the hum of their engines drown-
ing out and throttling Zeerid's and Aryn's laughter. The
bent panels of the fighters' wings formed parentheses
around the central fuselage.

"That doesn't look right," Zeerid said. "Imperial
ships over Coruscant."

"No," Aryn said. "It doesn't."

Zeerid looked higher up in the sky, trying to spot any
sign of his destroyed ship. He saw nothing. *Fatman* had
served him well and nearly gotten them away from the
cruiser.

He smiled, thinking that engspice addicts all over Coruscant would soon go through withdrawal. But after
those few days of torture, they'd have freedom, should
they choose it.

Zeerid felt a peculiar sense of freedom, too. He had
not delivered spice. That pleased him. In a way, the Empire had freed him from his treadmill, had destroyed it
in a hail of plasma fire.

Of course, The Exchange would try to kill him. He'd
have that to contend with.

"What are you thinking?" Aryn said.

"I'm thinking about Arra," he answered, as the weight of his situation overburdened the relief he felt at surviving a fall of fifty klicks.

The man who had stood beside the Sith Lord on the bridge of the cruiser had been the same man that Zeerid had seen back at Karson's Park on Vulta, the same man who had led the ambush on him and Aryn in the spaceport.

Vrath Xizor, Oren had named him.

Vrath knew about Arra and Nat.

And if Vrath decided for some reason to share that information with The Exchange, Oren would order more than just Zeerid's death. They'd make an example of him and his family.

He sat up with a grunt. "I have to get back to Vulta. Now."

Aryn sat up beside him. She must have felt the fear in him. "Because of the man on the cruiser?"

Zeerid nodded. "He knows about Arra."

"I don't understand why—"

"No one in my . . . work knows that I have a daughter, Aryn. They'd use her against me if they did. Hurt her. But now he knows. He saw me in the park with her. I *talked* to him." He put his face in his hands.

Aryn put a hand on his back. "Zeerid . . ."

He shook it off and climbed to his feet. "I have to get back."

"How?"

He shook his head. "I don't know, but I'm going. I owe you for saving me. I won't forget that, but—"

She held up a hand. "Wait. Just wait. Think it through, Zeerid. They're not going to let him leave, this man who knows about your daughter. No one has gotten off Coruscant since the attack. And no one will until the peace negotiations are concluded and the planet's disposition decided. They'll keep him on the cruiser or ground him on the planet. He's not going anywhere."

Zeerid considered the words. They made sense. His heart continued to pound, but slower.

"He's here, you think."

"Possibly. Maybe even likely. But he's not returning to Vulta, at least not yet."

Zeerid knew that Vrath already *could* have told someone else about Arra, but he thought it unlikely. No one gave away leverage. It was like giving away credits. No, Vrath had kept it to himself. Maybe to sell to The Exchange, maybe to use later. But he hadn't used it yet. He'd had to get to Coruscant from Vulta too fast. He must have left immediately after the ambush.

"Why didn't he use Arra against you back on Vulta?" Aryn asked. "Could've forced you to turn over the cargo."

Zeerid didn't know. "Maybe he would have. Maybe that was him in the stairwell of the apartment complex yesterday. Maybe we frightened him off. Or maybe he didn't have time. He had to follow me to ensure he could locate the spice. If he'd have grabbed Arra, he might have lost me, or I might have flown off with the spice without ever knowing he had her."

Aryn said nothing as Zeerid let his thoughts meander into the briar patch of the criminal underworld.

"Maybe he just wouldn't hurt a child," Aryn said.

"Maybe," Zeerid said, but did not believe it. He hadn't met many criminals who operated with any kind of ethical code.

"Listen," Aryn said. "I'll help you get off the planet or find him here. But first I need to get to the Temple."

"You came here to kill someone, Aryn. I cannot spare that kind of time."

Her face flushed, and he saw some inner battle going on behind her eyes. "I can just identify him." She said it as if trying to convince herself. "I can find him another time. But I must have his name. This may be my only chance." She blew out a deep breath. "I would welcome your help."

"Been real useful so far," he said.

"You got me here."

"I got us blown out of space."

"And yet here we are."

"And here we are."

"Let me get a name and then I'll help you get off-planet. Agreed?"

He made up his mind, nodded. "All right, I'm with you, but we have to do this fast."

MALGUS WAITED for Eleena to awaken, his mind moving through possibilities, still trying to square a circle. He was beginning to think it could not be done.

Eleena emerged from the bedroom of his quarters, barely covered in a light shirt and her undergarments. As always, her beauty struck him, the grace of her movement. She smiled.

"How long did I sleep?"

"Not long," he said.

She poured tea for both of them and sat on the floor near his feet.

"I have something I need you to do," he said.

"Name it."

"You will take several shuttles to Coruscant. Ten members of my security team, Imperial soldiers, will accompany you."

In his head, he had already picked the men—Kerse's squad—men whose discretion he knew he could trust. He continued: "I will give you a list."

She sipped her tea, leaned her head against his calf. "What will be on this list?"

"Names and locations, mostly. Some technology and its location."

He had pulled it all from the Imperial database while she had been sleeping.

"What do you want me to do?"

"Find everyone and everything you can on that list and bring it to this ship."

She sat up straight, looked up at him. The question was in the pools of her eyes.

"The people are to be made prisoners," he said. "The technology confiscated as spoils of war."

The question did not leave her eyes. She gave it voice.

"Why me, beloved? Why not your Sith?"

He ran his hand over her left lekku, and she closed her eyes in pleasure.

"Because I know I can trust *you*," he said. "But I'm not yet entirely sure whom else I can trust. Not until things progress a bit further."

She opened her eyes and pulled away from him. Concern creased her forehead. "Progress further? Are you in danger?"

"Nothing that I cannot deal with. But I need you to do this."

She leaned back into him, her arm draped over his legs. "Then I will do it."

The smell of her clouded his thoughts and he fought for clarity. "Tell no one else of this. Report it only as a routine transfer of cargo."

"I will. But . . . why are you doing all of this?"

"I'm simply taking precautions. Go, Eleena."

"Now?"

"Now."

She rose, bent, and kissed first his left cheek, then his right.

"I will see you soon. What are you going to do while I am gone?"

He was going to disobey Angral's orders yet again and return to Coruscant. "I am going hunting."

THE SMELL of smoke and melted plastoid hung thick in the air. Aryn and Zeerid picked their way on foot through the streets and autowalks of Coruscant. Aryn was conscious of the fact that level after level of urbanscape extended into the depths below her. She realized that she had never put a boot to solid ground on Coruscant. Not really. Instead she, like so many, simply trod the network of walkways and duracrete streets on the surface level, unaware of most that went on in the lower levels. She had lived on the planet for decades but did not know it well.

The sun pulled itself into the sky, slowly, as if it did not want to reveal the ruin. Her eye fell on a distant, isolated skyrise that leaned precipitously to one side, the attack having damaged its foundation. It, like all of Coruscant, like the entirety of the Republic, had been knocked off-kilter.

In the distance, the black dots of a few aircars and speeders populated the morning sky. Sirens blared from somewhere, rescue teams still searching the wreckage, pulling the living and dead from the ruins.

Coruscant was coming to life for another day, the day after everything had changed.

As they traveled, they encountered piles of rubble, streets flooded by broken water lines, shattered valves spitting gas or fuel. It was like seeing bloody viscera, the innards of the planet.

A few faces regarded them from behind windows or

from balconies high above, the uncertainty and fear in their eyes the expected aftereffect of unexpected war, but they saw far fewer people than Aryn might have imagined. She wondered if many had fled to the lower levels. Perhaps the damage was less severe there. If so, the underlevels must have been thronged.

As the morning stretched, an increasing number of vehicles filled the sky. Medical and rescue ships screamed past. Swoops and speeders, bearing one or two riders to who knew where streaked over them.

Due to her empathic sense, Aryn felt the dread in the air as a tangible thing, a pall that overhung the entire planet. It wore on her, weighed her down. The towers of duracrete and transparisteel seemed ready to fall in on her. She felt hunched, tensed in anticipation of a blow. The dread was omnipresent, an entire planet of billions of people projecting raw emotion into the air.

She could not wall them out. She did not want to wall them out. The Jedi had failed them. She deserved to feel what they felt.

"Aryn, did you hear me? Aryn?"

She came back to herself to see Zeerid standing beside an open-topped Armin speeder. It was just sitting there in the middle of the street. His face twisted with concern when he saw her expression. His straggly beard and wide eyes made him look like a religious fanatic.

"Are you all right?" he asked. "What's wrong?"

"Nothing, I'm fine. It's just . . . fear is everywhere. The air is full of it."

Zeerid nodded, his lips pressed together and forming a soft line of sympathy. "I'm sorry you have to feel it, Aryn. Everyone on Coruscant knows what the Empire has done to some conquered worlds. But if they were going to do it here, I think they'd have done it already."

"It's only been a day," Aryn said, but still she hoped he was right.

A squad of Imperial fighters flew high overhead, the unmistakable hum of their engines cutting through the morning's silence.

Zeerid climbed into the speeder, stripped its storage compartment of four protein bars, a pair of macrobinoculars, and two bottles of water. He tossed a bar and bottle to Aryn.

"Eat. Drink," he said, and ducked under the control panel.

"What are you doing?" Aryn asked him. She guzzled the water to get the grit out of her throat, then peeled the wrapper on the bar and ate.

The speeder's engine hummed to life and Zeerid popped back up from under the instrumentation.

"I'm taking this speeder. We can't walk all the way to the Jedi Temple. Get in." He must have read the look on her face. "It isn't stealing, Aryn. It's abandoned. Come on."

She climbed in and strapped herself into the seat. Zeerid launched the Armin into the sky.

They made rapid progress. There was little traffic. Zeerid flew at an altitude of about half a kilo. For a time, Aryn looked out and down on Coruscant, but the rubbled buildings, smoldering fires, and black holes in the urbanscape wore her down until it all began to look the same. When she realized she had become inured to the sight of the destruction, she sat back in her seat and stared out the windshield at the smoke-filled sky.

"The Temple is ahead," Zeerid said, coming around. "There."

When she saw it, her heart sank. A hole opened in her stomach and she felt as if she were falling. She extended a hand to the safety bar and held it tight, to keep from falling.

"I'm so sorry, Aryn," Zeerid said.

Aryn had no words. The Temple, the Jedi sanctuary that had stood for millennia, had been reduced to a mountain of smoking stone and steel. The destruction wrought by the Sith on Coruscant generally had left her pained. The destruction of the Temple left her gutted. She had to remember to breathe. She could not take her eyes from it.

Zeerid reached across the speeder and took her hand in his. She closed her fingers around his and held on as if she were sinking and he was a life ring.

"I don't think we should set down, Aryn. No data cards survived that."

"Fly closer, Zeerid."

"You sure?"

She nodded, and he took the speeder in for a better look. Smoke leaked from between blackened stones. The remains of the towers lay in chunks across the ruins of the main Temple, as if they had folded over on it.

Broken columns jutted up from the ruins like broken bones. Aryn braced herself for bodies, but thankfully saw none. Instead, she saw broken pieces of statuary here and there, the jagged remains of the stone corpses of ancient Jedi Masters.

Thousands of years of honorable history reduced in a day to dust and ash and ruins by Imperial bombs. The fires would smolder for days, deep in the pile. Loss suffused her, but she was too dried out for tears.

How wonderful and terrible, she thought, was the capacity of the mind to absorb pain.

Zeerid had not released her hand, nor she his. "If your Master was here when the bombs hit, then he . . . he died in the blast. And it was just some anonymous Imperial pilot, Aryn. There's no one for you to find, no one for you to hunt down."

She was shaking her head before he'd finished speaking. "He did not die in a blast."

"Aryn—"

She jerked her hand from him, and some of the grief and anger she felt sharpened her tone. "I felt it, Zeerid! I felt him die! And it was no bomb blast. It was a lightsaber. Right here."

She touched her abdomen, and the memory of the pain she'd felt when Master Zallow had died made her wince.

Zeerid's arm and hand still stretched across the seat toward Aryn, but he did not touch her. "I believe you. I do."

He circled the ruins in silence. "So, what now?"

"I need to go down."

"That is not a good idea, Aryn."

He was probably right, but she wanted to touch it, to stand amid the rubble. She fought down the impulse and tried to quell her emotions with thought, reason. "No, don't go down. There is another way in."

"There's nothing standing."

"The Temple extends underground. One of the rooms where backup surveillance is stored is fairly deep. It may have survived the blast."

Zeerid looked as if he wanted to protest but did not. Aryn was grateful to him for it.

"Where is the other way in?"

"Through the Works," Aryn answered.

MALGUS'S PRIVATE shuttle bore him toward Coruscant's surface. Eleena and her team had left *Valor* in a convoy of three shuttles an hour earlier. They would already be well into their mission.

He sat alone, the steady rasp of his respirator the only sound in the compartment. Staring at his reflection in the transparisteel window of the shuttle, he tried to sort his thoughts.

Wild ideas bounced around his brain, thoughts that he dared not latch onto for fear of where they would carry him.

He knew only one thing with certainty—Angral was wrong. The Dark Council was wrong. Perhaps even the Emperor was wrong. Peace was a mistake. Peace would cause the Empire to drift into decadence, as had the Republic. Peace would cause the Sith to become weak in their understanding of the Force, as had the Jedi. The sacking of Coruscant was evidence of that decadence, that weakness.

No, peace was atrophy. Only through conflict could potential be realized.

Malgus understood that the role of the Republic and the Jedi was merely to serve as the whetstone against which the Empire and the Sith would sharpen themselves, make themselves more deadly.

Peace, were it to come, would dull them.

But, while Malgus knew that the Empire needed war, he had yet to determine how to bring it about.

"Entering the atmosphere, my lord," said his pilot.

He watched the fire of atmospheric entry sheathe the ship, and pondered something he recalled from his time at the Sith Academy on Dromund Kaas.

It was said the ancient Sith of Korriban purged their bodies with fire, learned strength through pain, encouraged growth through destruction.

There was wisdom in that, Malgus thought. Sometimes a thing could not be fixed. Instead, it had to be destroyed and remade.

"Remade," he said, his voice harsh through the respirator. "Destroyed and remade."

"Darth Malgus," said the pilot over the comm. "Where shall I fly you? I do not have a flight plan."

The fire of reentry had faded. The smolder in Malgus was growing into flames. Aryn Leneer's unexpected presence had started him down a path he should have trod long ago. He was grateful to her for that.

Below, the cityscape of Coruscant, pockmarked and smoking here and there from Imperial bombs, came into view.

"The Jedi Temple," he said. "Circle at one hundred meters."

If nothing else, he would soon have his own personal war. Aryn Leneer had come to Coruscant looking for him. And he had returned looking for her.

They would meet on the rubbled grave of the Jedi Order.

ARYN POINTED over the windscreen at an enormous building of duracrete and steel that could have held ten athletic stadiums. The peak of the dome stood several hundred meters high, and the innumerable venting towers and smokestacks that stuck from its surface looked like a thicket of spears. Not a single window marred the metal-and-duracrete façade.

"The Works," Aryn said. "Or at least one of the hubs. Set down there."

As Zeerid piloted the speeder down, Aryn looked back over the urbanscape, orienting herself to the relative position of the Jedi Temple. She could not see the actual ruins from their location—the intervening terrain blocked it—but she could see the smoke plumes.

The image of the ruined temple still haunted her memory.

Zeerid put the speeder down atop a nearby parking structure. Few other vehicles shared the structure. A single speeder and two swoops—both tipped onto their sides—were all that Aryn saw.

"Where is everyone?" Zeerid asked.

"Hiding in the lower levels, maybe. Staying home."

Though it seemed a lifetime ago, the attack had happened only a day before. The populace was still in shock, hiding perhaps, picking up what pieces they could.

They took a lift and autowalk to the Works hub. A large gate and security station provided ingress through the ten-meter duracrete walls. While the gate remained closed, the security station stood empty. Ordinarily it would have been well guarded. Aryn and Zeerid climbed over and through unchallenged.

The mammoth structure of the hub, larger even than a Republic cruiser, loomed before them.

Zeerid drew a blaster from his hip holster, then pulled another from a hidden holster in the small of his back and offered it to Aryn. She declined.

"Thought I'd ask," Zeerid said. "That lightsaber doesn't do you much good at twenty meters."

"You'd be surprised," she said.

The arched double doors that offered entry looked like something from an ancient Alderaanian castle built for titans. They were enormous. Aryn's Raven starfighter could have flown through them.

"Power is still on and controls are still live," Zeerid said, examining the console on the doors.

Aryn tapped a code she'd learned years before into the console.

Somewhere invisible gears turned, the groans of giants, and the doors began to rise.

The doors opened and they entered, walking empty corridors that smelled of grease and faintly of burning.

The metal floor vibrated under their feet, the snores of some enormous, unseen mechanical beast. The shaking increased as they moved deeper into the complex. Somewhere, metal ground against metal.

They cut away from the wide main corridor through which they'd entered and moved through a network of halls and offices sized not for vehicles but for sentients.

"I've never seen the inside of a hub," Zeerid said. "Not much to look at. Where are all the mechanisms?"

Aryn led him through a series of deserted security checkpoints until they reached a set of soundproofed doors that opened onto the central chamber under the dome.

EARWEAR AND HELMETS REQUIRED BEYOND THIS POINT FOR ALL NON-DROIDS read a sign on the door.

She pulled open the doors and sound poured out in a rush: the rhythmic clang of metal scraping metal, the hiss of vented air and gas, the discordant hum of hundreds of enormous engines and pumps, the beeps and whistles of maintenance droids.

Zeerid's arms fell slack at his side. His mouth hung open.

The Works was difficult to comprehend all at once. The central chamber itself was several kilometers in diameter and hundreds of meters tall. Tiered flooring and a network of stairs and cage lifts made the whole of it look like a mad industrial artist's take on an insect hive. Aryn always felt miniaturized when she saw it. It seemed made for an alien race ten times the size of humans: gears as large as starfighters, pipes wide enough to fly a speeder into, individual mechanisms that reached floor-to-ceiling, chains and belts hundreds of meters long. Hundreds of droids scurried, rolled, and walked among the workings, checking gauges, readouts, maintaining equipment, greasing mechanisms. The sound was overwhelming, a deafening industrial cacophony.

Compared with the advanced technology apparent elsewhere on Coruscant—with its sleek lines, compact designs, and sheer elegance—the Works looked primitive, garish in its enormity, like a throwback to ancient times when steam and combustion powered industry. But Aryn knew it was an illusion.

The Works stretched under Coruscant's crust from pole to pole, generally accessible only through the hubs. Its pipes, lines, hoses, and conduits formed the circulatory system of the planet, through which water, heat, electricity, and any number of other necessities flowed. It represented the peak of Republic technology.

"Follow me!" she shouted above the noise, and Zeerid nodded.

Following signs and calling upon her memory, Aryn led Zeerid through the maze of raised flooring, lifts, and autostairs. Droids moved past them, oblivious, and it occurred to Aryn that the droids in the Works would probably have kept doing their work even if everyone on Coruscant were dead. The thought struck her as grotesque.

Zeerid turned circles as they walked, trying to take it all in.

"This is unbelievable," he said to her. "I wish I had a holorecorder."

She nodded and hurried along.

They soon left behind the mechanical tumult of the hub proper. As the sound faded behind them, the corridors narrowed and darkened, and the wall-mounted lights became less frequent. Pipes and conduits snaked on and through the ceiling, the floor, the entrails of plantwide convenience. Zeerid pulled a chemlight from one of the pockets of his flight pants, snapped it in half, and held it aloft as they advanced. Both of them were sweating in the still air of the tunnels.

"There are security droids in these tunnels," she said. "We don't have a proper pass. They will try to stop us."

"Great," Zeerid said. Then, "You sure you know where you're going?"

She nodded, though she was beginning to feel lost.

From ahead she heard the whir of servos, the rattle of metal. A droid.

She pulled Zeerid to a stop and activated her lightsaber, fearing a security droid. Dust danced in the green light of its glow. Zeerid pulled his blaster, held the chemlight up higher.

"What is it?" he whispered.

A form moved in the shadows, small, cylindrical, a droid. Not a security droid but an astromech. It emerged into the light and she saw the flat, circular head and dun coloration of a T7. Scratches marred the droid's surface, and loose wires dangled from one of its shoulder joints. But she knew its color and felt as if she were seeing a ghost, a specter from her past haunting the dark tunnels of the Works. Deactivating her blade, she said, "Tee-seven?"

Her voice cracked on the words.

When he beeped a greeting in droidspeak, she knew it was him, his mechanical voice redolent somehow of very human joys, triumphs, and pain, the soundtrack of her time in the Temple, of her life with Master Zallow. Tears pooled in her eyes as T7 wheeled toward them.

"You know this astromech?" Zeerid asked.

"It was Master Zallow's droid," she said.

She knelt before T7, daubing at the dirt on his head as she might a small child. He whistled with pleasure.

"How did you get here?" she asked. "How did you . . . survive the attack?"

She struggled to follow his droidspeak, so rapidly did he spit out his beeps, whistles, and chirps. In the end, she determined that a Sith force had attacked the Temple, that Master Zallow had sent T7 away during the fight, and that T7 had sneaked back to the battlefield after all had gone quiet. Later, the Sith had returned, presumably to lay explosives, and T7 had fled to the lower levels.

"I know about Master Zallow, Tee-seven," she said.

He moaned, a low whistle of despair.

"Did you see his— Did you see him when it happened?"

The droid whistled a negative.

"Why did you go back after the battle?" Zeerid asked the droid.

A long whistle, then a compartment in T7's body slid open and T7 extended a thin metal arm from within.

The arm held Master Zallow's lightsaber.

Aryn recoiled, stared at it for a long moment, memories crowding around her, falling like rain.

"You went back to get this? Just to get this?"

Another negative whistle. Another long, hard-to-follow monologue in droidspeak.

T7 had gone back to see if anyone had survived but had found only the lightsaber.

Once more, Aryn stared determinism in the face. The Force had brought her to Zeerid at the exact moment when Zeerid was making a run to Coruscant. And now the Force had caused T7 to find Master Zallow's lightsaber so that the droid could give it to her.

Aryn decided that it could not be coincidence. It was the Force showing her that the course she pursued was the right one, at least for her.

She took the cool metal of the saber's hilt in her hand, tested its weight. The hilt was larger than hers, slightly heavier, yet it felt familiar in her hand. She remembered the many times she'd seen it in Master Zallow's hands as he had trained her in lightsaber combat. She activated it and the green blade sprang to life. She stared at it, thinking of her master, then turned it off.

She clipped it to her belt, beside her own, and patted T7 on the head.

"Thank you, Tee-seven. This means more to me than you know. You were very brave to return there."

The droid beeped with pleasure and sympathy.

"Have you seen any other survivors?" Zeerid asked, and Aryn felt ashamed for not asking the question herself.

T7 whistled a somber negative.

Zeerid holstered his blaster. "What about security droids?"

Another negative.

"I need to get to the backup surveillance station," Aryn said. "Is it still standing? Can you lead the way?"

T7 chirped with enthusiasm, spun his head around, and headed off down the corridor, wires still dangling from his shoulder joint. Aryn and Zeerid fell in behind him. Aryn felt the weight of the extra lightsaber on her belt, heavy with the memories it bore.

T7 led them on through the labyrinthine passageways of the Works, avoiding collapsed or blocked corridors, doubling back when necessary, descending ever deeper into the hive of pipes, gears, and machinery. Aryn was soon lost. Had they not encountered T7, they could have wandered for days before finding their way.

In time, they reached an area familiar to Aryn.

"We're near now," she said to Zeerid.

Ahead, she saw the turbolift that would take them up

into the lower levels of the Temple. T7 plugged into the control panel and the lift's mechanism began to hum. As the doors slid open, Aryn braced herself to see something horrible, but there was nothing behind them save the empty box of the passenger compartment.

The three of them entered, the doors closed, and the lift began to rise. Aryn could feel Zeerid's concern for her. He watched her sidelong, thinking she did not notice. But she did, and his concern touched her.

"I am glad that you're with me," she said to him.

He colored with embarrassment. "Yes, well. Me, too."

The doors opened to reveal a long corridor. The emergency lights overhead flickered and buzzed. T7 started ahead, and Aryn and Zeerid followed.

Aryn had walked the corridor before, long ago, yet to her everything felt different. It no longer felt like the Jedi Temple. Instead, it felt like a tomb. The Sith attack had destroyed more than merely the Temple's structure. Something else had died when the structure fell. It had been a symbol of justice for thousands of years. And now it was gone.

There was symbolism in that, Aryn supposed.

She wanted out as soon as possible, but first she had to see if there was any record of the attack.

T7's servos, and Aryn's and Zeerid's footsteps, sounded loud in the silence. Rooms off the main corridor looked entirely ordinary. Chairs, desks, comps, everything in order. The attack had destroyed the surface structure but left the core intact.

Maybe there was symbolism in that, too, Aryn thought, and let herself hope.

When they reached the secondary surveillance room, they found it, too, entirely intact. The five monitoring stations each featured a chair, desk, and a computer, with a large vidscreen suspended from the wall above it. All of the screens were dark.

"Can you get some power in here, Tee-seven?" asked Aryn.

The droid beeped an affirmative, rolled over to a wall jack, and plugged in. In moments, the room came to life. The overhead lights brightened. Computers and the monitors hummed awake.

"I want to see whatever we've got of the attack. Can you find that?"

Again the droid beeped an affirmative.

Zeerid wheeled a chair over to Aryn. She sat, her heart racing, her breath coming fast. Zeerid put a hand on her shoulder, just for a moment, then pulled up another chair and sat beside her. They stared at the dark security monitor, waiting for T7 to show them horror.

The droid let out an excited series of whistles. He had located the footage. Aryn gripped the arms of the chair.

"Play it," she said.

A single glowing line formed on the monitor and expanded up and down until it filled the screen. Images formed on it. The main security cam had a view opposite the main doors of the Temple, so it could record those coming in or leaving.

Aryn's mouth was dry. She was afraid to blink for fear of missing something, though that was ridiculous since T7 could freeze, replay, and even magnify any image on the screen.

They watched as a cloaked figure and a Twi'lek woman armed with blasters walked through the Temple's enormous doors.

"Does the Temple post guards?" Zeerid asked.

Aryn nodded.

Neither of them needed to say what must have happened to the guards.

As the pair walked brazenly down the entry hallway, the cam showed people gathering on the balconies above, looking down.

"They didn't know what to make of him," Zeerid said.

Aryn nodded.

"He is big," Zeerid said.

"Freeze on his face and magnify," Aryn said to T7.

The image froze, centered on the man's hooded face, and magnified. She could make out nothing in the shadowed depths of his cowl except what looked to be the bottom of a mask of some kind.

"Is that a mask?" Zeerid asked.

"I don't know. The Twi'lek, Tee-seven," she said, and T7 pulled the image back, recentered on the Twi'lek, and did the same.

The Twi'lek's face filled the screen.

"Skin color is unusual," Zeerid said. He leaned forward in his chair, peering intently.

She was beautiful, Aryn allowed.

And she was a murderer. Or at least associated with one.

"See the scar," Zeerid said. He stood and pointed a finger at the screen, at the Twi'lek's throat. There, a jagged scar cut an irregular path across her neck. "Between that and her skin, maybe we can identify her?"

"Maybe," Aryn said, and tried to swallow. She was less interested in the Twi'lek than she was in the hooded figure. "Continue, Tee-seven."

They watched as the two strode halfway down the hall. Aryn's breath caught when she watched Master Zallow emerge from off cam to confront the Sith and the Twi'lek. Six other Jedi Knights accompanied him.

"Freeze, Tee-seven."

The frame stopped, and Aryn studied Master Zallow's

face. He looked as he always had—stern, focused. Seeing him somehow freed her to grieve with something other than tears. She recalled some of their training sessions, how he had at first insisted that she fight with his style, but had later relented and allowed her to find her own path. The memory made her smile, and cry.

"Are you all right?" Zeerid asked.

She nodded, wiped away the tears with the sleeve of her robe. "Tee-seven, let me see the faces on the other Jedi."

T7 flipped through a variety of footage from recorders at different angles until it finally captured the faces of the other Jedi. Aryn recognized each of them, though she did not know them well. Still, she recited their names. She figured she owed them at least that.

"Bynin, Ceras, Okean, Draerd, Kursil, Kalla."

"Friends?" Zeerid asked, his voice soft.

"No," Aryn said. "But they were Jedi."

"It's not possible that this Sith and Twi'lek took down those Jedi and the Temple alone," Zeerid said, though he sounded uncertain. "Is it?"

Aryn did not know. "Continue, Tee-seven."

The footage started again. Master Zallow went face-to-face with the Sith. The other Jedi ignited their blades. Aryn stared at Master Zallow and the Sith warrior, seeing if they exchanged words, gestures, anything. They didn't, at least as far as she could see.

"Stang," Zeerid breathed.

"What?" Aryn said. "Freeze it, Tee-seven. What is it?"

The image froze. She saw nothing unusual happening between Master Zallow and the Sith.

"There," Zeerid said. He bounced out of his seat again and pointed at something beyond the Temple's tall entrance, something in the sky. Aryn did not see it.

"What is it?"

"A ship," Zeerid said. "Here. See it?"

Aryn stood and squinted at the screen. She did see it, though it was hard to distinguish against the sky through the slit of the Temple's floor-to-ceiling open doors.

"Note the silhouette," Zeerid said. "That's an NR-two gully jumper, a Republic ship. Like the kind I used to fly. See it?"

Aryn did, but she did not understand its significance.

"Magnify, Tee-seven," said Zeerid, and the droid complied. The ship came into clear view.

"No markings," Zeerid said. "But look at its nose, its trajectory. It's coming down, right at the Temple."

"You sure?"

"It doesn't look damaged," Zeerid said thoughtfully. "Back out to normal magnification and play it, Tee-seven."

They watched in awed silence as the gulley jumper crashed through the Temple's entrance, tore through the hall, collapsing columns as it went, a rolling mass of metal and flame, until it stopped right behind the Sith facing Master Zallow.

Neither the Sith nor Master Zallow had moved.

"Mid-section is still intact," Zeerid said. "It must have been reinforced." He looked over to Aryn. "There's something in it. A bomb, maybe."

"Not a bomb," Aryn said, beginning to understand.

They watched as a large hatch on the center compartment of the NR2 exploded outward and dozens of Sith warriors poured out, glowing red blades in hand.

Zeerid sat back in his chair. "Worse than a bomb."

Master Zallow ignited his blade, and many more Jedi rushed in from off cam to reinforce him. Aryn watched it all, her eyes fixed on the Sith. As the battle began, he discarded his cloak, showing his face at last.

"Freeze it," she said, and T7 did. Her voice was cold. "Magnify his face."

The image centered and grew to show the Sith. A bald head lined with blue veins, the scarred face, the intense eyes, and not a mask but a respirator.

"That's the same man from the cruiser!" Zeerid said.

"Darth Malgus," Aryn said, sudden tension forming at the base of her skull. "Darth Malgus led the attack." She stared into Malgus's dark eyes for a time, hardened herself for what she knew would be coming. "Continue it, Tee-seven."

She watched the battle unfold, trying to keep her passions in check. She imagined she could feel the emotions of the combatants pouring through the vid. Her entire body was tense, coiled, as she watched.

The flow of battle separated Master Zallow and Malgus from the outset. Both fought their way through enemies, obviously seeking the other.

"That's a Mandalorian," Zeerid said.

Aryn nodded. A Mandalorian in full battle armor appeared amid the battle, flamethrowers spitting fire.

"That's hotter than some war zones I've been in," Zeerid said.

It was. Flames burned everywhere, piles of rubble littered the hall, blasterfire crisscrossed the battlefield, and everywhere Jedi fought Sith. It became difficult to track any individual actions. Everything bled into the anonymous chaos of battle. She kept her eyes locked on Master Zallow as he moved toward Malgus, and as Malgus moved toward him.

As they closed on each other, she saw Malgus save the Twi'lek woman from a Padawan's attack, saw him respond with even greater anger when she was hit with blasterfire.

"I didn't know Sith cared about anything," Zeerid said.

She, too, found Malgus's response surprising, but had little time to consider it because Malgus and Master Zallow at last met in battle.

She rose from her chair as the duel began to unfold, stepping closer to the monitor. She watched them trade flurries, each test the other's skill. She watched Malgus throw his lightsaber, saw Master Zallow leap over it, saw Malgus knock him from the air in the midst of his leap and follow up with a leaping charge that Master Zallow avoided at the last minute.

Her heart was pounding. She kept hoping for something to intervene, to change the outcome she knew could not be changed. Barring that, she hoped to see a mistake from Master Zallow, or some treachery by Malgus, that would explain what she expected in moments— Master Zallow's fall to Malgus.

They engaged on the far side of the hall, Master Zallow loosing a torrent of blows. Malgus fell back under the onslaught, but Aryn saw that he was drawing Master Zallow in.

And then it happened.

Master Zallow slammed the hilt of his lightsaber into the side of Malgus's face, driving him back a step. He moved to follow up but Malgus anticipated it, spun, and drove his lightsaber through Master Zallow's abdomen.

"That's enough, Tee-seven," Zeerid said. "We've seen enough."

"We haven't," Aryn said. "Play it again, Tee-seven."

The droid did.

"Again."

"Again. He says something at the end. Close up on his mouth."

T7 did as she asked. Master Zallow's blow to Malgus's face had knocked his respirator aside and Aryn could see the Sith's scarred, deformed lips. He mouthed words to Master Zallow as Master Zallow died. Aryn read his lips, whispered the words.

"It's all going to burn."

She found that she was holding her side as she watched, as if it were she that had been impaled on a Sith blade. She relived the pain she'd felt on Alderaan when she'd felt Master Zallow die. And overlaying all of it: anger.

And now she had a focus for that anger—Darth Malgus.

"Again, Tee-seven."

"Aryn," Zeerid said.

"Again."

"Not again, Tee-seven." Zeerid turned around so that they were facing each other. "What are you doing? What more do you need to see?"

"I'm not seeing it. I'm feeling it. Leave me alone, Zeerid."

He must have understood, for he released her and she turned back to the monitor.

"Magnify Master Zallow's face and play it again, Tee-Seven."

She watched his expression as he died over and over. His eyes haunted her, but she could not look away. Each time, before the light went out of them, she saw in his eyes what he was thinking the moment he died:

I failed.

And then Malgus's words. "It's all going to burn."

Whatever walls she had built around her pain collapsed as thoroughly as the Temple. Her eyes welled and tears poured freely down her face. Yet still she watched. She wanted to remember her Master's pain, tuck it away and hold it inside of her, a dark seed to yield dark fruit when she finally faced Malgus.

Before she killed Malgus, she desperately wanted him to feel the same kind of pain Master Zallow had felt.

A gentle touch on her shoulder—Zeerid—brought her around. The monitor screen was blank. How long had she been sitting there, staring at a blank screen, imagining death and revenge and pain?

"Time to go, Aryn," Zeerid said, and helped steer her from the room.

T7 whistled sympathy.

"Are you all right?" Zeerid asked.

She knew how she must look. Using the sleeve of her tunic, she wiped the tears from her face.

"I'm all right," she said.

He looked as if he wanted to embrace her, but she knew he would not take the liberty without her giving him a sign that it was all right.

She gave him no such sign. She did not want relief from her grief, her pain. She simply wanted to pass it on to Malgus somehow.

"Keep a copy of that footage, Tee-seven," she said. "Bring it with you."

The droid beeped an affirmative.

They walked back through the Works and to the surface in silence. By the time they returned to their speeder, Aryn had rebuilt the walls around her emotions. She managed the grief, endured the pain, but put it within reach, so she could call on it when she needed it.

She and Zeerid lifted T7 onto the droid mount at the rear of the speeder.

"I need to get up to that cruiser," she said.

Zeerid activated the magnetic clamp to hold T7 in place. "You can't attack a cruiser, Aryn."

"I don't want to attack it. I just want to get aboard it."

"And face him. Darth Malgus."

"And face him," she affirmed with a nod.

"And how do you think that plays out if you get aboard? Are you just going to walk through all those Imperial troops? Think he'll just let you through and meet you in honorable combat?"

She did not like Zeerid's tone. "I'll bring the cruiser down. With him on it."

"And you on it."

She stuck out her chin. "If that's what it takes."

He slapped a hand in frustration on T7's body. The droid beeped in irritation.

"Aryn, you've been watching the HoloNet too much. It won't work like that. You'll get captured, tortured, killed. He's a Sith. They flew a ship into the Temple, killed dozens of Jedi, bombed Coruscant. Come on. Think!"

"I have. And I have to do this."

He must have seen the resolve in her eyes. He swallowed, looked past her, as if gathering his thoughts, then back at her.

"You said you would help me get offplanet."

"I know," she said.

"I can't follow you to the cruiser. I have a daughter, Aryn. I just want to get off the planet and get back to her before The Exchange or anyone else gets to her."

The heat went out of her in a rush. "You've done more than enough, Zeerid. I wouldn't let you come even if you volunteered."

They both stared at each other a long time, something unsaid hanging in the air between them. T7's head rotated from Zeerid to Aryn and back to Zeerid.

"You don't need to face him," he said to her.

Grime from the Works stained Zeerid's coat and trousers. Lack of sleep had painted circles under his brown eyes. He hadn't shaved in days and black stubble coated his cheeks. His appearance once more struck Aryn as that of a mad prophet, though it seemed she was the one acting out of madness.

"Yes, I do," she said.

She reached out a hand and wiped away some dirt on his cheek. At first he looked startled at her touch, then looked as if he wanted to say something, but did not.

"We go our separate ways here, Z-man," she said. She sensed his alarm at the thought. "You keep the speeder and Tee-seven. I'll figure something else out. Good-bye, Zeerid."

T7 uttered a doleful whistle as she walked away. Zeerid's words pulled her back around, just as hers had pulled him back around earlier in the day.

"Let me help you, Aryn. I'm not going at that cruiser, but I can help you get aboard."

"How?"

"I don't know. Maybe you stow away on an Imperial transport heading for it." He pointed at a distant black form moving across the afternoon sky. "They come and go regularly and always to the same spaceport. And I know that spaceport. I've parked *Fatman* there myself a few times. I'll figure out a way to get you aboard a transport while I find a ship to get me offplanet. So no good-byes yet. I still need your help and you still need mine. Good enough?"

Aryn did not have to consider long. She could use Zeerid's help, and she wanted to keep his company for as long as possible.

"Good enough," she said.

"And who knows?" he said as she climbed into the speeder. "Maybe you'll come to your senses in the meantime."

CHAPTER 11

ZEERID DROVE the Armin speeder low, hugging the urbanscape, until he reached a bombed-out apartment building. There was nothing particularly notable about it. It just seemed a decent place to hole up.

The façade had fallen away from the building's upper levels, exposing the interior flats and rooms. It looked as if the Empire had peeled the rind off the building to expose its guts. Zeerid supposed the Empire had done just that to all of Coruscant: they had vivisected the Republic.

The rubbled façade of the building lay in a heap of glass and stone at the building's base, a pile of ruin intermixed with furniture, shattered vidscreens, and the other indicia of habitation.

The interior remained largely intact, though the dust of pulverized stone coated everything. Shards of shattered glass like fangs hung from windows. A few live wires spat sparks. Water leaked from somewhere, formed a minor cascade pouring down from one of the upper floors. Not a single light glowed in the entire building. It appeared abandoned.

"This should serve," he said to Aryn and T7. He piloted the speeder around and through the rubble until he had it near one of the exposed lower apartments.

"Serve for what?" Aryn asked, and T7 echoed her question with a beep.

"I'm going to scout the spaceport. You both are going to stay here."

Aryn shook her head. "No, I should come."

"I work better alone, Aryn. At least when it comes to surveillance. Take some time—"

"I don't need time. I need to get to that cruiser."

"And this is the best way to do that. So take some time to eat and . . . pull yourself together." He winced as he said that last, thinking she'd take offense, but it appeared barely to register. "I'll be back as soon as I can."

He tossed her another of the protein bars he'd taken from the speeder's console compartment.

"Zeerid . . . ," she said.

"Please, Aryn. I'm just eyeballing it. I won't do anything without you."

She relented with a sigh and climbed out of the speeder. She unclamped T7 and lowered him to the ground.

"I'll return as soon as I can," Zeerid said. "Keep an eye on her, Tee-seven."

The droid whooped agreement and Zeerid sped off.

AVOIDING THE search-and-rescue teams working in the still-smoldering ruins, Zeerid made his way toward the quadrant's port, the Liston Spaceport. He could see it in the distance, framed against the night sky, the curved appendages of its large craft landing pads raised skyward like the hopeful arms of a penitent. It appeared undamaged by the attack, at least from a distance.

As he watched, the roof doors to one of the many small-craft landing bays opened in the main body of the port, a mouth spitting light into the dark air. He killed the speeder's thrusters and pulled to the side.

In the sky above the port, the running lights of three Imperial shuttles came into view as they descended into the port. The mouth of the doors swallowed them, closed, and killed the light once more.

At least he knew there were ships there.

Zeerid stayed where he was and for a time watched to see if there was more traffic. He saw none. In normal times, even a small spaceport like the Liston would have been buzzing with activity.

He fired the speeder back up and drove on, wanting to get a closer look. The area around the port to a distance of several kilometers had been hit hard by Imperial bombs. Burned-out buildings tilted like drunks on their foundations. Jagged, charred holes pockmarked the ground. Autowalks hung askew, forming a mad web of walking paths that led nowhere. Live wires spat angry sparks. Chunks of duracrete lay here and there, haphazardly strewn about by the force of the bombs.

He drove slowly, without lights, avoiding the hazards. He saw no one in the area, no movement at all. It felt like a ghost town. The stink of char hung in the air. So, too, the faint, sickly-sweet stink of organic decay. The ruins were the tombs of thousands. He tried to put it out of his mind, hoping that many had been able to flee into the lower levels before the bombing began in earnest.

He saw an unattended multistory parking structure. Half of it lay in ruins. The other half looked stable enough, and it was only a few blocks from the port. He drove the speeder into the lower level and parked it there. He'd cover the rest of the way on foot. He wanted to eyeball the port unseen and could do that best without a vehicle.

Republic flight school had taught him ground evasion—

to prepare him should his ship ever go down in enemy-held territory—and he put his skills to use. As unobtrusively as a shadow, he moved among the stone rubble and steel beams and abandoned vehicles, keeping undercover as much as possible to avoid being seen from the air. He knew the Empire sometimes used airborne surveillance droids.

Ahead, a ten-story hotel, The Nebula, stuck out of the smoking, rubbled urbanscape. Unlike almost everything else around it, it looked mostly intact except for a few shattered windows on the lower floors. Zeerid saw no lights in any of the rooms so he assumed it had no power and was unoccupied. He dashed across the street to the hotel, pried open the doors, and entered the lobby. No welcoming droids, no one at the concierge desk, deep darkness.

"Hello!" he shouted. "Anyone here?"

No response.

With the power out, he ignored the lifts and headed for the stairs. He was mildly winded by the time he reached the roof access door. He kicked it open, blaster in hand. Nothing. He ducked low and headed for the edge of the roof. From there, he had a good view of the spaceport. He pulled out the macrobinoculars he had taken from the Armin speeder and glassed the port.

The control spire was a dark spike of transparisteel, obviously unoccupied. All the entrances appeared locked down except one, and a dozen Imperial soldiers in full gray battle armor guarded it. Zeerid imagined there were more Imperial troops within the complex itself. It seemed the Empire had shut down all of the port save for a few of the small-craft landing pads, probably to give the already stretched troops less ground to secure.

Large transparisteel windows in the wall opened up

on the near pads. Through them, he saw the three Imperial shuttles that had just landed. All of them had a nu-
merical designation written above the word VALOR, the
name of Darth Malgus's cruiser.

"Looks like you'll get your wish, Aryn," he muttered.

He saw another ship there, too, a modified Imperial
drop ship, *Dragonfly*-class. He rolled a dial on the macrobinoculars to magnify the image.

No Imperial markings, and the landing ramp was up
as if it were ready to launch.

A couple of dozen workers in dungarees went about
the business of operating the port, as did half a dozen or
so droids wheeling among the ships, fuel lines, loading
cranes, and comp terminals.

A flash of lavender filled the binoculars' field of vision
and he backed out of the high modification.

A Twi'lek female had walked in front of the window
and temporarily filled the lenses with her lavender skin.

Lavender skin.

He watched as the Twi'lek and a squad of uniformed
Imperial soldiers in half armor put six hooded and man-
acled sentients into one of the shuttles. Zeerid tried to
keep the binoculars on the Twi'lek, who appeared to be
giving orders to the troops, but it necessitated hopping
the binoculars from window to window as she moved,
and he sometimes lost her.

Like the Twi'lek in the vid at the Jedi Temple, she wore
twin blasters on her hips. She also wore the tight-fitting
trousers and high boots.

"Has to be her," he said. But he wanted to confirm, so
he waited, and watched, and at last she turned her face to
the window and he saw it, the jagged scar on her throat.

"Gotcha," he said.

The Twi'lek spoke into her comlink, and the shuttle
with the civvies started to wind up. As it rose on its

thrusters, the roof doors of the pad slid open, once more spilling light into the night sky. When the shuttle broke the roofline, it engaged its engines and took off, presumably heading back to *Valor*. The doors closed behind it.

The Twi'lek and about a dozen troops remained on the pad. Workers, too, and droids. Zeerid watched a team of workers and the treaded box of a maintenance droid start refueling one of the shuttles from a thick hose connected to an underground tank.

Seeing that, Zeerid struck on a plan. He pocketed the binoculars and hurried back out of the hotel, to the speeder, and back to Aryn.

THE SHUTTLE flew a silent vigil over the ruins of the Jedi Temple. Malgus's pilot's voice carried over the intership comm. Boredom tinged his tone.

"Shall I remain here, my lord?"

"You will remain until I say otherwise," Malgus answered. "Internal and external lights are to remain off."

"As you wish, my lord."

Malgus's shuttle hovered over the ruins of the Jedi Temple at about three hundred meters. From that height, the Temple was little more than a tumble of stones in the starlight. He had lingered over the ruins for hours, as day had faded to night, and still Aryn Leneer had not shown.

But she would come. He knew she would.

ARYN UNWRAPPED and ate the protein bar Zeerid had given her. She and T7 had sheltered in one of the apartments. She sat on a dusty couch, the stink of a burning planet in her nostrils. She replayed in her mind Master Zallow's death, the look on his face. She saw once more the ruins of the Temple and she knew that his body lay beneath the mountain of rubble.

Fighting the rising tide of grief, she adopted a meditative posture, closed her eyes, and tried to drift into the Force.

"Still heart, still mind," she intoned, but both proved impossible.

Eventually, she sat back on the couch and stared up at the sky. The omnipresent smoke looked like black clouds against the stars. Now and again she saw a ship's lights in the distance and presumed them to belong to an Imperial patrol craft.

In time, her emotional and physical exhaustion chased her down and she drifted off to sleep.

She dreamed of Master Zallow. He stood before her on the ruins of the Jedi Temple, his robes billowing in the breeze. The cracked stone face of Odan-Urr watched them. Master Zallow's mouth moved but no sound emerged. He seemed to be trying to tell her something.

"I cannot hear you, Master," she said. "What are you saying?"

She tried to get closer to him, picking her way through the debris, but the closer she tried to get, the farther he moved away. Finally her frustration got the better of her and she screamed, "I don't know what you want me to do!"

She woke, heart pounding, and found T7 standing before her. He whistled a question.

"No, I'm fine," she said, but she wasn't.

She stood and pulled her cloak tight about her.

She checked her chrono. Zeerid had been gone for over an hour. He would probably be gone another hour, at least.

Her dream had left her shaken. She took the hilt of Master Zallow's lightsaber in her hands, turned it over, studied its craftsmanship. Its design mirrored his personality: solid, without flourish, but wonderful in its plainness.

She wanted to return to the Temple, to the scene where murder had occurred. She should have made Zeerid set down the speeder when they'd been over it earlier. She wanted to walk among the ruins and commune with the dead. She hooked Master Zallow's weapon to her belt.

"I have to go somewhere, Tee-seven. I'll be back soon."

He whistled another question, alarm in the beeps.

"Tell him I'll be back. There is nothing to worry about."

She left the ruined apartment building and headed back toward the Jedi Temple.

There was something there for her. There had to be.

WHEN ZEERID returned to their safehouse in the ruined apartment building, he found Aryn gone. Her absence put a lump in his throat. T7 whistled to him from one of the apartments.

"Where is she, Tee-seven?" he asked.

The small droid chattered, whistled, and beeped so fast that Zeerid could scarcely follow. In the end, he gathered that Aryn had left the apartment after a short rest, and that she did not tell T7 where she was going.

But Zeerid knew where she would go. She'd go to where Master Zallow died.

"Let's go, Tee-seven," he said, and loaded the droid up onto the speeder.

ARYN'S EMOTIONS roiled, her mood as dark as the night. Ordinarily, the artificial lights of hundreds of thousands of businesses and advertisements lit Coruscant's night sky. But the attack had knocked the power out over huge swaths of the planet, and the dark silence made the city feel like a mausoleum.

Aryn picked her way through the black darkness and approached the Temple along the wide, stone-paved processional that once had led to the Temple's grand main entrance. Malgus must have used the same approach, she realized, and it appalled her that the last person to walk the processional before the Temple's fall had been a Sith. She found it obscene.

She fancied she was retracing his footsteps, her boots effacing the wrongness of his passage.

She slowed, steeling herself, as the rubbled structure materialized out of the darkness before her. The attack had turned the Temple's once curved lines and elegant spires into a shapeless mound of ruin, a burial cairn for the Jedi Order.

The sight of it scratched the scab from the wound of her grief. As she approached, the ghosts of her past rose out of the ruin—her time in the Temple as a youngling, as a Padawan, the ceremony when she'd been promoted to Jedi Knight. The Temple had been her home for decades, and her father had been murdered in it.

In her mind's eye she saw the final blow that had slain her master, as clear as if she were once more watching the vid in the Temple's surveillance room. She saw Malgus spin, reverse his grip, and drive his lightsaber through Master Zallow. And once more she saw the look in Master Zallow's face as the light went out of his eyes, the despair there. He had failed and he had known it. Maybe he had also known, as Aryn now did, that the Jedi Order had failed, too.

The thought of her master dying with despair in his heart drove a hot spike of rage through the sore of her loss.

And yet . . . she could not shake the look she had seen in his eyes in her dream. It had looked like concern, a warning maybe. He had wanted to tell her something . . .

She shook her head. It had been but a dream, not a vision, just a projection of her own subconscious. She dismissed it.

She would find Malgus and she would kill him.

She reached the edge of the ruins, climbed the jagged chunks of stone. They still felt warm, still radiated the heat of their own destruction. She walked among them, the graves of dozens of Jedi, and wept through her anger.

A feeling seized her as the strings of her Force sensitivity vibrated with a discordant note. The feeling took her by the shoulders, shook her, and emptied her of grief, leaving only anger.

She knew the feeling's origin.

She activated her lightsaber and tried to pinpoint Malgus's location.

MALGUS FELT the signature of another Force-user, the uncomfortable pressure of the light side, and it pulled him to his feet. The pressure reminded him of how he'd felt in the presence of Master Zallow, and he knew that Aryn Leneer had come at last.

"Take the shuttle down to fifty meters," he said, adrenaline already coursing through his body. "And when I exit, you may leave."

"When you exit, my lord?"

Malgus did not respond. Instead, he overrode the in-flight safeties and pushed the button to open the side hatch. As the door slid open, as the night air poured in, redolent with the stink of a ruined Temple and a burned planet, he let anger fill him.

The ship descended to fifty meters. Below, the ruined Temple was dark, covered in the velvet of night. But he perceived the presence of Aryn Leneer as clearly as he would have under a noon sun.

He stepped to the doorway, drew on the Force, activated his lightsaber, and leapt out into the dark.

A ROAR, heavy with hate and rage, pulled Aryn's eyes skyward. Malgus descended like a meteor. His cape flew out behind and over him, a comma of darkness, and he held his lightsaber in a two-handed grip. Power went before him in a wave of visible distortion. The shuttle out of which he had leapt flew off into the night sky.

Aryn fell fully into the Force, raised her defenses, took a fighting stance, and parried Malgus's two-handed overhand slash. Still, he landed in a cocoon of power, hitting the ground in an explosion of might that shattered the stones around them and turned them into a hail of shrapnel. Unflinching, Aryn deflected them with the Force as she parried another slash from Malgus. The force of the Sith's blow made her arms quiver, but she gave no ground.

Blades locked, sparking, their eyes met.

Malgus's dark eyes burned with a rage that knifed through her. The anger he radiated was tangible to Aryn, made the air feel greasy, polluted. But she felt something else in it, something unexpected, an odd ambivalence.

"I know why you've come," he said, his voice a hiss from behind his respirator.

She forced words between gritted teeth. "You killed Master Zallow."

"And now I will kill you, too," he said. "In the same place I killed him." He leaned into his blade, pushed her back a step, and unleashed a Force-augmented kick at her ribs.

But she was the quicker, and a flip sent her over his head and fifty meters away, deeper into the mountain of ruins where her Master had died. She landed in a crouch atop one of the broken columns sticking out of the rubble.

"You will find that difficult," she called, and answered his anger with a wave of her own. "I assure you of that."

Malgus gestured with his left hand, and the column she stood on began to shake. She leapt off it to another nearby, then another, then another, leapfrogging her way across the ruins, back toward Malgus.

When she landed atop a large chunk of stone ten meters from the Sith, he made a cutting gesture with his free hand and two pieces of statuary rose from the rubble and rushed toward her from either side. She leapt into the air and they smashed into each other beneath her, spraying shards of rock. She landed atop the remains, lightsaber ready.

Malgus growled, leapt through the air from his perch toward hers. She slid to the side of his downward slash and his blade split the stone at their feet. She unleashed a crosscut that would have decapitated him had he not ducked under it.

She flipped up and over him onto another piece of rubble, fifteen meters away. Taking telekinetic hold of a large stone near Malgus, she flung it at him. He never moved, simply held his ground and split the incoming rock in two with his lightsaber. Red sparks and bits of stone rained down

Aryn could not find her calm. She was fighting angry, but did not care. Snarling, thinking of her Master, she bounded across the hill of rubble, leaping from one chunk of rock to another, closing the distance with Malgus. He answered her charge with one of his own, the two of them jumping across the gravestones of the Jedi Order until they closed to within striking distance.

Aryn stabbed low and Malgus slapped her blade out wide, reversed his motion, and unleashed a backhand swing at her abdomen. She leapt over it, pulling her legs in tight, and loosed a two-handed overhead strike as she came back down. Malgus parried crosswise with his blade and stepped into a Force-augmented side kick aimed at her ribs. She caught the kick with her free hand, closed her arm over his leg, spun, and flung Malgus twenty meters from her. He flipped in midair and landed atop the cracked face of the Odan-Urr statue that had once lined the processional approach into the Temple.

She took the hilt of Master Zallow's lightsaber in her off hand, crouched, and bounded into a leap toward him. He watched her come and at the apex of the leap's arc, he thrust his left hand at her, roaring, and veins of Force lightning squirmed toward her.

Ready for it, she activated Master Zallow's lightsaber, used it to form an X with her own, and intercepted the lightning on the two blades.

His power met her will. The lightning twisted around the glowing blades. The force of it stopped her downward descent and held her aloft in the air for a moment, suspended on a column built of the dark side.

And then she overcame it. The lightning dissipated to nothingness and she, unharmed by it, fell straight down, landing on her feet atop a shifting pile of rubble and deactivating Master Zallow's blade.

The moment she landed, Malgus was upon her, his blade slashing, stabbing, spinning. He tried to use his superior strength to force her off the stone, off balance, but she answered his strength with speed, sidestepping his blows, leaping over them, parrying, unleashing her own flurries. The hum of their weapons through the air, the sizzle of crossed blades, merged into a single song of speed and power.

ZEERID FLEW the speeder full-throttle at over a hundred meters in altitude. He watched an Imperial shuttle accelerate into the sky from the vicinity of the Jedi Temple.

Thinking of Aryn, he felt his stomach flutter. He flew still higher, hoping to catch a glimpse of her near the Temple.

And he did.

She and Darth Malgus bounded across the ruins of the Temple, their blades flashing, locking, the speed of their duel so fast Zeerid could barely follow their movement. Despite himself, he found the combat beautiful.

He slowed the speeder and T7 beeped a question.

Aryn had done what she had come to Coruscant to do—she was facing Malgus.

And Zeerid had seen what Malgus had done in the Temple. The Sith deserved death.

But he worried over Aryn's reasons. The line between seeking justice and seeking revenge was thin indeed, but Zeerid could see that Aryn had stepped over it. She wanted Malgus dead because she wanted revenge. And there would be no undoing it once it was done.

He knew that better than most.

He made up his mind and accelerated the speeder to full.

ARYN AND Malgus locked blades.

"I am more than your match, Sith," she said over the sparks of their joined lightsabers.

"Your Master was not," Malgus said, grunting, and shoved her with a telekinetic blast of such force that she flew backward and slammed into the rock and rubble. She used the Force to cushion the impact, but she still landed on her back and the impact blew the breath from her lungs.

Malgus leapt high into the air, shouting with rage, his blade held high for a killing stroke. She rolled aside as he came down and his blade sank to its hilt in the rubble of the Temple. She leapt to her feet and unleashed a backhand crosscut at his throat. He got his blade free and vertical to parry it, but at the same time she pointed the blade end of Master Zallow's lightsaber at Malgus and activated it.

He must have sensed his danger at the last moment for he slid partially aside. Still, the green line of Master Zallow's blade pierced his armor and side and elicited a snarl of pain and rage. Before Aryn could follow up, Malgus drove an open hand into the side of her face.

She was unready for the blow. The Force-augmented impact exploded a spark shower in her brain and sent her cartwheeling away from Malgus; she slammed into a rock and landed on her side ten meters away. Adrenaline pulled her to her feet, though she swayed unsteadily. She spat a mouthful of blood and held both lightsabers at the ready.

Malgus stood astride the ruins, his blade sizzling, eyeing the smoking hole in his armor, the furrow in his flesh.

Seeing an opportunity, she did not hesitate.

Using the Force to guide it, she hurled Master Zallow's lightsaber at Malgus. The blade cut a glittering green arc through the air as it spun end over end toward Malgus's head.

Despite his wound, the Sith slapped aside Aryn's Force-hold on the blade and snatched it out of the air, as quick as a sand viper. He deactivated the blade, held the hilt in his hand, studied it. He looked up and over at Aryn, his eyes burning. She imagined him smiling under his respirator.

"This weapon did not avail him and it will not avail you."

The sound of an engine pulled Aryn's head around. She whirled, her blade ready, and saw the Armin speeder roaring out of the sky like a comet, Zeerid in the driver's seat. T7 sat in the rear. He came in too hard and the thrusters could not completely stop the speeder from slamming into the ruins. Metal creaked. Dust flew up.

"Aryn!" Zeerid called. "Get in!"

Zeerid looked past her to Malgus, seemed to consider unloading a blaster shot, but thought better of it.

"Come on, Aryn!" Zeerid shouted, and T7 backed him up with an urgent whistle. "Please. You said you would help me."

She hesitated.

Malgus looked at her, brandished Master Zallow's hilt, a taunt to keep her there.

She made her decision.

She wanted to efface the smugness she'd heard in his tone, to see in his eyes what she had seen in Master Zallow's. Killing him was not enough. She wanted to see him in pain. She just had to figure out how to do it.

She leapt high into the air and landed beside Zeerid in the speeder.

"Death is too easy, Sith," she called to Malgus, the venom in her tone surprising even to her. "I am going to hurt you first."

The words left a bad taste in her mouth. She felt Zeerid's eyes on her and dared not look him in the face.

Malgus, too, seemed almost puzzled, to judge from his furrowed brow and the tilt of his head.

"Go," she said.

Zeerid accelerated and started to turn the speeder.

Anger went forth from Malgus. He reactivated Master Zallow's blade and hurled it after them. Zeerid tried to wheel out of the way but the blade curled and kept coming at them. T7 beeped in alarm.

Aryn watched the weapon spin, felt it, and before it reached the speeder, she reached out with the Force and snatched it from Malgus's mental grasp. The weapon turned upward over the speeder and descended hilt-first into her hand as Zeerid rose into the night sky and sped away. She deactivated it.

She looked back one last time to see Malgus standing atop the ruined temple, his blade in hand, his cape fluttering in the wind. He looked like a victorious conqueror.

And she hated him.

ZEERID FLEW low and fast through Coruscant's streets, wheeling around buildings, careering down alleys, descending into the lower levels as he went. Soon, the sky was lost to the density of structures above them. They were in an industrial underworld, a series of metal-and-duracrete tunnels that covered the entire planet.

"Anyone following?" he said.

Aryn did not answer. She sat in the passenger seat and stared at her Master's lightsaber hilt as if she'd never seen it before.

"Aryn! Is anyone following?"

"No," she said, but did not look back.

Zeerid shot a glance behind them, above them, and saw no one. He let himself breathe easier.

"Blast, Aryn, what were you doing?"

She answered in a tone as mechanical as a protocol droid's. "What I came here to do, Zeerid. Facing Malgus. What were you doing?"

"Helping you."

"I didn't need help."

"No?" He stared at her across the speeder's compartment.

"No."

Zeerid thought otherwise. "Why'd you get in the speeder, Aryn?"

"I didn't want you to get hurt. And I said I would help you get offplanet."

"A lie," Zeerid said. "Why not just stay there and finish it?"

She looked away from him as she answered. "Because . . ."

"Because?"

"Because killing him is not enough," she blurted. "I want to hurt him."

She hooked her Master's lightsaber hilt to her belt and looked over at Zeerid. "I want to hurt him like he hurt me, like he hurt Master Zallow before he died."

"Aryn, I don't have to be an empath to feel your ambivalence. Revenge—"

She raised a hand to cut him off. "I do not want to hear it, Zeerid."

He said it anyway. He owed her as much. "This doesn't sound much like you."

"We haven't seen each other in years," she snapped. "What do you know about me?"

The sharp tone cut him. "Not as much as I thought, it seems."

For a time, silence sat between them like a wall.

"I hired on with The Exchange for a good reason, I thought. To provide a good life for my daughter."

"Zeerid—"

"Just listen, Aryn!" He took a breath to calm himself. "And that one decision, that seemed so right, led to me running weapons, and then to running spice. One decision, Aryn. One act."

She shook her head. "This isn't like that, Zeerid. I know what I'm doing."

He wasn't so sure but decided not to press further. He changed the subject. "I think I can get us into the spaceport. There are ships there, from *Valor*, and Imperial troopers, but I have a plan."

Without looking at him, she reached across the seat

and touched his hand, just for a moment. "I'm sorry for the way I spoke, Zeerid. I'm not . . ."

He shook his head. "No apologies, Aryn. I know you're hurting. I just . . . don't want you to make it worse for yourself. I know how that can happen. Are you . . . seeing clearly?"

He felt ridiculous trying to provide an empath, of all people, with insight into her emotional state.

"I am," she said, but he heard uncertainty in her tone.

"In the end, you have to live with yourself."

He knew well how difficult that could get.

"I know," she said. "I know. Now, what's your plan?"

He told her.

She listened attentively, nodded when he was done. "That should work."

"Tee-seven can do it?"

Aryn nodded, and T7 beeped agreement.

"I will help you get in and get a ship," Aryn said. "But . . . I'm not leaving Coruscant."

"I figured you'd say that," he said, but in his own mind he had not yet conceded the point. He wrestled with whether to tell her about the Twi'lek.

"You are holding something back," she said.

He rubbed the back of his neck, torn.

In the end, he decided he owed her honesty, and he knew he could not make decisions for her.

"The Twi'lek we saw in the vid at the Temple . . ."

He trailed off. Aryn grabbed his forearm, squeezed.

"Tell me, Zeerid."

He swallowed, feeling complicit in a crime. It wasn't so much harm to the Twi'lek that concerned him, as it was harm to Aryn.

"I saw her at the Liston Spaceport. She was there."

Aryn's fingernails sank into his skin, but she seemed not to notice. He welcomed the pain. She stared off through the windscreen. He fancied he could see her weighing options in the scale of her mind. He held out hope she would choose the right one.

"I want to see her," she said. "Let's go."

That was not the answer Zeerid had been hoping to hear.

MALGUS SAT among the ruins, the fallen statues of his ancient foes, and pondered. The night breeze blew cool over his face. He replayed his confrontation with Aryn Leneer. Her power had surprised him. So, too, the anger that underlay it.

The anger he understood, even respected, but he didn't understand how she'd come by it. She had known that he'd killed Master Zallow when they had fought on the ruins. But she had *not known* when they had first seen each other on the ship-to-ship holo over Coruscant, when *Valor* had shot down the freighter. He was certain of that. He would have felt the knife point of her rage if she had known then.

So she must have learned in the interim that he had killed Master Zallow.

Either she'd seen it somehow—a surveillance recording pulled from the rubble, maybe—or she'd interrogated a witness, a survivor who had escaped, or maybe a droid who had crawled out of the destruction.

Either way, she now knew the details of the attack.

It pleased him that she knew. The destruction of the Jedi Temple was the greatest achievement of his life. He wanted the Jedi—wanted Aryn Leneer—to know it was he who had done it, he who had left the corpses of so many Jedi buried in the rubbled tomb of their onetime Temple.

But something worried at the edge of his mind. She

had not fled on the speeder out of fear. He would have felt that, too.

I am going to hurt you, she'd said.

How could she hurt him?

And all at once he knew. She knew the details of his attack on the Temple, so she knew Eleena had accompanied him. She might even have seen in Malgus's behavior what Lord Adraas had seen—his feelings for Eleena. She would hurt him the same way Adraas and Angral would try to manipulate him.

The realization sent a rush of emotion through him, a rush it took him a moment to recognize as fear. He activated his comlink and tried to raise his lover on their normal frequency.

No response.

A flutter formed in his stomach. He raised Jard.

"Jard, has Eleena returned to *Valor*?"

"She has not, my lord," returned Jard. "One of her shuttles has returned, but she was not aboard."

A fishhook of fear lodged in Malgus's gut and pulled him to his feet.

"When is the last time she checked in?" he asked.

"She has not checked in, my lord. Is there cause for concern? Should I send a team to retrieve her?"

"No," Malgus said. "I will find her myself."

There could be any number of reasons for Eleena to be out of contact. She could have simply turned off her comm.

But Malgus could not shake the unease he felt. He hailed his personal pilot and summoned the shuttle back to the Temple. He knew where Eleena and her team had set down—the Liston Spaceport. He would look for her there first.

DAY THREE

CHAPTER 12

THE SKY lightened to the east. Zeerid checked his chrono. Almost dawn. The night had disappeared on him. He was too wired to feel fatigue. He worked up the nerve to ask his question of Aryn.

"What are you going to do?" he asked.

She did not look at him, and he took that as a bad sign. "I'm going to get you into the spaceport and you're going to fly back to your daughter."

Assuming he could dodge Imperial cruisers on the way out, which would be no mean feat.

"That isn't what I mean, Aryn, and you know it. What are you going to do with *her*?"

Aryn did not answer, but the set of her jaw told Zeerid all he needed to know. He regretted mentioning the Twi'lek to Aryn. His honesty would cost Aryn her soul. Hunting the Sith who had murdered her Master was one thing. Killing the Twi'lek simply to hurt Malgus was something else. As he drove, he found himself hoping that the Twi'lek had left the spaceport.

Ahead, the port came into view. He scanned the sky, saw nothing. The control tower was still dark. The Empire had done a poor job of securing the port—they had far too few men guarding a location with many potential entry points—but Zeerid supposed they had limited troops and an entire planet to police. He was glad of it. Otherwise, his plan would have had no chance to succeed.

"I'll circle wide and we'll go up top. The key to this is speed."

"Won't they spot us on scanners?"

"The tower's dark and I don't see any hardware around. If they have orbiting surveillance on the port, well . . ."

He shrugged. If the Empire had orbiting surveillance or high-altitude surveillance droids watching the spaceport, he and Aryn would have problems.

"Speed is still the key," he said. "Even if they see us, if we can get in and out fast enough, we can still pull it off."

Aryn brushed her hair from her face. "Where did you see her? The Twi'lek?"

"There," he said, pointing at the large transparisteel windows that opened onto the small-craft landing pad where he had spotted the shuttles, the drop ship, and the Twi'lek. Without bringing his macrobinoculars to bear, all he could see through the windows were indiscriminate gray shapes, presumably the shuttles. Aryn stared at the windows for a moment, then nodded to herself.

"Let's go," she said.

He killed the running lights on the speeder and took it up to five hundred meters, just above the top of the main center structure in the spaceport. Pushing the thrusters as hard as he could, he accelerated toward it.

His heart raced, not out of fear that they would be caught, but out of concern that Aryn would find the Twi'lek.

He swerved around one of the large-craft landing

arms that reached up and over them. He hunched behind the controls, anticipating fire at any moment. But none came.

Below them perhaps a hundred meters, he could see the roof doors of the various small-craft landing pads. Aryn unstrapped herself, turned, and unlatched T7. The droid beeped.

Zeerid slowed the speeder but did not stop. If anyone had seen them approach, he wanted them to think that the speeder just kept on going.

"Ready?" he asked, and set the speeder's unsophisticated autopilot to fly on another ten klicks before setting down.

"Ready."

He released the stick, and he and Aryn quickly maneuvered onto the back of the speeder near T7. The wind pulled at them. He had trouble balancing but Aryn took him by the arm and steadied him. They sandwiched the droid between them, shared a look.

"Go," he said.

She nodded and they stepped off the back of the speeder.

T7 whooped as they fell. The droid's bulk did not allow them to control their descent; they were flipping end over end immediately. Zeerid's field of vision veered rapidly, wildly, between the starry sky and the top of the spaceport below. His stomach crawled up his throat and he gritted his teeth to keep down the protein bar he'd eaten.

End over end they spun, T7 whistling with alarm, until Aryn seized them in her power, ended the spinning, and slowed their descent. The metal and duracrete of the spaceport's roof rushed up to meet them. They had only a second, two. Aryn grunted, slowed them still further, further, until they touched down gently on the roof.

"Much better than last time," Zeerid said, grinning, heart racing. "I could go my whole life without another fall and feel I'd missed nothing."

Aryn did not so much as smile.

Zeerid gathered himself, took a blaster in each hand, and scanned the rooftop. He spotted a conduit access panel. "There."

They ran over to it and he shot off the metal cover with his blaster, exposing a viper's nest of wires. Ordinarily, a breached cover would have set off an alarm in the control tower, but the control tower was dark, unoccupied.

"Do it, Tee-seven."

A panel in the droid's abdomen opened and several thin, mechanical arms reached out. All ended in one kind of tool or another. T7 stuck the arms into the wires and began to work. Zeerid, still concerned that they may have been spotted, scanned the sky. He saw nothing.

T7 hummed while he worked.

"Come on, come on," Zeerid said to the droid. To Aryn, he said, "You all right?"

She seemed oddly calm, or preoccupied.

"I'm fine," she said.

The droid gave an excited series of whistles and whoops.

"He's into the safety and fire suppression system," Aryn said.

"Trigger it with a ten-second delay," Zeerid said to the droid.

The droid beeped acquiescence.

MALGUS BOUNDED into the shuttle as it set down near the Temple.

"The Liston Spaceport," he said to the pilot. "Quickly."

"Yes, my lord."

He tried again to raise Eleena on the comm but got no response. With each moment that passed his concern grew. He recognized that his emotions were driving him, controlling him, knew too the weakness it evidenced, but he could not let her come to harm, not by a Jedi.

Angral's admonition bounced around his brain: *Passions can lead to mistakes.*

The pilot's voice over the comm disrupted his train of thought.

"Have you heard the news from Alderaan, my lord?"

"What news?" Malgus said. His muscles bunched, as if in anticipation of a blow, or combat.

The blow came and hit him hard.

"There are rumors that an accord has been reached and that a peace treaty will be signed later today. In exchange for the turnover of certain outlying systems to Imperial control, Coruscant will be returned to the Republic."

The pilot's words pushed Angral's words out of Malgus's brain and ricocheted around in his head like blaster shots.

Outlying systems.

Coruscant returned to the Republic.

Peace.

The words applied heat to Malgus's already bubbling emotions. He thought of Angral and Adraas sitting somewhere together, drinking wine and thinking that they had accomplished something by forcing the Republic to surrender some insignificant systems, when in fact they had poisoned the body of the Empire with the venom of peace.

"Peace!"

He paced the compartment, fists clenched, a wild animal tiring of its cage. His thoughts veered between Eleena on the one hand, Angral and Adraas on the other.

"Peace!"

He slammed his fist into the bulkhead, welcomed the pain.

They thought they could tame him, Angral and Adraas, thought they could use Eleena to domesticate him. And wasn't that what she wanted, too? She, who sought to be his conscience. She, who asked him to put love before his duty to the Empire.

Malgus's brewing anger boiled over into rage. He slammed his fists down on the worktable, denting it. He picked up a chair and threw it against the bulkhead, drove his fist through the small vidscreen built into the wall.

"Is everything all right, Darth Malgus?" the pilot called over the comm.

"Everything is fine," Malgus said, though nothing was.

"Coming up on the spaceport now, my lord," said the pilot.

ZEERID WATCHED T7 work, anxious. His internal clock was running. They needed to keep moving.

Having jacked into the spaceport safety and fire suppression system, T7 was to send a false signal into the network, tricking the sensors into detecting a fuel gas leak in the landing bay where the Imperial shuttles had landed. An alarm indicating the leak of highly explosive fuel gas should trigger evacuation and venting procedures.

Or so Zeerid hoped.

The droid's metal arms worked their magic. T7 cut a wire here, soldered there, reattached several cables here, then plugged into the interface he had rewired. His low whistles and chirps told Zeerid he was communicating with the spaceport's network. After a short time, the droid retracted his metal arms into the cylinder of his body.

"Done?" Zeerid asked.

T7 beeped an affirmative.

Zeerid slapped him on the head and the droid protested with a low beep.

"Then let's go," Zeerid said.

He and Aryn sprinted across the roof toward the launch doors, with T7 wheeling after them. Zeerid counted down from ten in his head. Just as they reached the launch doors, just as he finished his countdown, sirens began to wail, audible even from the roof. A mechanical voice spoke over the facility's speakers.

"A hazardous substance spill has occurred in landing bay sixteen-B. There is significant danger. Please move rapidly toward the nearest exit. A hazardous substance spill has occurred in landing bay sixteen-B . . ."

"If Tee-seven did his job," Zeerid said, and the droid beeped indignantly, "the system will detect the fuel gas leak in the pad right below us. When it does, it should open the launch doors automatically to vent the gas—"

The roof vibrated as the launch doors unsealed and started slowly to slide open.

"Nicely done," Zeerid said to the droid.

AHEAD, MALGUS saw the small spaceport the Empire had commandeered. It looked somewhat like an upside-down spider with a few too many legs, with large-craft landing arms sticking out from the bloated body and raised skyward. Launch doors over the various small-craft landing pads dotted the spider's body. All were closed save one. Light spilled out into the sky through the open doors.

"There is a crowd near the port's entrance," the pilot said.

Malgus looked away from the open launch doors to see dozens of people pouring out of one of the entrances to the spaceport and milling about. Most were port workers in dungarees, citizens of Coruscant whom the Empire had pressed into service to do menial labor at the port, but he counted perhaps twenty Imperial soldiers, a dozen navy sailors, and a handful of other soldiers in half armor.

He pressed his face to the window to look more closely at the soldiers. He saw Captain Kerse, one of those he had picked to accompany Eleena.

But he did not see Eleena.

"Set down near the doors," he said. "Quickly."

The shuttle touched down with a heavy thud and Malgus hurried out. Upon seeing him, the Imperial soldiers snapped to attention and offered a salute. The workers backed away, fear in their eyes. Perhaps they'd heard of what he'd done at the hospital.

Malgus walked up to Captain Kerse, a powerfully built man whose bald head sat like a boulder upon his thick neck. Malgus towered over him.

"Darth Malgus, there is a fuel gas leak in the small-craft landing area. We evacuated while the safety system—"

"Where is Eleena?" Malgus asked.

"She is . . ." Kerse looked around the crowd. His skin turned blotchy. To one of his men, he said, "Where is the Twi'lek?"

"I saw her near the other shuttle, sir," replied another of the soldiers. "I assumed she followed."

Malgus grabbed Kerse by his plasteel breastplate and pulled him nose-to-nose.

"She was with you before the gas leak?"

Kerse's head bobbed on his neck. "Yes. She—"

"Take me."

"The fuel gas, my lord."

"There is no fuel gas! It is a ruse to get to Eleena."

To get to *him*.

"What?" Kerse said.

Malgus threw Kerse to the ground and strode past him for the port's doors. Behind him, he heard Kerse call out for the other soldiers to follow. By the time the doors slid open before Malgus, he had six elite soldiers with blaster rifles in orbit around him.

"This way, my lord," said Kerse, taking position beside him.

"SPEED AND precision," Zeerid said, as much a reminder to himself as to Aryn. "Speed and precision."

They watched the launch doors pull back to vent nonexistent fuel gas. The open doors revealed the landing pad below. Zeerid saw the two Imperial shuttles, the *Dragonfly*-class drop ship. The sirens continued to scream. The automated voice on the speakers continued to drone on.

Zeerid would hijack the drop ship. He'd have to dodge Imperial fighters and cruisers on his way out of Coruscant's space. The shuttles would fly like the square heaps they were, and he'd get shot down as soon as he cleared the atmosphere. The dropship, at least, would give him a decent chance of getting clear.

He took Aryn by the bicep. "You can still come with me, Aryn."

She looked him in the face and he saw once more, for the first time since seeing her again, the deep understanding that lived in her eyes.

"I can't," she said.

"You can," he insisted. "You've honored your Master's memory."

"Time to go," she said. "Speed and precision, you said."

He bit back his reply and once more they wrapped T7 in their shared grasp and leapt into the void. Again Aryn's power slowed their descent and cushioned their landing.

They hit the pad's metal-and-duracrete floor, assaulted on all sides by the wail of the sirens and the relentless voice on the loudspeakers. Zeerid took quick stock of the situation.

He saw no one in the landing area and the only way out—a pair of double doors leading into a long corridor beyond—were open. Everyone must have evacuated.

Both of the Imperial shuttles had their landing ramps down. The drop ship did not and the canopy of its cockpit was dimmed, as opaque as dirty water.

"Tee-seven, I need you to crack open that Dragonfly. Right now."

The droid beeped agreement and wheeled toward the drop ship's rear door. Zeerid looked to Aryn and gave it another try.

"Reconsider, Aryn." He stood directly before her, forcing her to see him, to hear him. "Come with me. Please." He smiled, trying to make light. "We'll start a farm on Dantooine, just like I said."

She smiled, seemingly amused by the thought, and he was pleased to see it. "I can't, Zeerid. You'll make a good farmer, though. I'm going to find the Twi'lek and—"

She stopped in mid-sentence, her eyes fixed on something over Zeerid's shoulder.

He whirled around to see the Twi'lek descending the near shuttle's landing ramp, a rucksack thrown over her shoulder. Two Imperial soldiers in plasteel breastplates flanked her to either side. Each had a blaster rifle slung over his shoulder. All three wore breathing masks. They had not left their ship when the alarm sounded, had instead just donned masks. Perhaps there was something on the shuttle they were unwilling to leave unguarded. Everyone froze, and for a moment no one moved.

Then all at once everyone moved.

The Twi'lek dropped her rucksack, her eyes wide behind the lens of her mask, and went for her blasters. The soldiers cursed in muffled tones, unslung their rifles, and tried to bring them to bear.

Aryn ignited her lightsaber.

Zeerid, one of his blasters still in hand, fired at the soldier on the right. Two shots screamed into the soldier's chest. Armor ablated in a puff of smoke and the force of the impact knocked the man from the ramp, turned his mask sideways on his face. He hit the deck and lay there, scrabbling for cover. Zeerid fired again, and a hit to the man's midsection made him go still.

The Twi'lek got her blasters clear and fired two, four, six shots at Zeerid. Aryn slid before him and her blade deflected all of the shots, two of them back at the other soldier, which opened small holes in the soldier's mask. He fell forward onto the ramp, dead.

"Get out of here, Zeerid," Aryn said over her shoulder. She started walking toward the shuttle, toward the Twi'lek.

"Aryn," Zeerid called, but she did not hear him. He imagined she heard only the voice of her dead Master now.

Zeerid realized it was no longer his fight. He holstered his blaster and watched. There was nothing else he could do.

Aryn strode toward the shuttle while the Twi'lek backed up the landing ramp, taking aim. Before the Twi'lek could fire, Aryn gestured with her left hand, and both of the blasters flew from the Twi'lek's hands and landed at Aryn's feet. The Twi'lek mouthed something lost in the muffle of her mask. Aryn stepped over and past the blasters.

The Twi'lek, wide-eyed, turned to flee into the shuttle's compartment. Again, Aryn gestured and a blast of power went forth from her, slammed into the Twi'lek's back, and drove her hard into the bulkhead. She collapsed within the shuttle's compartment, only her feet sticking out far enough for Zeerid to see.

Aryn deactivated her blade. She stopped for a moment and lowered her head, thinking.

Zeerid let himself hope, almost called her name again.

But then she raised her head and walked for the landing ramp, stepping over the corpse of the soldier.

Zeerid hung his head for a moment, saddened. It was her decision, her fight. He gathered himself, turned, and shouted at T7.

"Get that Dragonfly open, Tee-seven. It's time to go."

VRATH AWOKE to the sound of blasterfire, the high-pitched whine of sirens, and the voice on the port's speaker system saying something about a fuel leak. He'd taken a sleeptab to put him out and it took a few moments for his head to clear. He'd fallen asleep in the cockpit. He checked his chrono. Almost dawn, or just after. He'd been out the better part of the night.

Something thudded into *Razor*'s hull, a blaster shot.

"What in the—"

He undimmed the cockpit's transparisteel canopy and looked out on the landing pad. *Razor*'s angle offered him a very small field of vision so he could see little, merely part of one of the Imperial shuttles docked near him. Strangely, he saw no workers, no Imperial soldiers, no droids.

He heard a few more blaster shots from behind the ship. He had no idea what was going on and had no desire to find out. He did not yet have permission to leave Coruscant, but he would not leave his ship in dock in the midst of a firefight or whatever was happening out there. He figured he'd just take *Razor* into the air and stay in-atmosphere. He put the dull monotone of the spaceport's automated announcement on his in-ship comm.

"A hazardous substance spill has occurred in landing bay sixteen-B. There is significant danger. Please move rapidly toward the nearest exit. A hazardous substance spill . . ."

On the wall near him, written in large black letters, were the words: LANDING BAY 16-B.

He double-checked to ensure *Razor* was still sealed tight. It wasn't. The rear door was open. He cursed. He swore he'd closed it. He hit the button to close it but it still flashed as unsealed and open. Something was keeping it open, or there was a malfunction in the circuit.

He would have to close it with the rear switch or cargo would fall out as he flew. He started *Razor*'s auto-launch sequence, rose, and headed for the rear of the ship. Halfway there, he realized he'd left his blaster and blades in the cockpit. He'd stripped them off when he'd grabbed some shuteye.

No matter. He wouldn't need them.

ARYN FELT light-headed as she walked up the shuttle's landing ramp. She held her lightsaber hilt in her hand, held anger in her heart.

She slowed when the Twi'lek stirred, groaned, and turned over to watch her approach.

Aryn held up her free hand and almost said, *I won't*

hurt you, but walled off the words before they escaped her mouth.

She did not want to lie.

The woman scrabbled backward crabwise, eyes showing no fear, taking Aryn in, until she bumped into the bulkhead. She slid up the wall so that she was standing. Aryn stopped two paces from her. They regarded each other across the limitless gulf of their respective understandings.

Outside, the sirens howled. Aryn could no longer see Zeerid. More important, he could no longer see her.

The Twi'lek's eyes fell to Aryn's lightsaber hilt. Aryn felt no fear radiating from the woman, just a soft, profound sadness.

"You have come to kill me."

Aryn did not deny it. Her mouth was dry. She belted her own lightsaber, took Master Zallow's in hand.

"I see your anger," the Twi'lek said.

Aryn thought of Master Zallow and hardened her resolve. "You don't know me, woman. Do not pretend that you do."

She ignited Master Zallow's lightsaber. The Twi'lek's eyes widened and a flash of fear cracked her calm façade.

"I don't," the Twi'lek acknowledged. "But I know anger when I see it. I know it quite well."

A sad smile illuminated her face, overcoming the fear in her expression. She was thinking of something or someone other than Aryn and the sadness she radiated increased, sharpened.

"Anger is just pain renamed," she said. "This I know well, too. And sometimes . . . the pain runs too deep. Pain drives you, yes?"

Aryn had expected resistance, a fight, a protest, something. Instead, the Twi'lek seemed . . . resigned.

"You will kill me, Jedi? Because of Darth Malgus? Something he did?"

Hearing Malgus's name uttered stoked the heat of Aryn's anger. "He hurt someone I loved."

The Twi'lek nodded, gave a single, short outburst that might have been a pained laugh. "He hurts even those he himself loves." She smiled, and her soft voice sounded like rainfall. "These men and their wars. His name is Veradun, Jedi. And he would kill me if he knew I told you. But names are important."

Aryn had to work to keep hold of her anger. The Twi'lek seemed so . . . fragile, so hurt. "I don't care what his name is. You were there with him. In the attack on the Temple. I saw it."

"The Temple. Ah." She nodded. "Yes, I was with him. I love him. I fight at his side. You would do the same."

Aryn could not deny it. She would have done the same; she *had* done the same.

The anger she'd carried since feeling Master Zallow's death began to shrink, to drain out of her in the face of the Twi'lek's pain and sadness, in the realization that her own pain was not the moral center of the universe. The loss of her anger startled her. Since his death, she had been nothing but anger. Without it, she felt empty.

Pain by another name, the Twi'lek had said. Indeed.

"Please be quick," the Twi'lek said. "A clean death, yes?"

The words sounded not so much like a challenge as a request.

"What is your name?" Aryn asked.

"Eleena," the Twi'lek said.

Aryn stepped toward her. Eleena's eyes went to Aryn's blade but she did not shrink from Aryn's approach. She stared into Aryn's eyes and Aryn into hers, each measuring the other's pain, the other's loss.

"Names are important," Aryn said. She flipped her grip on her dead Master's lightsaber, deactivated the blade, and slammed the pommel against Eleena's temple. The Twi'lek collapsed without a sound.

"And I won't kill you, Eleena."

In so many ways, Eleena was already dead. Aryn pitied her.

She still felt compelled to avenge Master Zallow, but she could not murder Eleena to make Malgus suffer. Master Zallow would never have countenanced it. Aryn could not avenge him by betraying what he stood for. Perhaps he had failed. Perhaps the Order had failed. But both had failed nobly. There was something to that.

She remembered the dream she'd had of Master Zallow, of him standing on the Temple's ruins silently mouthing words at her that she could not then understand.

She understood them now.

"Be true to yourself," he had said.

Hadn't Zeerid been trying to tell her the same thing all along?

"I AM sorry, my lord," Kerse said as they hurried through the spaceport. "I assumed they had evacuated, and we had not yet had a chance to take a head count—"

"Save your excuses, Kerse," Malgus said and resisted the urge to cut the man in two.

The long main corridor within the port felt kilometers long. Counters lined it, businesses, even vendor carts, all of them abandoned. Vidscreens sat dark on the walls of lounges and clubs.

Smaller corridors branched off the main one, leading to commercial passenger pads, to lifts that led to the large craft staging areas, and to the small-craft pads.

"Move," Malgus said to them, and they did. To Kerse, he said, "Show me where you saw her last."

Kerse pointed to a side corridor far ahead, near the end of the main corridor. "It's there, my lord. Pad 16-B. On the left."

Malgus thought 16-B was close to the launch doors he had seen open upon his arrival at the spaceport. He augmented his speed with the Force and blazed along the hall, leaving the soldiers far behind. The walls, signs, and floor were a blur to him as he sped toward the landing pad, toward Eleena.

T7 HAD the rear hatch open on the Dragonfly and was still plugged into the control panel. Zeerid spent a few long moments turning his head from the Dragonfly to the Imperial shuttle where Aryn had disappeared with the Twi'lek, then back again. He finally started to head for the Dragonfly, but Aryn's voice pulled him around.

"Zeerid!"

He turned to see Aryn emerge from the shuttle, carrying the still body of the Twi'lek in her arms. Zeerid could not tell whether the Twi'lek was dead or alive. He walked toward Aryn slowly, his eyes not on the Twi'lek but on Aryn.

"Do I want to know?"

He dreaded the answer.

"I didn't kill her, Zeerid. It was important to me that you knew that."

Zeerid let himself breathe. "I'm glad, Aryn. Then you'll come with me, now?" He jerked a thumb over his shoulder. "Tee-seven has the Dragonfly opened."

"I can't, Zeerid, but I'm . . . all right now. Do you understand?"

"I don't, no."

Aryn opened her mouth to speak, stopped, and cocked her head, as if she'd heard something from far off.

"He's coming," she said.

The hairs on the back of Zeerid's neck rose. "Who's coming? Malgus?"

Aryn knelt and laid the Twi'lek down as gently as she might a newborn child.

The sirens suddenly stopped wailing, the sound cut off as if by a razor. The unexpected silence felt ominous. Zeerid eyed the open double doors of the landing pad. A dark corridor stretched beyond them.

Aryn rose, closed her eyes, inhaled.

"Go, Zeerid," she said.

"I'm not leaving," Zeerid said, and drew his other blaster. He ran his tongue over lips gone dry.

She opened her eyes and grabbed him with her gaze. "You are leaving and you're leaving now, Z-man. Think of your daughter. Go right now. Go . . . be a farmer."

She smiled and pushed him away. He stared into her face, knowing she was right.

He could not make Arra an orphan, not even for Aryn. Still, he was unwilling to leave her. He stepped closer to her, and her expression softened. She reached up and touched his face.

"Go."

Driven by nothing more than impulse, he grabbed her by the shoulders and kissed her full on the mouth. She did not resist, even returned it. He held her away from him at arm's length.

"You are a fool, Aryn Leneer," he said.

"Maybe."

He turned and headed for the Dragonfly. The feel of her lips lingered on his, a ghost of softness he hoped would haunt him forever. He only wished he had kissed her longer.

He imagined her eyes on him and he dared not look back for fear of losing his will to leave. He thought of the holo of Arra he used to keep on *Fatman,* her smile, her laugh, thought of his promise to Nat that he would not take unnecessary chances.

Hard as it was, he kept his back turned to Aryn Leneer.

"Get aboard, Tee-seven," he said as he walked up the landing ramp.

T7 beeped a sad negative.

"You're not coming?"

Again, a sad negative.

Zeerid patted the droid on his head. "You are a brave one. Thank you for your help. Take care of Aryn."

T7 whistled an affirmative, followed that with a somber farewell, and wheeled away from the Dragonfly.

The ship's engines were already winding up. T7 must have started the launch sequence.

VRATH PICKED his way through *Razor's* narrow corridors until he reached the rear compartment, which he'd converted from troop carrier to cargo hold. Stacked crates magnetically sealed to the deck dotted the hold, forming a rats' maze. He hurried through it to the rear door. The firefight outside seemed to have abated, so he allowed himself to relax.

ZEERID WATCHED T7 move away. He hit the control panel to close the rear door, and it began to rise. He waited until the latches sealed. Still thinking of Aryn, he put his hand on the cold metal of the door.

The Dragonfly lurched as it rose on its thrusters. He needed to get to the cockpit. He could not have the autopilot flying the ship when the Imperials started shooting.

He hurried through the converted cargo bay, made into a labyrinth by the many storage crates that dotted it. Rounding a corner, he nearly bumped into another man.

It took a moment for recognition to dawn—the small frame, the neatly parted dark hair, the deep sockets with their dead eyes, the thin mouth.

It was the man from Karson's Park.

It was the man who had betrayed Zeerid and Aryn to the Sith.

It was the man who knew about Arra and Nat.

"You!" Vrath Xizor said.

"Me," Zeerid affirmed.

ARYN WATCHED the Dragonfly lift off, missing Zeerid already. She tried to summon the rage that had brought her to Coruscant to face Malgus, but she no longer felt the same heat. She reached into her pocket, found the bead from the Nautolan bracelet, held it between forefinger and thumb.

She would face Malgus. She had to. But she would face him as her Master would have wished, with calmness in her heart.

She stood over Eleena's body and waited. Malgus's presence pressed against her as he drew nearer. His anger went before him like a storm.

MALGUS RUSHED through the large double doors and into the landing bay. Vrath Xizor's ship, *Razor*, rose on its thrusters toward the open roof doors. Two Imperial shuttles sat idle on the landing pad.

"Eleena!" he shouted, hating himself for his vulnerability but unable to contain the shout.

He reached out with the Force as *Razor* continued its rise, tried to take it in his mental grasp. Its ascent slowed.

He held forth both of his arms, made claws of his hands, and shouted with frustration as he sought to hold back the power of the ship's thrusters.

He felt a tightness in his mind, the string of his power being drawn taut, stretching, stretching. He would not release the ship. Its thrusters began to whine. He held it, teeth gritted, sweat soaking his body, his breath a dry rattle through his respirator.

And then the string snapped and the ship flew free, lifting clear of the roof doors.

He roared his rage as the ship's engines fired and it headed for the heavens. Seething, he activated his wrist chrono.

"Jard, the spicerunner's drop ship has just left the Liston Spaceport. Eleena may be aboard. Secure it with a tractor beam and detain everyone aboard—"

The hum of an activating lightsaber cut off his words. Another followed it. He looked across the landing pad and saw Aryn Leneer, a lightsaber in each hand, standing over the body of Eleena.

CHAPTER 13

THE PURE hate and raw rage pouring off Malgus struck Aryn like a physical blow. She braced herself against it as she might a hailstorm. She realized how strongly he felt for the Twi'lek, how he sublimated all of his emotion for her into hate and rage.

He ignited his lightsaber and his eyes and the plates of his armor reflected its red glow. He reached a hand behind him, made a sharp, cutting gesture, and the doors to the hangar slammed closed. Another gesture and the emergency locks turned into place.

"Just us," he said, his voice as rough as a rasp. He had not taken his eyes from Eleena.

Aryn indicated the Twi'lek. "She is alive, Sith. And I know your feelings for her."

"You know nothing," Malgus said, and took a slow step toward her.

"Let the drop ship go. Give the order, or I will kill her."

"You lie."

Aryn placed Master Zallow's blade at Eleena's neck.

Raw emotion surged out of Malgus, a gust of rage.

"I promise you I will do it," Aryn said.

Malgus's free hand clenched into a fist. "If you have

harmed her permanently, I will see that you suffer. I promise you *that*."

Aryn understood less and less about Malgus with each word he spoke. Still, she maintained her bluff. "Give the order, Malgus!"

Malgus glared at her, snarled, spoke into his comlink. "Jard, belay my previous order. The drop ship is to be allowed to leave the system."

"My lord?"

"Do it, Jard!"

"Yes, my lord."

Malgus walked toward Aryn, the slow movements of a hunter that smelled prey.

"And now, Jedi? You cannot leave here."

"I don't want to leave, Malgus."

His eyes smiled. "No. You want to kill me. Need to, yes? Because of your master?"

The feelings the words mined out of the dark parts of her soul felt uncomfortably close to the rage flowing from Malgus. A day earlier and her feelings might have mirrored his. That they didn't she owed to Eleena.

And Zeerid.

And Master Zallow.

"I wanted to hurt you, Sith. Hurt you by hurting her. But I won't add to her pain. She suffers enough already."

Malgus stopped in his advance. His eyes went to the Twi'lek, and to her surprise, Aryn felt something akin to pity radiate from him, just a flash, quickly washed away by hate.

"Enough words," he said, returning his gaze to Aryn. "Make your attempt, Aryn Leneer. I am here."

He discarded his cape, stood up straight, and saluted her with his lightsaber.

She hefted her lightsaber, Master Zallow's lightsaber,

felt the weight of both in her hands. She fell into the lines of the Force, at peace, calm.

Still heart. Still mind.

She had trained in dual lightsaber combat when she had been a Padawan, but she rarely fought with two blades in a genuine combat situation. She would now, here, today. She thought it fitting that she do so.

She did not wait for Malgus. She bounded across the hangar, her speed augmented by the Force, the lines of her blades leaving a blur of light in their wake. Malgus held his ground, blade ready.

She stabbed low with her primary blade, high with her secondary. Malgus leapt over both, flipped, landed behind her, and crosscut for her neck.

She ducked under it while spinning into a reverse leg sweep that caught his feet and tripped him. When he hit the ground, she rose, turned, raised both blades, and drove them down in a parallel overhand slash. Malgus somersaulted backward, and Aryn's blades cut gashes in the floor of the hangar. Sparks flew.

Malgus bounced up from the somersault and loosed a telekinetic blast that lifted Aryn from her feet and blew her across the hangar. She slammed into one of the shuttle's bulkheads, but used the Force to cushion the blow so that it did no harm. Bouncing off the cool metal, she charged Malgus. As she ran, she cast first her own lightsaber at Malgus, then Master Zallow's, using the Force to guide both.

The attack caught Malgus unprepared, and Aryn's blade bit into his armor. Sparks flew and Malgus winced, snarled with pain. He ducked under Master Zallow's blade, and Aryn recalled both to her hands as she ran. The moment she had them, she cast them both at Malgus again.

But this time he was ready. Augmenting his speed with

the Force, he flipped high into the air and out of the way of both. She anticipated his movement, however, bounded forward to cut him off and landed a flying kick in his chest. He used the Force to diminish the blow's impact but it drove him back a step and she heard his breath hitch through the sound of his respirator.

He recovered, roared, raised his blade high to cut her in two, and brought it down. But she had already summoned her own blade back to her hand and interposed it in a parry.

Malgus's strength drove her to her knees. She held out her other hand and pulled Master Zallow's blade to her hand, stabbed for his stomach with it.

Malgus sidestepped the stab, though it skinned his armor and showered sparks. He pushed her blade to the side with his own and kicked her in the face. The strength behind the blow blew through her defenses, caused her to see stars, loosed teeth, and sent her head over heels backward. She landed on her knees, stunned, seeing double.

She rose, swayed on her feet, seeing four blades in her hands rather than two. Something was in her mouth and she spat it out—a tooth, the root forked and bloody.

"You are a child to hate," Malgus said, his tone incongruously soft as he stalked toward her. "Your anger barely smolders. You are a fraction of what you could be."

She needed time to recover her senses, some distance from Malgus. She backflipped high into the air and landed atop the Imperial shuttle. Her mind was beginning to clear.

"Your Master was also misguided. He thought to defeat me with calm, but failed. You thought to defeat me with anger, but carry too little, despite your loss."

Aryn's vision began to clear. She felt more herself.

"Be grateful for that, Jedi. Anger exacts its own price."

Again she felt the odd sense of sympathy or pity adulterating the otherwise pure hate flowing from Malgus. His eyes went to Eleena, her body crumpled on the landing pad's floor.

As Aryn prepared to leap at Malgus, he held forth a hand, almost casually, and lightning sizzled through the space between them. Aryn interposed her lightsabers, but the power in the lightning exceeded anything she had felt from Malgus before. It blasted through her defenses and both lightsabers flew from her hands. The lightning seized her, lifted her up, and threw her from the top of the shuttle.

As she flew toward the deck, she smelled burning flesh, heard screaming, realized that it was her flesh, her screams. She hit the ground hard and her head bounced off the ground. Sparks erupted in her brain, pain, and everything went dark.

ZEERID'S MILITARY training responded faster than his thoughts. He made a knife of his right hand and drove it at the smaller man's throat. But Vrath, too, must have been trained. A sweeping side block with his left hand threw Zeerid's arm out wide, then Vrath seized the arm by the wrist, shifted his feet to get him closer to Zeerid, and rotated into a hip toss. Zeerid saw it coming, rode with the throw, hit the ground in a roll, and came up with his E-9 drawn and aimed.

A kick from Vrath sent the blaster flying and it discharged into the bulkhead. Vrath followed the side kick into a spinning back kick but Zeerid anticipated it, took the blow to the side to capture the leg, stood, and drove his fist into the man's nose.

Bone crunched and blood exploded outward.

Vrath flailed wildly with his left hand, driving his

straightened fingers into Zeerid's throat, a blow that would have killed him if the man had been able to put more into it. As it was, the blow caused Zeerid to release Vrath's leg and recoil.

Zeerid reached behind his back for his second blaster and started to pull it loose. But Vrath charged him before Zeerid could bring it to bear, drove Zeerid up against one of the cargo crates. The sharp point of the crate's corner pressed into Zeerid's back, and he grunted at the pain. Vrath's hand snaked around Zeerid's, caught him by the wrist, levered it, and slammed it against the crate. The second blaster fell to the floor and the man kicked it away.

Zeerid grunted with effort and shoved Vrath away from him.

They regarded each other from three paces, both gasping. Vrath's eyes watered. Blood poured out of his nose. Zeerid had trouble breathing through his damaged trachea.

"Guess it had to come to this," the man said, his voice made nasal by his broken nose. "Didn't it, Zeerid Korr?"

He covered first one nostril, then the other, blowing out blood and snot in turn.

"I'm Vrath, by the way. Vrath Xizor."

Zeerid barely heard him. He took the time Vrath had used to clear his nose to recover his own breath and eye the floor for either blaster. Both weapons had disappeared under crates during the scrum.

Vrath felt the damage to his nose with a two-finger pincer. "What are you? Harriers? Commandos?"

Zeerid's breathing cleared and the two men began to circle.

"Havoc Squadron," Zeerid said, sizing up the smaller man.

"First in," Vrath said, reciting one of the squad's mottos.

"You?" Zeerid asked.

"Imperial sniper corps."

"A skulker," Zeerid said.

Vrath lost his smile at the insult. "I killed over fifty men in a Republic uniform, Korr. You'll be just another number to me."

"We'll see," Zeerid said, as calm as the quiet moments before a thunderstorm.

Vrath feinted, drawing a response from Zeerid. Vrath grinned, his teeth bloody with runoff from his nose.

"Jumpy, yeah?"

Zeerid watched for an opening as they circled. When he saw one, he feinted high and lunged in low, thinking to take Vrath down where Zeerid's size would give him the advantage. Vrath sprawled to avoid the takedown, but Zeerid used his weight to drive him up against the bulkhead. Vrath threw a short elbow, grazing Zeerid's head, another, catching him on the cheek.

Grunting, Zeerid pushed himself away from the smaller man to get some room to work. When he had it, still holding Vrath's arms, he put a knee into his abdomen, another, another. Vrath grunted, turned his body to keep his hips in the way.

Vrath's fingers slid up Zeerid's shoulder to his face, toward his eyes. Zeerid shook his head but Vrath's fingers found the sockets, started to burrow.

Zeerid shoved him away and backed off, blinking, covering his retreat with a front kick.

Vrath lunged at him, seized him around the thighs, lifted him off the ground, and threw him back down. Zeerid's head hit the deck hard and he saw stars. Vrath squirmed atop him, fast, elusive, his arms and legs everywhere, wrapping Zeerid up. Soon he had his body atop Zeerid.

Elbows and fists poured down, one after another. Zeerid took a blow to the cheek, the temple, another to the cheek, the top of his head. The last opened him up and blood ran warm and slick down his pate, smeared his face, darkened Vrath's elbow.

Desperate, he reached for Vrath's arms but the man was too fast and the blood made his skin slick, more difficult to get a grip. Zeerid wrapped his arms around Vrath's back, pulled him close to disallow him the room he needed to ply his elbows.

And then Vrath made a mistake. Trying to pull himself back up to loose more elbows, he put his face above Zeerid's with only a few centimeters between them. Zeerid threw his head up and slammed his brow into Vrath's already broken nose.

Vrath cried out in pain, instinctively recoiled. Taking advantage of the opportunity, Zeerid seized one of Vrath's wrists, rolled him over, threw his legs on either side of Vrath's shoulder, extended Vrath's arm, then extended his own body to lever the arm at the elbow.

Vrath screamed as the hyperextension turned into an audible break. The arm went loose in Zeerid's grasp, the joint shattered.

He released Vrath's elbow, rolled, and bounded to his feet. Vrath, his face twisted in pain, crawled for where the E-9 had disappeared under a crate. Zeerid cut him off, picked him off the floor, and shoved him hard toward the bulkhead. Vrath careered into the metal wall, off-kilter. He tried to catch himself with his broken arm but it just hung limp from the joint and he caught the side of his head flush. His eyes rolled and he went down in a heap.

Zeerid jumped atop him, punched him square in the eye, thinking he was only stunned, but the man stayed limp beneath him. Blood dripped from Zeerid's head onto Vrath's face.

Gasping, Zeerid checked Vrath's pulse. Still alive.

All at once the adrenaline that had fueled him during the combat drained out of him. His entire body ached. His breath came ragged and he had no strength. Stabs of pain in his face and head echoed each beat of his heart. The entire fight had taken maybe forty seconds. He felt as if he'd been beaten for hours.

He stared down at Vrath, wondering what to do with him. He searched the man's pants, jacket, coat. He found several IDs and other personal items. He also found flex binders. He flipped Vrath over and pulled his arms behind him.

He felt the bones in the broken arm grind together and Vrath groaned.

"Sorry," Zeerid said. There was nothing he could do about the arm.

Once he had the man's arms secured, he slung him over his shoulders and carried him on shaky legs through the ship to the cockpit. A Dragonfly had no brig and there was no way Zeerid was letting Vrath out of his sight.

By the time he reached the cockpit, the ship had cleared the spaceport and angled upward for the atmosphere. Zeerid studied the instrumentation. His face was swelling and his eye was damaged from Vrath's fingers so he had to squint. He took off his shirt and used it to apply pressure to his head wound. He didn't want to bleed all over the controls.

A weapons belt with a GH-22 blaster and several knives lay on the pilot's seat. Vrath's weapons, presumably. Zeerid belted them on and sat.

He'd never flown a *Dragonfly*-class drop ship before, but he could fly any kniffing thing that tramped the stars. He'd need to get past the Imperial blockade and get into a hyperspace lane.

"Time to dance between the raindrops," he said, and disengaged the autopilot.

He looked down out of the canopy at the spaceport far below, wondering what had happened with Aryn. He'd have paid a lot of credits to have her beside him right then.

ARYN OPENED her eyes. Malgus stood over her, his bloodshot eyes fixed on her face. He held the Twi'lek, still unconscious, in his arms. He also held both of Aryn's lightsabers. His own lightsaber hilt hung from his belt.

He had not killed her. She had no idea why.

He stared down at her and she felt his ambivalence. He was struggling with something.

"Take them and go," he said, and dropped both of her lightsabers. They hit the floor in a clatter. "Take the shuttle. I will ensure you have safe passage away from Coruscant."

She did not move. The lightsabers were centimeters from her hand.

His eyes narrowed. "Unless your need to avenge your Master requires you to die, you should do as I command, Jedi."

She pushed herself up with one hand, took both of the lightsabers in the other. The metal was cool in her palm. "Why?"

"Because you spared her," he said, his voice soft behind the respirator. "Were our situations reversed, I would not have done so. Because your presence made me aware of something I should have known long ago."

Aryn rose, still cautious, and clipped the lightsabers to her belt.

"We will be leaving Coruscant, you know," he said, almost sadly. "The Empire, I mean. All that remains is to sign the treaty. Then we will have peace. Does that please you?"

"Please me?" She still did not understand. She inventoried her injuries. Lots of bruises and lacerations. Nothing broken. She inventoried her soul. Nothing broken there, either.

She looked into Malgus's face. She did not know what to say. "Perhaps we will meet again, under other circumstances."

"If we meet again, Aryn Leneer," Malgus said. "I will kill you as I did your Master. Do not mistake my actions for mercy. I am repaying a debt. When you leave here, it is paid."

Aryn licked her lips, stared him in the face, and nodded.

"Do you know your own Order betrayed you, Jedi?" he said. "They informed us that you might be coming here."

Aryn was not surprised, but the betrayal still hurt.

"I no longer belong to an Order," she said, her throat tight.

He laughed, the sound like a hacking cough. "Then we have more in common than anger," he said. "Now, go."

She did not understand and resigned herself to never understanding. She turned, still disbelieving, and headed for the shuttle. T7 emerged from hiding near the ship and beeped a question. She had no answer. Together, they boarded the shuttle. When she reached the cockpit and sat, she realized that she was shaking.

"Still heart, still mind," she said, and felt calmer.

Exhaling, she engaged the thrusters. She had no idea where she would go.

* * *

AS THE blue of Coruscant's sky gave way to the black of space, Zeerid started to sweat. He eyed the sensors for Imperial ships. They would have detected him by now. A cruiser showed on his screen, maybe *Valor,* maybe another one. He wheeled the drop ship away from it, accelerated for the nearest hyperlane. He just wanted to jump somewhere, anywhere.

A beep from the panel drew his attention. It took him a moment to realize it was a hail. It took him another moment to figure out how to operate it. He slapped the button, opening the channel. If nothing else, he'd curse out the Imperials before they shot him down.

"Drop ship *Razor,* you are cleared to leave."

Zeerid assumed it had to be a ruse, a bad joke. But he saw nothing on the scanner, and the cruiser did not move to interdict.

He flew for the hyperlane. He let the navicomp calculate a course and tried to believe his luck. Vrath's voice startled him.

"Not bad, Commando. I'm impressed."

"Impressing you isn't my concern, skulker."

Vrath chuckled, but it turned into a cough and a wince. "There are pain pills in the medbay. You mind?"

"Later," Zeerid said.

"It hurts pretty bad, marine."

"Good."

"It's just business, Korr."

Zeerid thought of Arra, Nat, Aryn. "Right. Business." He'd had all he could take of business.

"We're done as far as I'm concerned," Vrath said. "I was hired to stop that engspice from getting to Coruscant. I did that. Which means we're done. I report back and we never see each other again. I'd like my ship back, though."

Zeerid resisted the urge to punch a restrained man. He was behaving as if they'd just had a friendly sparring match, that they'd go out for drinks later.

"The Exchange probably won't be as forgiving though, eh?" Vrath said. "I hear they don't tolerate lost shipments. You and your family are going to have a hard row there."

Vrath's words made Zeerid's breath hitch. Hearing them changed everything. His knuckles turned white on the stick as options played out in his mind. Adrenaline filled him to his eyes. He stared straight out the cockpit window.

"They don't know I have a family."

"Not yet," Vrath said. "But they will. They always do—"

Too late Vrath seemed to realize he'd stepped on a mine. He tried to chuckle it away but Zeerid heard the fear behind the laughter.

"Or maybe they won't. I'm just talking here."

"You talk too much," Zeerid said while he hardened his expression, hardened his mind. The alchemy of necessity distilled his list of options down to one.

He put himself on autopilot and stood.

"On your feet, Vrath."

When the man did not stand right off, Zeerid pulled him roughly to his feet. Vrath groaned with pain.

"Easy there, marine. Pain meds now, yeah?"

He sounded doubtful.

"Walk," Zeerid said.

"To where?"

Zeerid stuck the GH-22 in his back. "Move."

Reluctantly, Vrath let Zeerid push him through the corridors of the ship. The man moved slowly, as if he knew Zeerid's intent, and Zeerid had to push him along.

A few turns, a few corridors, and Zeerid saw an air lock door. He steered Vrath to it, stopped before it.

"Turn around."

Vrath did. His face was blotchy, but whether from the beating or from fear Zeerid could not tell.

"This is about your daughter, yeah? Well, I already told my people, Korr. They already know."

Zeerid heard the high pitch of a lie in Vrath's tone. "A lie. You already told me you didn't. You said, 'Not yet.'"

He moved Vrath out of the way with the blaster and activated the internal doors on the air lock. They unsealed and slid open with a hiss. A red light set into the ceiling lit up and began to spin.

Zeerid showed him the blaster. "You want this?" He nodded at the air lock. "Or that?"

Vrath looked at the weapon, the air lock, swallowed hard.

"It doesn't have to go this way, Korr. I won't tell anyone about you or your family. You can even keep the ship."

"I can't take that chance."

Vrath tried to smile, but it looked like a death grimace. "Come on, Korr. If I say I won't talk, I won't talk. I'm nothing if not a man of my word."

Zeerid thought of the promise he'd made to Nat, that he'd take no unnecessary chances. "Yeah. Me, too."

Desperation crept into Vrath's voice. He shifted on his feet. "You'll have to bear this, Korr. This will make you a murderer. Kill a man with his own weapon. You want that weight?"

Zeerid knew what he was doing. Or at least he thought so. "I can carry it. And I don't need a lecture about murder from a skulker."

Fear made Vrath's eyes water. "That was war, Korr. Think about it. Think hard."

"I have. Pick, or I pick for you. Just another number, right?"

Vrath stared into Zeerid's face. Maybe he saw the blankness, the resolve. "To hell with you, Korr. To hell with you."

Zeerid pushed him into the air lock.

"I could have killed her, Korr. Both of them. Back at the park on Vulta. You know I could have. But I didn't."

"No," Zeerid said. "You didn't."

He activated the seal and the door started to close.

"I wish I had killed them now! I wish I had!"

Zeerid stopped the door, a sudden flash of anger rekindling his strength. He reached into the air lock and grabbed Vrath by the shirt, shook him. "If you had harmed her, this would be coming to you with a sharp blade and a slow touch. You hear me, skulker? Do you?"

He kicked Vrath in the stomach, doubling the man over with the blow. While Vrath gasped for breath, Zeerid reactivated the door and it sealed shut. Vrath stared at him through the tiny transparisteel window, all wild eyes, snarls, and teeth.

Zeerid hit the button to evacuate the air lock. The warning alarm wailed.

He gave one more glance at Vrath, saw the fear there, then he turned and walked back toward the cockpit.

Murderer.

That's what he was.

The siren stopped and he felt a soft rumble as the external air lock door opened.

A pit opened in his stomach.

Emotion, nameless and raw, caused his eyes to water. He wiped them clear.

He *was* a murderer, and he felt heavy already.

But he would carry it—for Nat, for Arra. He expected

he'd carry it the rest of his life and the weight would never diminish. He'd killed men before, but not like that, not like he'd killed Vrath.

For the first time, he understood, really understood, why Aryn had returned to Coruscant.

He prayed to gods he did not believe in that she reconsidered what she had come to do. She felt things too keenly to feel what he felt. She could never carry it. It would destroy her. Better she should die.

All of a sudden, he just wanted to sleep.

He overrode the navicomp's random course and plugged in the coordinates to Vulta. His hands shook the whole time.

In moments, *Razor* jumped into hyperspace.

He had always flown alone, but he'd never felt alone in the cockpit, not until that moment.

Sitting back in the chair, he tried to sleep.

And tried not to dream.

MALGUS WATCHED the shuttle piloted by Aryn Leneer rise on its thrusters. He raised Jard on the comm.

"A shuttle is lifting off from Liston," he said. "It is also clear to leave Coruscant's space."

"Yes, my lord," Jard answered.

Malgus could have broken his word to the Jedi, could have shot Aryn Leneer from the sky. But he would not. He kept his promises.

But he realized, more than ever, that the Jedi were too dangerous for him to allow them to exist. They were to the Sith what Eleena was to him—an example of peace, of comfort, and therefore a temptation to weakness. Angral did not see it. The Emperor did not see it. But Malgus saw it. And he knew what he must do. He must destroy the Jedi utterly.

He knelt beside Eleena, cradled her head in his left

arm. He studied her face, its symmetry, the line of her jaw, the deep-set eyes, the perfectly formed nose. He remembered the first time he had seen her, a cowed, beaten slave barely out of her teens. He'd killed her owner for his brutality, taken her into his house, trained her in combat. She had been his companion, his lover, his conscience ever since.

Her eyes fluttered open, focused. She smiled. "Veradun, you are my rescuer."

"Yes," he said.

"Where is the woman?" Eleena asked. "The Jedi?"

"She is gone. She will never hurt you again."

She leaned her head back into his arm, closed her eyes, and sighed contentedly. "I knew you loved me."

"I do," he acknowledged, and her smile widened. He felt tears forming in his eyes, his weakness made manifest.

She opened her eyes, saw the tears, reached up an arm to put a hand on his cheek. "What is wrong, my love?"

"That I love you is what is wrong, Eleena."

"Veradun—"

He steeled himself, stood, ignited his lightsaber, and drove it through her heart.

Her eyes widened, never left his face, pierced him. Her mouth opened in a surprised gasp. She seemed as if she wanted to say something, but no sound emerged from her mouth.

And then it was over and she was gone.

He deactivated his blade.

He could no longer afford a conscience, or a weakness, not if he was to do what must be done. He could serve only one master.

He stood over her body until his tears dried.

He resolved that he'd never shed another. He'd had to

destroy what he loved. And he knew he would have to do it again. First the Jedi, then . . .

Behind him, Kerse and his soldiers were worrying at the landing bay doors, trying to cut their way in.

Malgus knelt and picked up her limp body. She felt as light as gauze in his arms. He would give her a funeral with honor, and then he would begin.

His vision on Korriban had shown him a galaxy in flames. But it was not just the Republic that required cleansing by fire.

EPILOGUE

NIGHT, AND controlled rage, wrapped Malgus. His anger smoldered always now, and his thoughts mirrored the caliginous air. He had taken a ship in secret from the Unknown Regions, where he was currently stationed, and made his way to the planet. No one knew he had come.

He focused on keeping his Force signature suppressed. He did not want anyone to learn of his presence prematurely.

A sliver of moon cut a narrow slit in the dark sky, painted everything in grays and blacks.

The stone wall of the compound, eight meters tall, rose before him, its surface as rough and pitted as Malgus's mien. Drawing on the Force, he augmented a leap that carried him up and over the wall. He landed in a well-tended garden courtyard. Sculpted dwarf trees and bushes cast strange, malformed shadows in the moonlight. The gentle sound of a fountain mixed with the night hum of insects.

Malgus moved through the garden, a deeper darkness among the shadows, his boots soft on the grass.

A few lights lit the windows of the rectangular manse

that sat in the center of the grounds. The manse, the garden, the fountain, all of it, looked similar to some soft world in the Republic, some decadent Jedi sanctuary where so-called Force scholars pondered peace and sought tranquillity.

Malgus knew it was folly. Empires and the men who ruled empires could not stay sharp when surrounded by comfort, by peace.

By love.

Low voices sounded from ahead, barely audible in the stillness. Malgus did not slow and made no attempt to hide his approach as he emerged from the darkness of the garden.

They saw him immediately, two Imperial troopers in half armor. They leveled their blaster rifles.

"Who in the—"

He drew on the Force, gestured as if he were shooing away insects, and sent both of the troopers flying against the wall of the manse hard enough to crack bone. Both sagged to the ground, unmoving. The black eyes of their helmets stared at Malgus.

He walked between their bodies and through the sliding doors of the manse, reminded of his attack on the Jedi Temple back on Coruscant.

Except then Eleena had accompanied him. It seemed a lifetime ago.

Thinking of Eleena blew oxygen on the embers of his anger. In life, Eleena had been his weakness, a tool to be exploited by rivals. In death, she had become his strength, her memory the lens of his rage.

He resided in the calm eye of a storm of hate. Power churned around him, within him. He did not feel as if he were drawing on the Force, using it. He felt as if he *were* the Force, as if he had merged with it.

He had evolved. Nothing split his loyalties any longer.

He served the Force and only the Force, and his understanding of it increased daily.

The growing power whirling around him, leaking through the lid of his control, made the suppression of his Force signature impossible. All at once he lowered all of the mental barriers, let the full force of his power roil around him.

"Adraas!" he shouted, putting enough power into his voice to cause the ceiling and walls to vibrate. "Adraas!"

He strode through the rooms and hallways of Adraas's retreat, toppling or destroying everything within reach—antique desks, the bizarre, erotic statuary favored by Adraas, everything. He left ruin in his wake, all while shouting for Adraas to show himself. His voice rang off the walls.

He rounded a corner to see a squad of six Imperial troopers in full armor, blaster rifles ready, the front three on one knee before the other three.

They had been waiting for him.

His Force-enhanced reflexes moved faster than their trigger fingers. Without slowing his pace, he pulled his lightsaber into his hand and activated it as the blasters discharged. The red line of his weapon spun so fast in his hand it expanded into a shield.

Two of the blaster shots ricocheted off his weapon and into the ceiling. He deflected the other four back at the troopers, putting black holes through two chests and two face masks. Another two strides and a lunge brought him upon the surviving two troopers before they could fire again. He crosscut, spun, and crosscut again, killing both.

He deactivated his lightsaber and continued on through the manse until he reached a large central hall, perhaps fifteen meters wide and twenty-five long. Decorative wood columns that supported upper balconies lined its length at even intervals. A pair of double doors stood on the far side of the hall, opposite those Malgus had entered.

Lord Adraas stood within the open doorway. He wore a black cloak over his elaborate armor.

"Malgus," Adraas said, his voice showing surprise, but his tone turning Malgus's name into an insult. "You were in the Unknown Regions."

"I am in the Unknown Regions."

Adraas understood the implication. "I knew you would come one day."

"Then you know I am here for you."

Adraas ignited his lightsaber, shed his cloak. "For me, yes." He chuckled. "I understand you, Malgus. Understand you quite well."

"You understand nothing," Malgus said, and stepped into the room.

Malgus felt the hate pouring off Adraas, the power, but it paled in comparison to the rage and hate roiling in Malgus. In his mind's eye, he saw Eleena's face as she died. It poured fuel on the flames of his rage.

Adraas, too, stepped into the room. "Do you think that your presence here is a surprise? That I have not long foreseen this?"

Malgus chuckled, the sound loud off the high ceiling. "You have foreseen it but you cannot stop it. You are a child, Adraas. And tonight you pay. Angral is not here to protect you. No one is."

Adraas scoffed. "I have hidden my true power from you, Malgus. It is you who will not leave here."

"Then show me your power," Malgus said, sneering.

Adraas snarled and held forth his left hand. Force lightning crackled from his fingertips, filled the space between them.

Malgus interposed his lightsaber, drew the lightning

to it, and started walking toward Adraas. The power swirled around the red blade, sizzling, crackling, pushed against Malgus, but he strode through it. The skin of his hands blistered but Malgus endured the pain, paid it as the price of his cause.

As he walked, he spun his blade in an arc above his head, gathering the lightning, then flung it back at Adraas. It slammed into his chest, lifted him bodily from the ground, and threw him hard against the far well.

"Is that your power?" Malgus asked, still advancing, cloaked in rage. "That is what you wished to show me?"

Adraas climbed to his feet, his armor charred and smoking. A snarl split his face.

Malgus picked up his pace, turned the walk into a charge. His boots thumped off the wood floor of the hall. He did not bother with finesse. He vented his rage in a continuous roar as he unleashed a furious series of blows: an overhand slash that Adraas parried; a low stab that Adraas barely sidestepped; a side kick that connected to Adraas's side, broke ribs, and flung Adraas fully across the narrow axis of the hall. He crashed into a column and the impact split it as would lightning a tree.

Adraas growled as he climbed to his feet. Power gathered around him, a black storm of energy, and he leapt at Malgus, his blade held high.

Malgus sneered, gestured, seized Adraas in his power, and pulled him from the air at the apex of his leap.

Adraas hit the ground in a heap, his breath coming in wheezes. He climbed to all fours, then to his feet, favoring his side, his blade held limply before him.

"You hid nothing from me," Malgus said, and the power in his voice caused Adraas to wince. "You are a fool, Adraas. Your skill is in politics, in currying favor with your betters. Your understanding of the Force is nothing compared to mine."

Adraas snarled, started to charge toward Malgus, a last-ditch attempt to salvage his dignity if not his life.

Malgus held forth his hand and the rage within him manifested in blue veins of lightning that discharged from his fingertips and slammed into Adraas. The power stopped Adraas's charge cold, blew his lightsaber from his hand, caught him up in a cage of burning lightning. He screamed, squirming in frustration and pain.

"End it, Malgus! End it!"

Malgus unclenched his fingers and released the lightning. Adraas fell to the ground, his flesh smoking, the skin of his once handsome face blistered and peeling. Again he rose to all fours and looked up at Malgus.

"Angral will avenge me."

"Angral will suspect what has happened here," Malgus said, and strode toward him. "But he will never know, not for certain, not until it is too late."

"Too late for what?" Adraas asked.

Malgus did not answer.

"You are mad," Adraas said, and leapt to his feet and charged. He pulled his lightsaber to his fist and activated it. The attack took Malgus momentarily by surprise.

Adraas loosed a flurry of strikes, his blade a humming, red blur as he spun, stabbed, slashed, and cut. Malgus backed off a single step, another, then held his ground, his own blade an answer to all of Adraas's attacks. Adraas shouted as he attacked, the sound that of desperation, filled with the knowledge that he was no match for Malgus.

Finally Malgus answered with an attack of his own, forcing Adraas back with the power and speed of his blows. When he had Adraas backed up against the wall, he crosscut for his head. Adraas ducked under and Malgus cut a column in two. As the huge upper piece of the column crashed to the floor and the balcony lurched above them, Adraas fell to one knee and stabbed at Malgus's chest. Malgus spun out of the way and rode the spin into a chop that severed Adraas's arm at the elbow. Adraas screamed and clutched his arm at the bicep while his forearm fell to the floor along with the column.

Malgus had taught the lesson he'd come to teach.

He deactivated his lightsaber, held up his left hand, and made a pincer of his fingers.

Adraas tried to use his own power to defend himself but Malgus pushed through it and took telekinetic hold of Adraas's throat.

Adraas gagged, the capillaries in his wide eyes beginning to pop. Malgus's power lifted Adraas from the floor, his legs kicking, gasping.

Malgus stood directly before Adraas, his hate the vise closing on Adraas's trachea.

"You and Angral caused this, Adraas. And the Emperor. There can be no peace with the Jedi, no truce." He clenched his fist. "There can be no peace, at all. Not ever."

Adraas's only answer was continued gagging.

Seeing him there, hanging, near death, Malgus thought of Eleena, of Adraas's description of her. He released Adraas from the clutch of his Force choke.

Adraas hit the ground on his back, gasping. Malgus had a knee on his chest and both his hands on his throat before Adraas could recover. He would kill Adraas with his bare hands.

"Look me in the eyes," he said, and made Adraas look at him. "In the eyes!"

Adraas's eyes showed petechial hemorrhaging but Malgus knew he was coherent.

"You called her a mongrel," Malgus said. He removed

his gauntlets, took Adraas by the throat, and began to squeeze. "To my face you called her that. Her."

Adraas blinked, his eyes watering. His mouth opened and closed but no sound emerged.

"You are the mongrel, Adraas." Malgus bent low, nose-to-nose. "Angral's mongrel and you and those like you have mongrelized the purity of the Empire with your pollution, trading strength for a wretched peace."

Adraas's trachea collapsed in Malgus's grip. There was no final cough or gag. Adraas died in silence.

Malgus rose and stood over Adraas's body. He pulled on his gloves, adjusted his armor, his cloak, and walked out of the manse.

THE RISING sun peeked over the mountains on Dantooine, and the thin clouds at the horizon line looked to have caught fire. Shadows stretched over the valley, gradually receding as the sun rose higher. The trees whispered in a breeze that bore the scent of loam, decaying fruit, and the recent rain.

Zeerid stood in the midst of the damp dirt and tall grass, under the open sky, and faced the fact that he had no idea whatsoever about what he should be doing.

Probably sowing seeds, he supposed, or grafting vines, or testing the soil or something. But it was all a guess. He glanced around as if there might be someone nearby whom he could ask for assistance, but the next nearest farm was twenty klicks to the west.

He was on his own.

"Same as always," he said to himself with a smile.

After getting clear of Coruscant, he'd flown to Vulta, scooped up Nat and Arra, and fled deeper into the Outer Rim. There, he'd sold *Razor* and its cargo on the black market and, with the credits he'd earned, bought Nat her

own home and bought him and Arra an old vineyard—
long unused for growing—from an elderly couple.

He'd become a farmer, of sorts. Or at least a farm
owner. Just as he'd told Aryn he would.

Thinking of Aryn, especially her eyes, made him smile,
but the smile curled down under the weight of bad
memories.

He had never seen her again after leaving Coruscant.
For a time he'd tried to learn what had happened to her,
but a search of the HoloNet turned up nothing. He
knew, however, that Darth Malgus had lived. He presumed that meant Aryn had not, and he'd been unable
to tell Arra why Daddy sometimes cried.

And he still secretly hoped the presumption was
wrong, that she'd escaped somehow, remembered who
she was.

He thought of her every day, her smile, her hair, but
especially her eyes. The understanding he saw in them
had always drawn him to her. Still did, though he was
drawn only to her memory now.

He hoped she had found whatever she'd been seeking
before the end.

He looked around his new estate, at the large home he
and Arra rattled around in, at the various outbuildings
that held equipment he did not know how to operate, at
the row upon row of trellises that lined the fallow vine
fields, and he felt . . . free.

He owed no one anything and The Exchange would
never find him, even if they somehow realized that he
was still alive. He owned land, a home, and had enough
credits left over to hire a crew that could help him turn
the land into a decent winery within a year or two. Or
maybe he'd convert the farm and grow tabac. Months
earlier, he could not have imagined such a life for himself.

Grinning like a fool, he sat down in the center of his plot of dirt and watched the sunrise.

A black dot above the horizon drew his eye.

A ship.

He watched it, unconcerned until it started to get larger. He could not yet make out its lines, but he could see its course.

It was heading in his direction.

A flash of panic seized him but he fought it down. His eyes went to the house, where Arra slept. He turned his gaze back to the ship.

He disliked unidentified ships descending from the sky in his direction. They always reminded him of the gully jumper he'd watched crash into the Jedi Temple. They always reminded him of Aryn.

"They could not have found us," he said. "It is nothing."

The ship grew still larger as it closed the distance. It was moving fast.

From the tri-winged design he made it as a BT7 Thunderstrike: a multi-use ship common even out on the Rim. He stood as it closed. He could hear the deep bass hum of its engines.

"Daddy!"

Arra's voice turned his head around. She had come out of the house and sat in the wooden swing chair on the covered porch of the house. She smiled and waved.

"The rain's gone!" she said.

"Get in the house, Arra!" he shouted, pointing at the door.

"But Daddy—"

"Get inside right now."

He did not bother to see if she complied. The ship probably had not seen him yet. The trellises and their veins of browning vines would have concealed him from an airborne viewer. He ducked low and darted toward the edge of the field, sheltering as best he could behind one of the trellises. He pulled some dead vines from it so that he could look through to the open area at the edge of the field where the ship was likely to put down.

If it was coming to his farm.

He spared a glance back at the house and saw that Arra had gone back inside. He reached down to his ankle holster and pulled out the E-3 he kept there, then reached around to the small of his back for the E-9 he kept there. He chided himself for not wearing his ordinary hip holster with its twin BlasTech 4s. Arra disliked seeing the weapons, so he'd taken to wearing only those he could carry in concealed holsters. But little E-series popguns would have trouble doing much to someone in ablative armor.

Again, *if* the ship was coming to his farm.

The ship came into view, and he noted its lack of markings. Not a good sign. It slowed, circled the farm, and he tried to make himself small. Its engines slowed and its thrusters engaged. It was coming down.

He cursed, cursed, and cursed.

Tension coiled within him but he still felt the habitual calm that always served him well in combat. He reminded himself not to shoot until he knew what he was facing. It was possible that whoever was in the Thunderstrike intended him no harm. Another local, maybe. Or an official in an unmarked ship.

But he doubted it.

If they were agents of The Exchange, he wanted to take at least one alive, to find out how they'd tracked him down.

The ship set down, its skids sinking into the wet ground. The engines wound down but did not turn off. He could see the pilot through the transparisteel canopy—a human

man in the jacket, helmet, and glasses that seemed to be the bush pilot uniform out on the Rim. He was talking to someone or someones in the rear compartment, but Zeerid could not see who.

He heard the doors on the far side of the ship slide open, then close. He still could not see anyone. The ship's engines wound back up slightly, the thrusters engaged, and it started to lift off. He gave it a few seconds to get up in the air and engage its engines fully then stepped out from behind the trellis.

A single figure walked toward his home, a human woman with short hair, dressed in baggy trousers and a short coat. He leveled both blasters at her back.

"Do not take another step."

She stopped and held out her hands to either side.

He started to circle so he could see her face.

"Are you going to shoot at me every time we meet?"

The sound of her voice stopped him in his tracks, sent his heart racing, stole his breath. "Aryn?"

She turned, and it was her. He could not believe it.

The first words out of his mouth were ridiculous. "Your hair!"

She ran her hand through her shorn hair. "Yeah, I needed a change."

He heard the seriousness in her tone and answered in kind as he walked toward her. His legs felt unsteady under him. "I know what you mean."

She smiled softly, and it was the same as it had ever been, as warm as the rising sun.

"I looked everywhere for you," she said. "I wanted to make sure you were all right."

"I looked for you, too," he said. "But there was nothing. I watched every holo story about the Jedi. It said they were leaving Coruscant . . ."

Her expression fell. "I resigned from the Order, Zeerid."

He stopped in his tracks. "You what?"

"I resigned. Like I said, I needed a change."

"I thought you meant your hair."

She smiled at that, too, then indicated the blasters with her eyes. "Are you going to put those away?"

He felt himself color. "Of course. I mean, yes. Right."

He holstered both his weapons, hands shaking. "How did you find me?"

"You said you'd become a farmer on Dantooine." She held her arms out to the side, indicating the landscape. "And here you are."

"And here I am."

"Don't worry," she said, anticipating his concern. "No one else could find you. Just me."

"Just you. Just you."

He was smiling stupidly, echoing her words, and probably looked like a fool. He didn't care. She was smiling, too, and he could take no more.

"Stang, Aryn!" he said. He ran toward her and scooped her into his arms.

She returned his embrace and he pulled her tighter, felt her body against his, inhaled the smell of her hair. He enjoyed the moment then held her at arm's length.

"Wait, how did you . . . get off Coruscant? Malgus—"

She nodded. "We reached an understanding, of sorts."

He wanted to ask about the Twi'lek but was afraid of the answer. Perhaps she felt his emotional turmoil, or perhaps she knew him well enough to anticipate the question.

"Even after you left I did not hurt her. Eleena, I mean. I left her with Malgus. I don't know if I did her any favors, though."

He hugged her again, more relieved than he would

have expected. "I'm glad, Aryn. I'm glad you did that. And I'm glad you're here."

Tears leaked from his eyes. He was not sure why.

She pushed him back and studied his face. "What is it? You're upset."

Words pushed up his throat but he kept them behind his teeth. He remembered the air lock on *Razor*, but shook his head. Vrath was his weight to carry.

"It's nothing. I'm just glad to see you. An understanding with Malgus? What does that mean?"

"He let me go."

"He what?"

Aryn nodded. "He let me go. I still don't understand why. Not fully."

"Are you . . . still hunting him?"

A shadow passed over Aryn's expression, but her soft smile brightened her face and chased it away. She put her fingers on a necklace she wore. A stone hung from a silver chain. Zeerid thought it was a Nautolan jewel of some kind.

"No, I'm not hunting him. When I faced him I felt his hate, his rage." She shuddered, wrapped her arms around her slim body. "It was like nothing I'd encountered in a Sith before. He lives in a dark place. And I . . . did not want to follow him there."

Zeerid understood better than she knew. He lived in his own dark place.

"You don't want to carry that," he said to her, to himself.

"No," she said. "I don't want to carry that."

He shook off the darkness and forced a smile. "Will you be staying for a while?"

Before Aryn could answer, Arra's voice carried from the house. "Daddy! Can I come out now?"

He waved her out and she threw open the door, bounded across the porch, down the stairs, and across the swath.

Aryn grabbed him by the arm. "She's running, Zeerid."

"Prosthetics," he said, and his eyes welled anew to see her running toward him with Aryn at his side.

When Arra reached them, she stopped before them, out of breath, her curly hair mussed, her eyes curious and her smile wide. She extended a small hand, all serious. "Hello. My name is Arra."

Aryn knelt down to look her in the eye. Taking her hand, she said, "I'm Aryn. Hello, Arra. It's nice to meet you."

"You have pretty eyes," Arra said.

"Thank you."

Zeerid spoke his hopes aloud. "I think Aryn is going to stay with us for a while. Won't that be nice?"

Arra nodded.

"Aren't you, Aryn? Staying for a while?"

Aryn rose and Zeerid's hopes rose with her, fragile, ready to be dashed. When she looked at him and nodded, he grinned like a fool.

"Do you like to play grav-ball?" Arra asked her.

"You can teach me," Aryn said.

"How about some food?" Zeerid said.

"Race you!" Arra said, and sprinted for the house.

Zeerid and Aryn fell in behind her, all three of them laughing, free.

FATE OF THE JEDI

THE SAGA CONTINUES

FOR OVER three decades, the *Star Wars* universe has been expanding. New drama, new adventures, and new revelations have played out in the pages of bestselling *Star Wars* novels. Now, almost forty years after the end of *Return of the Jedi*, Luke Skywalker, Princess Leia, and Han Solo are living legends, starring alongside a new generation of heroes in their endless struggle to bring peace to a beleaguered galaxy.

This is the start of Fate of the Jedi, the newest *Star Wars* saga: nine books, three authors, one spectacular epic adventure!

Read on for a brief refresher course on the current standing of the characters and worlds of the galaxy far, far away . . . or skip straight to a sample from the first book of *Star Wars: Fate of the Jedi: Outcast,* by Aaron Allston!

THE STATE OF THE GALAXY

The Clone Wars are distant history. The Galactic Civil War between the Empire and the Rebel Alliance is a fading memory. In the four decades that followed the deaths of Darth Vader and the evil Emperor, the galaxy has known only a few scant stretches of peaceful times.

The Rebel Alliance transformed from a revolutionary military force to a legitimate government—the New Republic—in a long process as it liberated worlds from the iron grip of the Empire. The Senate was restored. Luke Skywalker rebuilt the Jedi Order.

Then, the Yuuzhan Vong came. A violent species of alien invaders, they destroyed entire worlds in their quest to conquer the galaxy. The New Republic teamed with the shrinking Imperial Remnant to counter this threat, and although the alien menace was defeated, the galactic government was just one of many casualties of this brutal war.

From the fragments of the New Republic emerged the Galactic Alliance, but its attempt to enforce order on a war-weary galaxy proved difficult. Isolationists and independent-minded cultures like the Corellians did not bow down to Alliance rule. When the Galactic Alliance came under the draconian rule of a fallen Jedi, Jacen Solo, who adopted the Sith guise of Darth Caedus, this tinderbox exploded into the Second Galactic Civil War. Violence erupted between the Alliance and a Confederation of worlds wishing independence. The Jedi Order split from the Alliance, going rogue to take down Caedus, slain by his twin sister, Jaina, the Sword of the Jedi.

By the end of this latest conflict, the galactic players were once again rearranged. The Galactic Alliance is still in power, but a new Chief of State has been installed: a former Imperial, Natasi Daala. The Galactic Empire's influence has grown, as beings everywhere see and appreciate its relative stability and order compared to the shaky years of Alliance rule.

But Daala has never had great love for the Jedi, and their willingness to abandon the Galactic Alliance has given some reason to doubt their reliability or even loyalty. How exactly the Jedi will fit comfortably into this new order remains to be seen. . . .

LUKE SKYWALKER
FARMBOY. PILOT. REBEL. JEDI.
GRAND MASTER. FATHER.

LUKE SKYWALKER has come a long way from the starry-eyed farmboy whose biggest concern was picking up power convertors from Tosche Station. After helping defeat the Emperor alongside his redeemed father, Skywalker carried out Yoda's dying command to pass on what he had learned.

At first, Luke's role was very similar to the one he had during the Rebellion. He continued serving as a pilot and military leader for the New Republic, but he gradually withdrew from this active service to pursue his studies in the Force. His travels across the galaxy led him to uncover fragments of Jedi knowledge that the Emperor and his agents had not wholly eradicated. Luke, though, had to improvise in his teaching methods, adopting practices that would have been considered forbidden during the time of Obi-Wan Kenobi and Anakin Skywalker. For example, there was no age limitation placed on prospective students, and the idea of romantic attachment was not taboo among this new generation of Jedi.

For many years, the idea of settling down and starting a family seemed impossible to Luke, who was much more focused on larger galactic matters. But fate has a way of laying unexpected paths before a Skywalker. He fell in love with and married Mara Jade, a former Imperial agent who was also powerful in the Force. Together, they had a son, Ben, during a time of great conflict in the galaxy—the invasion of the violent Yuuzhan Vong.

The Yuuzhan Vong War tested the Jedi Order, and ultimately forced Luke to adopt the mantle of Grand Master of the Jedi and reinstate the Jedi Council. The new Jedi Order found difficulty in fitting into the structure of the Galactic Alliance, a situation made worse when the Alliance began adopting some draconian methods of enforcing loyalty among its member worlds. Jacen Solo, Luke's nephew and former student, grew powerful in the Force and—like his grandfather Anakin Skywalker—turned to the dark side in a Faustian bid to bring order and protection to the galaxy and his loved ones. He emerged as Darth Caedus, a Sith Lord, and brought more war and heartbreak to the extended Skywalker family, including murdering Mara Jade Skywalker.

Though tragic, the death of Mara Jade brought Luke and Ben closer than they had ever been before. In the Fate of the Jedi series, father and son will depart on an important quest together that will test that bond and their formidable Jedi skills.

HAN SOLO

NO ONE could have predicted that a Corellian smuggler would someday become a First Husband of the New

Republic and the father of a new generation of Jedi. But these unlikely events came to be. As Han would say, "Never tell me the odds." After the defeat of the Empire, Han was branded as "respectable" by the rogues and pirates he had once done business with. Solo's role as a general in the Rebel Alliance meant that he became a key player in the New Republic's formative years. His numerous underworld contacts helped the New Republic in its continued battle with the shrinking Imperial presence in the galaxy. Han eventually married Princess Leia, and together they had three children—the twins, Jacen and Jaina, and their younger brother, Anakin.

Han's most recognizable traits were passed on to his children—they all exhibited a mix of his sense of humor, his mechanical aptitude, and his amazing piloting skills. But the three Solo children were known foremost as some of the most capable Jedi of their generation. It was a world that was alien to Solo—he could not touch the Force and couldn't experience this particular connection the children shared with their mother. He was nonetheless often dragged into the affairs of the Jedi, in much the same way that he ended up pulled into Leia's political involvements.

The Yuuzhan Vong War took a heavy toll on the Solo family. One of the earliest casualties of the invasion was Solo's oldest friend, his beloved Wookiee co-pilot Chewbacca. Chewie's death hit Han hard, and for a time, he turned his back on his family to exorcise his demons in some of the shadiest corners of the galaxy. Han smartly returned to the love and security that Leia and his family offered him; he would need it, for the next tragedy was the death of his sixteen-year-old son, Anakin Solo.

By war's end, Jacen and Jaina would take on principal roles in defeating the Yuuzhan Vong—this war was to their generation what the original struggle against the

Empire had been to Han, Leia, and Luke. Jacen in particular proved to be irrevocably changed by his experi-
ences in the war. During the growing conflict between
independent-minded Corellians and an overreaching
Galactic Alliance, Jacen succumbed to the dark side in
an attempt to enforce order in the galaxy.

Jacen became Darth Caedus, an evil warlord whose
actions resulted in even more destruction and betrayal.
To Han, his son was no more—a casualty of the last
war. The abomination who replaced him, Caedus,
needed to be stopped no matter the cost. It fell to Jaina
to defeat and ultimately kill her brother. His reign of terror ended, Jacen left a surprising legacy—a young
daughter, Allana, born to the Hapan Queen and former
Jedi Tenel Ka. To keep Allana safe, Han and Leia have
now resumed the role of parents, adopting the young
girl and raising her under the alias "Amelia."

LEIA ORGANA SOLO

SINCE HER teen years, Princess Leia has been trying to
make the galaxy a better place. Once a Senator from
Alderaan, she later served as a leader in the Rebel Alliance. When she discovered she was Luke Skywalker's
sister, she found she had to make a choice as to what her
role in the changing galaxy would be. Would she pick up
the lightsaber?

The needs of politics won out. Leia became one of the foremost leaders of the New Republic, eventually serving as Chief of State. Another important role she played was that of mother—she married Han Solo, and together they had three children. The twins, Jacen and Jaina Solo, and their younger brother, Anakin, all proved strong in the Force. Leia practiced her skills as a Jedi with her brother, but a galaxy of distractions kept her from reaching her full potential.

It was the turmoil of the Yuuzhan Vong War and its fallout that caused Leia to return to her Jedi studies with renewed focus. The tragic deaths of Chewbacca and her youngest son, Anakin, greatly tried the bonds of the Solo family, but they emerged stronger from that terrible crucible. Leia would rarely leave Han's side, and she became the *Millennium Falcon*'s co-pilot, capably filling the role left void by the loss of the mighty Wookiee.

Once more, Leia had to let go of one her children, when it became apparent that Jacen had succumbed to the dark side. It was one of Leia's longest held and deepest fears—that one of her children might one day follow a dark path similar to that of her father, Darth Vader. That it fell to Jaina to kill Jacen was all the more appalling, but Jaina did her duty as a Jedi Knight.

After a lifetime of struggle to keep the galaxy from falling apart, Han and Leia have no real grasp of the concept of retirement. By all rights, they could retreat to a remote and peaceful world and live out a quiet life together, but they are once again thrust to the center of galactic conflict. A new wrinkle this time is that now, decades after their last child reached adulthood, they are once again playing the role of parents. Han and Leia have adopted the daughter that Jacen Solo left behind and are raising her as their own.

LANDO CALRISSIAN

THE CONSUMMATE gambler and lady's man, Calrissian is always looking for angles and opportunities. Though he stepped up to a larger calling by serving as a general in the massive space battle that saw the destruction of the second Death Star and the deaths of Darth Vader and the Emperor, Calrissian quickly returned to his entrepreneurial ways after the war. In the four decades since, he has started many businesses and made and lost a few fortunes along the way. Always looking for a challenge, he tackled the biggest one when he decided to find a wife.

After a lengthy search for a possible partner compatible in both business and romance, he discovered Tendra Risant. She was a wealthy businesswoman, and together they founded several mining ventures and other profitable enterprises. They are the co-founders of Tendrando Arms, a weapons-development firm that was a key supplier during the Yuuzhan Vong War.

Lando is now the father of a young boy, Lando Calrissian, Jr., whom he nicknamed "Chance." Lando and Tendra currently own and operate the spice mines of Kessel and remain close friends of the Solo family.

BEN SKYWALKER

THE SON of Luke and Mara Jade Skywalker, young Ben was born at a time of brutal war. The vicious Yuuzhan Vong destroyed entire worlds in their crusade to conquer the galaxy, and targeted the Jedi specifically as heretics that needed to be destroyed. As the son of Luke Skywalker—grandson of Anakin Skywalker—Ben was genetically predisposed to be an immensely powerful Force user. But, as a young boy, Ben shied away from his connection to the Force. He withdrew, possibly retreating from the constant disturbances in the Force caused by the terrible destruction of the war.

Only one person seemed to be able to coax Ben from out of his shell—his cousin, Jacen Solo. Ben grew connected to Jacen, learning the ways of the Force as his apprentice. When Ben was a teenager, Jacen's explorations of the Force's strange, darkened corners, as well as the growing conflict between Galactic Alliance and independent-minded Corellians, led Jacen to the dark side.

Ben did not see it at first. He saw Jacen as being forced to take the necessary steps to enforce order in the galaxy. Jacen founded a secret police—the Galactic Alliance Guard—to deal with insurrectionists or any who would threaten the peace of the Galactic Alliance. Ben became one of its youngest members, learning effective investigation and combat techniques.

In time, Ben came to realize what Jacen was willing to sacrifice in his obsessive pursuit of order. He even discovered the horrible truth that Jacen was a Sith Lord, and that he had murdered his mother, Mara Jade.

The loss of Mara brought Luke and Ben closer together. Ultimately, Jacen was defeated, but at great cost to the Jedi Order and its standing in the galactic government. During the Fate of the Jedi series, Luke will leave the comfortable borders of the Galactic Alliance, heading to parts unknown to find clues to whatever may have twisted Jacen Solo's fate to the dark side. Ben will accompany Luke, bringing his fresh insight, as well as a hard-earned pragmatism far beyond his teenage years.

JAINA SOLO

THE DAUGHTER of Leia and Han Solo, Jaina Solo is, sadly, the last remaining Solo child. She was born a twin, with her brother Jacen. Only a few years later, they were joined by their younger brother, Anakin. All three were very strong in the Force. As a child, Jacen exhibited a compassion for animals and a natural attunement to the Force. Jaina's skills leaned toward the mechanical, for she, more than her brothers, inherited her father's talent for piloting and mechanics.

During the Yuuzhan Vong War, Jaina, Jacen, and Anakin were all pressed into frontline service, fighting against the brutal alien invaders. Jaina became an ace starfighter pilot, flying an X-wing in the legendary elite unit Rogue Squadron. This war would claim many of Jaina's closest friends, and her brother Anakin, as well. It would also force her to mature and recognize her role in the future of the Jedi Order. Luke Skywalker branded her "The Sword of the Jedi" during the ceremony that saw her elevated to Jedi Knight.

It was this role that required her to confront and defeat her brother Jacen once he had turned to the dark side. Jacen Solo, in an effort to enforce order in a rapidly fragmenting Galactic Alliance, succumbed to the dark side and emerged as the Sith Lord Darth Caedus. It was only Jaina who could confront and defeat him. She studied new deadly combat techniques from armored Mandalorian warriors, coupling them with her natural Jedi abilities and her attunement to her brother to ultimately defeat him.

For a long time, Jaina's role as a Jedi prevented her from establishing a romantic connection to anyone, though she had no shortage of would-be suitors. It was often Zekk, a fellow Jedi, or Jagged Fel, a fellow pilot, who would vie for her affections, but she could not let herself choose between them or allow herself the luxury of romance. Now, though, after having faced the hardships and threat that she has triumphed over, she recognizes how fleeting moments of peace and tenderness can be in a war-torn galaxy. She has lowered her guard to let Jag into her heart.

JAG FEL

JAGGED FEL is an amazing pilot, the son of a legendary Imperial flying ace. Jag was raised in an extremely regimented environment, a militaristic upbringing surrounded by coldly methodical aliens known as the Chiss. This resulted in a very serious, disciplined, and focused young man. Opposites truly attract, for this coolly collected, even-tempered man established a strong connection to the fiery-tempered child of the fates Jaina Solo. The two shared a love of piloting and a skill behind the controls of a starfighter, and during the war against the Yuuzhan Vong, they found that their complementary approaches to problems balanced each other well.

As part of the fallout of the Second Galactic Civil War, the ruling council of the Imperial Remnant was reprimanded for its attempt to take advantage of the internal strife plaguing the Galactic Alliance. Luke Skywalker negotiated terms with the Imperial Remnant, and surprised everyone when one of his conditions of peace was the installation of Jagged Fel as head of the Imperial state. As Luke explained it, the Empire suffered from no shortage of overly ambitious short-sighted leaders, and needed someone in command who did not crave power for its own ends. Jagged Fel fit the bill perfectly.

NATASI DAALA

NATASI DAALA is a former Imperial officer who is now
serving as Chief of State of the Galactic Alliance. She sat
out much of the Galactic Civil War, sequestered in a top-
secret Imperial weapons think tank. She is one of the
very few high-ranking female officers in the Galactic
Empire. Some whisper that she landed her position only
because of an illicit love affair with Grand Moff Tarkin,
but talk like that belittles her command skills.

When the Empire was defeated at the Battle of Endor,
Daala never knew of the government's fate, for no one
knew of her secret installation in the Maw. No news of
the Rebellion or the New Republic's victory ever reached
her ears. When she emerged from the facility, in command
of a task force of Star Destroyers, she attempted to continue the war against the enemies of the Emperor, even
though he was long dead. She was eventually defeated,
and she retired from galactic view and military life.

Daala returned decades later to stop Darth Caedus,
and her forces helped in the defeat of the Sith Lord. She
was installed as Chief of State of the now leaderless Galactic Alliance, as she was the only choice that all the
various fragmented factions could agree upon. But the
haste to find leadership resulted in the Galactic Alliance
now being led by someone with strongly voiced anti-
Jedi sentiments.

THE NEW JEDI ORDER

LUKE SKYWALKER'S Jedi Order is in many ways different from the previous generation of Jedi Knights that produced such legends as Obi-Wan Kenobi, Anakin Skywalker, and Mace Windu. The necessity of rebuilding the Order from scratch and the lack of records of its predecessors forced Luke to allow exceptions to long-standing Jedi traditions. In this new order, prospective candidates were allowed to undergo training regardless of their age. No longer was anyone "too old" to begin training. A Jedi Master could also have multiple apprentices at the same time—the old Master-Padawan one-on-one relationship was left in the past. Furthermore, the concept of attachment as it pertained to romantic relationships or family was no longer forbidden. Jedi were encouraged to stay connected with their families or to start families of their own.

AMONG SOME OF THE MORE NOTABLE
MEMBERS OF LUKE SKYWALKER'S JEDI ORDER

TAHIRI VEILA: She was a young girl from Tatooine who befriended Anakin Solo during their time as young Jedi students. As they grew older, a romance between the two began to blossom but was tragically cut short by Anakin's death at the hands of the Yuuzhan Vong. Tahiri has never really recovered from that loss, and her instability was recently exploited by Darth Caedus, who attempted to groom her to be his apprentice. After Caedus was defeated, Tahiri's life was spared, and she has withdrawn from the Jedi in an attempt to understand her own motives and find her true destiny.

TAHIRI VEILA

CILGAHL: A gentle Mon Calamari, this Jedi Master is also a biological scientific expert and renowned healer.

TEKLI: A short, bat-faced alien Chadra-Fan, she is a Jedi healer.

CILGAHL

KYP DURRON: When he was a teenager, he was possessed by the spirit of a long-dead Sith Lord and wreaked much havoc on the galaxy. He has long since reformed and is now one of the most powerful of the current Jedi, with a reputation for recklessness that did not prevent his elevation to the rank of Master.

KYP DURRON

SABA SEBATYNE: A powerfully built, lizard-like Barabel alien, she is a natural hunter who, as a Jedi Master, also served as an instructor for Leia Organa Solo.

CORRAN HORN: A former Corellian security officer turned Jedi Knight, he is now a highly respected Jedi Master.

CORRAN HORN

KENTH HAMNER: A former colonel in the New Republic military who resigned his commission to study in the Jedi Order, he is a level-headed, extremely reliable Jedi Master.

KENTH HAMNER

VALIN HORN: The son of Corran Horn, he was a child during the Yuuzhan Vong War, one of many sequestered from the fighting in the hidden base in the Maw. He became a Jedi Knight and served during the Second Galactic Civil War.

ZEKK: A friend of Jacen and Jaina Solo since childhood, Zekk climbed up from the lower levels of Coruscant to become a prominent Jedi Knight. He was very close to Jaina, but her focus on her role as a Jedi prevented them from exploring their strong connection any further. He vanished from sight and from the Force during the final battle against Darth Caedus, and his current whereabouts are unknown.

ZEKK

READ ON FOR AN EXCERPT FROM
STAR WARS: FATE OF THE JEDI: OUTCAST
BY AARON ALLSTON
PUBLISHED BY DEL REY BOOKS

CHAPTER 1

GALACTIC ALLIANCE DIPLOMATIC SHUTTLE,
HIGH CORUSCANT ORBIT

ONE BY one, the stars overhead began to disappear, swallowed by some enormous darkness interposing itself from above and behind the shuttle. Sharply pointed at its most forward position, broadening behind, the flood of blackness advanced, blotting out more and more of the unblinking starfield, until darkness was all there was to see.

Then, all across the length and breadth of the ominous shape, lights came on—blue and white running lights, tiny red hatch and security lights, sudden glows from within transparisteel viewports, one large rectangular whiteness limned by atmosphere shields. The lights showed the vast triangle to be the underside of an Imperial Star Destroyer, painted black, forbidding a moment ago, now comparatively cheerful in its proper running configuration. It was the *Gilad Pellaeon*, newly arrived from the Imperial Remnant, and its officers clearly knew how to put on a show.

Jaina Solo, sitting with the others in the dimly lit passenger compartment of the government VIP shuttle, watched the entire display through the overhead transparisteel canopy and laughed out loud.

The Bothan in the sumptuously padded chair next to hers gave her a curious look. His mottled red and tan fur twitched, either from suppressed irritation or embarrassment at Jaina's outburst. "What do you find so amusing?"

"Oh, both the obviousness of it and the skill with which it was performed. It's so very, *You used to think of us as dark and scary, but now we're just your stylish allies.*" Jaina lowered her voice so that her next comment would not carry to the passengers in the seats behind. "The press will love it. That image will play on the holonews broadcasts constantly. Mark my words."

"Was that little show a Jagged Fel detail?"

Jaina tilted her head, considering. "I don't know. He could have come up with it, but he usually doesn't spend his time planning displays or events. When he does, though, they're usually pretty . . . effective."

The shuttle rose toward the *Gilad Pellaeon*'s main landing bay. In moments, it was through the square atmosphere barrier shield and drifting sideways to land on the deck nearby. The landing place was clearly marked—hundreds of beings, most wearing gray Imperial uniforms or the distinctive white armor of the Imperial stormtrooper, waited in the bay, and the one circular spot where none stood was just the right size for the Galactic Alliance shuttle.

The passengers rose as the shuttle settled into place. The Bothan smoothed his tunic, a cheerful blue decorated with a golden sliver pattern suggesting claws. "Time to go to work. You won't let me get killed, will you?"

Jaina let her eyes widen. "Is that what I was supposed to be doing here?" she asked in droll tones. "I should have brought my lightsaber."

The Bothan offered a long-suffering sigh and turned toward the exit.

They descended the shuttle's boarding ramp. With no duties required of her other than to keep alert and be the Jedi face at this preliminary meeting, Jaina was able to stand back and observe. She was struck with the unreality of it all. The niece and daughter of three of the most famous enemies of the Empire during the First Galactic Civil War of a few decades earlier, she was now witness to events that might bring the Galactic Empire—or Imperial Remnant, as it was called everywhere outside its own borders—into the Galactic Alliance on a lasting basis.

And at the center of the plan was the man, flanked by Imperial officers, who now approached the Bothan. Slightly under average size, though towering well above Jaina's diminutive height, he was dark-haired, with a trim beard and mustache that gave him a rakish look, and was handsome in a way that became more pronounced when he glowered. A scar on his forehead ran up into his hairline and seemed to continue as a lock of white hair from that point. He wore expensive but subdued black civilian garments, neck-to-toe, that would be inconspicuous anywhere on Coruscant but stood out in sharp relief to the gray and white uniforms, white armor, and colorful Alliance clothes surrounding him.

He had one moment to glance at Jaina. The look probably appeared neutral to onlookers, but for her it carried just a twinkle of humor, a touch of exasperation that the two of them had to put up with all these delays. Then an Alliance functionary, notable for his blandness, made introductions: "Imperial Head of State the most honorable Jagged Fel, may I present Senator Tiurrg Drey'lye of Bothawui, head of the Senate Unification Preparations Committee."

Jagged Fel took the Senator's hand. "I'm pleased to be working with you."

"And delighted to meet *you*. Chief of State Daala sends her compliments and looks forward to meeting you when you make planetfall."

Jag nodded. "And now, I believe, protocol insists that we open a bottle or a dozen of wine and make some preliminary discussion of security, introduction protocols, and so on."

"Fortunately about the wine, and regrettably about everything else, you are correct."

AT THE end of two full standard hours—Jaina knew from regular, surreptitious consultations of her chrono—Jag was able to convince the Senator and his retinue to accept a tour of the *Gilad Pellaeon*. He was also able to request a private consultation with the sole representative of the Jedi Order present. Moments later, the gray-walled conference room was empty of everyone but Jag and Jaina.

Jag glanced toward the door. "Security seal, access limited to Jagged Fel and Jedi Jaina Solo, voice identification, activate." The door hissed in response as it sealed. Then Jag returned his attention to Jaina.

She let an expression of anger and accusation cross her face. "You're not fooling anyone, Fel. You're planning for an Imperial invasion of Alliance space."

Jag nodded. "I've been planning it for quite a while. Come here."

She moved to him, settled into his lap, and was suddenly but not unexpectedly caught in his embrace. They kissed urgently, hungrily.

Finally Jaina drew back and smiled at him. "This isn't going to be a routine part of your consultations with every Jedi."

"Uh, no. That would cause some trouble here and at home. But I actually *do* have business with the Jedi that does not involve the Galactic Alliance, at least not initially."

"What sort of business?"

"Whether or not the Galactic Empire joins with the Galactic Alliance, I think there ought to be an official Jedi presence in the Empire. A second Temple, a branch, an offshoot, whatever. Providing advice and insight to the Head of State."

"And protection?"

He shrugged. "Less of an issue. I'm doing all right. Two years in this position and not dead yet."

"Emperor Palpatine went nearly twenty-five years."

"I guess that makes him my hero."

Jaina snorted. "Don't even say that in jest . . . Jag, if the Remnant doesn't join the Alliance, I'm not sure the Jedi *can* have a presence without Alliance approval."

"The Order still keeps its training facility for youngsters in Hapan space. And the Hapans haven't rejoined."

"You sound annoyed. The Hapans still giving you trouble?"

"Let's not talk about *that*."

"Besides, moving the school back to Alliance space is just a matter of time, logistics, and finances; there's no question that it will happen. On the other hand, it's very likely that the government would withhold approval for a Jedi branch in the Remnant, just out of spite, if the Remnant doesn't join."

"Well, there's such a thing as an *unofficial* presence. And there's such a thing as rival schools, schismatic branches, and places for former Jedi to go when they can't be at the Temple."

Jaina smiled again, but now there was suspicion in her

expression. "You just want to have this so *I'll* be assigned to come to the Remnant and set it up."

"That's a motive, but not the only one. Remember, to the Moffs and to a lot of the Imperial population, the Jedi have been bogeymen since Palpatine died. At the very least, I don't want them to be inappropriately afraid of the woman I'm in love with."

Jaina was silent for a moment. "Have we talked enough politics?"

"I think so."

"Good."

HORN FAMILY QUARTERS, KALLAD'S DREAM VACATION HOSTEL, CORUSCANT

YAWNING, HAIR tousled, clad in a blue dressing robe, Valin Horn knew that he did not look anything like an experienced Jedi Knight. He looked like an unshaven, unkempt bachelor, which he also was. But here, in these rented quarters, there would be only family to see him— at least until he had breakfast, shaved, and dressed.

The Horns did not live here, of course. His mother, Mirax, was the anchor for the immediate family. Manager of a variety of interlinked businesses—trading, interplanetary finances, gambling and recreation, and, if rumors were true, still a little smuggling here and there— she maintained her home and business address on Corellia. Corran, her husband and Valin's father, was a Jedi Master, much of his life spent on missions away from the family, but his true home was where his heart resided, wherever Mirax lived. Valin and his sister, Jysella, also Jedi, lived wherever their missions sent them, and also counted Mirax as the center of the family.

Now Mirax had rented temporary quarters on Coruscant so the family could collect on one of its rare occasions, this time for the Unification Summit, where she and Corran would separately give depositions on the relationships among the Confederation states, the Imperial Remnant, and the Galactic Alliance as they related to trade and Jedi activities. Mirax had insisted that Valin and Jysella leave their Temple quarters and stay with their parents while these events were taking place, and few forces in the galaxy could stand before her decision—Luke Skywalker certainly knew better than to try.

Moving from the refresher toward the kitchen and dining nook, Valin brushed a lock of brown hair out of his eyes and grinned. Much as he might put up a public show of protest—the independent young man who did not need parents to direct his actions or tell him where to sleep—he hardly minded. It was good to see family. And both Corran and Mirax were better cooks than the ones at the Jedi Temple.

There was no sound of conversation from the kitchen, but there was some clattering of pans, so at least one of his parents must still be on hand. As he stepped from the hallway into the dining nook, Valin saw that it was his mother, her back to him as she worked at the stove. He pulled a chair from the table and sat. "Good morning."

"A joke, so early?" Mirax did not turn to face him, but her tone was cheerful. "No morning is good. I come light-years from Corellia to be with my family, and what happens? I have to keep Jedi hours to see them. Don't you know that I'm an executive? And a lazy one?"

"I forgot." Valin took a deep breath, sampling the smells of breakfast. His mother was making hotcakes Corellian-style, nerf sausage links on the side, and caf was brewing. For a moment, Valin was transported back to his childhood, to the family breakfasts that had been somewhat more common before the Yuuzhan

Vong came, before Valin and Jysella had started down the Jedi path. "Where are Dad and Sella?"

"Your father is out getting some back-door information from other Jedi Masters for his deposition." Mirax pulled a plate from a cabinet and began sliding hotcakes and links onto it. "Your sister left early and wouldn't say what she was doing, which I assume either means it's Jedi business I can't know about or that she's seeing some man she doesn't *want* me to know about."

"Or both."

"Or both." Mirax turned and moved over to put the plate down before him. She set utensils beside it.

The plate was heaped high with food, and Valin recoiled from it in mock horror. "Stang, Mom, you're feeding your son, not a squadron of Gamorreans." Then he caught sight of his mother's face and he was suddenly no longer in a joking mood.

This wasn't his mother.

Oh, the woman had Mirax's features. She had the round face that admirers had called "cute" far more often than "beautiful," much to Mirax's chagrin. She had Mirax's generous, curving lips that smiled so readily and expressively, and Mirax's bright, lively brown eyes. She had Mirax's hair, a glossy black with flecks of gray, worn shoulder-length to fit readily under a pilot's helmet, even though she piloted far less often these days. She was Mirax to every freckle and dimple.

But she was not Mirax.

The woman, whoever she was, caught sight of Valin's confusion. "Something wrong?"

"Uh, no." Stunned, Valin looked down at his plate.

He had to think—logically, correctly, and *fast*. He might be in grave danger right now, though the Force currently gave him no indication of imminent attack. The true Mirax, wherever she was, might be in serious trouble or worse. Valin tried in vain to slow his heart rate and speed up his thinking processes.

Fact: Mirax had been here but had been replaced by an imposter. Presumably the real Mirax was gone; Valin could not sense anyone but himself and the imposter in the immediate vicinity. The imposter had remained behind for some reason that had to relate to Valin, Jysella, or Corran. It couldn't have been to capture Valin, as she could have done that with drugs or other methods while he slept, so the food was probably not drugged.

Under Not-Mirax's concerned gaze, he took a tentative bite of sausage and turned a reassuring smile he didn't feel toward her.

Fact: Creating an imposter this perfect must have taken a fortune in money, an incredible amount of research, and a volunteer willing to let her features be permanently carved into the likeness of another's. Or perhaps this was a clone, raised and trained for the purpose of simulating Mirax. Or maybe she was a droid, one of the very expensive, very rare human replica droids. Or maybe a shape-shifter. Whichever, the simulation was nearly perfect. Valin hadn't recognized the deception until . . .

Until *what*? What had tipped him off? He took another bite, not registering the sausage's taste or temperature, and maintained the face-hurting smile as he tried to recall the detail that had alerted him that this wasn't his mother.

He couldn't figure it out. It was just an instant realization, too fleeting to remember, too overwhelming to reject.

Would Corran be able to see through the deception? Would Jysella? Surely, they had to be able to. But what if they couldn't? Valin would accuse this woman and be thought insane.

Were Corran and Jysella even still at liberty? Still *alive*? At this moment, the Not-Mirax's colleagues could be spiriting the two of them away with the true Mirax. Or Corran and Jysella could be lying, bleeding, at the bottom of an access shaft, their lives draining away.

Valin couldn't think straight. The situation was too overwhelming, the mystery too deep, and the only person here who knew the answers was the one who wore the face of his mother.

He stood, sending his chair clattering backward, and fixed the false Mirax with a hard look. "Just a moment." He dashed to his room.

His lightsaber was still where he'd left it, on the nightstand beside his bed. He snatched it up and gave it a near-instantaneous examination. Battery power was still optimal; there was no sign that it had been tampered with.

He returned to the dining room with the weapon in his hand. Not-Mirax, clearly confused and beginning to look a little alarmed, stood by the stove, staring at him.

Valin ignited the lightsaber, its *snap-hiss* of activation startlingly loud, and held the point of the gleaming energy blade against the food on his plate. Hotcakes shriveled and blackened from contact with the weapon's plasma. Valin gave Not-Mirax an approving nod. "Flesh does the same thing under the same conditions, you know."

"Valin, what's *wrong*?"

"You may address me as Jedi Horn. You don't have the right to use my personal name." Valin swung the lightsaber around in a practice form, allowing the blade to come within a few centimeters of the glow rod fixture overhead, the wall, the dining table, and the woman with his mother's face. "You probably know from your research that the Jedi don't worry much about amputations."

Not-Mirax shrank back away from him, both hands on the stove edge behind her. "What?"

"We know that a severed limb can readily be replaced by a prosthetic that looks identical to the real thing. Prosthetics offer sensation and do everything flesh can. They're ideal substitutes in every way, except for requiring maintenance. So we don't feel too badly when we have to cut the arm or leg off a very bad person. But I assure you, that very bad person remembers the pain forever."

"Valin, I'm going to call your father now." Mirax sidled toward the blue bantha-hide carrybag she had left on a side table.

Valin positioned the tip of his lightsaber directly beneath her chin. At the distance of half a centimeter, its containing force field kept her from feeling any heat from the blade, but a slight twitch on Valin's part could maim or kill her instantly. She froze.

"No, you're not. You know what you're going to do instead?"

Mirax's voice wavered. "What?"

"You're going to *tell me what you've done with my mother!*" The last several words emerged as a bellow, driven by fear and anger. Valin knew that he looked as angry as he sounded; he could feel blood reddening his face, could even see redness begin to suffuse everything in his vision.

"Boy, put the blade down." Those were not the woman's words. They came from behind. Valin spun, bringing his blade up into a defensive position.

In the doorway stood a man, middle-aged, clean-shaven, his hair graying from brown. He was of below-average height, his eyes a startling green. He wore the brown robes of a Jedi. His hands were on his belt, his own lightsaber still dangling from it.

He was Valin's father, Jedi Master Corran Horn. But he wasn't, any more than the woman behind Valin was Mirax Horn.

Valin felt a wave of despair wash over him. *Both* parents replaced. Odds were growing that the real Corran and Mirax were already dead.

Yet Valin's voice was soft when he spoke. "They may have made you a virtual double for my father. But they can't have given you his expertise with the lightsaber."

"You don't want to do what you're thinking about, son."

"When I cut you in half, that's all the proof anyone will ever need that you're not the real Corran Horn."

Valin lunged.